**I'M IN TIME**

*Requests for information should be directed to:*

ZizaCreative Publishing, Inc.

718.708.3348 | raseacinc@gmail.com

New York

ZizaCreative
PUBLISHING, INC.

Cover & Interior Design by ZizaCreative Publishing, Inc.
Cover Photograph © Thanayu Jongwattanasilkul

Printed in the United States of America

ISBN: 978-0-692-86559-0

# I'M IN TIME
Lisa Walden

# DEDICATION

*This novel is dedicated to the memory of my mother who selflessly helped and prayed for everyone who crossed her path. She had such a compassion for winning souls for God's kingdom and although people talked about her or thought she was crazy, it did not stop her from spreading the Gospel wherever she went because she was truly on fire for the Lord!*

*Many Christian parents want to see their children saved and living for God, and I know my mother, being a single parent, wanted nothing more than just that!*

*I remember when she had us all sit in a circular position on the floor and poured into us the things of God and the facts of life. She would share some of her mistakes and how we should avoid them by putting God first. My mother had an extremely hard life and no matter how many times life dealt her a bad hand, she was determined more than ever to never give up on God's promises!*

*Mommy, thanks to you, I now know how to wait on God. I know how to keep praying until God answers my prayers. I know how to pray over my house when uninvited spirits want to take residence. I know how to encourage myself when people or situations seem to let me down.*

*Mommy, I will always love you and be forever grateful to you for being both a mother and father to me as you held down the fort with God's help! Although you are not physically here on earth any longer and would have loved to see all of your children being used of God, He is still answering your prayers.*

# INTRODUCTION

Have you ever thought about how God answers your prayers according to His time? It's so amazing that man cannot go without looking at the time whether it's seconds, minutes, hours, days, weeks, months or years. When we are all waiting for our prayers to be answered, time does not move God any faster. But God can answer prayers right away, or He can let some days or weeks pass before answering our prayers. Maybe even months or years. Why? Because God's movement or answering our prayers is not dictated by time as we know it. God created man in time, which is a concept of the universe, but He is supernaturally watching over mankind outside the universe in His own time. The Bible tells us that a day is like a thousand years to God!

When you think that God is not limited by time, yet He is always on time, it makes you want to praise His name even more!

Think about it. Visualize the word 'TIME' in your mind. The second letter of the word is 'I'. When reading that word, it refers directly to you. Now the second and third letters of the word 'TIME', spell 'IM'. By adding an apostrophe, it becomes the word 'I'M', this again refers directly to you. The third and fourth letters of the word 'TIME', spell 'ME'. So no matter how you look at the word 'TIME', whether it spells I, I'M or ME, we are all there - wrapped up in time! Even though God is outside of time, He still controls time!

Another thought: When God hears a sincere prayer from one of His children, and because He is a God of order, who strategically plans everything, He responds accordingly. But we do not know the order of God. Believe it or not, there are times when before God can answer your prayer request, He may have to answer someone else's. So although there may be a delay in your prayers being answered within your expected time frame, it does not mean that you are being denied by God.

God is God and does not have to answer to anyone. Do not think that He has to share His plan of action with you. You may never know the circumstances behind the delay—why God has not answered your prayers as you anticipated. You may conclude that the delay is due to sin in your life or that God is simply trying to build up your faith. Granted, both can be true, but I personally believe that sometimes it could be that answering your prayers is contingent upon Him answering the prayers of others.

Let's say, you are praying for a promotion on your job, which would involve God changing the heart of your boss so that you would be favored by him for a promotion. What if that same boss is dealing with an overly ambitious wife who neglects her wifely duties and he has developed distaste for any woman trying to get ahead. Now, your boss is also praying to God that his wife does not have to work all the time and can spend her hours at home with him so they can concentrate on starting their own family.

Initially your prayer only involved you and your boss, but now, according to God's plan, your boss needs a change of heart, and so does his wife. Every Christian should know that God can do all things, but go along with me for a moment. Now let's say your boss's wife has taken on that type of ambitious attitude because she saw how hard her mother single-handedly took on two and three jobs cleaning houses and scrubbing floors so that her children would have a better opportunity in life than she had. Let's say after all those years of hard work, her mother still did not have enough health insurance coverage or money to pay for her medications for all the illnesses she developed over the course of years: chronic pain in her hands, knees, and back, as well as asthma.

Now, the boss's wife is also praying that God would heal her mother's body so that she would not have to work so many long hours at the job and take on the extra expenses from helping her mother pay for her prescribed medications.

Hence, according to God's plans before He answers your prayers, He must heal your boss' wife's mother's body. Then, He must change your boss' wife's heart to become more domesticated and to be a better wife to her husband. Then God must change your boss' heart and teach him to appreciate hard-working women, and last but not least He can grant you your promotion.

Look how the order changed. It all started out with you asking God for a promotion, but your prayer ended up on the bottom of the prayer list. But as the saying goes, "He may not come when you want Him, but He is always on time!"

# PROLOGUE

Walking away from the home I knew for more than fifteen years filled my heart with such comfort that words could never tell. As the heavy prison gates made a loud slamming sound behind me, it also reminded me of when I first stepped foot into that horrible place. My identity was instantly snatched away from me and I was told I no longer would be identified by my birth name, but by the number assigned to me. All of the new arriving inmates were told that our lives no longer belonged to us, but were now placed into the capable hands of the North Carolina Z. Correctional Facility. I could not help but get upset, as they carelessly used the word "capable"—they were "capable" alright, by beating submission into us whenever we disobeyed a direct order! They told us when to wake up, what time to eat, when to leave our cells, what time to go to bed, and the list was endless.

After several years passed, a part of me did not even feel alive anymore. My self-will and self-determination left me and I faded away with time. The correctional facilities' staff was supposed to help rehabilitate the inmate population into changed individuals. But instead, they treated and talked to us like we were inhuman, like we were not even a part of the human society. Meanwhile, the government insists on calling it a "correctional facility." They should just stick with the word "prison." At least they would live up to its definition, "a building for the confinement of accused persons awaiting trial or persons sentenced after conviction."

There was nothing correctional about this place because all they did was beat people into good behavior. Heck, anyone will follow rules and regulations if they are constantly being beaten into submission. This correctional facility would like for outsiders to believe if someone comes into this prison, whether bipolar, mentally-challenged, emotionally-damaged, suicidal or a serial killer, they would be treated with the best medical care that could be offered until they were released back into society as a changed person. Yeah right!

Ironically, the outside appearance of the correctional facility makes a person believe that this is truly a caring, rehabilitating institution. But looks are deceiving! While on this side of the wall, I noticed the neatly paved sidewalks outside, which looked nothing like the grounds on the inside. There were several cracked grounds and some of the cracks had holes so deep a person wearing a size twelve sneaker could comfortably place his foot inside the crack and his entire ankle would be hidden. Going forward, I knew I had to protect myself from ever going back there again.

Leaving this place made me feel alive again and suddenly everything within me began to matter. Looking straight ahead, I saw a familiar face, my father's baby brother, Uncle Brad. There he was patiently waiting as he leaned against his navy blue SUV, looking sharp as ever with his blue and white sweat suit with matching colors in his shirt and sneakers. Uncle Brad was always someone I could talk to when things were really bad between me and my parents. He believed in me and never turned his back on me while I was incarcerated.

I used all the strength I had to embrace my Uncle Brad showing him that I really appreciated him. I asked him how he was doing. But before he could reply, I told him that I was so grateful for him not only remembering my release date, but for taking the time to drive all the way to North Carolina to come and get me.

"I'm fine Junior. I'm just so surprised to see how big you have gotten since we last saw each other. It looks like my nephew who was this wimpy little boy when he went into prison is now this full-blown, grown man who has more muscles than his uncle," Uncle Brad said, as he jokingly threw a punch into the left side of my stomach.

"Uncle Brad, I know you heard me set goals and make promises over the years and I do not expect you to believe me, but I want you to know that I'm a different person now, and trust me, it did not have anything to do with this place rehabilitating me."

My uncle formed a big confident smile on his face and said, "Would the personality change have anything to do with you surrendering your life back to God, Junior?"

As a result of the question, I lowered my head like a little boy being reprimanded by his parents and said, "No, I backslid again, Uncle Brad and I did not surrender my life to God this time."

Now my uncle's smile turned to a frown when he heard the disappointing news and he said, "Junior, after all those visits we had together, walking you through the steps of salvation? What about all those Bibles and other Christian literatures I gave you to read so that you could grow in God? Did it not mean anything to you, Junior?"

"Yes it did, Uncle Brad!" I exclaimed. "I do not want you to feel that your visits and ministering to me were in vain all those years. I tried reading the Bible as well as the other Christian materials you gave me, it just wasn't for me. However, I've learned through our studies that God gives man their own free will in life."

"Yes, He does Junior, but there are only two choices, life or death! If you are not following God and choosing life, then you are choosing eternal death, which is separation from God forever."

"Uncle Brad, I know how disappointed you are with my decision, and being a pastor, a man of the cloth, you would love for everyone in the world to accept God into their lives. But truth be told, that is not going to happen and you have to be willing to let me make my own choices in life. Both my parents tried to force me into believing in the Bible, which is by the way, full of a whole lot of fairy tales."

"Junior," shouted Uncle Brad. "Now you are going to disrespect God and His Word by saying that the Bible is full of fairy tales? I see. You wait just one minute young man! Everything in the Bible is real and did happen whether man believes it or not or whether man can prove it or not!"

"Uncle Brad, how do you explain the story about a man who was swallowed by a whale and was spat out alive onto dry land after three days? Let's even go with the fact that he was still alive after three days! But spat out onto dry land? Come on Uncle Brad! Then the Bible speaks about Jesus walking on water and then asks someone else to join him, but I forgot his name. These things are impossible with man and the law of gravity."

"Junior, Jonah was swallowed up by a big fish and Peter was the one who Jesus asked to walk on water. You are right. These things are impossible with man but not with God! Junior, just because you are out of jail and feel like you do not need God anymore does not give you the right to disrespect Him or His Word only because you want to explore your own free will and not include God in your life. I find it very strange, Junior. As long as you were locked up, we read the Bible together and prayed together. But now you do not want to have any-thing to do with God. Was that all a joke to you?"

"No, Uncle Brad it was not. I just decided to change my direction and reach towards my own goals again."

"But Junior, you can still do all of those things in the Lord, plus you will have God guiding you every step of the way. Junior, God loves you and He only wants the best for you. Why throw a valuable gift away that God has given you—His gift of salvation? God has a calling on your life, Junior, and you cannot run or hide from your calling. You are going to submit one way or another because your entire family has been praying for you for too long."

"Honestly, Uncle Brad, I'm so grateful for you being in my life, but I just really want to go home now, take a shower, sleep in a real bed and enjoy a good home cooked meal or at least a decent take-out meal."

"Okay, Junior. Perhaps we started off wrong. Let's go home and enjoy each other's company."

But Uncle Brad was silently praying that God would present anoth-er opportunity for him to minister to his lost and dying nephew.

Hours passed and we made several stops to stretch, eat, and use the restroom. So to kill time while on the road, I decided to ask my uncle one simple question. "Uncle Brad, how does it feel to plan out your life's goals and see them finally come to pass?"

But before he responded, under his breath Uncle Brad thanked God for another opportunity.

"Well, Junior, I know that you do not want to hear this, but not all of my plans worked out the way I wanted them to. God had plans for my life as well and I had to give up some of my desires and be obedient to God's calling on my life. Eventually, He opened up other successful doors for me and one door led to a successful pastoral life."

"But, Uncle Brad, there are so many successful people in the world who do not believe in God or read the Bible, and yet they are successful. How do you explain that?"

"Junior, we cannot negate the fact that in life, if you sacrifice, you will benefit; working hard eventually brings about good results. How-ever, in Romans it says, 'For the gifts and calling of God are without repentance.' In other words, there are some people who are naturally born with talents and skills. But, Junior, only what you do for Christ will last. Remember God gives and God takes away!

"You can have everything in life that you set out to achieve, but if it does not bless God, it means nothing. The Bible also says in Mark chapter 8, 'For what shall it profit a man, if he shall gain the whole world, and lose his own soul? Or what shall a man give in exchange for his soul?' Just because someone has riches and seems to be successful does not mean that they have joy and peace of mind. I'm talking about the joy that only God can give you on the inside when everything on the outside is turned upside down.

"No one can take this peace of mind from you. Just like the peace you felt leaving the prison today. At that moment, nothing could have taken the feeling of those prison doors slamming behind you. Although you did not have much money in your pocket when you left prison, the peace of mind and joy you felt was worth it all. Money does not buy you joy or peace of mind. Only God can give you joy and peace.

"Junior, the kind of fulfillment you are talking about is happiness, which is based on happenings. Most people look like they are happy because they have lots of fame and fortune in their lives and can obtain anything that their hearts desire, but if God took those possessions from them, would they still have happiness? When you were in prison, God gave you that peace and joy that no man could have taken away from you if they tried, but now that you are free, you want to try life without Him. This is a very dangerous game you are playing, Junior!

"The Apostle Paul said it best in Romans 11, '...Be not high minded, but fear: for if God spared not the natural branches, take heed lest he also spare not thee.'"

"Uncle Brad! I only want to achieve my goals in life like other successful people. There is always someone in this family who tries to control the way I think or either disagrees with the path that I would like to take in life. It's hard enough to decide what you want to be in life, and even harder when your family members try to make those decisions for you and in the process shoot down your dreams and goals."

"Junior, you are full of anger and bitterness towards your parents and anyone else who tries to tell you the same thing. I'm asking you to cast all of your cares upon God. He can turn all your wrongs into rights. He can give you joy where there is sorrow. He can make you strong where you are weak and He can build up what has been torn down! Junior, the devil is filling your head with all these negative thoughts by reminding you of your past, but God can make you feel positively whole again if you allow Him to work in your life as you move towards your future dreams and goals."

"Uncle Brad, no disrespect to you, but God just does not have any time for a person like me who has so many issues. He already showed me how much he cared about me—look where you picked me up from."

"That is not true, Junior. God has plenty of time for people like you. In fact, that is what God loves to do best—help His people solve their problems. The main reason why God sent His Son was for people like you, Junior—the lost and broken-hearted. And He was born, suffered and died for all of mankind's sins."

Then I held up my hand in a stop position and said, "Okay, okay Uncle Brad! I know what you are trying to do and where you are going with this, but I prefer not to talk about God right now. The subject alone really makes me angry! I know all the failures and wrong turns I made in life, but right now I have plans and they DO NOT include God! Uncle Brad, I know that there will be struggles, but if I can endure the correctional facility for fifteen years, I think I can endure life without God!"

"Well, Junior, I'm not going to pressure you any longer. As you mentioned earlier, I am a man of the cloth and would love to see everyone get saved. God will not force His ways on any man and neither will I. Know that if you ever change your mind and would like to accept the Lord Jesus Christ as your personal Savior, I will be here for you. Just remember, Junior, you can run, but you cannot hide from God. Whatever purpose He has for your life, it shall come to pass, willingly or unwillingly."

"Wait, wait Uncle Brad. What do you mean "unwillingly?" I was always taught that God would not force man to follow His ways."

"Yes, that is true for some people, Junior, but there are others who have a calling on their lives to preach the Gospel and God will use them to save thousands, if not millions of people. Junior, you are one of those people who have a calling on your life and God wants to use you in ministry. God's hand of protection is on your life, so even if the devil tries to kill you, he will not succeed because God has dispatched an army of angels to protect every move and step you make. Junior, you are called by God whether you like it or not and there are many souls counting on you to lead them to Salvation. So you see, you must walk in God's ways and keep His Commandments!

"God will allow you to have your playtime for a while, but when God created you, He placed a special gift in you that needs to be fulfilled, and many people are waiting to hear from you. When God has had enough and is ready for you, your playtime will be over and things will no longer line up the way you planned. He will block all your plans until He gets your undivided attention!

"Trust me, Junior. You do not want to go down that road with God; it is not a pleasure walk in the park."

I turned my head towards the car window. I had heard enough about God, and said in a loud voice, "Whatever, Uncle Brad! We are no longer having any more conversations about God. I just would like to go home now."

# CHAPTER ONE

Unable to sleep, Lois Rose tossed and turned in bed all night. But it was not new to her because she experienced insomnia for so many years in her adult life. Her doctor tried different prescriptions to address her sleeping disorder but none worked. Besides, Lois Rose, better known by everyone as Mother, a title given to senior women who had been a church member for years at The Love Church of God Assembly. Mother Rose was fully aware of all the side effects that medication had these days—depression, liver damage, blindness, strokes, thoughts of suicide, or even worst, sudden death.

Mother Rose did not want to be the doctor's human experiment and was not willing to keep trying different types of medication that could potentially kill her. She also knew, although people took medications, they were not really healed by them. Medications only controlled their illnesses, meaning people would probably be taking medications for life, causing additional illnesses along the way. As she thought about how many drug dealers were arrested daily, she wondered about these pharmaceutical companies. To her, they were the biggest drug dealers.

So she had her own remedy, and that was praying and reading the Bible, which always seemed to help her fall asleep. But this particular night no matter how much she prayed and read the Bible, sleep was absent from her body. Mother Rose began to get frustrated, but then realized the enemy had stolen her sleep from her and now he was trying to steal her joy as well. She quickly recognized the devil's devices and began to rebuke him and told him that he did not have any place in her home!

Mother Rose decided to make herself a cup of tea with honey, which always seemed to help her relax. She got out of bed, put on her bathrobe and made her way to the kitchen. Sitting down at the kitchen table while the teakettle was heating, her mind drifted back to her past again, a past she wished to forget.

She knew giving up on God was not an option. She continued to walk and trust God all these years because He was truly her lifeline. God knew that He could trust her with those trials and she would still be faithful to Him. Many opportunities arose where Mother Rose could have turned her back on God, but when she was ten years old, she remembered giving her heart to the Lord. She had sworn to God back then that she would serve Him until she died. Although she was at the tender age of ten, she meant it then and still means it today.

Walking and trusting God was easier said than done. She distinctly remembered telling her parents when she was about nineteen years old, "Living for God is not so difficult; just simply follow God's Word and everything will be alright because He knows how much everyone could handle."

She also remembered both her parents' reactions; they had this strange look on their faces as they stared at each other. They knew then that she would later discover that living for God can be difficult at times, but her parents did not want to discourage her from her walk of faith. Because she was so young in the Lord, it would be better for her to discover it on her own.

Whenever you are denying your own self-will and taking up your cross to follow God's will, there will be many challenges and tests. But one thing Mother Rose was right about — and it's still true today — God does not give us more than we can handle, and He gives us the grace to go through. Nevertheless, God allowed her past to happen and she still survived! If she had to say so herself, she turned out to be a pretty good person spiritually, as well as morally, praise God!

Suddenly a loud whistling sound broke Mother Rose's concentration as she jumped and raced towards the stove. Having her cup ready, she began to sip the tea with delight. Feeling more relaxed after finishing her tea, Mother Rose looked at the clock on the kitchen wall and realized it was her favorite time of the day, 5:00 a.m., prayer time. As she reached for the phone to dial her prayer partner's number, her phone rang; her prayer partner beat her to it. She picked up the phone eagerly ready to pray, and said, "Good morning, Mother Williamson! Praise the Lord!"

Mother Williamson was just as excited as Mother Rose and replied, "Praise the Lord and good morning to you too! How are you doing on this beautiful day that the Lord has made?"

"Well," said Mother Rose, "the enemy has been trying to steal my sleep and rest from me during the night and he keeps reminding me of my life's mistakes and failures." Mother Williamson got upset because she was tired of the enemy attacking her best friend's sleep. So she told Mother Rose to remind Satan that he's a defeated foe and remind him of his future, and fight back in prayer. Then Mother Williamson asked her to lead prayer.

She agreed. "I would love to pray." She paused for a few minutes with tears in her eyes and said, "God, You are so awesome!"

After prayer, Mother Rose turned on the television to find out the weather that the Lord was going to bless Atlanta with. The forecast was about 75 degrees and no chance of rain so she decided to cook her twin daughters their favorite breakfast—pancakes, eggs and turkey bacon.

Anytime she wanted to wake the girls early so they could enjoy a fun-filled day, she would just cook their favorite breakfast. Just the aroma alone would give them that burst of energy they needed to get out of bed and get dressed quickly. Now breakfast was ready, and Mother Rose did not even have to tell them to come and eat because they were already seated at the kitchen table.

Still rubbing her eyes, Eva said, "Mom, we are hip to your morning tricks."

Mother Rose smiled with her back towards the girls while she prepared their plates.

"What are you talking about? What tricks?"

Ava, agreeing with her sister, said, "Yeah, Mom, we know that if you want to wake us up early, you always cook our favorite breakfast. But any other day, we just get the regular treatment."

Both girls high-fived each other as they giggled.

When everyone was seated at the table holding hands, Mother Rose prayed, "Father, I thank you for allowing me to raise beautiful, bright twin girls who love You with all their hearts, minds and souls. I thank You so much for their godly values and how You have given them a mind to want to learn about life and all that it has to offer them. Thank you for giving them favor to excel in all their classes in school. I am very proud of both girls, and know that as long as they stay committed and grounded in You, God, I know You will give them the desires of their hearts."

Eva opened one of her eyes and said, "Mom, can we eat? You are praying off the grid again with those long prayers."

Her sister, Ava, sighed and thanked Eva for pointing out the obvious.

Mother Rose chuckled. "God, thank you for this food. Bless the hands that had anything to do with preparing it and take out all impurities so that it will be healthy to our bodies. Amen!"

After breakfast, Mother Rose mentioned that the day was going to be beautiful. She thought that they could go bike riding in the park, grab lunch and if they were not too tired, visit the park's free circus show in the evening. Before she could complete her sentence, both girls were showering her with kisses of thankfulness and appreciation.

Being a single parent and trying to raise twin, teenage daughters was not easy, but neither girl asked for much because they understood her financial circumstance. Besides, the girls were involved in a lot of activities at church and school, which kept them very busy and not involved with expensive activities.

Mother Rose and the church members always referred to Ava and Eva as the "girls" and they were comfortable with that. When they traveled, they took public transportation. If a trip was not too far, the girls and Mother Rose would just ride their bicycles to their destination. Although she managed to obtain her driver's license after all these years, buying a car with her retirement salary would be more like a dream come true. Who knows? Maybe one day she will be able to buy a car.

In Atlanta, The Love Church of God Assembly was preparing to celebrate its 50th anniversary, which was being held in the basement of the church. Although The Love Church of God Assembly was considered a small church, whenever these types of events took place, all the mothers of the church would get involved to make sure everything was done with elegance and excellence.

Of all the mothers, there was only one person who could coordinate everything with perfection leading up to a fun-filled joyful night, and that was the one and only Mother Rose! With her years of experience, she was always the driving force behind these types of preparations; she was definitely the right mother for the job!

To avoid paying extra outside expenses, the church would always cater their own events and hold them in their basement as opposed to renting a costly hall and hiring a caterer. This was where all the mothers played a key role in making these types of events a huge success—they prepared the food.

However, the leader of the church, Pastor Paul, was carrying a heavy burden on his shoulders that most of the members were not aware of. Although the church was planning its 50th anniversary, they did not realize there was not enough money to purchase food to feed everyone. To add salt to the wound, the air conditioners in the basement were not working.

Pastor Paul had not confided in anyone about the church's financial challenges; only the church's treasurers were aware. After all, how many times could he stand before the congregation asking for funds? After several months of receiving offerings, the church still had not met the targeted amount. Pastor knew that if God did not come through for them, their anniversary would have to be postponed! He was not willing to quit or give up because he knew that during the darkest hours is when your break-through comes from the Lord.

Pastor Paul was frustrated because he could not figure out why so many seasoned Christians were not faithful in giving God their tithes and offerings as the Bible instructed. Though their financial struggles were real, honoring God with tithes and offerings would bring abundant blessings because of obedience. Needless to say, all they were doing was passing up their blessing.

He sighed and whispered a prayer, "Oh God, how I just wish people would grab a hold of Your concepts! Everything belongs to You, God! You are allowing us to keep the ninety percent and all You ask is that we give ten percent to help finance the House of God.

"If everyone followed this simple concept, not only would they be blessed individually, but the congregation would also be blessed corporately. God, help me to teach your people that honoring their financial commitment to you will reap great dividends."

Pastor continued, "God, Your Word states in the book of Numbers that You are not a man, that You should lie. Your Word also states in Malachi to 'Bring ye all the tithes into the storehouse, that there may be meat in mine house, and prove me now herewith, saith the Lord of hosts, If I will not open you the windows of heaven and pour you out a blessing that there shall not be room enough to receive it.'

"Father, many may argue that this was for the Old Testament times, but God, whether it is coming from the Old Testament in Malachi or the New Testament in Hebrews, You are speaking and we should listen. God, please help them to see the bigger picture and that it takes finances to keep the house of God functioning. Your Word also says in Luke chapter six, 'Give, and it shall be given unto you; good measure, pressed down, and shaken together, and running over, shall men give into your bosom.' God, when they are obedient to Your Word, You will cause their enemies to give unto them when they do not even know why!"

Pastor Paul was really disappointed and saddened because they had not even scratched the surface on the amount of money needed to support this church event. He felt this was not the time to stop praying because he knew that his God is faithful. He began walking around the sanctuary praying:

"Father, I do not put my confidence in what I see, but I put my confidence in You and Your Word. Father, I ask that You allow my thoughts to be victorious, prosperous and successful as we plan our church's 50th anniversary. Father, I refuse to think negatively. I choose to think big and expect that You will do awesome things on behalf of this ministry. Eyes have not seen nor ears heard the things You have prepared for this ministry. Your Word says in Psalm 37:25, 'I have been young, and now am old; yet have I not seen the righteous forsaken, nor his seed begging bread', so I thank You in advance for bestowing a financial miracle on this ministry because You are the God who specializes in all types of miracles.

"Father, just as You spoke the world into existence and said, 'life and death is in the power of the tongue', so I decree and declare that this ministry shall be lenders and not borrowers! I command the church financial circumstances to line up with Your Word. God, You are Jehovah-Jireh, the Lord that will provide, and I thank You for providing everything we lack today. In Jesus' Name, Amen!"

Pastor, not wanting to trouble his heart any longer about his members, decided to place them into God's hands and believed that they would be obedient and develop a strong desire to want to help finance the house of God.

Pastor Paul realized his cell phone was ringing in his office earlier, but he made it a habit not to answer his phone during prayer so he let it go straight to voicemail. Almost everyone knew, including his family, that if he was talking to God on his behalf or praying for someone else, all calls would have to wait because he did not like interrupting his conversation with God for anyone!

After praying, Pastor Paul headed towards his office and checked his cell phone to see who had been trying to reach him. He was staring at his phone for a couple of seconds because he did not recognize the number displayed. Then he listened to the message, but could not make out what the person was saying on the phone because there was so much background noise making it very difficult understanding the person.

Finally he gave up and decided to press the redial button. When a voice said hello, Pastor Paul introduced himself. A cheery voice on the other end of the phone gave him a calm feeling that this was not one of his emergency calls where he would either have to rush off to the hospital, the police station or comfort someone due to death in the family.

"Oh hello, Pastor Paul. This is Sam from the Super Tender Meat Market around the corner. I was trying to call you."

"Hello Sam. Sorry I did not recognize your number. I could not make out what you were saying in your message so I just hit the redial button. How are you doing?"

Sam answered, "I'm sorry about that. Perhaps I should have called you during our least busy time at the store. But I understand, Pastor, it's not like we call each other on a daily basis. I would not expect you to be familiar with my number. So to answer your question, I'm fine and thanks for asking.

"On another note, I was speaking with your wife earlier today and she mentioned that your church was celebrating its 50th anniversary and she wanted to invite me and my family. I was so excited I told her that The Love Church of God Assembly has been a blessing to this community for 50 years and I felt it was now time that the community gave back to the church. Pastor Paul, you have been praying for our sick and troubled family members for years and no matter how late or how far we needed you to go, you were always there. You are a true man of God.

"I clearly remember how you were right there for my wife as she passed by your church and went into labor with our middle child. She told me that you took care of her as if she were your own wife and you even went to the hospital with her and stayed right by her bedside until you were able to get a hold of me. So, as our gratitude towards you, I called some of my friends and other neighborhood stores to help out with this special celebration. I would like to stop by today to discuss exactly what the church still needs to finalize everything as our humble way of saying thank you so much for your dedication to the community!"

Hearing nothing, Sam said, "Hello? Pastor Paul, are you still there or engaged in another conversation with someone else?"

Then Sam realized that he was praising God because he was so overwhelmed with joy.

Finally Pastor Paul managed to say, "I'm still here, Sam. I'm just so lost for words right now. I would like to thank you on behalf of The Love Church of God Assembly for helping us out in this time of need. I'll be at the church until 7:30 p.m. today. If you would like to stop by any time before then, you are more than welcome. But if you are really busy, I can also stop by The Super Tender Meat Market."

"No, Pastor, that is quite alright. I can stop by in thirty minutes and gather a list of things that you need."

Pastor Paul replied, "Thank you so much for allowing God to use you, Sam. You are a good man and God is going to tremendously bless you."

Pastor Paul was so amazed at how fast God answered his prayers from this morning. He went straight into giving God praise and before he knew it, the doors of the church swung open and the sanctuary was illuminated with strong sunlight from outside. Looking at his watch, he was even more stunned because he could not believe that he had been praising God for thirty minutes already. It felt as if he had just hung up the phone with Sam.

When Sam arrived at the church, Pastor Paul immediately greeted him. Both gentlemen embraced each other as if they were old high school buddies. As he led Sam into his office, he asked him to have a seat and then offered him a cold glass of water. Sam explained that he did not have much time to stay, so if he did not mind, they could go straight into discussing what food the church still needed to purchase.

Pastor looked puzzled so Sam said, "I do not want you to be shy. Please, tell me where the community could help. For instance, exactly what types of meats would you like me to donate, and what other types of food choices do you want to serve?"

"Oh no, Sam. I'm not being shy about asking for anything because the church could really use a helping hand. I'm just not too sure what dishes are being served so here is my house number. Speak with my wife and Mother Rose about what types of dishes they plan on serving."

Pastor Paul then asked Sam if he know of anyone who could fix air conditioners. He would only be able to pay the person in small monthly installments.

"Well, it's funny you should ask me about air conditioners. That is why I also wanted to stop by. When the people in the neighborhood saw your banner announcing the church's 50th anniversary, the community decided to assist by receiving a collection. We know that we all couldn't fit in the basement, so we decided to go this way instead."

Sam reached in his pocket and retrieved his phone to make a call. Then he asked Pastor Paul to follow him to the main sanctuary. More than three dozen people from the local neighborhood came walking through the church doors. With everyone around, Sam announced to Pastor Paul that the community wanted to contribute seven thousand dollars to The Love Church of God Assembly for their

50 years of servicing the community.

"What! Praise God!" shouted Pastor Paul.

He was steadily praising God and the people were just as excited as he was. Some were crying, some were just smiling and others were praising God that they were able to be a blessing. After everyone calmed down, Sam decided to make another announcement to Pastor Paul who could not believe how God was causing people to give in abundance so readily.

Sam said, "Pastor Paul, as far as getting your air conditioners fixed, I will ask my son to stop by next week to install brand new air conditioners all expenses paid."

Pastor Paul could not believe it as he buried his face into his hands and wept like a child.

Then he said, "You all do not know what this truly means to us and how much we appreciate your acts of kindness."

Pastor Paul grabbed Sam's hand and asked that everyone join hands so that he could pray for the community as a whole. After he prayed and everyone was about to leave, Sam handed his business card to Pastor Paul and told him if there was anything else he could do to help out, just give him a call.

Pastor Paul said, "I know that everyone cannot fit in the basement, but I'm expecting to see some of your faces at the church's celebration." Pastor Paul was mostly looking at Sam. He continued, "It will not only be an honor, but a blessing to have some of you with us."

Most of them said they would really try. Sam did not want to commit, but said he would let the Pastor definitely know in a couple of days. If he could not, he would make sure someone from his family would be there to represent him.

Pastor knew that the hand of God was upon The Love Church of God Assembly making sure that the ministry did not lack anything. Earlier, the church did not know how God was going to bless them. Now, God not only caused them to be blessed financially, but He opened the windows of heaven and poured out so many blessings that they did not have room enough to receive them. God made a way where all the church's anniversary needs were met, and some of the other church expenses were also paid. God is awesome and marvelous are His works!

Who wouldn't want to serve a God like Him, a God who cares and can supply all our need according to His riches and glory?

# CHAPTER TWO

Preparation time for the church's 50th anniversary had begun. Almost all the Mothers of the church were in the kitchen helping out wherever their hands were needed making sure everything was cooked with perfection. Mother Rose especially liked micro-managing her crew, which had become an occupational habit because she was truly a perfectionist and wanted things done with excellence. She was very strict about a clean kitchen and everyone had to wear hairnets and gloves at all times; it was not an option while handling the food. Mother Rose made it a habit of walking around the kitchen floor making sure that no one fell behind on their tasks because time was of the essence.

All the Mothers came together to start prepping their individual dishes. Mother Rose noticed from the corner of her eyes that Mother Curtis had a slight cough and was sampling various foods with the same stirring spoon and licking it afterwards. She was shocked and could not believe what her eyes were seeing.

From across the kitchen, Mother Rose shouted at the top of her lungs, "Mother Curtis, what are you doing?! We have a strict policy here, not to sample any food with the same utensils that you are cooking with. Also, if you are not feeling very well, excuse yourself from the kitchen area. You are spreading your germs while you are coughing and I should not have to remind everyone that people will be eating this food!

"Mothers, this kitchen should be a healthy and clean environment and our visitors should be able to trust the church to feed them delicious food, not contaminated food that will make them sick! It would be a complete disaster if after having a beautiful celebration, our hospital ministry has to go visit and pray for the sick, not to mention deal with lawsuits later."

She continued, "Mother Curtis, I really appreciate your help and I'm glad that you really wanted to assist today, but it seems that you are a little under the weather and should not be cooking. Please go home and attend to that cold of yours and if you are feeling better tomorrow, perhaps you can help out in another area like grocery shopping, working with the decoration or the cleanup committee. I'm sure they can use a helping hand."

Realizing she had all the Mothers' attention, she asked them to be smart about how they were cooking. "Just as the people of this community were a blessing to our church, we also want to be a blessing to the community."

Finally after several months of planning and preparing, the day arrived for the celebration. The entire room was decorated in white and gold. There were white and gold web light bulbs hanging from the ceiling and also at the top of each wall. There were floating white balloons with gold strings and floating gold balloons with white strings. The tables were set to seat eight people and covered with a rich, gold color tablecloth with white trimmings at the edges. Each table had a fresh bouquet of white roses as the centerpiece with a 50th anniversary sign placed in the middle.

The tables were dressed with eight matching sets of floral gold and white plates, desert plates and salad bowls stacked on top of each other. Some tables had solid white napkins, cups, forks, knives, and spoons while other tables had solid gold items. Every seat had a tall clear glass for toasting. To top things off, the entire evening was being recorded.

The atmosphere of the room was filled with love and fellowship as everybody sat down in their best black and white attire to enjoy each other's company while the meals were served. The volunteer waitresses and waiters took everyone's entrée and beverage order.

The main course choices on the menu were salmon served with twice-baked potatoes with strips of cheese on top and fresh steamed string beans, or blackened chicken served on a bed of dirty rice and asparagus, or sirloin steak served with mashed potatoes and gravy with a mixture of steamed broccoli and cauliflower. All the dishes were served with a house salad and every table had a basket of warm, baked bread and a plate filled with pats of butter and margarine.

While the people ate, there were all sorts of games and prizes for both the children and adults. There was a cash prize of three lots of fifty dollars totaling one hundred and fifty dollars.

The women were interested in winning the centerpieces. Everyone was handed a raffle ticket as they entered the festivities. The only way someone could go home with the beautiful arrangement was if his or her raffle ticket number was called. There was one strict rule: you could not be a winner twice because it would not be fair to everyone else. But there was enjoyment and delight written across everyone's faces as the night continued.

There was live entertainment. It started with two performances from a group of mimes. They slid their bodies across the floor like they were floating on thin air. Then they made you believe they were inside a box when they walked around in a square "touching" imaginary sides; it was so believable. There were also four soloists, and two separate comedy acts that were absolutely hysterical. Nowadays, most people do not agree with Christian comedy, but as long as it is not disrespectful to God's Word, they do agree that laugher is medicine for the soul. There were also two skits: one was about the three Hebrew boys and the other was about the ten virgins. Both skits were outstanding and could have been off-Broadway shows.

To top off the night of entertainment, there were three selections from the one and only The Love Church of God Assembly Choir, also known as TLC Choir. Their choices of songs were so uplifting and inspiring; they sang as if this were their last night on earth. By the time they were finished, only half the TLC Choir was still standing on their feet because the other half was slain in the Spirit, lying on the floor.

Now the hour was getting late and Pastor Paul had to be the one to bring all of the fun and entertainment to a halt. He decided to take over the festivities and give some people a chance to testify about The Love Church of God Assembly before closing out the night. Now everyone wanted to get up and say a few words, but time would not permit, so only a handful of people were able to testify of God's goodness. One member got up and introduced himself as Minister Jimmy Gold and began to give God praise for where He brought the church from to where it was today. He remembered when The Love Church of God Assembly had only seven faithful members and now God increased the membership to over three hundred.

He walked away glorifying God saying, "God is worthy to be praised!"

Then another member stood up and introduced herself as Minister Kimberly Wards and testified how she remembered when Pastor Paul could not afford to heat the church during the winter months and also could not afford to cool the church during the summer months. So, she explained that during the winter months, everyone sat close together during the services with their coats, hats and gloves on and some of members wore extra layers to keep themselves as warm as possible. She said that during the summer months, everyone fanned with whatever they could get their hands on to relieve themselves from the heat. But, she declared that whether it was too cold or too hot, it never discouraged Pastor Paul from preaching the Word of God or the members from praising God for that matter.

Then Minister Wards said, "The saints of God are dedicated and know how to endure hardship as good soldiers and it paid off because today, the church has air conditioners in every room and enough money to pay the gas bill in order to heat up the entire building. God is so good!"

Pastor Paul gave a few more people a chance to give testimonies and everyone was praising God for all He had done over the past fifty years in The Love Church of God Assembly.

Some of the local neighborhood guests also testified how God used Pastor Paul to be a blessing in their lives and community, and also how he did not discriminate but was there for everyone. But the testimonies that topped it all off were from the men and women who were ex-offenders. They got up and testified how they spent years in prison and when they were released, they did not know what direction their lives would go. They thanked God for using the church's prison ministry to introduce them to Christ. The saints taught them how to trust God as He gave them favor every single day. They mentioned how the saints did not judge or reject them. Instead, they were embraced, prayed for, nurtured, and encouraged daily.

They testified about how God promoted some of them to become deacons, ministers, and evangelists in the church; some were working in successful positions with big corporations because the favor of God was on their lives. Some testified how they thought marriage would never come their way, but they met their husbands and wives and now have beautiful families of their own. One gave a testimony that he was able to start a very small business, and hires other ex-convicts to help them get started back into society; they have jobs and are able to support their families. Others stated that they were inspired by God to go back to the very same prisons to minister to other inmates.

Pastor Paul minimized the testimonies because he also wanted to allow time to honor some of the saints because of their tremendous dedication in making the church's 50th anniversary a huge success.

"First," he began, "I would like to thank the community who gave generously when we needed help the most."

He asked everybody who contributed to proudly stand as the rest of the church applauded them. The ushers walked around and gave them a statue of men and women extending their hands out to help someone. The inscription at the bottom of the award read: "We are our Brother's Keeper." They also passed out small plants to the women and gave the men a gift bag that contained toiletries. Everyone began to praise and bless God for opening the hearts of such a caring group of people. The church's members stood, giving them a standing ovation.

Pastor Paul also wanted to recognize everyone who dedicated their time to decorating, cooking and cleaning. He asked that if anyone had a hand in any of these committees to stand as well, while the church thanked them. Once again the ushers walked around passing out large gift bags full of various items to the men and women.

Last, but certainly not least, Pastor presented all the head Mothers with a large arrangement of flowers and a gift certificate to an all-day spa for a full body massage, facial, pedicure, manicure and lunch. Everyone stood, blew whistles, and clapped their hands. Some shouted out that the Mothers did an excellent job! Pastor walked over to Mother Rose and personally handed her an envelope with a love offering telling her that she just keeps outperforming her own self. He hugged and kissed her and told her that she was truly appreciated and loved.

There were so many wonderful memories to take home that night.

The video team worked extremely hard burning DVDs so everyone could leave with a recording of the event. Now that the event had come to a close and everyone was starting to leave, all the Mothers and the cleanup committee pitched in to prepare the basement for Sunday school service the next day. Cleaning up did not take much effort at all because the Mothers cleaned up as they served. All they needed to do to complete the job was to fold all of the tables and chairs. Within less than one hour, everything was finally finished.

All the Mothers who did not have cars were taken home by some of the deacons in the church who were patiently waiting outside for them.

Arriving home from church, Mother Rose was physically wiped out. She carefully placed all her gifts on the kitchen table and kicked off her shoes. The girls were equally as tired and went straight to their bedroom to prepare for bed.

Mother Rose kept admiring the beautiful bouquet of flowers. She knew that they needed to be put in water so she managed to gain enough strength to get up out of her comfortable chair and quickly looked for a vase. She searched in her kitchen cabinets for a suitable one and finally laid her hands on the perfect one in which to place the flowers.

Immediately sitting back down, she reached for the pearl-handled spa gift bag with the words 'Thank You' all over it in various languages, font sizes and colors. The bag contained a gift certificate for an all-day spa treatment along with the latest Christian magazines, and her personal bathrobe and slippers to take with her to the spa. Everyone who knew Mother Rose also knew how picky she could be whenever she had to wear someone else's clothing, so they thought it would be best if they purchased her a personal robe and slippers.

Next, she picked up the envelope from the table and pulled out a card that seemed to be signed by the entire church. Inside the card were all new crisp one hundred dollar bills. When she counted them, they totaled five hundred dollars. Mother Rose buried her face in the card and wept all over it. Then she looked up and gave God thanks. She was not a person who believed in taking handouts from people. She was raised to believe in working for anything you wanted in life. But with this church gift, she was willing to make an exception because she did not want to block her blessing or anyone else's blessing for that matter. Deep down in her heart, she knew that the church really could not afford to bless her with this amount of money so she thanked God again.

The girls had already prepared themselves for bed and came out of their room to give their mother a good night kiss. That was when they saw all the hundred dollar bills laying on the table. They looked with amazement but were too tired to engage in a conversation about the money. They both kissed Mother Rose on each cheek and told her again that she did a fabulous job with the celebration.

Once again, Mother Rose was extremely tired but sleep was absent from her body so she went to the kitchen to prepare a hot cup of tea to relax as she began reading the Bible.

# CHAPTER THREE

It was 6:00 a.m. on a cool Sunday morning. Joseph was known by all of his neighbors as a loner. No matter where you saw Joseph, he would always be alone even during the busiest holiday seasons. Today, he was outside taking his usual morning stroll and feeding the birds along the way as this was a daily routine for him since he had retired seven years ago.

This particular morning while walking he remembered how bad the storm was the night before and the evidence was clearly everywhere. Some streets were flooded while others were covered with puddles of water. This made it almost impossible for him to walk a straight line. With every step he took, Joseph almost felt like a kid again playing the hopscotch game. He could not help but laugh because if no one else was enjoying the aftermath of the rain, the birds were enjoying every bit of it as they were bathing and playing in the puddles of water.

All of a sudden from a distance, he noticed that one of the huge puddles in a flooded area had an object protruding from it. Joseph cautiously approached the area and recognized that it was a handrail from a bicycle. As he drew nearer, his eyes widen with shock because now the handrail looked very familiar. He grabbed a balled up handkerchief from his pocket and pulled the object all the way out of the puddle. To his surprise, he immediately identified the bicycle as belonging to one of his neighbors named Miss Rose. To further validate his claim, he also saw her name inscribed across the back of the bicycle seat!

Joseph was totally confused at this point and could not imagine how Miss Rose's bicycle wound up immersed in a pool of water blocks from their apartment building complex. Questions began racing through his head. *Did she get stuck in the bad weather with her bicycle last night and decide that she could no longer ride in the storm, leave it and take a cab home instead? Or did someone give her a ride home but the bicycle could not fit in the car? Certainly not,* thought Joseph. *Miss Rose loves that bicycle with all her heart and I just cannot see her leaving it on the side of the road to get run over by other vehicles.*

Joseph had no answers to his questions. He started looking around further to see if he could also spot her daughters' bicycles as well, but there were no signs of their bicycles anywhere. Now his concerns intensified and he became very concerned about Miss Rose and her daughters. To find Miss Rose's bicycle and not her daughters' bicycles was very odd because they frequently rode their bicycles together.

⸙

During Sunday morning service at The Love Church of God Assembly, everyone was still excited from the celebration, which was a big success. But many of the members could not help but notice that there were three empty seats where Mother Rose and her daughters usually sat, especially Mother Williamson who was Mother Rose's prayer partner and best friend. She could not help but wonder what may have happened to her best friend who missed their 5:00 a.m. prayer call and wasn't in the Sunday morning service. *Perhaps she got sick and was unable to answer the phone when I called this morning,* thought Mother Williamson. But after further thought she dismissed the idea because the girls would have answered the phone. There were very few Sundays that the Rose family missed. In fact, Mother Williamson could not recall the last time they did not come to church. What made their absence even more strange was that it was the Sunday morning service after the church's 50th anniversary event.

Mother Williamson was not the only one who wondered why the Rose family did not show up to church. That morning while Pastor Paul was thanking everyone again for their help in the church's celebration, he didn't see Mother Rose, who basically organized everything. This seemed really odd and he hoped that everything was okay with her. After service, many of the concerned members approached him to find out if he heard or knew the whereabouts of Mother Rose and the girls, but he was as clueless and shocked as everyone else. Still puzzled, Pastor Paul recommended that after service one of the church members try to find Mother Rose's best friend, Mother Williamson, and see if she had heard from Mother Rose or the girls.

Hastening through the crowd outside the church, Mother Williamson had one thing on her mind and that was to go to Mother Rose's apartment and find out why she and the girls did not show up for Sunday service. One of the church members recognized that Mother Williamson was rushing through the crowd and not stopping to speak to anyone, which was very unusual for her. Sister Winn called out her name twice and finally got her attention. When she caught up with her, she began asking all sorts of questions about the Rose family. Mother Williamson interrupted and told Sister Winn that she is just as shocked as everyone else and was on her way to Mother Rose's apartment to make sure everything was okay and she would contact the church later.

Joseph suddenly noticed another familiar neighbor who did not live in their apartment building complex but who he would see speaking with Miss Rose on a regular basis. He also noticed Miss Rose's wet bicycle lying on the ground next to a huge puddle of water and wondered why it was left outside her apartment unattended while neither she nor her daughters were anywhere nearby to be found.

Both gentlemen formally introduced themselves with a handshake. Joseph introduced himself as a retired private investigator while Zachariah introduced himself as the neighborhood handyman claiming to be able to fix anything. Zachariah asked Joseph when last he had seen Miss Rose.

"Just yesterday morning. We always meet during the morning hours," replied Joseph. "Oh, by the way," he continued, "Please do not touch the bicycle with your bare hands." Then he quickly apologized. "Please excuse me. It is a habit I picked up over the years as a PI."

Joseph asked Zachariah did he know where Mother Rose lived.

"Of course I do. I've fixed and installed plenty of things inside her apartment," he replied.

"Great! Can you please do me a favor and go knock on her door to see if anyone answers? Also, try calling her as well. Meanwhile I will contact the police and make sure no one else tampers with the evidence, I mean the bicycle. Sorry again, these types of habits are really hard to break."

"No apologies. Sure I will go," said Zachariah as he started walking towards her apartment building. Minutes later, Zachariah returned with the most concerned look on his face and Joseph knew at that moment, based on his PI experiences, that they should prepare themselves for the worst. Zachariah's voice began to crack as he spoke. "No one answered the door when I knocked. I even banged on the door and called her name, but still no answer."

"Okay," replied Joseph, and he told Zachariah that he had called the police and they were coming to assess the situation. Joseph knew it was very important to do things quickly in case this was a missing persons incident because every second counted. While in conversation with Zachariah, Joseph noticed one of Miss Rose's close friends who he would always see her with from time to time going toward Miss Rose's apartment building. Trying to get her attention, Joseph began waving both of his hands high in the air. Mother Williamson noticed Joseph and waved back to let him know he had gotten her attention. She did not know him too well, but was wondering if this man knew anything about her best friend.

Mother Williamson quickly walked over to him and introduced herself, but immediately looked down and noticed Mother Rose's bicycle lying on the ground by a huge puddle of water. She burst into tears and Joseph began comforting her. He told her how he had discovered it moments ago and pulled it out of the water and just definitely identified the bicycle as Miss Rose's. He also informed her that Zachariah knocked on her door and even tried calling her, but there was no answer. He would have knocked on some of the neighbors' doors, but it was still early and everyone was probably still in bed.

Mother Williamson frantically asked, "How did my friend's bike get here? Has something happened to her while she was riding to church?"

While wiping the tears from her eyes, Joseph asked in a nervous voice, "Miss Williamson, we were hoping you knew where Miss Rose was."

Mother Williamson shook her head and said, "She did not answer my phone calls this morning which was extremely odd because we always have prayer at 5:00 a.m. to start off our day."

Zachariah noticed that Miss Williamson had a scared look on her face.

She started to cry again and said, "I hope nothing bad happened to my friend and her daughters."

Zachariah tried calming her down. He said, "You just came from church. Obviously you are a God-fearing lady. Just pray and believe God that everything is all right concerning them."

Joseph asked her if she knew of any other living relatives she might have gone to visit in an emergency and if they could contact them. Then Mother Williamson began to cry hysterically as she struggled to speak. She shook her head.

"Mother Rose has no living relatives that she ever mentioned to me. I have never heard her talk about calling or visiting anyone for as long as I have known her."

Zachariah thought to himself that things weren't looking good for Miss Rose and her two daughters. It was as if they just vanished into thin air and a bicycle was left outside her apartment building to remind everybody of their presence.

Mother Williamson said, "I wish I had a key to her apartment but she never offered one to me. We must call the police and report the family missing! I asked some of the girls' friends at church this morning if they spoke with either of them, but no one heard from them today."

Joseph assured her that they had already contacted the police and they should arrive shortly. He also suggested that Mother Williamson stick around because the police may want to question her because she was more familiar with the family than anyone else. As they were speaking, the police drove up to the scene.

Detective Thomas and Detective Lee introduced themselves to the small group of neighbors and spectators, while uniformed police followed. Detective Thomas started asking questions while Detective Lee and the officers combed the area for anything suspicious or odd.

"Can someone explain what happened and what is this about a

bicycle lying in a pool of water?"

Considering that he was the first to find the bicycle, Joseph started off by introducing himself as Joseph Walker and explaining that he was the one who contacted the police and how he discovered his neighbor's bicycle immersed in water and did not know her whereabouts. He went on to say that he would normally see the Rose family riding their bicycles almost every day so he is very familiar with their bicycles.

Detective Thomas asked, "Among you all, who would have been the last person to have seen Miss Rose and her family?"

Mother Williamson slowly raised her hand and said, "That would be me, Detective.

Detective Thomas replied, "When and where was the last place you saw the missing people?"

"Last night, at my church's 50th anniversary celebration. The family must have left around 12:00 a.m. after the celebration in Deacon Brown's car."

Mother Williamson explained how Deacon Brown would offer some of the Mothers of the church a ride home after late night services, which is why she knew that the family did not ride their bicycles to church last night. While Detective Thomas asked questions, Detective Lee began to comb the area for additional clues and told all the spectators who had gathered around to stand clear of the area.

"So you are saying that Miss Rose and her family live in your apartment building which is about three blocks from here, Mr. Walker?" asked Detective Thomas.

"Yes, that is correct, sir."

"So how did Miss Rose's bicycle get outside and so far away from where she lives? Did she keep the bicycle chained outside of the apartment building at night?"

Mother Williamson said, "No."

Her mouth was now twisted to the side of her face as she thought, *Okay Lord, he is definitely not the sharpest tool in the shed. He is supposed to be helping us find out the answer to why her bicycle is outside her apartment.*

Detective Thomas interrupted her thought and asked her, "Did she attend church service this morning?"

As he continued to question her, Mother Williamson went to a nearby bench to sit and change her shoes into something more comfortable. She always carried around a second pair just in case her feet started to hurt or if she planned on doing a lot of walking. Mother Williamson answered no to his question.

"I was heading to her apartment to see if everything was okay when I was stopped by her neighbors, Mr. Joseph and Mr. Zachariah. Mother Rose never keeps her bicycle or the girls' bicycles chained up outside under no circumstances so I'm not sure how this one got here. When I tried to call her this morning for prayer she did not answer."

Detective Thomas quickly asked, "Around what time was that?"

"5:00 a.m.," she replied with tears in her eyes again wondering if something terrible happened to her best friend.

"Miss Williamson, how old are the girls?"

"They are only fifteen years old." Then Mother Williamson began to pray softly under her breath, "Lord God, please wherever they may be, please keep them safe from all hurt, harm and danger."

"Now considering that there are minors involved, you're her best friend, and no one knows if she has relatives nearby, we'll need you to come down to the police station and answer some more questions," explained Detective Thomas. "The police department will follow-up with the super to open the apartment door. Hopefully, we will hear from her soon, but if not, we will have to put out an all-points, missing persons bulletin on the entire family. Normally, when an adult is missing, we do not take action until after the person has been missing for more than forty-eight hours, but since there are two minors involved, we'll take immediate action. If we do not hear from them in a couple of days, we will start a reward fund in the amount of one thousand dollars, and hope that someone will come forward with information."

"That's a blessing," replied Mother Williamson, "but hopefully it will not have to come to that!"

Mother Williamson agreed to cooperate and then reached inside her pocketbook to retrieve an old family photo of them that she kept in her wallet and handed it to Detective Thomas before he could even ask.

"Thanks Miss Williamson. I was just about to ask you, but you beat me to it. Is this a recent photo of the family?"

"Sorry Detective Thomas, but that picture is about five years old."

"Okay, well thanks anyway; it's a start. Miss Williamson, do not worry. We are going to do everything in our power to find them." Both detectives walked towards their patrol car.

Both Joseph and Zachariah were taken back by what transpired concerning the Rose family. Joseph ran to Miss Williamson and handed her his business card.

"Please give me a call if you learn anymore news about Miss Rose and her two daughters."

"I certainly will," replied Mother Williamson. "Nice to have met the both of you and thanks so much for your understanding hearts."

Detective Lee ordered the area to be taped off by one of the rookies so that no one would walk in and accidentally damage any additional clues that could be in the area. Joseph knew that there were children going missing daily and the police department did not have the resources to dedicate their time to one case. He and Zachariah would have to take matters into their own hands and do some investigating of their own.

Miss Rose meant something to everyone in the neighborhood—to Joseph especially, because during the lonely holiday seasons, she always made him feel wanted like he was a part of her family. As for Zachariah, he knew that she did not have much so he always tried to fix anything of hers that broke and not charge her for it. Being the person she was, she always insisted on giving him something even if it was just a plate of food or a hot cup of coffee and a donut.

Both gentlemen exchanged business cards so they could meet the next day to go over their own investigation plans.

# CHAPTER FOUR

When Mother Williamson entered the police station late on Sunday, she noticed all of the eerie photographs of missing people hanging on the walls. Trying to redirect her attention elsewhere, she could not help but notice people who had been recently arrested were all handcuffed and every available chair in the police station was occupied. Detective Thomas caught her attention and asked her to follow him down a long corridor that eventually led to his office. He asked her to be seated in a dark brown worn-out leather chair that told its own story of all the people who had sat in it.

While she was sitting, he offered her coffee or soda, and she simply replied that water would do just fine. Detective Thomas excused himself and went to the vending machine.

Mother Williamson began looking around his office and noticed how messy the conditions were. There were extremely large amounts of files all piled on top of each other and if anyone would hit the pile with the tip of their finger or accidentally bump into his desk, all those files would go tumbling to the floor. She thought, *how on earth can he find anything in those piles of paper? Why doesn't he use those file cabinets in his office to file them away?* When Detective Thomas entered the room, he could read her mind by the expression on her face.

"Do not be concern about my messy office, Miss Williamson. I know where everything is. If I really needed to get my hands on a file quickly, I would probably be able to find that file faster than you could find your makeup bag in your pocketbook. I also know you are probably thinking what if someone mistakenly bumps into the pile and knocks it down to the floor? Well, for starters, hardly anyone comes into my office and besides, I keep it locked whenever I'm not around."

Mother Williamson felt embarrassed and at the same time very impressed by his responses as she thanked him for the water.

"Now that we have cleared the air, can we get started?"

With a smile of comfort on his face, he pulled out a missing person report and an extra writing pen. Mother Williamson nervously gripped the bottle with both hands because, for one moment, she had forgotten why she was there. Detective Thomas told Miss Williamson that he would like her to answer a few questions he had before filling out the missing person report.

"So, did Miss Rose have any enemies?"

"No," replied Mother Williamson. "She is the sweetest person and everybody loves her."

"Did she seem upset about anything this past week?"

"No. As a matter of fact, she was happier than ever because everything was working out so well for the church's 50th anniversary celebration."

"Do you know any of her close relatives or other friends within or outside the states?"

"No. I do not believe she has any other living relatives other than her twin daughters because she has never spoken to me about any other family members."

"So, you are not sure if she has living relatives or not?" asked Detective Thomas.

Mother Williamson looking as if she was giving it a lot of thought finally responded, "No!"

"How about other close friends other than the ones in the church? Does she have any friends outside Georgia?"

Having learned her lesson on how to respond to Detective Thomas' questions when she was not certain, Mother Williamson simply said, "I am not sure."

"Do you know if she was having any financial trouble that would make her want to leave without telling anyone?"

Mother Williamson gave Detective Thomas a look as if to ask, what does her financial status have to do with anything?

Once again, he read the expression on her face and said, "I know this question seems a little weird, but you would be surprised what some people will do when they are financially troubled."

"Oh," replied Mother Williamson. "Well, she is not rich but she survives by God's grace."

Detective Thomas noticed that he was upsetting Miss Williamson so he told her she could start filling out the report. As she began filling out the paperwork, he let her know she could leave once she was done and he would give her a follow-up call if she didn't mind leaving her number with him.

As Mother Williamson filled out the report for her best friend and her family, Detective Thomas made a copy of the family photo that she gave him earlier. When he returned it, he had one last question to ask her, "What is her full name?"

Mother Williamson had to think for a split second because she was so used to calling her Mother Rose. Then it hit her. "Her full name is Lois Rose, but everyone at church calls her Mother Rose."

"Sorry I know I said one last question, but I forgot about her daughters. What are their names?"

Once again Mother Williamson began twisting her lips to the side and said, "Detective Thomas, won't all of this information be on the report?"

"Yes, but I would have to wait until you are finished. I need the information now for something else."

"Oh, I'm sorry. Their names are Ava and Eva."

"Do Ava and Eva also have the same last name as well?"

"Yes they are twins. Ava Rose and Eva Rose are their full names."

Mother Williamson had almost finished filling out the entire report, but there was one question she was unable to answer. She informed Detective Thomas that she would have to leave one question blank because she did not know anything about Mother Rose's marital status.

Detective Thomas looked over his eyeglasses at her and leaned forward on his desk and said, "How many years were you friends?"

"We have been friends for at least fifteen years. I met her when the girls were babies."

Then in a gentle tone, Detective Thomas said, "You mean to tell me that you do not know if she was ever married or not?"

"No, I do not. Why is that so strange?" replied Mother Williamson as she had about enough of his questioning. Nevertheless, she proceeded to explain, "Although we have been good friends for years, some people like to keep certain things private so out of respect, I never asked."

Detective Thomas shook his head as if to say I understand and decided to leave the question alone.

As Mother Williamson got up to leave his office, she handed him the completed report and her phone numbers. He thanked her for all her time and promised her again that the police would do everything in their power to find out what happen to the Rose family. Detective Thomas shook her hand then gave her his business card and told her to give him a call if she should hear or remember something else.

"Oh, I forgot to remind you to please stay close to home just in case she tries to contact you."

"I will, Detective Thomas," replied Mother Williamson as she walked out of his office.

Monday morning did not seem real to Mother Williamson because she and Mother Rose would have already prayed together by now and praying alone at 5:00 a.m. did not feel the same. While still in deep thought, the phone rang. She leaped with excitement and hurried to answer it. "Hello!"

It was Detective Thomas. "Good morning, Miss Williamson. How do you feel this morning? Did you receive any news or phone calls from your friend last night?"

"I'm afraid not," replied Mother Williamson sadly. "I tried calling her again this morning, but no one answered the phone."

"Okay thanks. I just wanted to let you know that a search team, as well as an all-points bulletin were released this morning. I told you that we will do everything in our power to find them."

Mother Williamson profusely thanked Detective Thomas for all his dedication to their case.

"Oh, Miss Williamson?"

"Yes, Detective Thomas?"

"Can you please tell me where I can find or how to contact this Deacon Brown?"

"Sure, hold on while I retrieve his contact information from my address book."

While searching through her address book, she asked herself if this was part two of a bad dream or if this was really happening. When she got back to the phone, she gave him all Deacon Brown's information, which included his home and cell phone numbers along with his address.

"Thank you," replied Detective Thomas. "I need to ask him some very important questions that need answers. I will check in with you a little later, Miss Williamson. Let me get back to concentrating on the Rose case and get in touch with this Deacon Brown."

Hearing his house phone ring felt a little strange to him because his family members hardly ever call him and when they did, it was bad news or some special family gathering that they wanted him to attend. Joseph knew that it was Zachariah calling, but it seemed strange that someone he just met was calling him; everyone to him was just a polite hello or good-bye. Being a PI, he typically did not want too many friends because one day those same friends could potentially be a person of interest and he would have to gather information on them.

"Hello?"

"Hi Joseph," replied Zachariah. "I'm on my way to your apartment."

"Okay, ring the intercom and I will buzz you in."

It seemed like only seconds passed by and Zachariah was ringing the intercom. Joseph opened his apartment door and saw that Zachariah was ready for duty dressed in his casual jeans and a T-shirt with a tool belt attached to his waist. Joseph asked him if he would care for an ice-cold bottle of water, which was all he had to offer because he had not yet gone grocery shopping.

"No, thank you," replied Zachariah. "I have my own. If we are going to work together, please call me Zach, as all of my family and friends do."

Joseph was delighted to hear that and asked Zach to call him Joe as all of his friends and family did. "So now that we have gotten over the formal name calling, Zach, let's focus our attention on how we can help the police solve this case."

Joe suggested that they first try to track the family's last steps and find out things like who was the last person to see them.

Zach said, "According to Miss Williamson, a gentleman by the name of Deacon Brown supposedly drove the entire family home after their church's anniversary service."

Joe replied, "Then that settles it. Our first step is to get in contact with this Deacon. Maybe we can get his contact information from Miss Williamson."

Joe then suggested that they create missing persons flyers and post them in the lobby, laundry room and recreational center. Hopefully someone will respond. Next, they decided to knock on each neighbor's door in the entire building to see if there were any witnesses who saw Mother Rose and her family getting dropped off by Deacon Brown. Perhaps a neighbor saw them leaving the building after the Deacon dropped them off. Joe explained to Zach that the apartment building has seven floors including the basement apartments and each floor has six apartments. Zach volunteered to knock on all the apartments with the letters A to C while Joe agreed to cover the apartments with the letters D to F.

Both grabbed a pad and pencil from Joe's coffee table and entered the elevator to go to the sixth floor. Zach rang the doorbell of apartment 6A, but there was no one home. Meanwhile Joe received an answer at apartment 6D. Joe introduced himself as a neighbor and then held up the missing persons flyer with no picture, only details of the Rose family. The neighbor shook Joe's hand and told him the last time he saw the Rose family was on Saturday morning around 10:00 a.m.

"Do you know if she seemed upset or worried about anything when you saw her?" asked Joe.

"No. As always, she spoke very politely by saying hello, but she did seem like she was in a bit of a hurry, and she was carrying a lot of grocery bags wherever she was heading."

"How about the girls? Were they with her?"

"Yes, most of the time they're with her and they were also carrying a lot of grocery bags. I wondered what they were doing carrying all those bags."

"I'm not sure, sir, but thanks so much for your time and if you happen to hear or think of anything else, please call this number on the bottom of the flyer which has been posted throughout the entire building."

"Well," the neighbor said, "now that you mention it, I remember Miss Rose was always outside talking to people early in the morning and trying to hand out spiritual pamphlets to everyone who passed by. Perhaps someone got really angry at her for trying to force them into taking the pamphlet and decided that they had enough and tried to hurt her."

"What? Thanks for your time and helpful information."

As Joe walked away, he thought about how some neighbors were just busybodies and was always in everyone's business and, most of the time, they had the story all wrong.

Now Zach finished talking to the neighbors in apartment 6B. They were familiar with Miss Rose, but they had not seen her because they had just gotten back into town Sunday night from visiting their daughter and grandchildren in New York City.

Joe moved on to apartment 6E, but did not receive an answer. After two and a half hours of conversing with Mother Rose's neighbors, both Joe and Zach were completely exhausted and decided to return to Joe's apartment to go over some of the notes they had gathered so far. They had a lot of work to do.

# CHAPTER FIVE

Detective Thomas reached inside his pocket to get the contact information for this Deacon Brown. He dialed his home phone first. Deacon Brown answered the phone as if he was asleep.

"Hello?"

"Hello, my name is Detective Thomas and I got your contact information from one of your fellow church members by the name of Miss Williamson."

"Oh yes, how can I help you?"

"If I understand correctly, you dropped the Rose family home on Saturday. If so, I would like to ask you some questions regarding their disappearance."

"Absolutely Detective, I would be more than happy to come down to the precinct to answer any questions that may help law enforcement find the Rose family."

"But," Detective Thomas interrupted, "I am already in your area and it will only take me ten minutes to arrive at your home. If you can spare thirty minutes now both my partner, Detective Lee, and I can stop by."

Deacon Brown agreed.

Dealing with such cases like these in the past, Detective Thomas knew that if someone was considered a suspect, it would take days trying to arrest the person and, if the police wanted to get a search warrant without probable cause, most of the time the request would get rejected by the judges. This is why Detective Thomas and Detective Lee would call the suspect and try visiting him or her at home first. This way, if they declined their offer to stop pass the home, there was a strong possibility they were hiding something from the police.

Detective Thomas parked the patrol car in front of Mr. Brown's home. To his surprise, it was very well kept. The bushes and the grass were manicured and the house outside really looked great. As Detective Thomas reached to ring the doorbell, the door swung open. Deacon Brown looked shocked as he was wearing only his bathrobe and slippers and holding a bag of garbage in his hand. He stepped back and asked that Detective Thomas and his partner come inside and take a seat in the living room while he placed the garbage in the trashcan.

"I'm sorry, Detectives. I was tidying up the place and thought I would have more time to get dressed. I did not think that you would come so soon."

Detective Thomas assured him that his appearance did not bother them at all and that they would not take up too much of his time. They only had a few questions that needed to be addressed.

Deacon Brown felt glad and asked if they cared for some hot tea and a slice of pound cake he just bought from the grocery store. Detective Thomas declined the offer and introduced his partner, Detective Lee, who took Deacon Brown's offer of a hot cup of tea. Happy to oblige, he began reading off a list of different types of teas he had in the house.

"I have regular tea, decaffeinated tea, lemon tea, cinnamon apple spice tea, peppermint tea, green tea and black tea. So which one would you prefer, Detective Lee?"

"I'll have the decaffeinated tea with one pack of sugar and a slice of fresh lemon, please."

Deacon Brown said, "Okay," and excused himself while he prepared the tea.

This gave the detectives a chance to roam around his living room. Detective Thomas could not help but notice that there were no family pictures on the wall, nor were there any on the fire place. As Deacon Brown returned, Detective Lee quickly complimented him on his well-kept home. He reached for his hot cup of tea and thanked him for taking the time to prepare it.

"Why thank you, Detective Lee. I cannot stand a messy house."

Detective Thomas asked, "Was there ever a Ms. Brown living in the house with you?"

Deacon Brown said, "Nope. Fortunately I will take all house compliments for myself."

He turned his head away from the detectives and explained with a smirk on his face that he had never found the right woman.

"But I do thank God for my mother who taught me how to keep a tidy house and cook homemade meals for myself."

Detective Thomas smiled and said, "Well, let's get started."

Deacon Brown nodded in agreement. "Yeah, because I would really like to help as much as possible with this case."

"So, you are very familiar with Mother Williamson?"

"Yes," replied Deacon Brown, "she is one of the Mothers in our church and a very dear friend of mine as well."

It was now Tuesday morning and Mother Williamson felt like she was going crazy not knowing where her best friend and her daughters were. Not knowing if they were hurt or alive, she found herself getting upset with Mother Rose, especially if she could have called her by now, but then Mother Williamson dismissed those thoughts because she knew better.

Later on, the house phone rang and Mother Williamson stumbled over her bedroom slippers while racing to answer the phone. With what little breath she had left, she mustered out a hello as she desperately prayed that Mother Rose's voice would be on the other end of the phone. It was Pastor Paul.

"Hello," Pastor Paul said, "thank God that you are okay. The church has been trying to call you since yesterday morning. Several members even stopped by your apartment, but they did not get an answer so we began to worry about you as well."

"I'm sorry, Pastor Paul. I was with some of Mother Rose's neighbors trying to figure out how her bicycle ended up in a pool of water after the storm, blocks away from her apartment building."

Pastor Paul said, "Wait a minute. I'm not aware of what has been going on and I need you to take a couple of steps back and fill me in on all of the details."

Mother Williamson started out by saying that although Deacon Brown drove the family home after Saturday's service, somehow Mother Rose's bicycle that she kept inside her apartment was found a couple of blocks away from her apartment building complex submerged in a pool of water.

Pastor then asked, "Are you sure she did not ride her bike to the church early Saturday night to maybe drop something off for the anniversary?"

Mother Williamson said, "I'm positive because Deacon Brown helped us transport several items from her apartment to the church that day and her daughters and I were in the van helping unload those items."

"Could she have possibly left the church to retrieve something from her apartment that she forgot and rode her bike back to the church?"

"No sir, because we were glued at the hip while setting up the church to make sure things ran as smoothly as possible."

"Okay. Have the police come up with any leads?" asked Pastor Paul.

Mother Williamson responded, "An all-points bulletin and a search team were released this morning and they will notify me if they hear anything new."

Pastor Paul said, "I just cannot understand why Deacon Brown did not tell the church that he dropped Mother Rose and the girls off when we were all asking questions on Sunday about the Rose family. I find that behavior to be very strange. What do you think, Mother Williamson?"

"You're absolutely correct, Pastor Paul. I think that Deacon Brown should have voluntarily told the church what happened that night when he dropped the family home."

"Do you know if the police were able to contact him about what exactly happened the night when he dropped the family off?"

"I'm not sure." Mother Williamson let Pastor Paul know that she gave Deacon Brown's contact information and address to the police and hopefully they have contacted him by now.

"I personally went down to the police station the other day," she said, "and filled out a missing persons report on their behalf and I'm hoping that we get good results soon."

"Thank God for you, Mother Williamson."

Pastor Paul said a few words of prayer. Before he hung up the phone, he decided to give her his personal cell phone number and told her not to hesitate in calling him no matter the time of day and also told her the church would continue to pray for the Rose family and pray for her strength in the Lord as well.

"Thanks, Pastor Paul. I will call you immediately if any new evidence comes up that Detectives Thomas or Lee share with me. God bless!"

Detective Thomas asked Deacon Brown, "Around what time did you drop Miss Rose and her family off at their apartment building?"

"It was 12:32 in the morning before the storm," replied Deacon Brown.

"How are you so sure that it was exactly 12:32 a.m.? "

"Because I remember looking at the car's clock and estimating how long it would take me to get home," replied Deacon Brown.

"Do you know if Miss Rose or her daughters were upset about anything when you last saw them?"

Deacon Brown hesitated and then said, "No one seemed upset. Everybody was talking about how wonderful the church's 50th anniversary event turned out."

"Did Miss Rose happen to mention anything to you that would have caused her to worry?"

"No, and if she had anything that was troubling her, no one would have ever known because she only had one thing on her mind and that was to try to make everything as perfect as it could be that night," replied Deacon Brown.

"I was told you drove the Rose family home frequently. Did any of them ever mention other family members beside church members during these rides home?" asked Detective Lee.

"Well, Mother Rose spoke proudly of her girls, but I do not recall her ever mentioning other family members. I know that this is going to sound strange, but you would be surprised to find out how common this occurs in churches."

Deacon Brown's face began to change from a pleasant look to a concerned one as Detective Lee asked him, "Just how close were you and Miss Rose?"

Deacon Brown sighed and said, "We are just good friends and there is nothing else going on between us I assure you, Detective Lee!"

As Deacon Brown answered the question, Detective Thomas looked deep into his eyes because it is said the eyes are the windows of one's soul. Both detectives tried to detect any sudden body movement that would be an indication that he was not being truthful or perhaps hiding something. But the only body movement from Deacon Brown was the disappearance of his smile and the appearance of a frown on his face.

Trying to give him another chance to come clean, Detective Lee asked him again, "Are you sure that there was nothing going on between you and Miss Rose?"

Getting extremely frustrated Deacon Brown answered the question this time with more sternness, "There is absolutely nothing going on with Mother Rose and me! We're just merely close friends!"

Still not convinced, Detective Lee and Detective Thomas nevertheless decided to leave it alone, but Deacon Brown was aware that they did not believe his responses. Detective Thomas apologized for taking up so much of his time but he had one more question to ask him before they left.

"Did Miss Rose have any enemies that she ever mentioned to you? Whether it was in or out of the church?"

Deacon Brown let out one of the biggest laugh. "Out of the billions of people on this planet, she would probably be the only person that was loved by everyone."

"Well, as funny as that may sound to you, Deacon Brown," Detective Thomas replied, "everyone has someone who does not like them so there is someone who didn't like Mother Rose. We just do not know who at this time."

Both detectives decided to wrap up the questioning for now and assured Deacon Brown that they really appreciated him taking the time out of his personal schedule to address all of their questions. Detective Lee especially thanked him for the cup of tea because his throat was a little itchy and it helped tremendously. They shook hands and left. Although they were leaving, Detective Thomas still had this funny feeling that Deacon Brown was not being completely honest with them and believed that he knew more than what he was telling them.

As they left his house, Deacon Brown also knew this would not be the last time they would be seeing each other. Detective Lee took out his business card from his pocket and told him if he should remember something later on to please give him a call immediately; Detective Thomas handed him his business card as well.

# CHAPTER SIX

It was Wednesday morning and four days had gone by and there was still no word from the Rose family. Mother Williamson thought, *I can no longer just sit in my apartment and do nothing.* She decided to call Detective Thomas to see if they heard anything and if she could help with the search team. But as Mother Williamson reached for the telephone, her doorbell rang. She quickly ran to the door while fixing her headscarf and asked who was there. It was Detective Thomas and Detective Lee. Mother Williamson could not open the door fast enough hoping that they had some good news, but from the expression on their faces, she knew they were also hoping the same thing from her.

"Good morning, Miss Williamson," said Detective Thomas. "May we come in for a few minutes?"

"Sure," she replied.

But before Detective Thomas could completely enter her apartment, Mother Williamson started attacking him with all sorts of questions—she was interrogating him this time. "Have you heard from anyone in the Rose family? Do you have any other leads since I last spoke with you? How is the search team working out and can I also assist in the search?"

"Calm down," replied Detective Thomas. He couldn't keep up with her list of questions. He asked her to sit down while he discussed some concerns with her and addressed any questions she may have afterwards.

"Miss Williamson, I spoke with Deacon Brown yesterday afternoon and I did not feel that he was being truthful about everything."

"What do you mean?"

"Well, I have been a detective for many years now and one thing I do best is read people's facial and body language. Miss Williamson, he is definitely hiding something, but I'm not sure what. Do you know if he and Miss Rose were more than good church friends?"

Mother Williamson looked as if Detective Thomas had slapped her clean across the face with the back of his hand as she held one hand on her right cheek, her mouth wide open.

"Why that is the craziest accusation I have ever heard and quite frankly, I find it very insulting to answer!" she stormed. "No, there is nothing going on between the two of them, nothing whatsoever! I'm not sure I like the way this round of questioning is heading."

"Okay," replied Detective Thomas. "I just really needed to see if perhaps you had that same look on your face as Deacon Brown."

Mother Williamson said, "I do not appreciate the implications you are making towards my friend at such a vulnerable time in her life and especially when she is not here to defend herself."

"Now, now, Miss Williamson, it is part of my job. I needed to make sure that the two closest people in Miss Rose's life were not hiding any secrets from me. I'm sorry if I upset you but, you really would be surprised at the confessions that I hear from church members. Now to address your questions, we did not hear from anyone yet about the Rose family and I do not have any additional information that I'm obligated to share with you at this time because it may interfere with the investigation.

"Oh, the search team is still on active duty, but so far nothing. I also know that you would like to help out as much as possible, but I really would like you to remain in your apartment because if Miss Rose would reach out to anyone, it definitely would be you. I cannot take the risk of missing her. You are the most important person of contact right now and if you really want to help, please remain in your apartment in case she does call or visit."

"All right," replied Mother Williamson as both detectives stood up to leave.

"By the way, Miss Williamson," Detective Thomas said, "if you have to leave the apartment for any period of time, which I hope not, please make sure you leave a neighbor that can be trusted to watch the apartment until you return. Will you do that for me or better yet, for the Rose family? I know that you are getting bored and impatient, but it's very important that your phones are monitored at all times."

Deep down inside, Mother Williamson knew what Detective Thomas was asking her to do was important so she nodded her head in agreement.

"Detectives, I do not think that Deacon Brown had anything to do with Mother Rose's disappearance. I know him and he would not harm a fly."

"Time will tell," replied Detective Lee. "Time will surely tell!"

---

As Deacon Brown began cleaning up the dishes, he could not help but think about the questions that Detective Thomas and Detective Lee asked concerning Mother Rose and his relationship and their implications. *Should I be worried about whether or not they consider me a suspect because I was the last person to have seen the family? Should I protect myself by obtaining a lawyer before they try to charge me with the disappearance of the Rose family? I only tried to help the Rose family in giving them a ride home and now I might be considered the prime suspect.* Thinking fast, Deacon Brown called his pastor, but to his surprise, he was unable to reach him at his office. *That is strange,* thought Deacon Brown, *because he is always there during this hour.* He searched for his cell number in his phone directory and hit the call button. The phone rang and then Pastor Paul heard a hello sound on the other end of the line.

"Hello Pastor Paul, it is Deacon Brown."

"God bless you, Deacon Brown. Is everything okay? Did you hear any updates about the Rose family case?"

"Everything is fine for now, Pastor Paul, and no I have not heard anything about their case. But I wanted to speak with you concerning a police matter. By the way, they just left my house. They were questioning me because I was the last person to see the Rose family and I just feel like everyone is looking at me as a suspect."

"What do you mean, 'a suspect', Deacon Brown? Is there something you are not sharing with the police or maybe you would like to get something off your chest now, because in all of my years of pastoring, I have heard people confess to all sorts of things and I will not judge you."

Deacon Brown thought, *now you are treating me the same way, just like a suspect.* "No, Pastor Paul. I simply just want to protect myself by getting a lawyer because the police have a very bad habit of wrongfully convicting people and I do not want to be one of their statistics."

"Okay, Deacon Brown, you're absolutely correct, I just wanted to make sure that you told the police everything they needed to know. Here is the contact information for Minister Keith, who is the church's lawyer as well. Let him know that I passed his information on to you. We must continue to keep the Rose family in prayer. I'm so deeply moved by all of this and we must believe God that wherever they are, He will not let any harm come to them and will return them home safely. God bless you, Deacon Brown."

"God bless you as well, Pastor, and thank you."

⸙

Being led by God, Pastor Paul decided to ask all the elders, ministers and deacons in the church to go on a fifty-day consecration and if others wanted to join, he asked them to talk to their physicians and get medical approval first. The church would be open twenty-four hours a day, and there would always be someone kneeling before the Lord expecting the Rose family's safe return. Truly there was strength in numbers because when everyone got together in prayer, it felt as if they were all bombarding heaven with prayers and was right in the presence of God Himself and His angels. God was certainly in the midst of His people since they were all on one accord. The Love Church of God Assembly was once again gathered together, only this time, for a not so pleasant occasion.

⸙

Mother Williamson was a lot calmer, but she really wished that she could get out of her apartment because it would help her relax. But Detective Thomas made it very clear that she was one of the most important contacts for this case. She thought, *Lord, I thank you for your strength to overcome these feelings.* The phone rang and Mother Williamson reached for it as quickly as her arm would move.

"Hello?" There was no answer. "Hello?" she asked again. Still no answer. Then Mother Williamson said, "Hello, is anyone there?"

Then an eerie deep-toned voice whispered, "Hello, Miss Williamson." The phone went dead. All she could hear was the dial tone.

Mother Williamson immediately looked at the Caller ID, but both the name and number read "Unknown". Still thinking quickly, she dialed #95 to call the number back, only to receive a recorded message that said, "Sorry, we are unable to reach the party by this method. Please hang up and try your call again". By this time, Mother Williamson was pacing back and forth nervously waiting to see if the person would call back. She wondered if it was Mother Rose trying to call her for help. A couple of minutes went by and nothing happened. She decided to give Detective Thomas a call.

"Hello, Miss Williamson!"

"Hi, Detective Thomas."

"Is everything all right?" asked Detective Thomas. He thought something was wrong because she sounded out of breath.

"Yes, I'm okay, but someone just called my house phone. At first, they did not say anything after I said hello a couple of times, then a voice said, 'Hello, Miss Williamson' and then the phone went dead."

"Do you know if it was a male or female voice?"

"No, I could not tell because it was not a normal voice tone, I think that someone was using a mechanical device of some sort to disguise their voice."

"Do you have Caller ID and were you able to retrieve their phone number?"

"Yes, I have Caller ID, but both the name and number showed up as Unknown."

"Did you hear any sounds in the background?" Detective Thomas questioned.

"No, I did not!"

"Do you have Call Waiting?"

"Yes, I do. Do you think that they will call back?" asked Mother Williamson.

"I'm not sure," replied Detective Thomas. "Sometimes those types of calls are unpredictable."

"How did that person get my number and know my name? They called my name as if they knew me."

"Miss Williamson, you would be surprised how people in general, especially hackers, can get your information. If the call is related to a kidnapping, the caller will call back again, so do not, I repeat, do not say anything while picking up the phone the next time you get an unknown name and unknown number. Instead, just try listening for any familiar noises in the background, like vehicles, planes, trains etc. I will be sending a team over to your apartment later today so that they can tap your phone line. They will also instruct you on how to properly handle a traced call. Just try to keep yourself busy."

"Sure," she replied sarcastically as she silently whispered another prayer underneath her breath, "Lord, continue to strengthen me".

No sooner had she hung up the phone that it immediately rang. Mother Williamson nervously answered the phone. The Caller ID displayed an unknown name and unknown number and she did not say anything.

Then Detective Thomas revealed himself as the caller and said, "I was just testing you to make sure that you did not say anything. Great job, Miss Williamson. You passed the test." He told her he would talk to her another time as he hung up the phone.

Thirty minutes later, the entire wiretapping team was inside Mother Williamson's apartment. It seemed to take hours to setup everything and to explain how to properly communicate with the caller on a tapped line so it can properly be traced. After setting up, a few stuck around in case she received another unknown phone call.

Lately, the sound of the phone ringing meant everything to Mother Williamson. While everyone was standing to their feet to rehearse their part, the phone rang. The ringing phone waited to be answered. Mother Williamson picked up the phone and hesitated to say hello so the caller decided to say hello first.

"How are you related to Miss—," then the phone went dead again.

"Hello, hello!" shouted Mother Williamson but the only sound heard was the dial tone. The wiretap team knew that Miss Williamson did not have a chance of trying to keep the caller on the phone in order for the call to be traced. They started explaining to Mother Williamson that they did not have enough time to get the location of the call. Detective Staples from the team notified Detective Lee that they received another call, but it could not be traced because the caller hung up too quickly. However, they were able to verify the time—it was 7:27 p.m. Mother Williamson tried to figure out what the person was going to say before they hung up the phone.

About an hour later, while the team was conversing about the last phone call, Mother Williamson heard a suspicious sound like the sound of paper being pushed under her apartment door. Nervously, she approached the door only to discover that her ears were not deceiving her. An envelope was, in fact, lying on the floor of her apartment. Mother Williamson stood there in shock looking at the envelope wondering if she should pick it up. She decided not to tamper with evidence, but to call the detectives over so they could examine it.

Mother Williamson now had everyone's attention in the apartment as they slowly walked towards the door. They ordered her to get away from the door. One of the detectives opened the apartment door, while another ran out and searched the elevator, hallway and staircase. After they could not locate anyone, Detective Staples decided to give Detective Thomas a call to keep him abreast of what was going on.

"Oh hi, Detective Thomas. I was about to leave you a voice message."

"What's going on? Did we get another call from the person?"

"Yes, but something else transpired. Someone slipped an envelope under the apartment door while we were discussing the suspicious phone call. Miss Williamson heard the sound of paper being pushed under her apartment door."

"The envelope. Did any of the detectives apprehend a suspect?"

"No sir, we were not able to catch anyone."

"Okay, how is Miss Williamson at this time?"

"She is a little shaken up because now the suspect knows her name, telephone number and her home address."

"Please tell me that she did not open the envelope?"

"No, she did not even touch the envelope," replied Detective Staples.

"Okay, good. May I speak with her?" asked Detective Thomas.

"Sure." The detective handed the phone to her.

Immediately, she began to vent. "Why, Detective Thomas is this person targeting me? I just do not understand. Why? Can you please come over to my apartment?"

"Sure, Miss Williamson but I need you to get a hold of yourself or you are going to become mentally drained. I'm on my way, so please do not go near the door, and let one of the detectives open your apartment door when I get there. Besides, they are more familiar with my voice than you are."

"Okay, Detective Thomas. I think I would like that much better if you were here."

"Okay, I'm on my way now."

"Thanks, Detective Thomas."

Mother Williamson walked over to her rocking chair and grabbed her Bible. She began to quote Psalms 91:1 to herself while she rocked back and forth: "He who dwells in the secret place of the Most High shall abide under the shadows of the Almighty."

Back in Joe's apartment, Zach remembered Joe had offered him a cold glass of water earlier and decided to take him up on his offer. While Joe sat there trying to make sense of this whole ordeal, he told Zach to help himself in the kitchen. Zach returned, but could not help noticing that Joe was posing like The Thinker sculpture.

"Joe, I know that this is your line of work - and I know that you know what our next move should be - but I really think that we should go after our last solid clue which is questioning this Deacon Brown."

"You're right, and I could not have said that any better, Zach. Someone should have seen him drop off the Rose family. I remember giving Miss Williamson my contact information but she has not called me yet. Maybe we can look up Miss Rose's church's name. I should know it by heart because she must've given it to me a hundred times while we were taking walks in the mornings witnessing to me."

Joe found the address to The Love Church of God Assembly online.

"So what is the pastor's name?" asked Zach. They both began searching the web. "Okay, here we go, Joe. Here is the pastor who is the overseer of The Love Church of God Assembly. Everyone calls him Pastor Paul. Hopefully he can provide us with both Miss Williamson's and Deacon Brown's contact information. Joe, do you really think that this pastor will just give two strangers their personal information?"

"Well do not forget, although I'm retired, my license is still current and my PI badge should carry some weight. You must also keep in mind that everyone wants answers, so I believe he would be more than willing to assist in this matter rather than decline our help."

"Okay," replied Zach, "but can we please stop and get something to eat first? My stomach is telling me to feed it and then we can stop by the church afterwards."

"Sure," Joe said as he got up. "Let's go and get something to eat."

They both walked out discussing their findings so far.

One hour later, both of their stomachs were full after leaving the local neighborhood sandwich shop. They started heading towards the church. When they arrived, both gentlemen felt very nervous entering because it had been years since either one of them had crossed over the threshold of a church. They heard noise, like people praying, and began to get even more fearful to go all the way inside. But they knew the quicker they retrieved this information from Pastor Paul, the better their chances were of getting their questions answered and they would be one step closer to solving the Rose family case.

They saw someone who looked like he could be the pastor of the church. Joe introduced himself as a private investigator working on the disappearance of the Rose family and Zach as his assistant. The gentleman introduced himself as Pastor Paul and said that he was extremely happy to hear that this case was receiving so much attention from the law enforcement.

"Please follow me into my office."

He explained to them that the congregation was on a 50-day con-secration praying for the Rose family's safe return. Joe and Zach could see some of the people kneeling and crying, while others were walking around the sanctuary lifting their hands. There were even some huddled in the corners of the church, rocking back and forth.

"Please come in and sit down," offered Pastor Paul. "Do either of you gentlemen care for a cold glass of water?"

"No," replied both gentlemen.

"Thanks for the offer though" said Zach and stated that they just finished having lunch.

"Do you know if there are any recent leads on the Rose case?" asked the pastor.

Joe replied, "No, there are no updates at this time, but we were wondering if you could help us out."

"Me?" replied Pastor Paul.

"Yes. Both Zach and I were introduced to a Miss Williamson where the bike was found a couple of days ago. Unfortunately, I seem to have misplaced her contact information and we were hoping that you would have it on file?"

"Why certainly!" replied Pastor Paul. "Anything to help out."

As he was about to go retrieve the information, Zach decided to ask him if he would also have the contact information of a Deacon Brown.

Pastor Paul suspiciously turned around and started looking at both gentlemen and said, "Wait a minute. Are you the gentlemen who spotted Mother Rose's bicycle in the street?"

"Yes, we are," replied Joe hoping that Zach had not messed things up for them.

Pastor Paul then said, "This is strange. Neither Detective Thomas nor Detective Lee mentioned anything about a private investigator working on the case. Can I please see some identification proving that you are private investigators?"

"Sure." Joe quickly displayed his private investigator credentials from his pocket.

Zach pretended to search for his badge while Joe distracted Pastor Paul by telling him that Miss Williamson had shared with them that Deacon Brown was the last person to see the Rose family because he dropped them home after the church's anniversary celebration.

"By the way, congratulations on fifty years," said Joe.

"Thanks!" replied Pastor Paul. "So, yes that is true. Deacon Brown dropped them off after our celebration service on Saturday."

Although Pastor Paul felt they were not being completely truthful with him, he still had this comfortable and peaceful feeling that they were working for the good of the Rose family. While he left the room to locate the contact information for Mother Williamson and Deacon Brown, Joe was happy inside and thought, *I did not forget all of the tricks of the trade because Pastor Paul totally forgot to validate Zach's credentials.* Joe whispered to instruct Zach to remain quiet and allow him to do all the talking because after all this was his line of work and he was more skilled at it. Zach whispered back that he was sorry.

"That was a close call and you are right because I could have messed everything up." Zach threw in a little humor. " Don't forget, when it is time for me to show off my handyman skills, I'll take the lead because I'm more skilled at them," he smirked.

Pastor Paul came back smiling with the information in his hands. "Gentlemen, I have one question for you."

Their hearts skipped a beat.

"What would that be?" replied Joe.

"Do you think that Deacon Brown is considered a suspect at this time?" asked Pastor Paul.

Joe cleared his throat relieved that Pastor Paul was not concerned about their credentials.

He replied, "The police still do not have any leads so to be perfectly honest with you, everybody is considered a suspect at this time, even you right now, Pastor Paul." Joe had the biggest grin on his face. " Thanks again for all of your help and we will come back if we need your services or assistance."

They both shook the Pastor's hand.

"God bless you," replied Pastor Paul. "Please bring home the Rose family and do not be a stranger to the church." Joe nodded his head in agreement and started walking towards the church doors.

When they got outside the church, Joe prayed, "God, please forgive us for lying in the house of God."

Zach added, "Yes God, please forgive us!"

Joe, looking at the contact information, said, "So, let's give Miss

Williamson a call. Hopefully she can inform us of any new leads."

---

Now that Mother Williamson had her apartment back to herself, she decided to read her Bible again and pray. Afterwards, she felt like taking a hot bath and going to bed early because she had one emotional day. While slipping into bed, the telephone rang and her heart skipped a beat. She jumped with uncertainty and expectancy. Although she did not recognize the phone number displayed, she was prepared after being coached by the wiretap team.

She slowly picked up the phone and then she pressed her ear hard against the phone trying to listen for any familiar sounds.

Then a strong deep male's voice said, "Hello, Miss Williamson?"

Feeling a little more at ease, but still not familiar with the voice, she said, "Hello. This is she."

"Miss Williamson, this is Joseph, the gentleman who discovered Miss Rose's bicycle."

"Oh yes," replied Mother Williamson. "How are you doing?"

"Actually, that is something I should be asking you. How are you doing? I know that Miss Rose means so much to you."

"Mr. Joseph, I feel so helpless and Detective Thomas does not want me to be involved in anything and demanded that I not leave my place under any circumstance. So to answer your question, I'm not doing very well. Besides, some mysterious things have been occurring at my place."

"Really? Like what?" replied Joe.

"For starters, I've received two suspicious phone calls on my phone so Detective Thomas thought it would be best if my telephone line was tapped. He sent a wiretap team over to my apartment. Then shortly afterwards an envelope was slipped under my apartment door."

"You have got to be kidding me!" exclaimed Joe. "What did the caller say?"

"Well, the first time the caller just said, 'Hello Miss Williamson' and hung up! The second time, the caller said, 'How are you related to

Miss' and the phone went dead."

"Wow, I cannot believe that happened! Do you know what was inside the envelope?" inquired Joe.

"I know it was a letter, but nothing else. None of the detectives were obligated to share any information with me probably because they did not want me to jeopardize the case in any way."

"I cannot even begin to imagine how you must feel. You are a strong woman. Keep holding on."

"Thanks so much for that wise counsel, Mr. Joseph." Not missing the opportunity to witness to a soul, she asked him, "Do you know the Lord as your personal Savior?"

"No, Miss Williamson, but I need to and to start going back to church as well."

"Will you be willing to receive Him now?"

"As I always told Miss Rose, I need to and will let you know when I'm ready," replied Joe.

"Okay, but you are always welcome to attend my church anytime and bring Zachariah too."

"Thanks for being concerned about our souls. By the way, Miss Williamson, going forward please call me Joe instead of Joseph and call Zachariah, Zach. It just seems so formal otherwise and we are all passed that stage now."

"Okay, that is not a problem as long as you gentlemen call me Mother Williamson going forward."

"Okay," replied Joe, "will do. It's funny that you invited both Zach and me to your church because we just left there and, Mother Williamson, I hope that you do not mind, but I retrieved your contact information from your Pastor. When I did not hear from you, we both decided to get your contact information another way."

Immediately she began to apologize, but Joe told her it was alright and he was glad they had the opportunity to talk.

"Joe, did you come across any additional information since we last spoke?" asked Mother Williamson. "Or did any of the neighbors see Deacon Brown when he dropped the Rose family off?"

"No, they hadn't but we still have not spoken to everyone in her building. Now that you mention Deacon Brown, I also retrieved his information from your Pastor as well and will be giving him a call."

"Oh," replied Mother Williamson, "is everything okay with Deacon Brown?"

"Well, I would not know. I just like to question him myself."

"Joe, please be honest with me. It seems that everyone wants to talk with Deacon Brown and no one is saying anything after they speak with him."

"Mother Williamson, this is all just procedure. Because he supposedly was the last person to see the Rose family, it is quite natural he would be questioned the most. This does not mean anything, unless Deacon Brown's statement does not line up. Then your friend will have some serious explaining to do. But I promise you, after speaking with Deacon Brown, I will give you a courtesy call, Mother Williamson."

"Thanks, Joe." She hung up the phone.

Lifting a fork full of homemade shrimp scampi with creamy pasta sauce into his mouth, Deacon Brown could taste the garlicky ingredient in the meal and was enjoying every bit of it. His phone rang, interrupting his dinner.

Deacon Brown thought, *Ah, man!, Whenever you are caught up in a pleasurable moment, disturbance always pays you a visit.* Refusing to be disturbed, he kept eating his food and said, "Sorry, but whomever is calling will just have to leave a message."

The answering machine came on and Deacon Brown heard someone leave a message: "Hello, Deacon Brown, my name is Joseph and I'm a close neighbor of the Rose family and I would really like to speak with you."

Although he was enjoying his meal, he felt that matter was much more important so he raced to answer the phone.

"Hello!" he quickly said before the person hung up the phone. "Can I help you?" he shouted.

"Good evening, Deacon Brown. As I stated before, I am a close neighbor of the Rose family and my name is Joseph Walker. I'm a private investigator as well and would like to ask you a few questions. I know that you are probably wondering how I got your contact information."

"Yes, I would like to know, Mr. Joseph."

"Well, I stopped by your church and spoke with your pastor and he willingly provided me with both Mother Williamson and your contact information."

Deacon Brown hesitated for a few minutes then told Mr. Joseph that he was already questioned by Detective Thomas and Detective Lee and if there was anything he needed to know, he should contact them at the 1002nd precinct. Joe then explained that he would like to conduct his own questioning in order to find out what happened to the Rose family. Deacon Brown sighed, but then thought, *what if one of my family members had gone missing? I would certainly want everyone who could to show that same kindness and help out.*

"Okay, how can I help you?"

"Well, for starters, can my partner and I stop by your residence to go over a few questions?"

"Where are you now?" asked Deacon Brown.

"Actually, both my partner Zachariah and I are only a few blocks from your church so if you could provide us with your home address, we will stop by now," stated Joe.

"Okay, take down my address and it should take you about forty minutes to get to my house from the church and that will give me time to finish my dinner and clean up."

"Thanks so much," replied Joe. "We will see you in forty minutes if not sooner."

Deacon Brown said, "There is no need to rush. Please, by all means, take your time!"

After a couple of weeks searching the wooded areas, no one was able to find anything that could help solve this case. Now the cost of a search team was becoming very expensive, both Detective Thomas and Detective Lee were instructed to suspend the search team. Delivering this news to Miss Rose's neighbors, who voluntarily gave their time, did not go so well. Nevertheless, everyone was still hoping for the safe return of Mother Rose and her daughters.

As good as the home-cooked meal tasted, Deacon Brown decided to save it for later because there were more important matters to attend to. He remembered how he had procrastinated about calling Minister Keith so that he or someone else from the law firm could represent him. Becoming upset with himself, he wished that he had thought about proper representation before accepting Joseph's invitation. Now it was too late for him to back out of the appointment.

At first, it slipped Deacon Brown's mind where he had placed Minister Keith's contact information. Then suddenly it hit him—he had placed it in the top drawer of his dresser. Quickly retrieving it, he began dialing the number and thankfully Minister Keith answered the phone.

"Hi, Minister Keith. It's Deacon Brown from the church."

"Oh hello, Deacon Brown. What can I do for you?"

"Well, for starters, in case you are wondering how I got your phone number, Pastor Paul was kind enough to give it to me."

"That's fine!" replied Minister Keith

"I think I'm in a bind."

"How so?"

"Well, I know that you are aware of the disappearance of the Rose family."

"Yes, the whole church is aware," stated Minister Keith.

"Well, I'm not sure if you know that I was the last person to see them."

"Yes I am. Go on."

"The police have been questioning me and now some private investigators want to stop by my house to ask me a couple of questions. So I was wondering if you could represent me or give me some legal advice about speaking to these private investigators."

"Deacon Brown, you do not want to speak with anyone from the law enforcement without having an attorney present with you because they can, and trust me, they will twist your words around. Now I know that you want to defend your innocence but you also must be very careful."

"Minister Keith, I think I already put my foot in my mouth by accepting the private investigator's request to come to my house tonight."

"Well then, I will represent you, Deacon Brown. Give me your address and I will be there during their questioning and if they should arrive before me, please stall them until I get there."

"Okay, thanks so much for your help. I really appreciate it especially on such short notice."

"You're very welcome, and don't forget, do not start until I arrive. Also, it will be in your best interest if you do not tell them that I'm coming."

"Absolutely, I'll see you when you get here."

"One more question before we hang up the phone. Would you happen to know the names of these private investigators?" asked Minister Keith

"Sure, but only their first names. Joseph and Zachariah."

"Where did I get Thomas and Lee from?"

"Detectives Thomas and Lee are the officers assigned to the Rose family case."

"Okay, that explains it. I will see you shortly."

Deacon Brown could not help but wonder how he was considered somewhat of a prime suspect. The doorbell rang and Deacon Brown opened the door. Both Joseph and Zachariah introduced themselves and Joseph quickly flashed his PI badge. Deacon Brown smiled and asked them to come in and have a seat in his living room as he pointed the way.

He offered them something to drink, but both declined. Just when he was about to sit down in his favorite chair, Joe asked him, "Can you tell us your full name?"

"It's Alfred Brown, Jr."

"So, Alfred Brown, Jr. where were you born?" asked Joe.

When he realized that he was starting without Minister Keith, Deacon Brown asked them again if they cared for anything to drink or maybe if they cared for some chocolate chips cookies. Once again they declined his offer.

"Well, I would like to get myself some hot tea with lemon. My throat is feeling a little dry."

He knew it would take the water a while to boil and that would force him to excuse himself to take a couple trips into the kitchen area.

Deacon Brown began praying in the kitchen that Minister Keith would show up soon because he did not know what else to do to stall them any further. As he shouted, "I'll be there in a couple of minutes," the doorbell rang. He thanked God. Minister Keith had arrived.

Deacon Brown guided him into the living room area and introduced him to both Joseph and Zachariah as his lawyer. Joe and Zach began to get a little uncomfortable when they heard the word "lawyer", but did not want Minister Keith to become suspicious so they got a hold of themselves. Returning with his hot tea, Deacon Brown asked Minister Keith if he would like something to drink. He declined.

"Okay, we can get started gentlemen," Deacon Brown said as he sipped his tea with delight. "I believe, Mr. Walker, you were asking me where I was born."

"Yes, that is correct."

"Well, I was born in Tampa, Florida on September 18, 1951 to Alfred and Kathy Brown."

Reading the facial expression of Minister Keith, Deacon Brown knew that he had given more information than was asked.

"Are you close with your family?"

"I'm very close to my family. That is the way my parents raised all their children."

Then Minister Keith asked, "What do these questions have to do with the Rose family case?"

Deacon Brown interjected, "I do not mind addressing these questions." He continued, "Well, my parents would always remind us that family should come first, because when your friends are gone, family will always be there."

Minister Keith asked, "Deacon Brown, can I speak with you on the side for one minute?"

"Sure, excuse us."

Deacon Brown took him into the kitchen.

Minister Keith blurted, "You called me and asked me to represent you, correct?"

"That is correct. Why? Did I say something wrong?"

"I just want you to remember what we discussed earlier today. Please let me do my job in representing you. If I'm not comfortable with their questions, it is for a reason."

"I'm sorry. Please forgive me. Let's try this again."

They walked back into the living room. Minister Keith explained to Joseph and Zachariah that he informed his client that he should only stick to answering the questions pertaining to the case and nothing else. Deacon Brown began retracing his steps the night of the disappearance of the Rose family.

Just before he did, his mind took him back to when he got upset with Mother Rose. He offered her a ride home and it was late but she continued to converse with her friends. He truly felt that she was being inconsiderate because all she could think about was sticking around to chat with the other Mothers of the church. What made it worse was that they were all going to see each other again the next day! Deacon Brown was glad that he did not volunteer this information to Detectives Thomas and Lee because they would have blown the whole situation out of proportion.

Then Minister Keith began asking both private investigators a couple of questions concerning the Rose family case.

"Are the both of you working with the police department? Do you have any new leads on the whereabouts of the family? Have the police found anyone else who may have seen them after my client dropped them off?"

Meanwhile, Deacon Brown started thinking back to when he was a teenager and finding himself in trouble with the law so many times. He remembered an incident when he was arrested which involved the disappearance of a young lady. As fear began to grip his heart, he could not help but wonder if that incident still appeared on his record after so many years even though he was cleared of all charges. He tried to remember her name again. Ah, it finally came back to him; her name was Linda Snow. He began to remember about that night:

*It was summer many years ago. I asked Linda out on a date. We went to a local carnival. Exploring a few of the rides was not an option because I only had enough money for one ride. So we decided to get on a ride called The Cup and Saucer. Linda was popular and all the boys liked her. The only reason I was able to take Linda out on a date was because our parents just happened to be friends.*

*The night of our date, I went to buy Linda some cotton candy and a soda pop that we both could share. Linda was standing behind me when I went to purchase the items, but when I turned around to hand her the cotton candy and soda pop, she vanished. I walked around the park for two whole hours looking for Linda, but there was no sign of her. So I decided to go to her house to tell her parents, but as I was walking home, I noticed Linda sitting in some older guy's car and he was kissing all over her. I was still holding the cotton candy and soda pop when I raced over to the car window and screamed, "Hey, what are you doing with this guy, Linda? You are supposed to be out on a date with me!"*

*Linda straightened herself up and leaped out of the car smiling and then snatched both the cotton candy and soda pop from my hands.*

*I could not believe this was happening to me. There were no words to say. With unbelief and pain in my heart, I simply walked away like a dog with his tail between his legs. All I could hear from the both of them was: "Thanks for the cotton candy and soda pop, Alfred!"*

*Tears began to well up in my eyes and all I could think about was how could she? How could she do this to me?*

*The most embarrassing part of the night was arriving home and finding my parents and her parents listening to music, playing board games and singing along to the songs that were playing on the radio. When I entered my house, everyone immediately saw the sad look on my face but I could not let them know how I just got dumped by my date. So I lied and told them that my stomach was upset and I needed to end the night early. Linda's parents were concerned about her and asked if she was home, and once again, I lied and said yes—I dropped her off first. My mother immediately took me to my bedroom and asked me to get ready for bed. She went and got some medicine for my make-believe upset stomach. Knowing that nothing was really wrong with me, I had to suck it up and take the nasty medicine anyway. Then she kissed me and said good night as she went right back to entertaining her company.*

*I laid in my bed practically all night thinking about how I could repay Linda for using me as her scapegoat. She made her parents believe she was going on a date with me when she really had plans to be with some other guy all along.*

*My eyes finally began to feel heavy and I could no longer keep them open. Before I knew it, I fell asleep to the sound of my parents' music.*

———— ✺ ————

Praying as she worked, Mother Williamson never had any problems cleaning her own apartment. She looked around and decided to end her chores and began to pray. But not knowing where her best friend or her daughters were, she found it to be very difficult concentrating on anything even praying. Mother Williamson could not believe how popular her house phone had become as she, once again, was startled by its ringing.

Sort of recognizing the number but was not completely sure, Mother Williamson said, " Hello!"

"Hello, this is Joe."

"Who?"

Joe explained, "I'm the gentlemen who discovered Mother Rose's bicycle outside, remember?"

"Oh, I'm sorry. Please charge it to my head and not my heart. There is so much going on these past couple of days. How are you?"

"Good," replied Joe. "I'm calling because some of the neighbors saw the flyers at various locations and wanted to take up a collection for Mother Rose and her daughters."

"My Lord!" gasped Mother Williamson. "That is such a thoughtful act of kindness. God is so good! You have to thank everyone for caring so much for my friends. So how much was collected?"

"Well, there were a lot of people involved in this collection including supermarkets, corporations, and at least thirty blocks of neighbors. The amount collected was a total of nine thousand dollars. They wanted to add it to the one thousand dollars startup reward money donated by the police department."

Joe heard some screaming coming from the other end of the phone.

"Oh my God! Thank you, Jesus!"

Joe said, "Hello, hello, are you okay?" Then a faint sound came through the telephone followed by a sniffing sound.

"I'm here."

"Mother Williamson, is everything okay?"

"Yes." She struggled to speak. "I'm just so overwhelmed." Trying to control her emotions, she finally said, "God bless you and I pray that the grace of God blesses everyone who contributed!"

"You are welcome and thanks for your blessings upon our lives," replied Joe. "We just wanted you to know how much we love Mother Rose and her precious little girls. We also wanted you to know that the money has been handed over to the reward department at the precinct. Mother Rose will be so proud of all her neighbors and when God decides to bring her back home, and trust me, I believe He will, she will not stop thanking you all for what you have done."

"I personally do not have words to say," Mother Williamson said, "but on behalf of Mother Rose and the girls, I thank you for this tremendous act of love. I am ever so grateful and thank you from the bottom of my heart."

"It is our pleasure," replied Joe.

As Mother Williamson hung up the phone, she whispered a silent word of prayer to God, "Lord only You can cause such an act of kindness to happen in this magnitude. Thank you!"

This still did not feel real; it seemed like she was watching a movie. The only thing that made it a reality to her was seeing the story aired on the local news channel confirming that Mother Rose and the twins were really missing and there were no real leads after weeks. There were the photos of Mother Rose and her two daughters that she gave to Detective Thomas. As she turned up the volume, the newswoman was standing in front of Mother Rose's apartment building.

"Good evening, this is Sam Goody live from Channel 42 News with a breaking story. I'm standing in front of the building where three family members suddenly vanished without a trace and there are no leads so far. The Rose family members were last seen weeks ago and have not been heard of since. The question that everyone is constantly asking themselves is what could have possibly happen to an entire family?

"If anyone has information regarding the whereabouts of the Rose family or if anyone has seen someone fitting the appearance of the people in this family photograph, please call 911 immediately. Last reported, there was a ten thousand dollar reward for anyone who has any information leading to the arrest of the individual who may be responsible for the family disappearance. Once again, I'm Sam Goody from Channel 42 News. Back over to you, Dan."

Detectives Thomas and Lee decided to pay Mother Williamson another visit and tell her that they were going to allow a female detective to stay with her overnight until they figured out their next steps of safety measures. The way things were going, she was no longer safe in her own apartment. The one thing Detective Thomas could not figure out, was why after raising ten thousand dollars, no one had come forward or attempted to contact the police department.

Mother Williamson decided to plead with Detective Thomas and see if he would reveal what was inside the envelope.

"Miss Williamson, unfortunately I'm unable to reveal police evidence with you."

"Please tell me, did it have any bad news about the Rose family?"

As tears fell from her eyes, the female detective, who was assigned to guard the apartment and who had come earlier, went over and put her arms around Miss Williamson's shoulder and began to console her.

"Please, Detective Thomas, tell me what the envelope had inside!"

"Miss Williamson, I just told you that I cannot reveal what is inside the envelope because this case is still under investigation, and I'm not at liberty to say. But what I can tell you, so that you will not worry as much, is that it does not speak about any bodily harm to any of the Rose family members. We sent it down to the lab to see if we can retrieve any prints from the envelope or the letter. We already have your house line tapped, but unfortunately, neither phone call could be traced. So Miss Williamson, I will assign Detective Jackson to stay with you until further notice."

"God bless you, Detective Thomas. I would feel better if a female detective stayed with me until this case is resolved."

"Okay, that's it for now. I'll be in touch, but in the meantime, you will be safe with Detective Jackson."

Jackson pulled Mother Williamson close to her.

"Thank you again, Detective Thomas, for taking good care of me."

"Good night all," replied both detectives.

Jackson guided Mother Williamson to her bedroom and explained to her that they were going to have to move her to a safe house in an undisclosed location because she was not safe in this apartment.

"Stop! So I will have to leave my apartment and live somewhere else?" asked Mother Williamson in distress.

"Yes I'm afraid so, but we can talk more about the details tomorrow," Detective Jackson said as she slowly closed the bedroom door.

The next morning, Jackson awoke to the sound of pots and pans and she jumped up as if she were late for work. She rubbed her eyes and noticed that Mother Williamson was preparing breakfast. She asked her if she could help out.

"Daughter, I'm almost done with the cooking, but if you insist on helping out, you can prepare the table for three."

"Three?"

"Yes. I took the liberty of asking the officer standing outside the apartment to join us for breakfast and he kindly accepted. By the way, he's in the bathroom now getting ready for breakfast."

Detective Jackson's heart skipped a beat, and, from the expression on her face, Mother Williamson immediately picked up on her concern.

"What's wrong, daughter?" asked Mother Williamson.

"If the officer is in the bathroom, then who is keeping watch outside the apartment door?"

"No one. What's wrong with that?" replied Mother Williamson.

"Well, If someone happens to stop by and sees that there is no one on post, then one of us will get in serious trouble. It's called dereliction of duty."

Seconds later, Detective Smith appeared at the kitchen doorway. The officer's shadow fell over the doorway of the kitchen as he cheerfully said, "Good morning, Detective Jackson. I see you slept well last night."

"Yeah, but who relieved you of duty?" asked Detective Jackson.

"Detective Thomas called and told me that I could take a half-hour breakfast break."

After everyone was finished eating, they all gathered their plates and thanked Miss Williamson for the wonderful breakfast.

After breakfast, the phone began ringing again. This uninvited sound of the phone made everyone scramble into position like they were at war. Again, Detective Jackson advised Mother Williamson on how to answer the phone.

Speaking very softly, Mother Williamson said, "Hello?"

The voice said, "Hello, this is me. You can relax."

"Oh. Hi, Detective Thomas. Would you like to speak with any of the police on guard?"

"Yes please. Let me speak with Detective Jackson."

After speaking with Detective Thomas, Jackson called Mother Williamson to the phone because he wanted to discuss a few things with her.

"Hi, Miss Williamson. I know that Detective Jackson briefed you on the protective custody, correct?"

"Yes," replied Mother Williamson.

"Well, we have picked a location and we need you to start preparing to leave."

"Do I really have to go?"

"Yes, Miss Williamson, it's for your own protection. We do not know why you are being targeted or why this person is trying to scare you. So, for your own protection, we would like to keep you close and protect you."

"Oh boy, this is really happening, isn't it?"

"Yes, it is so I need you to pack all the personals you would like to take, contact two, at best three, of your loved ones and explain to them the situation and let them know they will not be able to visit or contact you until the case has been solved. Miss Williamson, please do not worry. We will protect you and watch over your home as well until you return. We just cannot take any more chances."

"I know," Mother Williamson replied, "but I also know who I serve and my God will win and get the victory out of all of this."

"That's right and that's the spirit, Miss Williamson. You must pray and do not let them win. Take care, and I hope this is all over very soon."

Detective Jackson looked over at Mother Williamson and began hugging and consoling her. "Would you like me to get anything from the kitchen for you?"

"No, thank you dear. I want to just go to my bedroom and lay down for a while."

Trying to clear her head, Mother Williamson decided to start making her phone calls. She chose to give Pastor Paul her first call.

"Hello?"

"Hello Pastor, this is Mother Williamson."

He wasn't sure if he heard correctly so he closed his office door to drown out the sound of the saints praying.

"I'm sorry. Who is this?"

"Pastor, it's Mother Williamson."

"Oh, okay. I could not hear clearly before. Have you heard anything else concerning the case?"

"No, unfortunately there are still no leads. But I called to tell you that the police are relocating me to an undisclosed area because they feel that I might be the next target due to all of the threatening phone calls and a letter being slipped under my door."

"What! When did all of this happen?"

"All of this took place over the last couple of days, and whoever is involved, really has me on edge. I know that the other saints will judge me, but if they were in my shoes, then they would have no comments to make."

"Jesus!" replied Pastor Paul.

"Now, Pastor Paul, they told me I will be leaving in a couple of days, so I'm just grabbing a few things to take with me. So can you also have the church keep me in prayer until this bad nightmare is finally over?"

"Yes, Mother Williamson, we will definitely pray for you. Be encouraged and know that God is watching over you. Do you think I can have a quick word of prayer with you now, if you have time?"

"Sure."

"Father, we thank you for being her Shield and Buckler. We also thank you for putting a fortress around her so that no harm comes to her. God, we know that Your hand of protection is already in the midst of this situation so even though attacks may come, God, they shall not prosper because You are her Protector from dangers seen and unseen. Father, help her to continue to wear the helmet of Salvation to protect her mind from fear and doubt. We ask that You do not allow this situation to alter Mother Williamson's peace of mind and faith. Remind her that You will never leave her nor forsake her and will be with her always. Father, we both will continue to believe that You will bring Mother Rose and her family back home safely. We may not know where they are right now, but God You do! Amen!"

Mother Williamson was in tears after Pastor Paul prayed, but she felt in her spirit that everything was going to work out for everyone's best interest. As they said their good-byes, Pastor Paul hung up the phone and was also wiping tears from his eyes, as he walked back into the main sanctuary.

———

During prayer, it seemed a spirit of heaviness fell inside the sanctuary. Pastor Paul decided to shift the atmosphere by asking anyone who could, to stand up and give a joyful testimony about the Rose family.

He emphasized that anyone who did come up to speak should keep their testimony to no more than ten minutes and the testimony must be of good times and not of anything that would remind them of their current situation. As everyone gave their testimonies about funny moments with at least one member of the Rose family, instantly the spirit of heaviness was gone and the sanctuary was filled with laughter and joy again.

# CHAPTER EIGHT

*I woke to a loud banging sound on the front door. Both my parents' heads lifted up from the couch where they had fallen asleep the night before. They rushed to open the door.*

*All I could hear was my father shouting, "Junior, do not open the door!" Then even louder voices from the other side of the door shouting, "This is the police! Open up this door!"*

*My father told me to take my mother into her bedroom and shut the door while he slowly opened the front door. All he could see was flashing lights and police with their badges pinned to their chest.*

*The chief of police forcefully pushed the front door wide open as he made his way inside the house.*

*Stumbling backwards, my father shouted, "Can I help you?" Almost all of them were practically inside the house at this time.*

*"Yes you can. I'm Chief Harris. Is there an Alfred Brown living here?"*

*"I'm Alfred Brown," my father replied.*

*"Is there an Alfred Brown, Jr. who also lives at this residence?"*

*"Why yes," my father said. "That would be my eldest child. What has he done and what do you want with him?"*

*"We need to take your son downtown for questioning. Where is he now?"*

*My father noticed that one of the officers had his hand on his weapon from the moment he stepped foot into the house.*

*"Why, he is in the bedroom with his mother! Chief, can I ask you what has my son done? You still have not told me what crime he is being accused of."*

*"Mr. Brown, we have reason to believe that your son may be involved in a missing persons case that was reported this morning."*

*"That is a ridiculous accusation!" shouted my father.*

*"We received a phone call at 7:00 a.m. this morning from a Morgan Snow stating that his daughter did not come home last night after going out on a date with your son, Alfred Brown Jr."*

*"What? That cannot be true! Both Mr. and Mrs. Snow were over our house last night and we all saw Junior come home from his date with their daughter. Perhaps their daughter went back out that same night to hang out with some of her friends."*

"Mr. Brown, can you please go get your son. We need to speak with him to clear all this up."

"Sure, let me call my son out here to answer your questions."

My father nervously called for my mother and me to come into the living room where the police were waiting. He told my siblings to remain inside their bedrooms.

"Yes, honey," replied my mother acting as if she did not overhear the whole conversation.

"Babe, it seems that there is some kind of a mix-up. Linda Snow is missing and these detectives are saying that Junior had something to do with her disappearance and they want to question him."

"Oh my God," gasped my mother. "Why would my boy want to hurt Linda Snow? Besides he is only sixteen years old."

"Mr. and Mrs. Brown," replied the Chief, "We would like to question Alfred Brown, Jr. at the police station and because he is a minor, one of you need to accompany him."

"I will accompany him," barked my father. "I'm his father and he needs me now so yes, I'll be the one going. Babe, you stay here with the girls until I come back home with Junior."

"Alfred, go get dressed so we can take you downtown for questioning," replied the Chief.

As I got into the back of the police car, I cried hysterically into my father's chest while he tried to comfort me the best way he could.

I'll never forget holding my father so tight as he whispered, "Do not worry, son. I'm not going to let nothing happen to you." Then he mumbled a prayer, "God please be with us and keep Your hand of protection over my family and let the truth come to the light. Amen!"

Mother Williamson offered Detective Jackson something to eat and she accepted. They both were starving. Detective Smith had received permission from Detective Lee to take a two-hour dinner break locally because he had personal business to address.

Jackson asked, "So, what's on the menu, Miss Williamson?"

"I plan to make some turkey meatloaf with redskin mashed potatoes and spinach."

"Wow, that sounds yummy. Can I help with the cooking?"

"Baby, I would not have it any other way because the Bible says if a man wants to eat, he must work. Please go wash your hands and let's get started. By the way, what is your first name?"

"My first name is Tracy, but unfortunately it would be best that you continue to call me Detective Jackson because Tracy is too personal and if the other detectives suspect that I'm on a case with someone I know personally, I will get pulled off this assignment."

"Done," Mother Williamson stated, "but I can at least call you Daughter sometime, right?"

"Sure, that should be fine. All right then let's start cooking this meal because I'm extremely hungry!"

Mother Williamson was gathering all the ingredients and cookware when Jackson returned from washing her hands. She was ready to start preparing the dinner.

"Detective Jackson, would you like to prepare the mashed potatoes and spinach and I'll prepare the meatloaf and make some fresh lemonade?"

"Yes, Mother Williamson, lemonade is perfect and I do not mind preparing the mashed potatoes and spinach. This is one of my favorite meals."

All you could hear in the kitchen was the banging of the pots and pans. Unexpectedly, Jackson asked Mother Williamson if she could pray for her sick son, Marcus Jackson.

"Certainly, my Daughter. God answers prayers and loves to show Himself to those who would trust Him and believe that He can perform the impossible."

Tears began to fall from Detective Jackson's eyes. Mother Williamson quickly wiped her hands with the dish towel and held both of Jackson's hands.

"Oh no," Jackson said pulling away. "Mother Williamson, I meant after we finished preparing the food because you mentioned that you were extremely hungry."

Mother Williamson reached for Detective Jackson's hands again and said, "Look, my child, some things are more important and need to be prayed about as soon as possible. Now, Daughter, would you like to share with me what illness Marcus is battling? It is up to you."

"Of course. He has a rare brain tumor that is cancerous and there are times he is alert and other times he is unconscious."

"My God! Well, Daughter, God can fix anything. Would you happen to have a picture of the darling little boy?"

"Yes, let me get my cell phone. I have plenty of pictures!" Jackson eagerly showed off her ten-year old son, Marcus.

"What a handsome young man and he looks just like you." Mother Williamson smiled.

"Everyone tells me that he looks like me until they see my husband."

"Is that so? Well, you know what they say when couples are together long enough—they both start looking and acting like each other. I have one more question to ask you before we begin to pray."

"Okay, go ahead, Mother Williamson. I have nothing to hide."

"Good. Do you know the Lord Jesus Christ as your Lord and personal Savior?"

"Huh? Well, I read my Bible sometimes and I attend church when I can which is not very often."

"I'm asking, have you ever confessed your sins with your mouth, believed in your heart that Jesus died for you, and accepted Him as your personal Savior?" asked Mother Williamson.

"Do you mean when they call people up to the front of the church after the service? Well no, Mother Williamson, I have never done that before. I just sit and watch other people ask God for His forgiveness, but I never have."

"Well, Daughter, it is time that you do accept the Lord Jesus Christ as your personal Savior."

"I'm ready. I would like to confess my sins, believe and accept the Lord Jesus Christ as my personal Savior. I want to be one of His prepared people as they say in church."

As she held Mother Williamson's hands tightly, Detective Jackson had a peaceful look on her face that all of the worries in the world could not erase. Then Mother Williamson began to pray, and she asked Detective Jackson to repeat after her.

"God, I believe Jesus Christ is Your Son, the Savior of the world. I believe He died on the cross for me, and bore all my sins. Please forgive my sins, save me, come into my life. I confess with my mouth and believe in my heart that I'm saved by Your Grace. In Jesus' precious name, Amen!"

After she finished, Mother Williamson asked Detective Jackson if she understood everything she just did.

Detective Jackson smiled. "Yes."

She embraced Mother Williamson, this time as a born again believer and Mother Williamson welcomed her into the Kingdom of God.

"My Daughter, the Bible says heaven is rejoicing over your one soul and I am too!"

Slightly confused, Jackson asked, "Mother Williamson, is heaven really rejoicing that I'm saved?"

"Yes, my dear! If God's Word says it, then we as believers accept it and that settles it! They are rejoicing that a new soul has been won for the Kingdom of God." They both smiled. "You are born again which means that your old nature has died and now you are a new babe in Christ. God desires that you grow into a mature Christian. My dear, just like you eat natural food on a daily basis, you must also be fed spiritually and be nourished by God's Word daily. Prayer is also very important and God wants you to talk to Him so that your relationship with Him will become stronger. God is now living on the inside of you. Ask God to lead you to a good church where they are teaching the Word of God and where you can fellowship with other Christians as you grow studying God's Word. Now that God has received you into His Kingdom, let's focus our attention back on your son. Detective Jackson, there is a scripture found in the Bible at Matthew 18:20 that states, 'For where two or three are gathered together in my name, there am I in the midst of them.'"

"What does that really mean?"

"That scripture means that when two or more people by faith, come together and believe, God is right there with them. It shows God that we are united in faith to believe Him to answer our prayers according to His will."

"Okay. Are you saying that it may not be the will of God to heal my son?"

"No, Daughter. God loves to heal all of His people and that includes Marcus. God's Word states in the third book of John at verse 2: 'Beloved, I wish above all things that thou mayest prosper and be in health, even as thy soul prospereth.' All I'm saying is that there are times that saints will pray for things that are not God's will for their lives."

Mother Williamson detected a confused look on Detective Jackson's face and further explained, "God will not give you anything that will harm you. God knows all things and He never makes a mistake, no matter what man may say. He is truly the God of impossibilities and can do anything, even things that seem impossible to man. He will never give you anything that can hurt you! So there are times God may say yes, or no to our prayers, but then there are times God will say wait for our prayers to be answered."

"But why, Mother Williamson? I do not understand why?"

"God will never give you anything that will hurt you, like saying yes to a woman who wants to get married to someone who's not good for her or give a job to a man who will compromise his relationship with God. Bottom line—some things may seem all glamorous in the beginning, but He knows all endings."

"Okay, I get it now. So, you are saying that God will not bless us with anything that will hurt us or our walk with Him."

"Yes, my dear. God loves us and will do whatever it takes to protect us from ourselves, if necessary. All He asks of us is to commit our lives to Him and walk by faith and not by sight and God will take care of the rest."

"So why do we pray if God is not going to answer our prayers?"

"Because God wants us to trust Him when we pray no matter what final decision He makes. We cannot see into the future or know the heart of man; only God can. When we pray, it's like a child asking their parents for permission to do something because the parents know best. It is the same thing with God. Now that you have accepted Him as your

Lord and Savior, He wants to have full control of your life. He is your Maker and does not want to see you get hurt, just like your parents, and once again He knows best."

Mother Williamson prayed, "God, we humbly come before Your presence, standing in agreement, believing that You will touch little Marcus' body. You are his Creator, the Maker of both his body and soul. We now ask that You be his Chief Physician. God, we hold fast to Your promises. Even though our vision tarry, we will wait for it! God, Your Word declares in Matthew, 'For verily I say unto you, if ye have faith as a grain of mustard seed, ye shall say unto this mountain move from here to yonder place; and it shall move.' God, we thank you for allowing Marcus' body to line up with Your Holy Word! We cancel everything that is not like You and we claim total victory! God, with just one touch from Your nail-scarred hands, Marcus will not have to go through any more chemotherapy because by Your stripes Marcus Jackson is healed! We also believe by faith that when Marcus goes for his next doctor's checkup, the reports will not show any signs of cancer in his body! We give You all honor and glory that is forever due to Your matchless name, Amen!"

Detective Jackson was crying like a baby as she wiped her eyes and Mother Williamson's face was also drenched with tears.

Finally, Mother Williamson said, "Okay, enough crying! Let's feed our hungry bellies and finish cooking!"

They both had delight in their hearts.

"My Daughter, put God first in your life! Join a good church that is preaching the true Word of God and if you do not know of one, you are always welcome to attend my church, The Love Church of God Assembly. The devil is not going to make things any easier in life for you. In fact, he is going to do whatever he can to try and discourage you and to make you give up on God. So you must get busy for the Lord, get involved in a church and be about your Heavenly Father's business. He will take care of your business and reward you openly."

"Yes, Mother Williamson. I think I would like to attend your church and thanks so much for all your help, especially leading me to Christ."

"God has work for you to do and I also believe with all my heart that God has already healed Marcus. Just continue to thank Him for Marcus' healing."

"Thank you for your prayers. I'm about to share some news with you. The CSI team found a fingerprint on the envelope that was slipped underneath your doorway."

"What! See, Daughter. God is working in the midst even right now! Praise the Lord!"

Going into a police station for the first time would be scary for anyone, let alone a young teenager. *A Detective Oldman took both my father and me into an interrogation room that had nothing in it but a table, chairs and a huge window. I didn't know that the huge window was a two-way mirror. He told both of us to take a seat while he explained the process to my father.*

*But then my father said to Detective Oldman, "My son is a minor and I'm going to be right by his side or this questioning will not take place without a lawyer!"*

*"Very well," replied Detective Oldman. He reiterated how he was going to ask me questions about the disappearance of Linda Snow and that everything would be recorded. Detective Oldman proceeded to read my Miranda rights to me and asked me if I understood my rights and then stated for the record that my father was present. As my father nodded his head in agreement, Detective Oldman pressed the play button on the recorder.*

*"Can you please state your full name?" asked Detective Oldman.*

*"My full name is Alfred Brown Jr.," I replied.*

*"How old are you presently?"*

*"I'm sixteen years old."*

*"Where were you on June 25th at 5:00 p.m.?"*

*"I was on a date with a girl name Linda."*

*"You mean Linda Snow to clarify the records?" asked Detective Oldman.*

*"Yes, with Linda Snow."*

*"Alfred, do you realize that Linda Snow did not return home after going*

out on a date with you last night?"

My father stood up from his chair and shouted, "Wait a minute! My son told me that he dropped Linda home last night."

"Please do not interrupt this questioning," Detective Oldman said.

I looked at my father's face. He was very upset but began to settle down. He also knew there was something wrong about the way the questioning was being handled.

"I'll repeat the question again and hopefully there will be no interruptions this time." The detective looked in my father's direction. "Do you realize you were the last person to see Linda Snow, Alfred?"

I began feeling embarrassed and knew that the issue was really getting serious. So I felt I'd better come clean and tell what really happened on our date.

"Well, actually," I began, "I wasn't the last person to see Linda yesterday and I wasn't the last person who spoke with her either."

Detective Oldman turned his entire body around to look at the window that occupied most of the wall. That's when I started to get suspicious that there was something or someone behind that window.

Suddenly another detective came rushing through the door and introduced himself as Detective Redford. My father began shaking his leg back and forth in the fastest motion I've ever seen him do.

Then he started rubbing both of his sweaty hands together with a scared look on his face and said, "Junior, what are you saying?"

Getting familiar with my father's interruptions, Detective Oldman completely ignored his question to me because at this point all he cared about was getting me to tell the truth. He explained to my father that Detective Redford came into the room to verify that I was not being provoked as a minor in any way to make that statement.

Detective Redford asked, "So you were saying that Linda Snow was with someone else besides you yesterday?"

"Yes," I replied.

"Well, what was the name of this other person?"

"I do not know!"

"What do you mean you do not know? Did you see her with someone else or not?" Detective Redford stood over me now.

In a calmer voice, Detective Redford said, "Alfred Jr., we need to hear the truth about what happened with Linda Snow. Was she with someone else or not?"

Detective Oldman offered me a cold can of soda and said, "Perhaps we are scaring you. Drink your soda because we need you to be calm and tell us the truth."

"Okay," I said, "this is what really happened yesterday evening. I picked up Linda Snow from her house at 5:00 p.m. and we walked down to the local carnival, which was about ten blocks from our houses. When we entered the park, I noticed that Linda kept looking around, like she was trying to find someone. We headed towards a ride called the Cup and Saucer, which is what all the couples ride. Then we went for soda and cotton candy. After paying for the items, I turned around to give them to her and Linda was gone. I called out her name, but with all the loud music, there was no way she could hear me calling her. So I frantically started searching all over for her, but I could not find her."

I now was feeling embarrassed as my father looked at me.

"How long did you search for her?" asked Detective Redford.

"I searched for about two long hours, but she was nowhere to be found."

"What did you do next, son?"

"I remember walking back towards her house thinking perhaps she got distracted and got lost, then went back home."

Now both detectives were standing over me and I got really nervous so I stopped to catch my breath.

Detective Oldman said, "Okay, please continue."

My father had embarrassment written across his forehead because he would have sworn on a stack of Bibles that I was not lying about last night.

Looking down, I proceeded. "I was walking to her house and I noticed a girl with the same outfit that Linda Snow had on in a car with an older guy. Then I realized that girl was Linda Snow and she was supposed to be my date that night, but instead she was in the car with another dude."

Detective Redford said, "Son I can tell when someone is lying to me and I believe you are lying."

"No! I'm really telling the truth this time!" I screamed.

Then Detective Redford began to yell at me. "Did you harm her, son, because she dumped you? Where is Linda Snow?"

*"I do not know! I'm telling the truth!" Tears ran down my face.*

*"Okay," said my father, "that is enough! Unless you have enough evidence to hold my son here, we are going home. I'm seeking legal counsel and this questioning is over! If further questioning is needed, we will come back to the station with his lawyer present. Junior, come on, we are leaving this God-forsaken place because these detectives are trying to trap you into a confession by accusing you of something you had nothing to do with!"*

*Detective Oldman replied, "Mr. Brown, your son is free to go, but do not leave town because your son is the prime suspect in the case of the disappearance of Linda Snow."*

Joe realized that when he was speaking with Mother Williamson earlier, they did not discuss any updates on the case. He called her. She recognized the number and politely asked Joe to hold on while she asked Jackson to watch the food until she got off the phone with a friend.

"It will be my pleasure," she replied humbly.

"Sorry about that, Mr. Joe. I'm back. How are you doing?"

"I'm good. I forgot to ask you a question while we were on the phone. Did any new leads develop since we last spoke?"

"No, but between me and you, I just found out the CSI team found one print on the envelope."

"That is fantastic news!" shouted Joe.

"Joe, I also have some more information to share with you," replied Mother Williamson.

"Okay, what else?"

"So, because of all the strange events taking place, the police do not want to take any more chances with my safety so I'm being placed in protective custody and I'm leaving in a couple of days."

"What? Are you serious?"

"Yes, and I was going to call you and tell you this but you beat me to it. I will call you after this is all over, according to God's timetable."

"Miss Williamson, I can hear it in your voice that you are afraid."

"I am very afraid of the unknown, Joe, but I'm in God's hands and I trust God that He wouldn't place me in harm's way."

"I agree with Detective Thomas. It's best for your own safety. I will have to contact one of my friends on the police force and find out more information; he owes me a favor," said Joe.

"Be careful, Joe, and I will be praying for you and Zach that God will protect and guide your steps."

"Thank you so much for your blessings and keeping me up-to-date. I'm sure that Zach would want to know as well. I know that God will take care of you, and I do not need to remind you of what God can do."

Mother Williamson smiled as she realized that Joe had learned something from this experience and that is, God would not forsake her.

"You take care of yourself, Miss Williamson."

"And you do the same, Joe."

She hung up the phone and turned towards the kitchen where Detective Jackson was setting the table. She had already made the lemonade, sliced the meatloaf and placed both the mashed potatoes and spinach into separate dishes. Mother Williamson was so surprised; all she could do was smile knowing that God was truly going to bless Detective Jackson and her family.

Jackson waved Mother Williamson in and said, "Come on. The food is getting cold so have a seat."

"I'm coming," she replied as her stomach growled. "Oh my goodness! You've done a fine job, young lady, in setting the table and with the cooking too."

"Why thank you, Mother Williamson. It's an honor to serve you after all you have done for me and my family."

"Well, there is only one thing to do now, my daughter. Would you like to pray for the food?"

"Sure, I don't mind, but I only know the prayer that I was taught when I was young girl."

"That's fine!" replied Mother Williamson. "Detective Jackson, God is not concerned about how elegant your prayer sounds. He is more interested in the sincerity of your heart. So, go ahead and pray."

Detective Jackson started, sounding very nervous, "God, we thank you for the food we are about to receive, Amen!"

"You did great!" Mother Williamson gave her a big smile of encouragement.

"Thank you" Detective Jackson returned the smiled. " Can you please teach me how to pray?"

"Sure, my dear, but let's eat first."

Her stomach made a loud growling sound again.

As Joe hung up the phone, he knew that his hands were full and he had to start working at this situation very quickly. Joe turned towards Zach who was waiting anxiously to find out what was discussed over the phone.

"Well," said Joe, "you are not going to believe all that Mother Williamson just shared with me."

"Try me," replied Zach.

Joe began explaining everything to Zach and when he finished, Joe said, "We need to work full time on this case until it's solved by us or the police."

Still surprised by what Joe just revealed to him, Zach said, "I'm ready to start now! Do you have any other game plans other than questioning our neighbors, Joe?"

"We don't know who to trust anymore because as long as that amount of money is up for grabs, anybody will do whatever it takes to retrieve it whether it leads to an arrest or not."

"Joe, you are right."

"Yes. I think it would be good if I started out by getting in contact with one of my buddies downtown in the police department. I want to find out the suspect's name, where he lives and who has he been working with. Oh by the way Zach, I picked up some cheese and turkey sandwich meat. They are in the refrigerator and I believe there are a couple bottles of juice as well. Help yourself while I look through my address book for my buddy's contact information."

Joe did not have to tell Zach twice because before he knew it, Zach was heading straight to the kitchen while he made his way to the bedroom.

# CHAPTER NINE

Joe searched through his box of business cards and immediately his hand was on Detective Kelly's card. *Wow, I thought I was going to have to search high and low, but instead the card was right on top of the pile.* Of course, Joe looked up and said, "Thank You, God," as he smiled because after being a PI for so many years, he had encountered dozens of acquaintances at the police department, but there was just one who was really close to him.

Joe picked up the phone and began dialing his cell number. Not getting an answer, he decided not to leave a message. He wanted Kelly to feel like he was reaching out to an old friend not just picking him for information. He dialed his office number and the phone rang twice. Then Joe heard a voice say, "Detective Kelly speaking. Whom do I have the pleasure of speaking with?"

"Hello, Detective Kelly! This is your old buddy, Joe."

"Mr. PI, is this really you?"

"Yes, I'm afraid so and I'm fine before you can get the words out of your mouth. What have you been up to?"

"Nothing, just counting down my years for retirement like somebody else I know," Detective Kelly chuckled.

Joe let out a big laugh and said, "Boy, it is going to feel so good knowing that you don't have to get up early in the morning and travel to work to pay your bills because you have paid your debt to the working society! But let me warn you that there are moments you will miss being mobile as crazy as that sounds."

"That is crazy, Joe. I'm never going to feel that way," replied Kelly.

Joe, knowing that he said that same thing just before he retired, thought to himself that Kelly would eventually understand what he meant. He immediately changed the subject. "So how are Mrs. Kelly and the kids?"

"Joe, the wife is doing fine. I just keep falling in love with her over and over again. As for the kids, they are all grown up. The boys are in college out-of-state. My one and only girl, who is the youngest of the family, will be finishing high school next year."

"Wow, you're right, Kelly. They are no longer kids; they are practically adults."

"How about yourself, Joe? How have you been occupying your time since your retirement?"

"Doing absolutely nothing. Just taking one day at a time and enjoying what each day brings."

"Joe, is everything okay? I know you would like me to believe that you're just calling an old friend, but I can hear it in your voice that something is troubling you."

"Well, Kelly, you guessed right. Do you have a little time to meet with me or can you call me back on your cell phone?"

"Sure, Joe. This sounds very serious. Can I call you back at this number?"

"Yes, you can," replied Joe.

"Okay, just give me about thirty minutes. There is something I have to complete and then I will return your call."

"Thanks so much, Kelly. I can always count on you," replied Joe as he ended the conversation.

Less than thirty minutes later, Joe's phone was ringing and he knew it was Kelly returning his phone call.

"Hello, Kelly."

"Hey, Mr. PI. So what is troubling you?"

"I will just get straight to the point, I know that you are aware of the disappearance of the Rose family, right?"

"Yes," replied Detective Kelly, "I'm very familiar with the case."

"Is there someone in custody who can potentially be connected to this crime?"

"Yes, there is. I'm well aware. I'm one of the assigned interrogating detectives. Why, Joe? Where is all of this leading? Do you know more about the case?"

"No," replied Joe, as he was relieved that his buddy was assigned as an interrogating detective.

"Is there something you want to tell me, Joe?"

"Okay, so I know the Rose family personally. They have lived in my building for many years. I was thinking I would take a break from my retirement to help the police with whatever it will take to solve this case."

There was silence for a couple of seconds and then Detective Kelly said, "Joe, there is no doubt that you are good at what you used to do, but I think that it will be best to let the police handle this case. What information can I tell you off the record that would help comfort you?"

"Kelly, please you do not know how much these people really mean to me. I need to start doing some groundwork and I wanted to start by getting some information on the suspect. Please help me."

"Joe, you know I don't mind helping you, but please do not get in the way of the police investigation - and I do not have to remind you that if you do get caught and questioned, we never spoke."

"Sure thing, Kelly! I would never reveal my sources, I haven't after all these years and I have not changed!"

"Okay, but I would rather we meet somewhere in person, just you and me. Besides it would be good to see you again," replied Kelly.

"That sounds perfect. This is just like the old days," stated Joe.

"Perhaps we can meet at a restaurant nearby. Oh I know. Let's meet at our favorite diner on Front Street," suggested Kelly.

"Great! I'll see you there in about one hour," replied Joe.

Joe did not own a vehicle and had to rely on public transportation. He told Zach to get as comfortable as he could until he returned. He explained he needed to meet up with his buddy and try to get additional information about the suspect.

"Sure," replied Zach. "I know that you cannot take me along, so I'll be here when you get back. Oh Joe, do you have any snacks in the house?"

"Sure. Look in the kitchen cabinet above the sink. There should be some sugar-free cakes and cookies up there," Joe said as he headed for the apartment door.

Zach said, "You sure know how to make a person feel at home." He rushed into the kitchen area.

Joe took the bus to the Front Street stop, which was directly across from the diner. As he entered the diner, there was Detective Kelly already sitting at a table reading a newspaper.

Joe walked over to him and said, "Hello, Kelly!"

"How are you, Mr. PI? It's good to see you after all these years."

They embraced.

"Grab a seat, Mr. PI. Today, I will be treating you for lunch. What are you drinking?" asked Kelly.

"I'll just have a glass of water," replied Joe, "because I really need to stay away from the sugar and the acid."

As they waited for the waitress to serve their table, they could not stop looking at each other.

Kelly said, "Boy, do you look great for a retired man!"

Joe smiled. "You don't look bad yourself for someone still working nine to five." They both grinned.

Kelly asked, "On a serious note, what do you want to know about the suspect?"

"So, I was wondering if you can provide me with the suspect's name."

"Sure. He goes by the name Fat on the streets, but his real name is Fredrick Albert Tanks. He is a hustler who mainly steals anything he can get his hands on to support his bad habits. This is why I'm suspecting that he does not know the whereabouts of the Rose family. He was just trying to scare Miss Rose's friend so he could convince her that he knew where the Rose family was and eventually try and get some of the ransom money.

The waitress finally came and took their orders. As she took the menus and walked away, Kelly said, "So where were we? Oh I know… we were talking about Fat. So he was never involved in any really big crimes, just petty thefts and that is why I think he is acting alone just to get some ransom money. As a matter of fact, he lives in the same building as the Rose family. He lives on the third floor in apartment 3C with his parents."

"Yes, yes! I know the apartment because I live in that building as well. Heck, I know just who you are talking about and I'm familiar with his mother. She is such a sweet lady. I would see her coming and going from time to time, but I never knew that was his mother."

"Professionally speaking, most of these types of people like to be alone because they are trying to support their own bad habits and they do not want to share with anyone else because it is less for them."

"Kelly, is there anything else you can tell me about this case?"

"Are you aware the letter was Fredrick Alfred Tanks' doing?" asked Detective Kelly.

When the waitress arrived with their food, Kelly thanked her and Joe shook his head no. He was not aware. Then they held up their glasses and toasted to their good friendship. In a matter of minutes, both gentlemen had devoured everything that was on their plates; even their drinks were completely gone.

"Kelly, I cannot thank you enough for lunch and for this helpful information. I noticed that you kept looking at your watch throughout the whole conversation. Is there some place you need to be?"

"Yes, Joe. Some of us are still on the clock and I have a meeting to attend so I must get back to work."

"No problem. You should get back to work because I would hate to see you get in any trouble."

"Yes, Mr. Retiree, but it was good seeing you again and hopefully we can get together under better circumstances."

Joe said, "Yes." Kelly left a tip on the table and they both shook hands and departed to go their separate ways.

Mother Williamson asked, "Detective Jackson, tell me a little about yourself?"

"Well, I was born and raised here in Atlanta, and I love to dance. Although I do not dance any more, I took modern, jazz and tap lessons until I was about twenty-five years old. I have a Master's Degree in Business and I love roller blading with my family. I have been married to my husband, Marcus, for about thirteen years."

"Oh, so your son is a junior?" asked Mother Williamson.

"Yes, he is and his grandfather's middle name is Marcus."

"How did you meet your husband?"

"I was first introduced to my husband while I was on a cruise going to nowhere with my family. During disco night, he asked me to dance and I said yes and the rest is history."

"Well, it certainly seems like the cruise did go somewhere! It took you to your next destiny in life to becoming Mrs. Jackson!" They both giggled.

"What about you, Mother Williamson?" asked Detective Jackson.

"Well, I too was born and raised in Atlanta, and when I was young, my girlfriends and I would just travel all the time. We traveled to fifteen states and twelve countries. I have never had the opportunity to get married and never had the pleasure of birthing any children."

Mother Williamson had a sad look on her face and was pouting.

"It must have been very lonely living by yourself all these years," Jackson said as she returned the sad facial expression.

"Daughter, I've always had God in my life for one thing and I also kept myself very busy for the Lord. In addition to traveling with my friends, I also allowed God to use me in various ministries in the church. My dear, God can keep you if you want to be kept, but you need a made-up mind to want to be kept and used by God."

Mother Williamson touched her stomach as she leaned back against the kitchen chair and said that her stomach was fully satisfied, literally full. Jackson stood up from the kitchen table and began gathering all the empty dishes and insisted that Mother Williamson relax while she took care of cleaning up.

"My God, thank you, Daughter! It's not often that I get company who helps me cook and then cleans up too. God bless you, Daughter."

Mother Williamson headed for the living room where she could sit more comfortably. It did not take long before her thoughts drifted off to Mother Rose and the girls and tears began to fall from her eyes. She asked God in a low voice, "Why did this have to happen to my best friend and her daughters?"

Jackson went into the living room after drying the last dish to ask where everything belonged and she noticed that Mother Williamson was silently crying.

Jackson immediately put down the dish towel and walked over to her and started hugging her with all the strength that she had. She told her in the most comforting way that everything was going to all work out!

Those words touched Mother Williamson so much that she stood up and began to wipe her eyes and said, "Yes they will be alright! Thank you again, my daughter. I must keep believing the report of the Lord and trust God that He is doing a perfect work in the midst of all of this confusion. Now that we have eaten, would you like to study the Bible?"

"Okay," replied Jackson, "let's do that."

As both women headed towards the dining room table, Mother Williamson agreed and opened her Bible to the book of Daniel. She felt this would be a good book to study together because Daniel had faith not to turn his back on God, even as he faced death. Mother Williamson asked Jackson to start reading Daniel 1:1 out loud while she reached for a pack of popcorn on the sideboard that she intended to make after Bible study; they could also drink some more of the lemonade that was left over from dinner.

A couple of hours went by as they studied God's Word. Jackson thanked Mother Williamson for always wanting to invest in her spiritual growth. Then she told her that she was going to make a short phone call to her son before he went to bed.

Mother Williamson said, "You are more than welcome to use the house phone to make as many calls as you want."

After speaking with both her son and husband, Detective Jackson took an incoming call from the precinct.

"Hello, this is Detective Jackson."

"Hello, this is Detective Lee. Just checking in. Is everything okay?"

"Yes, Detective Lee, everything is fine."

"Good. Has Detective Smith returned from his dinner break yet?"

"I believe that is him knocking on the apartment door now. Hold on."

She went over to the door and looked into the hall.

"Hello sir? Yes, that was him."

"Okay, tell everyone good night," as he hung up the phone.

Everyone decided to watch a movie and relax for the remainder of the evening. She happened to glance towards the television and realized the movie they selected had already started.

"Mother Williamson, the movie started!" shouted Jackson.

"Okay I'm coming," replied Mother Williamson, "The popcorn is almost finished!"

Jackson reached for her glass of lemonade while Mother Williamson held onto the popcorn bowl as she sat down. Quiet filled the room as they could not take their eyes off the movie about a rebellious teenager who runs away from home because she did not want to obey her parents' house rules.

After two hours, the movie finally came to an end and so did Mother Williamson. When Jackson looked her way, she was nodding off. She wondered at what part of the movie did Mother Williamson start to get sleepy. Slowly rising from the couch, she went to wake her up, but suddenly Mother Williamson's eyes popped wide open and she said, "Don't worry. I'm going to bed."

"Oh," replied Detective Jackson. "I thought that you were asleep."

"I was but I'm a very light sleeper. At the slightest movement, I'll wake up, especially when someone is standing over me like you were."

"I'm sorry, Mother Williamson! I did not mean to startle you."

"It's okay. I should be in bed anyway. So, you two get comfortable. Hopefully, you are allowed to lay down while you are on duty."

"No. Unfortunately, both Detective Smith and I have to remain on guard, but we will relax in each of the chairs in the living room."

"Well, I'm just glad that I have company."

Mother Williamson started making her way to her bedroom and said good night to both detectives.

"Mother Williamson?"

"Yes, my daughter? What is the matter?"

"Do you mind if I keep the TV on low volume throughout the night?"

"Of course not. I always sleep with my door shut anyway. Okay, good night."

"Good night, Mother Williamson."

Mother Williamson took a shower and began reading her Bible before getting into bed. Reading the book of Exodus helped her to remember that God did not forget about the suffering of His people and prepared a way for them to escape bondage. Mother Williamson knew that the same God would not forget about the Rose family and she was trusting God to make a way of escape for them as well.

One hour later, Mother Williamson's head began to bob up and down. She decided to close the Bible and knelt down beside her bed to say a quick word of prayer.

# CHAPTER TEN

My father began explaining to my mother that when the police have their eyes on someone as a suspect, they will dig into their past to find some incident that fits the current crime. She could not believe that they were going through something like this again with me. The next morning, my family and I were sitting down eating breakfast when the phone rang.

"You would not guess who was on the other end," said my father to my mother.

As I looked at the expression on my father's face, I knew it was the police and it had something to do with Linda. All kinds of thoughts went through my head: either they found Linda or they were going to arrest me for her disappearance. My father quickly hung up the phone and began frantically looking through the kitchen drawer.

My mother said, "Honey, what are you looking for?"

"I need to get hold of Howard's number. Where is the address book?"

"You mean our friend, Howard, the lawyer?"

"Yes dear. They are coming to arrest Junior based on some new evidence that came up."

"What!"

"Yes! They are coming for Junior. You better get dressed, son, because they are going to take you."

I began to cry. "This is not fair! Why doesn't anybody believe me? Mommy, I'm scared! Tell them that I do not want to go to jail!"

At this point, my entire family was upset and my father had to calm everyone down since he could no longer hear what Howard, the lawyer, was saying over the phone.

"Junior, Junior, you must get dressed because they are on their way for you and I do not want them to take you in your pajamas," shouted my father. "Baby, take the other kids next door to Barbara's house while Junior and I wait for Howard and the police to come."

"Okay, dear."

She hugged and kissed me and told me that she loved me and everything would be all right. A loud banging sound interrupted my parents. My father ran to the front door.

"Whose there?"

"It's Howard. Open up the door."

"Good morning," Howard quickly said. "Have the police arrived yet? Where is Junior?"

"No, Howard. They have not arrived yet and Junior is at the kitchen table scared to death."

"Okay," replied Howard as he quickly walked into the kitchen to talk to his client, me.

Howard sat down in the chair next to me.

He explained, "Here is what the police will do. They are going to read you your rights. Just listen to them and do not say a word. I will speak on your behalf. Also, Alfred, it is very important that you do not interfere with the arresting detectives because you, too, can get arrested. So, Junior, here is where it will get scary for you, but do not worry. Both your father and I will be right by your side. As the arresting detective reads you your rights, they are going to be placing handcuffs on your wrists. I will try to talk them out of it because of your age, but depending on the arresting detective, they can refuse. Please do not fight them or they will have another charge against you, which is called resisting arrest, and they can hold you on that technicality as well.

"Right now everything they are saying is just allegations and must be proven in a court of law. So, Junior, whatever you do, do not say a word to the police. Let me speak for you. Do you understand everything I've explained to you, Junior?"

I was still crying, but managed to nod my head yes.

Seconds later, a loud banging sound came from the door. "This is the police! We have a warrant for the arrest of Alfred Brown Jr.!"

My father nervously opened the door. About two or three detectives waved their badges and another waved a warrant. Howard introduced himself as the family lawyer and asked to see it. They then asked for Alfred Brown, Jr. and my father pointed towards the kitchen area. I was still crying as they approached me. My father wanted to console me, but he remembered what Howard stated earlier.

I shouted, "Daddy, Daddy! Please help me!"

My father's eyes were filled with tears as he looked on and the entire neighborhood watched as the police arrested me.

*Howard assured me that everything was going to be okay. My father asked Howard if he could ride downtown in the patrol car with me. "I want to make sure my boy is okay."*

*"I know, Alfred," Howard said as he tried to calm my father down. "The law is definitely on your side because Junior is a minor and he must be accompanied by an adult. So, yes you can ride in the patrol car with him and I will follow. Alfred, once we get downtown, here is how the process is going to work. They need to book Junior first by taking his picture and finger printing him before you or I can speak with him again."*

*My father just was not taking this very well. Howard told one of the detectives that my father would be riding in the patrol car with me and that he would be following them.*

*"Okay," the detective replied. "Let's go downtown."*

*My father thought to throw a jacket over my shoulders in order to cover up those handcuffs.*

*When we arrived at the precinct, the police told Howard and my father to be seated in a visiting area until they were called. Howard took the time to convince my father into telling him everything up front now so that there would not be any surprises along the way.*

*"Okay, Howard, what do you want to know?"*

*"When the police came to the house, they told me that they had new evidence that linked Junior to this disappearance case."*

*"All I remember is the other night, Junior went out on a date with a girl named Linda Snow, our neighbors' daughter. He came home by himself and it was earlier than we expected."*

*"What time did he come home?"*

*"It was about 7:15 p.m., but I told him he could stay out until 11:00 p.m. When he first came through the door, he told both me and my wife that he wasn't feeling very well. We just took his word for it."*

*"Did you notice how his clothing looked?"*

*"Actually, I did because it was his first serious date, and I remember checking him out from head to toe."*

*"Okay, so you are saying none of his clothing was torn and he did not have any scratches on his body, correct?"*

*"I wasn't able to see any torn clothing or scratches on his body. Besides, his*

*mother would have seen that stuff when she put him to bed that night."*

*"Alfred, if the police have new evidence concerning Linda's disappearance, could they be referring to another incident involving Junior?"*

*Howard noticed my father's facial expression change when he mentioned a past incident involving me.*

Joe saw a bus approaching a few blocks down as he quickly ran to the nearest bus stop to catch it. While riding back home, Joe had the wealth of information that he needed to start this investigation. After all, time was not waiting. Joe also did not feel that Detective Kelly was correct about Fat working alone. He knew, due to his many years of experience, that people with bad habits can be bought and made to do just about anything for money. *Zach and I really have our hands full*, Joe thought. But they were ready to take on the many tasks necessary to find out what happened to the Rose family. Looking out the bus window, Joe noticed that he only had two more stops to go.

Finally arriving home, Joe found Zach fast asleep on his couch as the TV just watched him. Joe tried to gently shut the apartment door, but accidentally slammed it. Zach popped his head up and gradually moved from his comfortable position on the couch as if he was awake all along.

"So, Joe, did you find out anything interesting?"

"Yes, we have some good information to start with and hopefully it will crack this case."

"Joe, please do not take this the wrong way, and I want you to know that I'm not concerned about the money, but what if we find the perpetrator, are we entitled to the reward money?"

"Actually I haven't given it much thought, but since you mentioned it, yes we would be entitled to the reward money. Keep in mind that it must lead to both an arrest and conviction."

"Well, the reason I'm asking is that I propose we split it with Mother Rose after all she has gone through, if we get the money."

"Zach, I think that is an excellent idea and very noble of you to suggest such kindness."

Zach felt proud to hear that coming from Joe as he watched him pull a pad from his shirt pocket to go over the information he gathered.

Detective Thomas was sitting at his desk and, of all of the cases that he had encountered over the years, he was unsure why the Rose family case kept plaguing his mind every single day. It was not like he really knew this family. In fact, he had never met the people before. No matter what other cases he was investigating, he always stopped to think about what more he could be doing to solve the Rose family case. This would really seem crazy to someone else because all cases should be just as important, but somehow he kept feeling a tugging to work harder on solving this particular case.

He was going through all the evidence files and thinking about what the police department could still do to expedite matters when his office phone rang.

"Hello, this is Detective Thomas. Who is calling?"

A soft-spoken female whispered, "Are you the right person to report information concerning the disappearance of the Rose family?"

Almost immediately, Detective Thomas snatched his eyeglasses off his face, and repeated in the same calm voice, "Who is calling?" He waved Detective Lee into his office.

"Huh? Well, I do not wish to reveal my name at this time, but I just wanted to let you know that I saw an older lady riding her bike late at night in the storm."

"Okay. Did you see anyone else with her or was anyone following her in a car?"

"Huh? I'm not too sure because it was late at night. But the weirdest part of all, she was wearing a very nice outfit while riding a bike in a storm."

Detective Lee grabbed another phone in the office so he could trace the call. "Ask her why is she coming forward now," he coached.

Detective Thomas asked, "Why come forward with this information now? It would have been very helpful earlier to the police."

"Hmm, I don't know. I was hoping someone else would report it first."

"Do you know what road she was riding on that night?"

As she named the street, both detectives looked at each other and they knew that she could have easily gotten that information from the news.

Detective Thomas asked, "What color was her clothing?"

"It was too dark to see," she replied. "Would I be eligible for the reward money?"

Detective Thomas could not believe his ears. "Are you joking? Really? First of all, I do not even know your name and secondly, I do not feel that you are being truthful. So unless you come down to the station and speak with one of our detectives, you cannot receive anything because you didn't tell us anything we didn't already know!"

"What? I just called you and gave you important information about what she was wearing that night, information that was not aired on the news. How is that not helping the police department?"

"Miss, I'm not going to stay on this emergency line going back and forth. Either you come down to the station or we do not have anything else to talk about because the information that you provided was vague and doesn't help at all."

Detective Thomas heard a loud slam in his ear. Both detectives looked at each other. They were concerned because no one ever talked about what Miss Rose was wearing the night of her disappearance.

Detective Thomas said, "Supposedly, Miss Rose was taken from her apartment which does not explain how her bike was lying in the middle of the road. I think the caller could have also gotten that type of information from the Internet. If she happens to call back, perhaps we can persuade her to provide her name or contact number, then we will bring her in for further questioning to see how much she really knows."

"Okay," replied Detective Lee.

A couple of days went by, but the female caller did not call again. Then a man called.

"I know where the Rose family is being held," he said adamantly. "I can also provide you with a description of the perpetrators."

Detective Lee took the lead on this call. "Sir, I understand that you can give us information on the whereabouts of the perpetrators, but can you tell me now if the Rose family is alive and well?"

"Detective, they are all alive and are being held inside an old warehouse, but I'm not saying another word until I at least receive half the reward money up front."

"Sure, we can provide you with half of the money now." Detective Lee winked at Detective Thomas. "We just need you to tell us your name and give us your address."

"Sure, sure but are you going to give me my money now?"

"Okay, we are willing to pay you up front, but we would need to validate your story and your identity as well."

"What if I do not wish to reveal myself at this time, is that okay?"

"Alright, we can respect that, but can you at least give us the exact location of this old warehouse. Time is of the essence for the Rose family, so if you can give that to me over the phone, we will have the entire police department there in seconds."

"Just kidding! At the tone you will be alone!"

The phone went dead. Once again, the police had another false alarm but this time, they were able to trace the call and retrieve information about the caller. They arrested him for interfering in a police investigation.

Although the police had received several leads concerning the Rose family, they still had no suspects and the Rose family was still missing after months of searching.

# CHAPTER ELEVEN

"Joe, let's go shopping for some material we will need for this investigation," said Zach. "But we should first draw up a check list of what we already have and then purchase the things that we need."

Joe looked at Zach in amazement. "Wow! You are sharp today. I thought I would have to coach you, but you are really on top of your game! So, Zach, would you like to jot down what we need to purchase?"

"Sure!" he replied with enthusiasm. "Okay, we both agreed that we will need a big billboard to list all the clues we found so far and markers to write on the board."

"We also are going to need batteries for our flashlights and some tape," replied Joe.

"Oh, we'll need small plastic bags to store the evidence in case we need to check for fingerprints," added Zach. "Oh, by the way, do you have a finger-printing kit that we can use?"

"Yes, I have all of that from my job."

"Great!" replied Zach.

"We will need a measuring stick, tweezers and a nail file," Joe said.

"No worries. I have that in my toolbox already," responded Zach. "So it looks like we may only need to purchase a few things. Let's go shopping. It's fine with me if we use my car and we do not have to split the cost of gas. Remember I'm still working and you are retired, my friend, so it's all on me." Zach displayed his teeth in a bright smile.

"Now that we have established everything we need, what are our next steps, Joe?"

"Well, I would like to go into Mother Rose's apartment."

"What!" exclaimed Zach. "You of all people should know that is called breaking and entering, and, may I add, Mother Rose's apartment is considered a crime scene now!"

"I know, I know! We need to get inside her apartment and I'm suggesting that should be our next steps. But if you do not feel comfortable coming along, then you can stay at my place or I'll meet you at yours."

"No, Joe. I'm in this all the way. I'm not backing out now."

"Okay," replied Joe with a concerned look on his face. "Zach, you should know that sometimes in order for PI's to retrieve the information required, it is not always done legally. Although they will never admit it, that is how it is done most of the times. So I need to know again, are you sure that you are down with our next course of action?"

"Yes, I'm in this all the way!"

Joe tried to let Zach off the hook one more time. "You know that I would never think any differently about you if you decided to bail out on me now, right?"

"I know, Joe, and I appreciate your concern for me, but I'm a trooper and troopers never quit!"

Now Joe was completely convinced that Zach had his back on this task. The men shook hands in agreement as they were about to step into dangerous and illegal territories.

Leaving Joe's place, Zach retrieved the tweezers, nail file and measuring stick from his toolbox and handed them to Joe. Joe suggested that Zach take the stairs to Mother Rose's apartment and he take the elevator because they should not be seen together. While approaching Mother Rose's apartment, Joe told Zach that he was going to need him to look out while he picked her lock.

"Sure, but I need to be doing something so I will not look so obvious or suspicious to the other neighbors if they happen to come in the hallway."

"Right," replied Joe. "Maybe you can take one of the flyers from off the wall and pretend that you are knocking on the neighbors' doors, trying to gather additional information about the Rose family."

Finally, Joe heard the clicking sound that confirmed he had unlocked the apartment door. Slowly turning the doorknob, he waved Zach on that he was inside the apartment and to be on the lookout. Unable to see anything, Joe nevertheless kept walking as he searched for his small flashlight in his pocket. Turning it on, Joe knew not to point the flashlight towards the window area just in case there was a patrol car downstairs monitoring any activity coming from the apartment so he flashed the light towards the floor. He also placed a sheer dark-colored cloth over the face of the flashlight to reduce some of the brightness.

Joe began to have flashbacks of when he would see Mother Rose on Saturday mornings or during the week feeding the birds. Whenever someone would walk by, she would talk to him or her about God's love for His people. He looked around her apartment. Most of the time, you can tell a lot about a person just by the way they live because their home displays some of their characteristics. Joe decided to search Mother Rose's bedroom first. He felt that his questions would be answered in her bedroom. It was not hard to distinguish her room from the girls' room. Joe could not help but notice, except for a few things out of order on her nightstand, how clean Mother Rose kept her room. The messy nightstand was probably due to the previous break-in Joe thought. He felt that it was extremely important to place everything back the same way it was found if he had to move anything.

As Joe searched her closet for any old letters or family photo albums, he stumbled upon a pile of pictures in an old, worn out shoebox. He kept pulling up his extra-large rubber gloves, which were sliding off his hands, as he carefully searched through the box.

Joe continued to comb through the pile of pictures and he noticed most of them were of the girls as they were growing up; the rest were of Mother Rose. Then Joe found a photo of Mother Rose and a man. Was it her husband? She was holding an infant child and both looked to be in their early twenties. Joe thought, *I wonder if this photo was taken before the twins were born because they would be a lot older than teenagers by now, and why would parents of twins take a picture with only one child at a time anyway.* There was another picture of the same baby standing up in a crib with the biggest smile and one leg kicked up in the air. Joe was unable to make out whether it was a girl or boy.

There were two more pictures of this same baby celebrating a first birthday. Whoever was taking the picture had zoomed in on the baby who was sitting in a highchair trying to blow out a big number one birthday candle. Joe still was unable to determine the gender of the child because the photo was black and white and the baby was wearing a bib that covered its outfit. The baby had on a birthday hat and the theme of the party was circus clowns.

All of these pictures sparked Joe's interest. The last picture he found was of Mother Rose and the same man he saw her with earlier standing in front of a house waving a piece of paper in the air.

Joe took the pictures and placed them inside his makeshift evidence bag, which was actually a plastic sandwich bag. Then he suddenly noticed an old suitcase that had not been used in years judging by the amount of dust collected on it. This suitcase also had tape wrapped around the handles probably because the handles had broken over time. He carefully grabbed the sides, pulled it out of the tight space in the closet and gently placed it onto a center rug in the bedroom.

As Zach was stealthily monitoring Mother Rose's apartment door a neighbor he could not reach before finally showed up. Ms. Grant was how she introduced herself and she told Zach that she saw two gentlemen standing outside of Miss Rose's apartment door Saturday evening around 8 p.m. and as soon as they noticed her coming out of her apartment, they walked away, turning their backs towards her. She recognized one of them because he was a tenant in the building.

Ms. Grant regrettably said, "I should have called the police, but because they left when they saw me, I felt everything was fine."

"Did you recognize the other person?"

Shaking her head no, she replied, "I never saw the other gentleman's face, but I'm almost certain that he does not live in this building."

Since Ms. Grant was unable to get a good look at the other gentleman, she could not give Zach a full description. But she told him she did notice that he was wearing all black.

Meanwhile, Joe was going though the suitcase. It had a lot of Mother Rose's personal items in it, which made him feel even more guilty for rummaging through her stuff. He considered her to be a dear and personal friend of his so it disturbed him, not like with the other clients.

Continuing to search, Joe came across two old blank envelopes with no addresses but with letters inside. Joe opened the letters and briefly read them. These letters had some nasty things to say about Mother Rose. He noticed that the letters did not have any information about the sender, but were signed as 'lost'. Only, Mother Rose knew who had sent such hurtful letters to her, yet she chose to keep them along with her other personal collections. Joe did not want to make a big deal about the old letters, but still wanted to hold onto them so he placed them inside one of his evidence bags.

Joe knew he had to finish up and decided to search her nightstands for a telephone book. He could not find one. Cleaning up, Joe made sure he put everything back in its rightful place, just the way he found it in Mother Rose's bedroom.

Now it was time to search the girls' bedroom in hopes of finding more clues that would help him determine the baby's identity and perhaps who wrote those letters. Joe could not find much of anything in the girls' room. Strangely, there were no recent photos of the girls displayed on their nightstands or dressers. Even the walls were bare contrary to what was typical for teenagers.

Joe decided to search the living room. He thought to himself that there had to be more photos somewhere around the house; it just did not make sense not to have any. In the living room, there were recent faded shadows on the walls where pictures once hung. There was a dust spot on the coffee table where some kind of large book had been, probably a photo album. Joe had this funny feeling that someone intentionally removed the album, but who? The police usually did not remove items unless they would help solve a case. He was certain, however, that the police did not because they would have marked the area somehow. Maybe it was someone connected to the disappearance of the Rose family.

Brainstorming, Joe now thought that perhaps there was an address book in the kitchen because the older generation usually kept their address books in one of the kitchen drawers. He made his way to the kitchen and began searching through all the top drawers. Then he noticed there were a bunch of magnet picture frames on the refrigerator door, but all of the pictures were missing. Joe, not thinking, opened the refrigerator door and quickly realized the light was shining brightly in the dark kitchen. He quickly closed the door. Then he decided to slowly open the freezer door a little bit to see what was inside, and to his surprise, Mother Rose barely had any food inside.

As Joe was about to close the freezer door, he noticed a smashed up cigarette butt lying on the kitchen floor. He carefully picked it up and put it inside one of his plastic bags. He could not understand how the police overlooked this important piece of evidence. Surely it did not belong to Mother Rose because he had never known her to be a smoker. *Wow*, thought Joe, *this evidence could lead us straight to the suspect if their DNA is in the system. I will have my friend, Detective Kelly, test this in the lab and hopefully we will be able to identify the owner of this cigarette butt carelessly left behind.* He did not believe the police would be so sloppy and smoke at a crime scene.

Joe realized that older women were mostly creatures of habit and they liked hiding things under their mattresses. Heading back to Mother Rose's bedroom, he checked under the mattress. There was an envelope wrapped in a dated plastic freezer bag. The envelope's contents surprised him. It was a deed to a house. Joe got to thinking to himself, *why would someone want to leave a deed to a house underneath a mattress? This should be kept in a safe place, like a safety deposit box. This deed belongs to a Mr. and Mrs. Rose. Why would Mother Rose live in a small two-bedroom apartment if she owned a house?*

Joe bagged the deed because it was time for him to get answers to the many questions he had. He was ready to start his investigation along with Zach. Before he left the apartment, Joe softly knocked on the door and waited for Zach to return the light tap, assuring him that he was in the clear.

As they rushed to the elevator, Joe said to Zach, "Boy, do we have a lot to discuss, but not here because we do not want anyone overhearing our conversation."

Zach replied, "Yes, we do!"

This time Joe took the stairs and Zach rode down in the elevator. They met by Joe's apartment door.

———— ✛ ————

*"Has Junior ever been diagnosed with any mental illnesses by his family physician or any other doctors?"*

*"No. The kids used to make fun of Junior by calling him a retard and by saying he had to take medication to act normal, but none of that was ever true," replied Mr. Brown.*

"Okay Alfred and Junior, I will leave you in the questioning room while I go check out this bogus charge they are trying to pin on Junior. I'll be right back," said Mr. Howard.

"So, Junior, you are telling me that Linda dumped you that night for another guy?" my father asked me.

"Yes, Dad. She made it seem like she was going out on a date with me, but she had made previous plans to meet up with this other dude. She used me because her parents would never let her go out with such an older guy."

"Junior, you are telling me, this was not someone Linda's age?"

"Dad, this guy was twice her age!"

"How old would you say he was?" asked my father angrily.

"Daddy, I'm not sure. He looked to be about late twenties or early thirties."

"What? Junior, why didn't you tell her parents when you got home? After all, they were right there in our home?"

"Because I was so embarrassed when I walked through the door that night. I never felt so humiliated in all of my born days. That is why I made up the story about not feeling well."

Mr. Howard returned to the room.

"Junior, I know that you feel uncomfortable being questioned by the police. They will try to question you about your last incident with the law, but I will advise you not to answer certain questions because they are irrelevant and unrelated to this case. So everybody, let's sit tight until they come back into the room," declared Mr. Howard.

"Yeah, because they are probably listening to every single word we are saying!" my father added. "Just as they do with all suspects."

Sure enough after we stopped conversing with each other, the interrogation room door swung open. Two detectives, Redford and Oldman, walked into the room looking grim.

One of them said, "Let's get started" while slamming a folder on the table.

"Hello everyone," stated Detective Redford. "We are going to be questioning Alfred Brown, Jr. on the disappearance of Linda Snow. Now we ask that everyone keep your opinions to yourselves. Also if we say anything out of line, I'm pretty sure your lawyer, Mr. Howard, will interrupt the questioning. So, gentlemen, may we begin with the questioning?"

Detective Redford pressed the play button on the recorder.

"So Alfred," began Detective Redford, "after further investigation, we came across another incident involving a disappearance which involved you. Would you like to tell us about it?"

But before I could open up my mouth, Mr. Howard abruptly said, "Junior, disregard that question! We are not here for any previous charges. Please move on to the situation we are here about today!"

"Well, Mr. Howard, Alfred will eventually have to explain one way or another. Perhaps in the court of law," stated Detective Redford.

Just before the detective could ask me the next question, another detective burst into the interrogation room and whispered into Detective Oldman's ear.

Immediately, he stood to his feet and leaned over the table towards me and asked, "If you saw the gentleman who was with Linda Snow on the night of her disappearance, would you be able to identify him?"

Mr. Howard quickly interrupted again. "What is this all about?"

"We have reason to believe, based on some new leads by other witnesses, that we may have the suspect in custody."

"Oh really?" replied Mr. Howard. "Okay, everyone just wait one minute. You are suggesting that we stop the questioning and have my client pick the suspect out in a lineup?"

"Yes, Mr. Howard. That is exactly what I'm suggesting."

Breaking his promise, my father stood to his feet and interjected, "Will this man be able to see my son's face? If so, I will not consent to him being subjected to danger."

"Mr. Brown, I understand your concern for Alfred's safety, but I assure you, none of the suspects that are participating in the lineup will be able to see your son's face. If it makes you feel better, you can go inside the room with him," replied Detective Redford. "But once again, Mr. Brown, we ask that you do not interfere with his decision because he has to identify the suspect on his own. Agreed, Mr. Brown?"

We all walked into a dark narrow room with a huge, tinted glass window. Men were lined up holding a big card with a number on it. All the men were staring straight ahead to make it easy for them to be identified.

I looked at Mr. Howard and said, "Are you sure that they cannot see me because it looks like they can see me right through the glass window."

Mr. Howard assured me that they could not see me. Almost immediately,

*I recognized the guy that Linda Snow ran off with that night.*

*Tears fell from my face, as I pointed and sadly said, "That is him! Number six! Then I said something that no one expected. "What did you do to my next door neighbor?"*

*Acting quickly, Detective Redford asked, "Are you sure Alfred, Jr.?"*

*Then I shouted angrily, "There is the guy who was with Linda Snow the night of her disappearance. I am absolutely sure! How can I forget that face that was protruding out of the car window as they both laughed at me while I walked away?"*

*"Okay, Alfred, Jr. We need you to take another look and make absolutely certain that this was the man who was with Linda Snow."*

*"Detective, I'm one hundred percent sure that number six is your guy!"*

*"Okay. You definitely sound like your mind is made up so we are going with number six. Thank you for being such a brave young man, and sorry we had to put you through all this trouble."*

Mother Williamson, still not clear, asked Detective Thomas, "What does this all mean? I thought I was in protective custody already."

"You sort of are," replied Detective Smith, "but the new protective custody is removing you from your familiar surroundings like your home and placing you in a discrete location where only a limited number of people know your exact location. Your family and church family members will not know where you are staying. Unfortunately, you will have to cut off all communication with everyone you know. No one, and I mean absolutely no one, will be able to contact you and you will not be able to call anyone as well!"

"Oh God," moaned Mother Williamson, "please give me strength to go through all of this. I do not know if I can bear much more."

"Mother Williamson, God will give you strength to go through all of this. Just as you encouraged me and God strengthened me," replied Detective Jackson.

"Yes, you are right again."

They embraced.

# CHAPTER TWELVE

*After all that the police had put me through, my father had enough of all these false accusations against me and was ready to leave.*

*He took my hand and said, "We are leaving this God-forsaken place right now!"*

*Mr. Howard agreed, and we all started walking towards the exit and got into Mr. Howard's car. Mr. Howard was trying to read my mind as he looked in the rear-view mirror with a stern look on his face that I will never forget.*

*He said, "Son, I want you to know this is not a game! You have to really be certain that you picked out the correct person because if you have any doubt in your mind that you made a mistake, perhaps we should turn around this instant."*

*"No, Mr. Howard. I'm absolutely sure that he was the one who was staring at us while we were on the cup and saucer ride."*

*Mr. Howard immediately pulled over on the side of the road and stopped the car. He and my father both turned around.*

*"What do you mean that he was staring at you and Linda on the cup and saucer ride?" screamed my father.*

*Mr. Howard quickly raised his hand to calm my father down and told my father to let him handle this. He wanted to develop a good bond with me I guess. My father obeyed Mr. Howard as if he was his biological father or something. Mr. Howard began to question my last statement to find out if it was a mistake or not.*

*"Junior, let me make one thing clear to you. If you had mentioned that statement in the interrogation room, the cops would have had a reason to believe that you were hiding information and probably would have arrested you on the spot. Now I need to ask you one more time and I repeat, this is not a game. Do you know where Linda is?"*

*"No!" I cried. "I'm tired and confused. No one believes me anyway. Everyone thinks I had something to do with her disappearance!"*

*"Okay, okay. Calm down, Alfred," Mr. Howard said. "I only want to help you so that you will not be put in prison. Be honest. The man you identified, did you see him with Linda inside the car or did you see him near the*

*rides? Remember, I'm here to help you."*

*My father's entire body completely turned around in his seat. The car was still pulled over on the side of the road.*

*"I meant to say near the car. I do not know why I said in the park by the rides. I don't... I do not know why!"*

*"Junior, stop crying. You are only going to make yourself sick. We believe you," replied my father.*

*Later that day when my father and I were resting at home, Detective Oldman called.*

*"Linda is back home, unharmed. She said that a gentleman by the name of Brett, also known as Bee, drove her out of state. She came down to the precinct with her family lawyer and pointed out the same gentleman as Alfred Jr. We will no longer need Alfred, Jr. to come down to the precinct, but we will need him to sign papers that he will testify in court, if need be," said Detective Oldman.*

*My father agreed. No sooner had he hung up the phone and turned to tell me the news that the phone rang. It was Mr. Howard. When I heard my father repeat what Detective Oldman told him, I began to smile, knowing that Linda was okay. Even though she dumped me, I still did not want anyone to hurt her.*

*After my father hung up the phone, I asked him excitedly if I could go over to see Linda.*

*"Are you crazy, boy? You are forbidden to go anywhere near Linda or her house. Son, I met other women before marrying your mother, and let me tell you, there are good girls and there are bad ones. I'm telling you that Linda is one of the really bad ones so you need to stay far away from that girl as possible!"*

*Being extremely close to my father, I knew when he was giving me good advice that I should take to heart so I took him up on it and decided to keep my distance from her forever. It was a no brainer for me. Besides, it was not so difficult to do. She ditched me for someone else while on a date. It showed what type of girl she was turning out to be. Even her parents felt embarrassed by their own daughter's actions and hardly hung out with my parents again.*

Coming back to reality, Deacon Brown was concerned because the police always have a way of digging up your past. *But I'm not afraid if this should come up*, he thought, *but I know that I did not do anything in my past that I'm ashamed of today so let them dig.*

Joe and Zach asked Deacon Brown a couple more questions and then they were ready to call it a night. He was hoping they did not see the look on his face when they said they were finished. Then he looked towards his lawyer's face and he was equally as excited.

Deacon Brown wanted desperately for the Rose family to be found. The more he thought about that night, he did remember seeing a gentleman leaning against a fence with his back towards the car as he pulled in front of Mother Rose's building. He turned to make sure Mother Rose and her girls made it inside the building safely and when he turned back around again, the gentleman was gone.

He wondered if he should share this information with the police department but then another thought popped up in his head. *What if the police think I'm making this all up to draw suspicion away from me? I think I better call my lawyer first!* But the more and more he thought about that man, the more and more he thought the man could very well have something to do with Miss Rose's disappearance. It was as if he was intentionally hiding his face when we pulled up to Mother Rose's building. So he decided to do what he did best - pray and ask God to guide and help him remember everything concerning that night, "Oh Lord, I pray out of duty, but also because I need You to bring back to my remembrance everything that happened the night I dropped the Rose family home. Oh Lord, order my steps in Your Word and guide me into all truth. Please let Your Word renew my mind and help me to remember every detail about that night in question because there was a gentlemen standing outside Mother Rose's apartment building, and both the police department and I need help solving this case. Lord, if that gentleman had anything to do with the disappearance of the Rose family, please bring it to the light. In Jesus' name I pray, Amen!"

The more he thought about this man, the more he thought the man definitely could be a suspect in this case. Now he felt it was his duty to report this to the police with his lawyer present. He had confidence in

God that He would keep her safe and that no harm would come to any of them.

Deacon Brown started preparing something to eat, and decided to dial Mother Williamson's number while the food was cooking. Since he was multi-tasking, he used the speaker phone feature.

Mother Williamson, recognized Deacon Brown's number and said, "Hello!"

"Hello, Mother Williamson! I'm calling because there is a strong possibility that the police will list me as one of their prime suspects since I was the last person to see the Rose family."

"Oh no," replied Mother Williamson. "Do they have any reason to suspect you other than you being the last person to have seen them?"

"I think that I'm their biggest lead and I'm all they have to go on right now, but you should know, Mother Williamson, that I would never do anything to harm the Rose family."

"I know," replied Mother Williamson.

---

Joe could not open his apartment door quickly enough because now both men were eager to go over all the clues that they discovered so far. Joe pulled out the big portable chalkboard from the shopping bag. They wrote down all the information that could help them solve this case.

"Okay, Zach you tell me what information you found out while I was inside Mother Rose's apartment and I will tell you what clues I found as well and we can take turns noting them on the board."

"Sure."

From going over every detail they received from the neighbors to reviewing all the documentation found in Mother Rose's apartment, they then agreed that what they had was a great start towards their investigation.

"Detectives Thomas and Lee are not leaking any information about the suspect they have," said Zach. "All we have to go by is his name, Fat.

So, where do you think we should begin, given your line of experience?"

"I think we should focus on who Fat was working for because as I stated earlier, I'm not one hundred percent sure that Fat is working alone. Zach, we just need to find out answers to the remaining questions. Like who was the man in the photo with Miss Rose, who was the baby in those photos and does Miss Rose still own that house? I will call Kelly and see if he can run a DNA test on the cigarette butt and find out the person's identity. I also will ask him if the police were able to get more information from Fat since now we know that he is definitely not working alone based on what the neighbor, Ms. Grant, stated that there was another gentleman with Fat. Let's walk to the local diner and have dinner and it is my treat."

"Now you know I'll never past up a free meal, especially when I know the food is good" said Zach as he smacked his lips.

Joe had to laugh at Zach. They left his apartment and decided to leave everything as it was, and when they returned, they would continue to brainstorm some more.

After enjoying their dinner, Zach said "Joe, I was wondering if Ms. Grant saw something that night, imagine how many more neighbors on the floor may have seen something as well and not reported it to the police."

"Yeah, it's definitely worth looking into Zach, but let's discuss this when we get back."

Joe paid for their meals and started walking back to his apartment building.

"Joe, I enjoyed that meal. It was really good. Thanks for treating."

"You're welcome, but now that I think about it, that sure sounds funny coming from someone who seems to always be eating!"

They both laughed.

After walking back to Joe's apartment building, Joe said, "Zach, I really believe that we will find the Rose family and we are making good progress."

"Yes, we are, Joe. Now that we have more information, things will start to get busier for the both of us."

"Zach, they messed with the wrong guys. I'm coming back tomorrow with answers about that house deed. We will put these pieces together and will eventually have a complete puzzle."

Both gentlemen slapped each other high-fives as Zach walked with Joe back to his apartment to stay a little while. But upon arriving at his apartment, both gentlemen noticed that Joe's door was slightly opened.

They slowly pushed the door open even more. Joe tried to turn on the lights, but they were not turning on. Then they noticed that Joe's apartment had been broken into. Everything was turned upside down. Some of his personal things were either broken or thrown everywhere. Clothing from his bedroom was now in the living room and his dishes were broken in pieces in the dining room.

# CHAPTER THIRTEEN

Mother Williamson calmly stated to Deacon Brown that technology was so advanced these days that just with the slightest bit of information, the police department can solve cases.

"Okay, Mother Williamson. You have convinced me. I'll call Detectives Thomas and Lee when I hang up from you. By the way, I can tell both Mother Rose and you have been friends for years because she also could convince me to do just about anything. Thank you for your wisdom and God bless you. I will let you know how my conversation goes with both detectives."

"You're welcome. Thank you for your bravery and I pray that God will bring everything back to your remembrance when speaking with them. Oh by the way, Deacon Brown, how is everything in the church going? I know that they are just as saddened as I am and I know that everyone is still continuing to pray for the family's safe return."

"Yes they are. One time when we were having prayer, you could feel discouragement all in the air and you could have cut it with a knife. Pastor Paul had to get everyone together to sing uplifting songs, and he also gave everyone the opportunity to testify about how the Rose family impacted their lives in a joyful way. You could tell that God led Pastor Paul because after everyone was finished, you felt peace and joy being restored!"

"Praise God!" exclaimed Mother Williamson. "That's Pastor Paul. He knows how to get a breakthrough when one is needed. One thing I can say about him—he is a man who is concerned about the souls of all men and women. It's no wonder that God led him to pastor his own church!"

"Yeah, he is full of wisdom. He also knows how to pray courageously and fearlessly. Although there is nothing wrong with short prayers, there are times they can be too short and ineffective. However, there are times when you need to hear a word from God and need to pray until you receive a breakthrough. That is why Pastor Paul chose to have intercessory prayer and shut-ins so that the people of God can pray without ceasing and get a real experience with God," replied Deacon Brown.

"Pastor Paul always felt that in order for a person to know God better, it required spending hours studying His Word and spending time in prayer. He calls it birth by fire! When you spend hours a day praying and reading His Word, you never doubt that your deliverance is on the way. You would hear him quote Ephesians 6:18: 'Praying always with all prayer and supplication in the Spirit, and watching thereunto with all perseverance and supplication for all saints,'" quoted Mother Williamson. "Deacon Brown, I'm so glad that God led me to this church many years ago because not only are we being fed the true Word of God, but we are also being taught how to pray wisely, consistently walk in the Spirit, and how to thoroughly study and rightfully divide the Word of God."

"I know that you miss Wednesday night Bible studies."

"Yes I do, Deacon Brown. I miss the teaching, which, by the way, is fantastic! But I also miss being around my spiritual family."

"This week, Pastor Paul's study came from Daniel 3:27. He began when Shadrach, Meshach, and Abednego were thrown into the burning fiery furnace. He expounded on how the devil will try to defame or destroy the saints, but God will turn the situation around as if nothing ever happened. Everyone, including the king, stood amazed at how Shadrach, Meshach and Abednego were not harmed; none of their flesh was burned, none of their clothes were burned, none of their hair was burned, nor did any of them smell like fire. God made it so that none of them looked like they had been inside a fiery furnace.

"That is what God will do in your life after you have gone through your trials and tribulations. He will turn your situation around as if nothing ever happened, as if Satan's devices never penetrated. Just as the fire did not have any power over the three Hebrew boys, neither will the enemy's stumbling blocks have any power over your life!"

"Wow, what a great teaching! That word had to touch everyone's heart and ignite their spirit to be on fire for the Lord all over again," shouted Mother Williamson. "God tells us in His Word that the gates of Hell shall not prevail. So no matter how much power the devil tricks you into believing that he has, he has no power over you. Greater is He that is in you, then he that is in the world!"

"That is so true. That is why I wanted to share Pastor Paul's message with you, hoping to encourage you while you are going through this mess. God has not forgotten about you and what you are currently going through. Just remember the story we read in Bible study the other night about the three Hebrew boys. Be encouraged! God not only delivered the three Hebrew boys out of the hand of the enemy, but He also allowed everyone who witnessed what they went through to believe also! Mother Williamson, take this opportunity to win as many souls for Christ as you can. God is in control and He has your back!"

"Deacon Brown, you are right. God bless you for sharing that word with me because although you are saved, every now and then, a person needs to hear a word of encouragement. May God's hand be upon your life to do great things. In Jesus' name!"

"Take care of yourself and I will prayerfully speak with you soon. God bless you, Mother Williamson, and good night!"

Back at the church, members who had known Mother Rose for years were not taking her disappearance so well. Pastor Paul did all that he could to keep everyone calm. He told them that they would have to trust God and let Him work everything out because He can do it best! Although he tried every week to teach the saints to have faith in God and take Him at His Word, there were always some who just did not get it and wanted to do things their own way. When his phone rang, Pastor Paul, all too familiar with Sister Jay's number because of her constant calling, did not want to answer the phone. All she was going to do was complain about how no one is doing anything to find the Rose family. He, nevertheless, decided to answer.

"Hello, Pastor Paul. This is Sister Jay Hassell again. I would like to know if there have been any updates since we last spoke." Not giving him a chance to reply, she went on, "Because this is ridiculous. How can a grown woman and two teenagers get abducted without a single soul seeing a thing? Pastor, there has to be something we can do other than just sit around and pray. I know that prayer changes things, but I know that they are scared because I can feel them in my spirit crying out for our help!"

Pastor Paul had just about enough of Sister Jay always complaining about the obvious and about how everyone else should come up with some kind of plan, but never suggesting any ideas to help out the situation. He almost lost it as he interjected, "Sister Jay, take a deep breath and relax. The police are doing all that they can do at this point. It is best that we allow God to move on their behalf. So unless the police get new leads, they do not have anything else to go on. Besides Mother Rose is a child of God and He is not going to let anything happen against His will for their lives. Sister Jay, we do not know the plans of God. Everything that is happening is bigger than us right know. Bigger than our feelings, bigger than our emotions. When God allows something like this to happen to a child of God, we have to continue to trust Him because He does not make any mistakes. Think of this situation as one big puzzle. There are many pieces that must be fit together properly. You and I are just one piece of this puzzle. So until God has strategically put all of the pieces together, we have to wait until God says it is finished!"

"Pastor, I do not understand how you can be so relaxed, not knowing whether they are alive or dead. Don't you care about the Rose family? Everyone is acting as if they know that she is going to be all right and that she will be home tomorrow. What is wrong with everybody? This is not some nightmare that we are having; this is real!"

"Sister Jay, let's get one thing straight. There is nothing wrong with the saints of God nor do we think that this is some kind of bad dream! It is real but what we are exercising now is called faith, Sister Jay. That's why everyone can relax because we are all trusting in God and leaning on His Holy Word that is full of His promises. I encourage you to follow suit and grab hold of God's Word so that you can learn to wait on Him as well.

"I often preach about how God is outside of time and you cannot rush God. Time does not dictate how God is going to operate, nor do our emotions. You being upset is not making God move any faster. He moves according to His plans! If God operated based on how we felt, then we would always have our way with Him. He wants us to trust Him under the most critical circumstances, even if it does not turn out the way we want it to."

"I understand what you are saying, but I still think that we should trust God and try to do something at the same time because I'm tired of waiting on the police when all they do is sit around and eat donuts all day long."

"Now, Sister Jay, that is not true. I will admit that they do not have the resources to dedicate a lot of detectives to this one case, but they are trying to go by whatever leads they may have right now so please be patient! What do you recommend that the church do to help the police find the Rose family?"

"Huh? Hmm, well I do not know. That is why I'm calling you so that everybody can put their heads together and come up with some kind of plan. You are the pastor. Isn't God leading you to share something with His people concerning Mother Rose and the girls?"

"Now wait one minute. You are out of order. Just because you do not know how to rest in God and wait on Him does not mean that everyone is not taking the situation seriously. The problem with you is that you are allowing the enemy to control your emotions. God has given you the peace that surpasses all understanding, but you are allowing the devil to steal it. You must resist him and he will have no other choice but to flee! Stop pointing your finger at others when you need to examine your ways and ask God to help you with your unbelief! Sister Jay, I have noticed that you stopped coming to Bible study on Wednesday nights and I also noticed that you are not staying for the whole service on Sundays. Any particular reason why?"

"Huh?" replied Sister Jay. "I did not think that anyone noticed. You are right, Pastor Paul. I do have to start coming to church more often and get back into reading and studying my Bible like I should."

"Keep in mind, backsliding does not happen in one day, but the enemy will gradually convince you to stop participating in Bible study at the church and, before you know it, you will stop coming to church altogether. This is how you stop growing in the Lord. If the devil can remove you away from hearing God's Word, he can steal your faith.

Remember, faith cometh by hearing the Word of God!"

Pastor Paul didn't hear anything so he said, "Hello?" He was not sure if she hung up on him or, for once, was at a loss for words.

"Yes, Pastor. I'm still here. You are right. I have been slipping and need to be about my Father's business by getting back into studying God's Word and stop blaming everyone else for my insecurities and unfaithfulness towards the things concerning the Lord. Please forgive me for all that I said tonight that was disrespectful towards you because you are absolutely correct. I have allowed the enemy to play me like some kind of instrument instead of giving God all the glory. I was allowing the enemy to use me by ridiculing everyone else and not looking at my own faults. Pastor, would you please pray for me? I'm not taking this situation very well."

"Sister Jay, it would be my pleasure. But I don't just want you to think that if I pray for you everything will instantly be okay. You have to apply yourself. In order to grow in God, you must spend time with Him in prayer and study His Word. When you first met your husband, you did not know him like you do now. But now you and your husband know each other so well that you both could probably finish each other's sentences. How did you get to know him so well? By spending time together and learning each other's personalities. Same with God. In order to know God, you must build a relationship with Him and the only way you can do so is to spend time with Him in prayer and in His Word. Daughter let us pray.

"Father, we bless Your Holy name. You are the God who sent Your only begotten Son to die for the world's sins. Even if we were the only people on earth, You still would have sent Your Son to die for us. That is how much You love each one of us and are concerned about every aspect of our lives. God, I'm calling on You on behalf of Sister Jay. God, she needs peace of mind. We both know that You are still in control and have everything already worked out because You know all beginnings and endings. Father, please give Sister Jay peace in her spirit-man until You are ready to bring this case to a close. God, You know all things and have Mother Rose and the girls in Your hand. Help us to trust and patiently wait on You, God. So we ask now, to keep Sister Jay's mind stayed on You because You are her Lifeline and Strength. Thank you for how You are going to increase Sister Jay's faith day by day. In Jesus' name, Amen!"

———— ∞∞∞ ————

"Mother Williamson, let's get started with your packing," said Detective Smith who was assigned to help her move. When she pulled out three large suitcases, Detective Smith was so surprised and asked, "Mother Williamson, why do you have so many large suitcases?"

"Well, if you must know, the brown suitcase can only be carried by hand, whereas the black suitcase can be pulled on two wheels, but the burgundy suitcase has four spinning wheels. It's called advancement," she replied as she winked her right eye at him.

Not expecting such a detailed description of each large case, Detective Smith just looked in amazement.

"Now if you are wondering why they are large, family-sized suitcases for little old me not being married, you should already know the answer to that question. Women have more baggage then men!"

Everyone was so busy packing that Mother Williamson had not noticed it was afternoon. She told everyone to take a lunch break.

"Can we have lunch in the living room so that we can watch a movie?" Detective Smith asked.

"Sure," replied Mother Williamson. "I want everyone to feel as comfortable as I do in my apartment."

"Thank you, Mother Williamson. I love enjoying my food and watching a good movie."

Detective Jackson made sandwiches for everyone and put them on the coffee table while Detective Smith handled the drinks. Mother Williamson prayed for the food, and the phone rang again. She quickly answered in an effort to get rid of the person before the movie started.

"Hello?"

"Mother Williamson, it's me, Detective Thomas. I need to speak with Detective Smith."

She handed over the phone.

"Hello, Detective Smith. I just wanted to let you know that the suspect was not working with anyone and it turns out that he does not have any idea where the Rose family is. I'm calling you to continue with the move since he is only confessing to slipping the envelope under the door. As for the phone calls, he said he did not make them. I believe him, but Detective Lee seems to think he is still hiding something. Once again, continue with the move and I will talk to you later."

Everyone still felt like relaxing by watching a movie and finishing their lunch. This issue of who was targeting Mother Williamson was draining everybody mentally and physically.

After the movie was over, everyone knew that they had to continue with the packing since a patrol car would be down stairs waiting to take them to a remote location. As they began to move her suitcases out of the apartment, Mother Williamson began to cry because she just wanted this to be a bad dream and to wake up to normalcy. Both Detectives Jackson and Smith held her hands as they walked out of her long-occupied apartment with her belongings. Mother Williamson looked back as if she would never see her place again.

It took hours for them to get to the remote location, but once they arrived, Mother Williamson was very pleased with the house. It seemed quiet and she felt safe and, most importantly, it was very clean. *Oh well, God I know You will watch over me, and I will not be disappointed living in my temporary quarters,* she thought. *God always has a way of making bad situations turn into good ones.* She walked throughout the house observing how beautifully the home was decorated with state-of-the-art appliances and furniture.

"Wow, this place is really not all that bad. Although it is not my home, I can get used to living here," she said as they began to unpack.

Detective Jackson said, "Today seems like it is going to be a beautiful day."

"My dear, every day is actually beautiful because it is the day that God has made and He wants us to rejoice in it," replied Mother Williamson. Then she began to think about all that God had done for them by keeping them safe and said, "Daughter, we should never reach a level of spiritual growth where we no longer need to offer thanks unto God."

Detective Jackson agreed.

The next day when Mother Williamson saw Jackson, she said, "Good morning! Good morning, my darling. How did you sleep last night?"

"I'm so excited this morning, Mother Williamson. I thank God for allowing me to meet you. What a change God has allowed me to feel on the inside. I have some great news to share with you. I was speaking with my husband last night and he told me that Marcus' doctor called the house and wanted to speak with us to discuss Marcus' condition in person. My husband indicated that I was out of town on business and asked if it would be okay if they discussed the news over the phone. The doctor agreed. My husband told me that his stomach felt like it fell to the floor as he prepared for the worst when the doctor began to speak, 'Mr. Jackson, just a few questions before I get to the reason for my call. Has Marcus been eating any new foods or taking any new vitamins?' My husband answered that he hadn't and the doctor said that something unusual was happening in Marcus' body because now he is cancer-free! My husband asked the doctor to repeat what he said. Again he said that the cancer in Marcus' body was gone. Then he said several other doctors ran different tests, but there still were no signs of the cancer anywhere!

"The doctor asked my husband if he believed in miracles. He said he did. The doctor said that the only way he could explain what happened was that it was a miracle. My husband almost passed out, but managed to compose himself and thanked God.

"My husband could not hang up fast enough to call me and tell me the good news. Mother Williamson, when he called me last night, he was overjoyed about the news. We cried like we were holding each other while on the phone. Suddenly, I thought about taking this opportunity to tell my husband about Jesus and how He came to save the world from sin. Being so overwhelmed about Marcus' miracle, my husband listened and accepted Jesus as his Lord and Personal Savior right then and there.

"Mother Williamson, I also told him about you, how you told me to read the entire gospel of John until I get understanding and that this will help him to understand God and also establish a personal relationship with Him. I also told him how we prayed every day, sometimes twice a day and that is when my husband told me that he would really like to meet you. So after this whole ordeal is over, I would like to introduce you to my family."

"Praise God!" shouted Mother Williamson. "Detective Jackson, God is our Healer and once He speaks healing into someone's body no devil in hell can take it away. When you and your husband go back to the doctor's office, the doctor still will be amazed because the results will be the same. Hallelujah!"

Mother Williamson did a victory dance!

Now both Mother Williamson and Detective Jackson began to praise God for all of His benefits. Detective Smith walked into the kitchen and saw how they were praising God, and decided to turn around, but Mother Williamson saw him and invited him in.

"Come, my son. It's about time that I speak with you."

Detective Jackson now holding her hands in a praying position and stepping right to left, began to smile inside because she knew what Detective Smith was about to experience.

"My son, do you know the Lord Jesus Christ as your personal Savior?" asked Mother Williamson with a frowning face.

"No offense, but I do not believe in the Bible," replied Detective Smith. "It's made up of all of these stories that could not possibly be true." Mother Williamson allowed Detective Smith to speak on how he felt about God's Word. "I was raised in church, but decided to turn away because I did not believe in it anymore as I got older."

Mother Williamson asked Detective Jackson if she could pray for him that he would accept her invitation. Then she asked him, "Can I ask you what caused you to stop believing in God, and please do not tell me it was just the stories in the Bible."

The question bothered him.

"Yes, it was," he replied. "It all stopped making sense to me. Like, how can a donkey talk, or a man walk on water? Or even better, someone who had been dead for three days come back to life? There are so many more stories in the Bible that just do not add up. Besides the Bible was written by man anyway."

"So, is there anything about the Bible or God that you do believe, Detective Smith?"

"Well, I do believe in God because somebody has to be controlling this world. Someone had to create the things of the world and the people too."

"Okay," replied Mother Williamson. "So you do believe in God, and that He created mankind? Are you familiar with how God created man?"

"Yes, I learned that in Sunday school. With dirt."

"Okay. What else?"

"God blew into his mouth or nose and man came alive."

"Good. It was his nostrils," replied Mother Williamson. "Do you know how He created woman?"

"I think every guy knows the answer to that question," he responded as he puffed out his chest with a confident look on his face. "She was made from man."

"But do you know how, Detective Smith?"

"Yes, that is easy. From man's rib that is how God made woman!"

"Do you really believe those two events written about in the Bible took place?" asked Mother Williamson.

"Of course. As I said earlier, I do believe that God exists and that He made mankind," replied Detective Smith.

"So, what you are saying is you believe that God can take dust from the ground to create man and take a rib from man to create a woman."

"Yes. Those are some of the few things that I believe about the Bible and no one can make me think differently."

"Detective Smith, that is very good to hear." Mother Williamson cracked a smile. "Here is my question to you, if you can believe God can make a woman from a rib, would you be able to prove that concept to someone else who does not understand it? How would you explain that to the next person who does not believe in the Bible?"

"I would tell them that God is God and He can do anything. He spoke the world into existence from nothing and He took the time to create male and female with His own hands."

"Okay, but do you really believe, although you show them what the Bible says, that person would take your word?"

"Maybe not," replied Detective Smith. "But it will explain that God has the power to do whatever He wants to do."

"Precisely! That is exactly what I wanted you to say and see for yourself. If you can believe that God formed man and woman by His holy hands and created the world from nothing, then why is it so hard for you to believe the rest of the Bible stories?"

Suddenly there was silence. Detective Smith was at a loss for words.

# CHAPTER FOURTEEN

Deacon Brown took a deep breath as he dialed Detective Thomas' number.

"Hello, this is Detective Thomas. To whom am I speaking?"

"Hello, Detective Thomas. You may not remember me. My name is Alfred Brown Jr., better known as Deacon Brown. You recently questioned me about the disappearance of the Rose family. You said if I thought of any additional information to contact you. I remembered something, but I do not know if it will help."

"Oh, I remember speaking with you, Mr. Brown. What additional information do you have that will help in the Rose family case?"

"Well, I remembered something that took place outside the apartment building."

"Okay, go on," replied Detective Thomas, as he stood frozen with his hand on his hip.

"Seemingly, I was the last person who saw the Rose family, but I also remember seeing a suspicious person standing nearby when I dropped them off. I don't know if it is useful in solving this case," stated Deacon Brown.

"Let me be the judge of that. Can you describe this person?"

"Actually, I would feel better if we could meet face to face to discuss this matter further."

"Sure. Detective Lee and I were about to make some rounds and ironically they are not far from your residence. We will stop by your place within the hour."

"Great. That would not be a problem at all," replied Deacon Brown.

"Okay then. We should be at your house around 4:30 p.m. Thanks so much for giving us a call."

As Deacon Brown hung up the phone, he immediately flashbacked to when Detectives Thomas and Lee were at his house asking him all kinds of questions insinuating that he had something to do with the disappearance of the Rose family.

Deacon Brown thought to himself, *"Perhaps I'm turning this situa-*

*tion into more than what it really is. I'd better be honest and tell the police that I was upset with Mother Rose that night when I drove her home. In addition, I need to tell them that I noticed a suspicious gentleman standing by the building and it seemed like he waved at everyone in the car when we pulled up. Let me see if I can reach Minister Keith because I do not want anyone adding anything to my story."*

He dialed Minister Keith's home phone and did not receive an answer. He looked at the clock and realized that perhaps he was still at work. He left a voice message telling him that he was going to meet with the Detectives just to give them some additional information that he remembered about the night of the Rose family disappearance.

Then he felt he should try and call his cell phone. Minister Keith answered the phone.

"Good evening, Deacon Brown."

"Oh hi. I'm just calling to let you know that I remembered some additional information about the Rose family disappearance and I wanted to see if you were able to stop by my house."

"Unfortunately, I'm in court and I do not know when I will be finished. We just happen to be taking a break and that's how I was able to see your call. Are you meeting with the police?" asked Minister Keith.

"Yes, both Detectives Thomas and Lee will be stopping by at 4:30 p.m."

"Okay. Here is what you should do. Let both detectives know that you would like to record the conversation because your lawyer is not present and when I do have a free moment sometime this week, I will stop by and listen to the recording. You should not have any problems because once both detectives agree to the recording, they will be on their best behavior."

"Will do. Thanks for the advice and I will speak with you later."

Deacon Brown went into the kitchen to put a pot of water on the stove just in case they wanted to have something hot to drink. At exactly 4:30 p.m., there was a knock on the door. It made him jump and his heart skipped a couple of beats.

"I'm coming!" he shouted as he walked quickly to open the door. "Oh boy, I did not expect you all to arrive on time. I thought you would at least be another fifteen minutes. Please have a seat in the living room."

Getting right to the point, Detectives Thomas asked, "So you have further information about the Rose case?"

"Yes I do, but before we begin, do any of you gentlemen care for anything to drink? I have all types of hot beverages or ice-cold bottles of spring water."

Simultaneously, they declined the offer. Deacon Brown then told them that his lawyer was unable to make the meeting and asked, "Do you gentlemen mind if I record this conversation?"

He held the recorder in his hand and ready to press the play button. Hesitating at first, they both agreed.

"That should not be a problem at all," Detective Thomas stated. "So, Mr. Brown, what is this new information that you want to share with us in person?"

Nervously, Deacon Brown looked at both detectives, not knowing how they would take the new information. Not knowing if they would believe a word he said.

"Well, I got to thinking about that night and remembered when I last saw the Rose family. I did not tell you that I was upset with Mother Rose."

"Oh?" replied Detective Thomas as he moved himself closer to the edge of the chair.

Deacon Brown now realized that he was on his own without any attorney present, but at least they had agreed to the recording of the conversation.

"Yes. The more I concentrated on that night, I remembered I failed to tell you that I was extremely upset with Mother Rose because she was conversing with everyone while I was waiting in the car to drive her and her daughters home. After all, it was late and the more I honked the horn, nothing happened. She kept on talking as if she did not hear it. So I had to get out the car and tell her that I was tired and I wanted to go home and would she please have some consideration - not to mention that I had to drive home after dropping them off."

"Hmm," replied Detective Lee. "Then what happened?"

"Mother Rose became upset with me because she felt I rudely interrupted her conversation with her friends. So on the way to her house, we did not speak to each other."

"How about the girls? Did they say anything?" asked Detective Thomas.

"It was small conversations with the girls. I asked them did they enjoy themselves. Both girls replied that they had a nice time and they wished it could have lasted much longer. There is one more thing."

"Okay," replied Detective Lee as he readied to take more notes.

"Just before everyone got out of the car, I remember apologizing to Mother Rose for getting so upset and told her that I would walk her to the door. She accepted my apology and thanked me for the ride home, but turned down my offer to walk her to her building. She told me that she would be okay and there was no need for me to get out."

"Was that strange?" asked Detective Thomas.

Deacon Brown lifted up his hand. "Wait. I have more to tell."

"Okay, sorry."

"Also I noticed when we pulled up that there was this suspicious gentleman standing in front of the building. He shielded his face because of my headlights being so bright and turned his back towards the car. But then he waved at everyone in the car and started walking away. I turned my head to make sure everyone was in the building safely and when I looked again he had vanished."

"Can you tell us what he looked like?"

"Well, not exactly," replied Deacon Brown, "because the headlights from my car were blinding and he shielded his entire face. But I did notice that he wore all black."

"So all you were able to see was his dark clothing?" asked Detective Thomas.

"Yes, that is all because everything happened so fast and my main concern was that Mother Rose and the girls made it into the building safely."

"Deacon Brown, this is great information. You have given us more to work with. Thanks so much for sharing this information with us. If you should think of anything else that can potentially help the police, do not hesitate to give us another call. Once again, thank you for being honest with us."

Deacon Brown reached for the stop button on the recorder. "Anything to help out."

Both detectives stood as Deacon Brown replied, "No problem at all. It is my pleasure to help out because I'm here to do whatever it takes to find out what happened to my friend."

Detective Lee added, "Deacon, we would like you to look for some more recent photos of the entire family so that they can be shown on all of the local news channels. Maybe someone saw something that night, but did not think it was worth telling, or just like you, forgot about it until now. The precinct has a substantial reward for anyone with information leading up to an arrest or with information on the whereabouts of the Rose family. Hopefully, somebody will step forward. Thanks so much for your time and help, Deacon Brown. Take care and be safe."

"Likewise!"

Joe told Zach not to touch anything, but to call the police from his cell phone.

"Oh no, what!" exclaimed Zach. "The billboard, photos and letters were all taken!"

Angrily Joe said, "I should have taken the evidence with me!"

"What about the house deed—did they take that too?" asked Zach.

"No, thank God. It's still in my jacket pocket along with the cigarette butt."

"I personally think you should stay at my place tonight because they turned your house upside down. I think that the intruders were probably looking for just that, the house deed. Joe, I really believe you are being watched. You must get in contact with Detective Kelly tonight!"

Suddenly, lights from a flashlight began to shine in both of their faces.

"Freeze! This is the police. Identify yourselves!"

Two police officers stood with their weapons drawn. Both gentlemen put their hands in the air, but managed to grab their wallets from their pockets beforehand

Joe said, "Officer, my name is Joseph Walker. This is my apartment and here is my identification!"

One of the officers asked, "Can we turn on the lights in the apartment or do I have to use my flashlight?"

"If you do not mind," replied Joe, "all of the light bulbs have been removed. Even the fuse was removed."

"Do you live here sir?"

"Yes. I stated that already. This is my apartment."

"Do you have a spare light bulb and another fuse?"

"Sure, but I do not want to walk over the evidence and damage anything. There should be some in the tray on top of the refrigerator, if it is still up there."

One of the officers shined his flashlight in that direction. He saw them on the tray and asked Joe to put in a light bulb and put the fuse in the box. The lights immediately came on. Seeing the apartment in the dark, it looked bad. When the lights came on, everything looked even worse. Joe could not believe how the intruders ransacked the entire apartment.

"What were they looking for?" Joe asked.

"Mr. Walker, do you know who would want to do something like this and why?"

Joe looked at the officers' dead in the face and said, "I have no idea who would want to do this to my apartment."

"Someone was definitely looking for something of importance," replied Zach.

"What is your name sir?" asked one of the officers referring to Zach.

"My name is Zachariah Cooke, sir."

"Okay gentlemen, now that the CSI team has arrived and finished taking pictures and dusting for finger prints, they will need both of your fingerprints to differentiate them from the suspect or suspects."

Joe and Zach agreed, as both gentlemen's fingerprints were taken. When the officers were finished, Zach and Joe knew that they were getting closer to the truth about something or to someone who did not want to be exposed. Joe decided to take Zach up on his offer by staying at his apartment.

"Sure," replied Zach.

Joe gathered some personal items to take with him to Zach's place. He made doubly sure that the house deed was with him. As Joe and Zach were putting the items into the car, they were also looking around just to make certain no one was watching them.

"Zach, do you mind staying in the car while I meet with Detective Kelly?" asked Joe.

"That will not be a problem. It would look like he was leaking out information to us."

"I'm glad you understand, Zach."

"No problem."

"No, really. Thanks for being a friend and being so understanding."

Now in the car, Joe decided to give Detective Kelly a call. "Hello Kelly, I think that I may have some new evidence that there are others involved in the Rose case. I would like you to check it out."

"Oh really?" replied Detective Kelly. "Would you like to meet up tonight at the usual place?"

"Yes," replied Joe, "I think it would be best."

"Okay. Let us talk about this further when we meet."

"Okay." They both hung up the phone. "Zach, I'm going to meet up with my friend at the diner downtown on Front Street."

"Okay. There is a burger joint about three blocks away. I'll just be waiting there. Just give me a call once you're finished and I will pick you up."

"Thanks again," replied Joe as he left Zach's late model car.

Detective Kelly spotted Joe as soon as he got out of the car. He stuck his neck out so far trying to see who was driving the car that he almost fell forward. Joe noticed Kelly trying to get a glance of the driver so he blocked his view to hide Zach's identity. Joe waved to Kelly and noticed he had a cigarette in his hand. *Hmm, I thought he told me that he quit smoking.* When Detective Kelly saw Joe approaching, he quickly put out the cigarette, trying to hide the fact that he was smoking, and went inside. When Joe entered the diner, both greeted each other and waited for the waitress to lead them to their table.

Detective Kelly looked at Joe and said, "They must really make a lot of money in this diner because it is always jam-packed with people."

"But most neighborhood diners are always crowded."

"Yeah, you are right," replied Detective Kelly.

"What's amazing is how we always manage to be seated as soon as we walk through the door."

Then Kelly looked at Joe with a grin on his face and said, "It's not what you know, but who you know!"

The waitress handed each of them a menu and waited for their orders.

"I'm treating today," Joe said.

Detective Kelly shook his head in disagreement. "You can pay me back when I retire. Today, I'm treating again."

Joe accepted and thanked him, but immediately felt there was something different about his friend.

"What are you having, Mr. PI?"

"I'll have my usual, cheese burger and sweet potato fries with a glass of water and lemon on the side," replied Joe.

"I'll have the same, but I would like a glass of ginger ale with no ice, please," said Detective Kelly as he handed their menus to the waitress. "So, Joe, what brings us together again?"

"Well, I'm about to admit I was doing some investigating on my own and I went inside Mother Rose's apartment. I stumbled upon some old pictures and other documents that would have given the police more leads."

Detective Kelly's eyes widen. He pounded on the table. "You did what? Joe, please do not tell me you went into a crime scene area! I do not even want to know how you broke into her apartment. I should be arresting you right now! But tell me, what types of documents?"

Joe apologized to Detective Kelly and told him that he would have shared it with the police. Detective Kelly asked him again, "What types of documents did you find inside the apartment that would have help the police?"

That's when Joe felt it again; he knew something had changed about Officer Kelly since the last time they had spoken. But what disturbed him the most was that he was very skilled at listening—private investigators are trained to listen—and Detective Kelly kept repeating the word "documents". The troubling part was how quickly he dismissed how Joe broke the law because he was only concerned about what documents he obtained. Joe was no longer sure if he should tell him about anything else because he did not know if he could be trusted.

Joe said, "Besides some old photos that I found, I found some old letters as well. But I came here today to tell you that my apartment was broken into and the robbers knew exactly what they were looking for. They took everything I took out of Miss Rose's apartment."

"Oh no," replied Detective Kelly, "Did they get everything?"

Now Joe had a third confirmation that he needed—Detective Kelly was definitely inside someone's pocket. He had been bought for a price!

"Well, mostly everything," replied Joe.

Joe remembered Kelly mentioning that he did not have long to retire and that was when most police detectives make their biggest mistakes. Yeah! Joe stared into Kelly's eyes without blinking and he knew that he was going to have to work on his own without confiding in Kelly about every little detail of this case. Just trust Zach and no one else. Knowing now that Kelly could not be trusted, he still wanted to get more information about the suspect known by everyone as Fat.

"So, Kelly, were the police able to gather any more information from the suspect and were they able to determine if there were any other suspects involved?"

"No, we have not been able to find out any new information."

"Do you still think that he was working alone?" asked Joe.

"I believe he was. At the end of the day, he was just another hustler trying to support his bad habits. But Joe, you mentioned on the phone that you had some new evidence that there may be someone else involved."

Joe thought to himself that he needed to be real careful now because if Kelly were inside someone's pocket, he was doing it to make big money. So if Detective Kelly thought for a single moment that he was lying to him or jeopardizing him from getting paid, there was no telling what course of action he would take to stop him from getting in his way.

"Joe, what kind of photos did you find in the apartment?"

"Well, I found some photos of Miss Rose when she was younger holding a baby in her arms."

"Okay. Was there anyone else in those pictures other than the two of them?"

Joe, feeling like this was a trick question, did not reply immediately. "There was a gentleman in the photo. I think it was her husband. I could not determine the sex of the child because the photos were all in black and white. The child was mostly in sleepers and there was one photo where the child had on clothing, but was covered by this giant bib." Joe knowing that he said too much began to feel afraid so he tried to change the subject. "How's the family?"

"Fine. Everyone is just fine, but jumping back to the pictures—were there other pictures of the same three people?"

"I really cannot say because I never got the opportunity to examine all of the photos."

"Come on, Mr. PI. Surely, you would have noticed if there were other people in the photos!"

"Kelly, I'm telling the truth. I never had the opportunity to examine all of the pictures before they were stolen from me."

The waitress interrupted their conversation when she came with their meals. Joe excused himself for a bathroom break, but he slipped out the diner's back door to try and find the cigarette butt that Detective Kelly threw on the ground in front of the diner. To his surprise, there was only one cigarette butt lying on the ground. Although it was pretty smashed up, Joe did not care. He was just glad that Kelly did not use the cigarette stand located in front of the diner because there were about two dozen cigarette butts sticking out of the sand. Joe picked up the butt and placed it in the same type of plastic bag that he used in Miss Rose's apartment.

Just as easily, Joe slipped back into the diner, and rushed into the bathroom to compare the cigarette butt with the one he found in Mother Rose's apartment. They did not match and this gave him a little comfort being around Kelly. Joe washed his hands and left the bathroom.

Returning, Joe looked at the food and said, "Wow! This looks delicious!"

"Oh come on, dude. You get the same thing all of the time!"

Joe looked at Detective Kelly. "Okay. You got jokes now!"

"When you called you also mentioned that you had something you wanted me to check?"

Joe decided to chew at a much slower pace to give him some time to think. Did he flush the cigarette butt he found outside down the toilet or did he leave it inside the plastic bag?

"Oh yeah, I totally forgot about that. I found this cigarette butt on Miss Rose's kitchen floor. Do you think that the police can identify who was smoking it? Maybe it belongs to another suspect."

Joe reached into his jacket pocket for the plastic bag. He was relieved that the bag only had one cigarette butt inside. Kelly's eyes opened wide. He knew that Joe found some evidence that the police seemed to have overlooked.

"Yes, I can have the lab run a DNA test and will let you know what the results are. Give me a couple of days to get back to you."

Joe agreed knowing that he would never know the true results because whomever Detective Kelly was working for would not reveal it.

"Joe, keep me posted on any more findings. By the way, who was that person dropping you off tonight?"

"Oh, one of my neighbors offered me a ride because he was heading in this direction," replied Joe.

Things did not seem to add up with Kelly. Joe just realized that he did not ask him if he was home when the break-in took place, or if he was okay, or did any of his personal possessions get taken, or was there any damage to his apartment. Joe started to suspect that he did not ask any of those types of questions because he knew Joe was not home and that all of his personal possessions were tossed around but nothing was taken.

"I sure will. I will call you if there are more findings."

"How are you getting home?"

"I was going to take the bus."

"Well, I can drop you off if it is not a problem for you. It is a long ride home on the bus."

"Okay," Joe replied as he got up from the table.

Joe felt that whoever was behind this robbery did not know about Zach yet and he intended for it to stay that way. Joe told Kelly he was going to make another bathroom stop while he paid for the meals.

Joe quickly called Zach and told him to meet him at his house in about three hours, but wait until he called him first before he came up.

"Wait, I thought I was going to pick you up," replied Zach.

"I know, Zach, but I'll explain everything to you in three hours. Don't forget to wait until I call you."

Joe met Kelly outside the diner. "Boy, you have been going to the bathroom a lot. Is everything okay with your health, Mr. PI?"

"I'm okay. Just drinking a lot more water these days."

On the way to Joe's home, Kelly complained about how all of the new rookies on the job were getting promoted quickly and how the job environment was changing for the worse.

"It seems like the younger generation just wants to get paid big bucks and they expect the seasoned employees to do all the work."

Joe heard the anger and frustration in Kelly's voice and did not know what to say. That was one of the reasons he retired when he did without losing his integrity. Joe reminded Kelly that he only had a few more months to go and that he should not do anything to jeopardize all that he's worked for for so many years.

"I know, Mr. PI, but when you see people getting promoted and not really doing any work, and especially getting promoted instead of you, it makes you very bitter. It takes all your strength not to quit because you really need your job."

"Kelly, you have to be smarter than the job. We both have always made an honest day's living. Do not stop now. You have so much to lose."

Detective Kelly looked at Joe as he pulled in front of his building and said, "Not always, Joe." He lowered his head. "There are some things I'm not proud of."

"We all make mistakes sometimes so lift your head and start afresh."

Joe reached to shake Kelly's hand and thanked him for both lunch and the ride home.

"Good night, Mr. PI. I'll let you know the results as soon as I hear from the lab."

"Okay. I'll let you know if I come across any new leads that the department may have overlooked. Thanks again for everything."

Joe walked towards his building. While he was walking, he could feel Kelly staring at him, and then suddenly, he realized he never gave Kelly directions to his house. It had to be almost ten years since Kelly had been to his house. How could he possibly know Joe still lived there or remember his exact address after all these years?

# CHAPTER FIFTEEN

Mother Williamson and Detective Smith were talking about events that took place in the Bible, but Detective Smith could not wrap his brain around one particular story in the Bible.

"Do you really believe that God parted the Red Sea so that His chosen people could cross over on dry land?" he asked.

"Yes, I do believe that God performed this miracle and He is perfectly capable of performing that same miracle today," Mother Williamson replied. "You told me that you believed that God created both man and woman and that no one can make you think differently, correct?"

Detective Smith nodded in agreement.

"So why is it so hard for you to believe that God was capable of parting the Red Sea?"

Detective Smith said, "Let's say that I did believe God parted the Rea Sea, but how do you explain the fact that they all crossed over on dry ground? Do you know how long it would take for the ground to dry before they could even walk on it? It would probably take years!"

"Once again, Detective Smith, you were the one who told me that God formed woman from a man's rib. How do you explain that? Son, you have to realize that everything God does will not make sense to us, but that doesn't mean God doesn't know what He is doing or that He is incapable of performing miracles. God spoke the world into existence. He created the entire world from nothing. Why would it be so strange for you to believe that He is also able to part the Red Sea and dry up the ground for His people to cross over? Think about it. If God had not dried up the ground, the children of God would have drowned because it would have been like they were walking on quicksand. Son, when it comes to God's Word, which is His Holy Bible, and by the way, He inspired man to write the Bible, it is best that you believe it all or not at all. God doesn't do things halfway. He is a wise God and makes no mistakes!

"Son, don't be double minded. The Bible speaks of such people in the book of James, 'A double minded man is unstable in all his ways.'

This refers to someone who has two different opinions at the same time like you right now. One minute you are telling me that you believe God can create a human being from another human being's rib. Then the next minute you doubt other things about what God did in the Bible. Son, this is why you need God in your life. Only He can remove confusion and declare you stable!"

Detective Smith stood silent for a moment. Finally, he said, "You are right, Mother Williamson. If I can believe that God created both male and female, then I should believe He is able to do much more considering He is the Creator of all things. I'm sorry. I should have more respect for God instead of doubting His Word."

"Detective Smith, that is perfectly okay. You were just trying to explain a heavenly event and measure it up with the laws of science. God's ways are not our ways and will never make sense to mankind."

"Mother Williamson, you helped me see God more clearly and, although I cannot explain how God does things, it does not mean that He is incapable of performing miracles and answering prayers."

Mother Williamson was now smiling from ear to ear because there was one thing she would not do and that was to debate the Word of God.

Then she asked him, "Do you think God is capable of performing miracles today?"

Detective Smith thought for a while. "I'm not sure if He can perform miracles today."

Detective Jackson waited for Mother Williamson to finish witnessing and then she shared the testimony about her son to Detective Smith. He listened with a skeptical look on his face.

Not believing her story, he asked, "So you are telling me that after the doctors told you your son, Marcus, did not have long to live, you still believed God for his healing?"

"Well, not at first. But when I met Mother Williamson, she basically told me that I did not have to accept what the doctors told me and that I could trust God for Marcus' healing. Smith, there are some things that will happen in your life that cannot be explained by man or science. Even today, the doctors still cannot explain how they don't see any signs of cancer in my son's body. My husband had a few of the doctors come to him after Marcus was considered cancer free and say that God healed our son, and there was no other explanation."

Detective Smith just could not believe that God performed this miracle.

"Could it be that the doctor's diagnosis was wrong from the beginning? How can cancer just leave someone's body just like that? You should check that out because you probably have a lawsuit on your hands. They probably misdiagnosed the problem from the beginning and now the hospital is calling it a miracle to cover up their mistakes.

"Ladies, I appreciate your concerns and what you are trying to get me to believe, but this is all a bit too much for me to take in right now. I believe that God performed those miracles back in the Biblical days. But now that I hear that your son was on his deathbed and God just took away the cancer like that—that is one big pill to swallow."

Mother Williamson asked, "Detective Smith, is it that you cannot believe or will not believe that God removed all of the cancer from Marcus' body and today he is a walking miracle?"

He buried his face in both hands and said, "I need time to clear my head. No disrespect to God, but this is all too much to comprehend! Can we concentrate on eating breakfast? I'm very hungry."

He looked at Detective Jackson. Mother Williamson lifted up her hand as if to tell her to leave it alone because the one thing she learned a long time ago was not to force people into believing God's Word. Just plant the seed and God will do the rest.

Weeks passed by and still there was no sign of the whereabouts of the Rose family. Mother Williamson missed her apartment and her bed the most. She was more than ready to go home to the place she had lived for so many years. She was way past boredom. She read the Bible so many times. She had also watched television, but she was sick of watching it now. After all how many movies can a person watch to pass the time? Besides, most of the channels were airing a bunch of trash anyway, which was polluting the minds of the people. So Mother Williamson decided to do what she did best and that was to pray.

Detective Jackson seeing the boredom and disappointment on Mother Williamson's face asked if she could join in the prayer. She seemed to be a different person when she was praying.

"Of course, my darling. I could never say no to anyone wanting to pray with me."

A call came in.

Detective Smith answered the phone. "Detective Smith. How can I help you?

"This is Detective Thomas."

"Oh, good morning, Detective Thomas. We all just finished eating breakfast. How are you doing, sir, and how can I help you?"

"I'm fine, but I'm afraid I have some bad news."

Detective Smith whispered to them that it was Detective Thomas. He said he'd take the call in the kitchen because he did not want to interrupt their prayer time.

"Sir, what happened and what bad news did you want to tell me?"

"Smith, you are actually the person I wanted to speak with. There was a bad accident. What I'm about to tell you would require you to be seated."

"Me?"

"Yes. It's about your wife, Sarita. She was struck by a speeding truck while crossing the street this morning."

"No!" he shouted as he stumbled backwards. "Please tell me that my wife is still alive! Please, Thomas, I need to know!" He began sobbing uncontrollably.

"Yes, but she is in critical condition."

"I need to go and see my wife and be at her bedside right now!"

After hearing Smith shout, Detective Jackson leaped to her feet and ran into the kitchen. Mother Williamson followed.

"Oh no!" she said. "What happened?"

Detective Jackson rushed to where Smith was standing in the kitchen and quickly grabbed the phone from his hand as he continued to weep bitterly.

"Hello, who is this?"

"This is Detective Thomas. Oh, hello Jackson. I just informed Smith that his wife, Sarita, was stuck by a truck while crossing the street this morning. We just received the news. She is still alive, but in critical condition. I did not get the chance to tell Smith, but a car will be there in twenty minutes to take him straight to the hospital. The doctors do not know if she will survive, but if we can get him to the hospital now, he will someday appreciate it."

"Okay," replied Detective Jackson. "Let me tell him and have him get ready."

She hung up the phone. Detective Smith's face was now in the bosom of Mother Williamson; she was trying to console him. Jackson placed her hand on his back and told him that a car would be coming in twenty minutes to pick him up and take him to the hospital to be by his wife's bedside. He looked up, revealing his teary face that had been buried since he received the news. He managed to gain strength to walk to his room.

Mother Williamson's eyes filled with tears as Detective Jackson shared the tragic news with her.

Smith grabbed a few things and waited outside for the car to arrive. No less than five minutes later, a patrol car arrived and he got in while another detective got out of the car. The car drove away. Both Jackson and Mother Williamson waved good-bye. Standing in the driveway with an overnight bag in his hand, was Detective Smith's replacement.

Detective Jackson spoke first. "Hello, Detective O'Brien. This is Mother Williamson."

"Please to meet you," Detective O'Brien said as Mother Williamson extended her hand.

"God bless you, Detective O'Brien. Please to meet you as well."

"Let's all get back inside the house," suggested Jackson. "By the way, Detective O'Brien, we just finished eating breakfast not too long ago. Do you care for anything to eat? We still have more food."

"Actually, I was able to eat something before coming here, but I would love a hot cup of coffee if it is not too much trouble for you."

"Not at all," replied Jackson. The group went into the house.

During the entire ride to the hospital, Smith could not stop crying. He could not imagine living without his wife. Questions kept running through his mind. Would she make it? Would she be as she was before the accident? Would she still have all of her five senses? Then he thought about the conversation he had with Mother Williamson during breakfast time.

"Oh God, please do not punish my wife because of what I said this morning about not believing everything in the Bible!" he prayed. "God please, I wasn't so sure if You could still perform miracles, but if You can, God I need one right now!" He looked up as he prayed.

Mother Williamson served Detective O'Brien a hot cup of coffee and asked him to get comfortable while both she and Jackson went into the bedroom to say a word of prayer on behalf of Detective Smith's wife.

Surprisingly, Detective O'Brien said, "If it is okay, I would like to join in on the prayer."

"Praise the Lord!" Mother Williamson shouted. "I take it that we have a God-fearing saint among us."

"Yes, you do," he replied. "God bless you, my sister. I have been saved for many years and I love the Lord. God is everything to me. What a great privilege it is to call Him my Father."

"God is awesome!" replied Mother Williamson. "He sure knows how to turn a sad situation into a joyous one because smiles are on our faces when moments ago, this house was filled with sadness."

They joined hands in prayer. Mother Williamson felt led to ask Detective O'Brien to lead them in prayer.

As he nodded his head in agreement, with a strong voice, he began to pray, "My God, we thank you that the effectual fervent prayers of the righteous avail much! God, we will not stop praying until we get an answer. We stand together in prayer on behalf of Sarita Smith, thanking you for sparing her life and that she is still in the land of the living. Lord, remove all doubt so that we can continue to trust You for Sarita's healing and will not speak words of doubt or disbelief! We thank you that all of her needs shall be met according to Your riches in glory!

"I pray that You send Your sweet Holy Spirit into Sarita's hospital room right now and raise her body from that sick bed! God, sometimes we do not know what to pray for or how to exactly pray, but we know whatsoever we bind on earth, You will bind in heaven! So, as we continue to stay steadfast in our prayers to You, we thank You for allowing the situation to change for the good of Sarita Smith. God, we speak life into Sarita's body, and we thank You that she will not have any permanent damage!

"You are the God of the impossible. You are the God who can build up everything that has been torn down in Sarita's body! You are the God who can make her strong where she is weak! You are the God who can bring joy where there is sorrow! My God, we are lifting up Sarita Smith before You. She needs a divine intervention, so Lord, we are asking that You touch her body and restore it anew!

"We do not believe the report of the doctors, but we shall believe the report of the Lord so by Your stripes, Sarita Smith is totally healed! We thank You for Sarita's speedy recovery and thank You for preserving all of her limbs and senses. We cancel out every plan or attack of the enemy, and by faith we decree and declare healing power in her body! We know that You will answer our prayers because we are praying according to Your Word. Amen!"

As they sang hymns and spiritual songs of praise to the Lord, a peace was felt throughout the entire house and as believers they knew, without a shadow of a doubt, that God was going to come through for them and heal Sarita. They believed He was not going to allow her to lose her limbs or any of her five senses.

At the hospital, Detective Smith entered his wife's hospital room and he thought he had the wrong room because he could hardly recognize his wife as he slowly walked closer to her. Both legs were suspended in the air, and both arms had casts on them and tubes were coming from every direction. Bandages were also covering her face and only her eyes, nose and mouth were exposed. A tube was inserted into her mouth so that she would not choke on her own saliva. The doctors had her heavily sedated. As Detective Smith leaned over his wife's seemingly lifeless body, tears just fell from his eyes.

A group of doctors came into the room and introduced themselves and began to ask questions about his wife's medical history. Detective Smith was already weak. The doctors informed him that there was a strong possibility that his wife would not make it and, if she did, she may never walk again because both legs were badly damaged by the accident.

One of the doctors, Dr. Sheet, asked, "Is she right-handed or left-handed?"

Detective Smith replied, "Right-handed. Why do you asked?"

The doctor proceeded to tell him that her left arm was so badly damaged, they were not sure if it could be repaired; she may never be able to use that arm again. Feeling a little faint, Detective Smith sat down at this point. Mother Williamson and the morning's discussion came to his mind. She believed that God could still perform miracles today, and he needed to reach out to her for prayer for his wife's healing.

"Doctors, are you absolutely sure there is no possible way that she will be able to walk or have use of her left arm again?"

"Well, Detective Smith, we were talking and none of us have ever seen a situation like this before, Sarita's organs are barely functioning on their own and many of her bones are broken. The way it looks right now, you should prepare for the worst."

"Doctors, are you telling me that she may not survive? What about her brain, is there any damage to her brain?"

Another doctor, Dr. Wallace, said, "It is too early to determine if there is any damage to her brain. Detective Smith, if your wife survives this ordeal, we are uncertain how much mobility she will have in both legs and her left arm. I recommend that you go home and try to get some rest or sleep because only time will be able to answer those questions."

"Doctors, Sarita has to pull through because I do not have it in me to take care of her if she is not able to walk or talk again! I just cannot do this!" he lamented.

"Detective Smith, do not worry about those things right now. Let's just concentrate on her recovery. Then if additional assistance is needed, we have a whole department that can guide you on how to take care of your wife."

Trying to calm him down, the doctor asked Detective Smith, "Do you have any children?"

"No. My wife and I were never able to have children. We both took tests and the results indicated that neither one of us had any medical issues preventing us from having a child. We have been having problems at home and I really think it is more psychological because there is nothing standing in our way medically."

"Okay, I just wanted to make sure that if you did, someone was picking up the children from school," replied Dr. Wallace. "This hospital provides overnight stays for spouses for as long as they need. Would you prefer to stay at your wife's bedside? We can have another bed put in the room. There is no additional charge."

"Yes, Doc. I would really appreciate that very much. I would love to be here when she wakes up."

At this time, Detective Smith thought about the many relatives he needed to inform about Sarita's accident, but the only person he could think about calling was Mother Williamson. So he decided to give her a call and then he would inform her family members afterwards. He was a little reluctant to call her because of their earlier conversation about miracles, but he managed to call anyway.

Detective Jackson handed the phone to Mother Williamson letting her know it was Detective Smith.

Mother Williamson said, "Hello, dear. How is your wife doing?"

"Sarita is really not looking good and the doctors are saying that she may not survive and if she does, she may never walk again and that she may not have use of her left arm."

Smith tried to control his emotions, but began to cry uncontrollably again. Mother Williamson just let him cry.

He said, "God, please do not take my wife from me. Please God!"

She told him that he has to be strong for Sarita because she needs him right now more than ever.

"God will be with you every step of the way no matter how long the journey will be," promised Mother Williamson.

Still crying hysterically, he said, "I'm not an emotionally strong person. I do not know what to do. How can I possibly take care of her?"

"Son, you have to turn it over to God. He is the One who can fix it. Over two thousand years ago Jesus was beaten and bruised for all mankind's sins and because of His sacrifice and His stripes, we are healed today! We no longer have to provide animal sacrifices to approach God's throne, but we can come boldly and make our requests known to Him. Jesus hung, bled and died on the cross so that we will have everlasting life. He wishes that no man will perish, but that all would come to repentance. Son, God is knocking at the door of your heart, He wants you to accept Him as your Lord and personal Savior. Will you try Jesus today, Detective Smith, and take Him at His Word? I cannot save you, nor can I heal Sarita - but Jesus can. He can make all your wrongs, right and turn Sarita's situation completely around. Will you trust Him today? God did not cause this to happen because He does not tempt any man with evil; He only gives perfect and good gifts. When you truly trust God and take Him at his Word, anything that you put in the Master's hands becomes possible."

"Mother Williamson, I know what you are saying to me is true because about a month ago I was shopping in the mall when a woman approached me and said that I was running from God. Then she proceeded to tell me that from that day forward everywhere I walked, there would be someone there who would witness to me until I surrendered my life to the Lord. Mother Williamson, I'm tired of running. I want to surrender my heart to God. I need God as my personal Savior. I need Him to take control of my life. Can you walk me through the steps of salvation like you did with Detective Jackson?"

"I will be honored."

Mother Williamson gave God all the glory. After she walked him through the steps of Salvation and said a word of prayer, Detective Smith began to cry uncontrollably, but the difference was those were tears of joy!

Mother Williamson encouraged him to cry because the best gift had just been given to him and he had every right to be excited. She said a prayer for him and for Sarita, that she would have a speedy recovery and that all of her limbs would be intact and she would have use of them all.

Detective Smith thanked Mother Williamson for her love for him and his family and for being so concerned about their lives. She told him to trust God, not to listen to what the doctors were saying about how she may not survive, and not to focus on how she looks right now, but believe the report of the Lord so he can watch and see how God works.

"Yes, Mother Williamson, I will and God bless you."

When they left, Deacon Brown felt relieved that he had gotten everything off his chest. He decided to give Pastor Paul a call to see how the reward collection was going and to see if the church could do something else to increase the reward amount.

He dialed Pastor Paul's number. He picked up the phone before the first ring was completed.

"Hello, Deacon Brown." He had identified him with the Caller ID.

"Hi, Pastor. I just finished speaking with Detective Thomas and Detective Lee. They recorded the additional information I gave them."

"That is great news," the pastor replied.

"Pastor Paul, I hope this does not sound selfish of me, but it would really be nice if we could raise another seven thousand dollars, which would bring the reward to fifteen thousand dollars. Surely, someone would come forth with convicting evidence!"

"That sounds like a fantastic idea! I'll call some of the other saints so they can make the announcement at Friday night's service. Perhaps there will be some volunteers with website programming skills."

"Thanks, Pastor. I know that God will not fail us. I just know it."

The next day, Deacon Brown wanted to call Mother Curtis to see what kind of ideas could be used to raise money. He picked up the phone to call her, but Mother Curtis had beaten him to it; there she was on the other end, saying, "Good morning, Deacon Brown!"

"Wow, this is creepy! I was just about to call you concerning our fundraiser events and there you are on the other end of the phone!"

"Well, we are on the same page because I was calling you about the same thing," replied Mother Curtis. "It turns out that Pastor Paul was going to contact the both of us today. Sister Jay felt that we should be doing more, and so she decided to start a collection on her own in her neighborhood."

"What?" replied Deacon Brown.

"Yes, and you will not guess how much money she raised so far?"

"How much?"

"Five thousand dollars! So you see, Deacon Brown, we are already at the targeted amount of twenty thousand dollars!"

"My Lord! God is so good and worthy to be praised! Oh, how good God is!"

"So when is the church going to hand over the money to the police?"

"Well, Pastor Paul mentioned that he would like to hold onto the money until after an arrest has been made," replied Mother Curtis.

"Okay that's fine, but that should not stop us from continuing to raise more money for this sad occasion. Actually, I was just speaking with Pastor about starting a website on behalf of the Rose family, and he stated that he is going to see if he can get some of the other church members to help me create the site."

"Great," replied Mother Curtis. "I may not have any programming skills, but I know how to do administrative work and if you need me, I would love to help out."

"Mother Curtis, we would love to have as many hands on deck as possible."

"Let me know what you need me to do."

# CHAPTER SIXTEEN

Joe, still sharp as ever, even after retirement, entered his apartment and looked for his RF Bug Detector. He wanted to make absolutely sure his apartment was bug free. After making sure there were no bugs in his apartment, he called Zach and gave him clear instructions not to leave his apartment and to safely put away the only document that could potentially identify the other suspect. He also told him that he thinks someone has Detective Kelly in his or her pocket. He let Zach know that they were just going to have to do their own investigation and not rely on or trust anyone else.

Peeking out the window, Joe could still see Detective Kelly in his patrol car watching his building like a hawk.

"Zach," Joe said into the phone, "it seems like I'm being watched so give me some time and I will head over to your place and we can talk further. Oh, by the way, how is your apartment, Zach?"

"Everything is fine here, but I'm concerned about you at your place, Joe."

"I'll be okay because Kelly does not suspect anything so far. He is trying to keep tabs on me by finding out who all of my friends and associates are. He wanted to know who dropped me off this afternoon, but I told him a neighbor who lives in my building. I don't think he knows about you yet and I would like to keep it that way. That is probably why he is following me around everywhere, hoping that he would catch both of us together. So going forward, we are going to have to be extremely careful if we do not want your identity revealed. Zach, once he leaves from in front of my building, I'll take the back road to your house and we can sort everything out there."

"Okay," replied Zach. "Joe, just make sure that he has not assigned someone else to watch your building when he leaves. Be careful and I will talk to you when you get here."

Suddenly, the doorbell rang. Joe immediately thought that it was Zach disobeying him by coming over because he was concerned about his safety. But looking though the peephole, he saw that it was Detective Kelly. His heart skipped a couple of beats. He nervously opened the apartment door and played off his nervousness by remaining calm.

He said, "Did I leave something behind?"

"No, no, but I have bad news. I wanted to let you know that Fat died sometime last week."

"What?" replied Joe. "But how?"

"I do not know all the details yet, but he supposedly fell down a flight of stairs. They are going to perform an autopsy tomorrow morning, which should take about two weeks to get the results, to determine the real cause of death."

Joe started thinking that Kelly already knew this information when they were having lunch so why tell him now? Did he hold onto this information just to get inside his apartment? Did he come back to make sure he or someone else did not leave anything behind?

As Detective Kelly looked around the apartment, he asked Joe, "Do you need help cleaning up anything?

"Thanks for the offer, but it is okay. I have everything under control. I'm sleepy and will be getting ready for bed soon."

Joe was hoping that Kelly would get the hint and leave which he did.

"Okay then. I'll let you get your rest, but if you need my help with anything, please give me a call."

"Will do," replied Joe. "Drive safely and good night."

Joe locked the door and all he could feel was relief because he thought Kelly was on to him and was going to threaten him in some way. He decided to turn off all the lights to make Kelly think he was heading to bed. After a couple of minutes, Joe looked out the window and saw that it worked—Kelly's patrol car was driving away from his building.

Joe grabbed some clothes and personal items and headed to Zach's house using the back entrance of his apartment building. When he arrived, Zach quickly opened the door, glad that he arrived safely.

"Come inside before anyone spots us together," Zach said. "Hopefully, you were not followed."

Joe shook his head no. "I slipped through the back way and was very watchful. Besides, I think I convinced Kelly that I did not have any more evidence that would lead us to other suspects. I gave him the cigarette butt and he is going to check the DNA and let me know the results."

"Oh, great!" replied Zach.

"Yeah right! He also told me that the suspect known as Fat, who the police had in custody, fell down a flight of stairs last week and died."

"Seriously?" asked Zach. "How did he fall?"

"Kelly didn't know, but as soon as he gets that information, he promised to tell me. But I do not trust him anymore and I do not think that we will ever receive the DNA results. So, here is what we need to do going forward, Zach. We cannot be seen together at all anymore. Either we will call each other or get together at nighttime at your place."

"Yes, you are right. So let's figure out all the actions beforehand. This way we both will be on the same page."

"Okay, but can we please wait until the morning? I'm totally exhausted and my brain will not be able to comprehend anything at this point."

"Okay, everything you need is in the spare bedroom. Hope you get a good night's sleep, Joe!"

In the morning, Joe woke up to the smell of bacon and eggs and strong coffee. He allowed his nose to direct him.

"Good morning, Zach."

"Good morning, Joe. I placed a towel and washcloth in the bathroom. Please get cleaned up for breakfast. It will be ready soon."

"You don't have to tell me twice! I'm starving as you would say, and it smells really good, Zach!"

"Yeah. I thank the Army for my cooking skills. You'll be satisfied. Don't worry."

While both men sat at the kitchen table eating bacon, eggs and grits with a couple slices of toast, Joe said that he could not remember the last time he had enjoyed breakfast in a house setting with someone since his wife of thirty-three years passed away five years ago.

"Wow," replied Zach. "Thirty-three years is a long time to be married. Did you and your wife have children?"

"Unfortunately not. She was unable to have children, and we decided not to adopt and just spend our lives together which we really enjoyed."

"What was your wife's name?"

"Oh, it was Loretta. She was my best friend. Loretta was such a loving and caring person just like Mother Rose. She was always caring for other people because she loved people and did not want to see anyone hurting or suffering. How about you, Zach? Was there ever someone special in your life?"

"Yes, there was, but unfortunately Rachel died at a very early age. She had breast cancer. She was only thirty-seven years old and pregnant with our first child."

"Zach, I'm so sorry to hear that."

"It's okay. It was a long time ago, but I never had the desire to get married again."

"I know what you mean, Zach. When you have found that special woman, no one can take her place. I personally feel that it's up to the individual if he or she wants to marry again, which, it seems, we both decided against. Zach, we have a lot in common, more than I could have ever imagined."

"Yeah, you're right, Joe. I do not believe people just meet one another accidentally. I think it is for a purpose in life," replied Zach. Changing his thoughts, he said, "Okay, so what do you think we should start working on today, Mr. PI?"

"I figured we could try to find out the location of that house or find out if it still exists or who are the current owners."

"I agree," said Zach, "because it seems that Kelly is looking for something as well and it could very well be this house deed that we have in our possession."

"The house deed is very old. We have to get another legible copy that will answer the many questions we need help addressing. Considering both of us are renters, let's call Information to find out where we have to go to get another copy of the deed."

"Okay, Joe. I'll clean up while you make the phone calls and we can decide who should go retrieve the copy of the deed. I think that you should be the one because of your PI skills."

"I'm fine with that, Zach. We just need to work out a plan."

As Zach reached for the dishes on the table, Joe picked up Zach's house phone to attempt to call Information when his cell phone rang.

Joe quickly got Zach's attention, and told him to turn off the water and be silent because Kelly was calling him.

"Good morning, Kelly. What a surprise to hear from you so early in the morning."

"Good morning, Joe. Sorry if I'm disturbing your breakfast, but I thought I would stop by to share some news with you. I did not receive an answer when I called your home phone. It seemed pretty early for you to be out of the house. Are you going to be home within the next hours?"

"Well, I always take a morning walk before it gets crowded on the street. As a matter of fact, this is when Mother Rose and I would bump into each other. It would be around this time."

"Oh, okay, so are you near your house?"

"I'm not too far," replied Joe.

"Well, in that case, should I just wait for you in front of your apartment building?"

"Hmm, I have a couple of errands to run today so I will not be heading back that way for quite some time."

"I can meet you and drive you back home if you do not feel like taking public transportation."

"No, that will not be necessary. By the way, what's the news you wanted to share with me? Does it pertain to Fat or about the DNA results?"

"Joe, you know how I feel about having these types of conversations over the phone. I would prefer if we met in person. How about I treat you to lunch again? Would that be okay with you?"

"Sure, I'll give you a call just before I finish my errands and we can schedule a time to meet then. Hopefully, it is not too late for lunch."

Then unexpectedly there was silence on the other end of the phone. Joe called out Kelly's name.

"I'm still here," he replied. "I was just thinking. If today is not a good day for us to meet, just give me a call."

"Great," replied Joe. "Either way, I'll call you. Bye."

Zach looked at Joe. "This Kelly is really starting to scare me. If I did not know any better, it seems like he is trying to figure out your whereabouts at all times."

"Yeah, you are right. He was insisting that I meet with him for lunch. I know he wants to pick my brain. Perhaps he is trying to figure out if I have the deed. I have to be especially careful because he knows how to read body language very well. Zach, I have to leave soon because although the police do not tell you, they can pinpoint your exact location from your cell phone, which will lead him straight to your apartment. I would not put it past him. He was probably the one who broke into my apartment looking for the deed anyway," stated Joe.

Zach quickly put away the dishes and began to wipe the kitchen table and counter as Joe dialed Information.

"Hello, my name is Joe and I have a friend who owns a house in Georgia and needs to get a copy of her deed because the one that she has is badly damaged. Can you please tell me where she would have to go?" asked Joe.

"Sure. She would have to go to the Department of Records. Here is the general toll free number for the state of Georgia."

"Thanks so much for your help."

After speaking with one of the clerks in the Department of Records, Joe wrote down its address and how much it would cost for him to obtain a copy of the deed.

"Zach, I think I'm going to meet with Kelly because the longer it takes for him to see me the more he is going to think I'm trying to hide from him. I'll leave first using the back door. If you do need to go somewhere, you should leave an hour afterwards so no one will ever think we were together."

"Sure," replied Zach. "But Joe, please be careful. I do not think that Kelly can be trusted and he's definitely working with someone."

"Exactly! So if I need to contact you, I will not use my cell phone, but will use a pay phone if I can find one. They still exist in some business areas."

Mother Williamson explained to Detective Jackson what a consecration was and suggested that they participate in it for seven days, and believe God for Sarita's speedy recovery. Detective O'Brien and Detective Jackson were more than excited to fast for their fellow co-worker's wife. As they prayed, read the Word and praised God in song, everyone felt in their spirit that a breakthrough had already taken place.

A week passed by, but they did hear from Detective Smith. Mother Williamson encouraged Detective Jackson. She told her that they had to wait on the Lord. She reminded her that delay did not mean denial.

# CHAPTER SEVENTEEN

Joe reached for his phone to call Kelly and tell him to meet him at the diner. They agreed to meet within thirty minutes.

After waiting for more than forty minutes Detective Kelly said, "Mr. PI, I almost did not think you were going to make it. I was hoping I did not say anything to upset you the last time we spoke."

"No," replied Joe. "I just needed to finish up some personal business. So what did you want to share with me, Kelly?"

"We can talk about it, but let's order our food first. Oh, I'm treating again so you can order whatever you want."

Kelly waved the waitress over to their table to take their orders.

"So Joe, I wanted to let you know the autopsy results on Fredrick Alfred Tanks' death," began Detective Kelly. "During his fall, he broke his neck."

"Oh, it really seemed like someone wanted him out of the way before he started dropping names. Do you think that his falling was an accident? Did someone get to him from behind bars?" asked Joe. "It's sad that he had to die that way. Besides, he could have been so helpful in solving this case. Have you heard anything about that cigarette butt I found in Mother Rose's apartment?"

"I have not yet. That will take a couple of days before we get the results from the lab. So Joe, who was the guy who dropped you off the other day? I know you mentioned he was just a neighbor. Does this neighbor have a name?"

Playing it off, Joe said, "Why are you so concerned about my neighbor, Artie? He lives a couple of doors down from me and occasionally offers me rides. He's getting up in age and feels better having someone in the car with him."

"So Artie is an older man?"

"Yeah why? He has to be about seventy something."

"Well it's just when I came to your house this morning, there was an older man ringing your doorbell," replied Detective Kelly.

"Was he a short and medium-build man?" asked Joe.

"That was definitely him, Mr. PI, but from the looks of him, he could pass for someone in their early 60's, certainly not someone in their 70's."

"Yeah, some people really age gracefully and look good for their ages."

Joe felt relieved when Kelly said that he saw Artie since he was still trying to figure out if someone was working with him and it was better that he focused on Artie and not look around for anyone else. Besides, Joe remembered that Kelly told him that he called his house phone, not stopped by his place. Boy, he was getting really scary. Kelly was trying to get into Joe's head. He started asking more questions, like cops tend to do, in order to trap the suspect in a lie. But he forgot who he was talking to since Joe also knew how to play those cop games as well.

"So, Mr. PI, what made you want to go to Mother Rose's apartment? Was there something in particular that you were looking for?"

"Truthfully, I do not think Fat was working alone and now that the only suspect is deceased, there is no one else that the police can question. Isn't that so convenient? Perhaps we will be able to make an arrest once we find out the person's identity from the cigarette butt," replied Joe.

"Yes. Hopefully something will turn up on the DNA test results or worse, we may never find the Rose family," stated Detective Kelly.

Joe was almost certain that he saw a look of gladness on Detective Kelly's face after he made that statement because he knew that Fat was the best lead so far.

"Mr. PI, you and I live in the real world and we have witnessed many cold cases which still have not been solved to this day. Hopefully this will not be one of those cases. We will not give up and will continue to search for them."

Joe agreed, but did not feel like Kelly cared whether the police found the family or not. Finishing his meal, Kelly told Joe that he had to get back to work, that he just wanted to share the autopsy news with him and that he would contact him when he heard more information about the DNA results.

"Okay," replied Joe. "Thanks again for lunch."

He shook Kelly's hand and left the diner.

The next day Joe went to the Department of Records and immediately saw the long lines as he walked through the swing doors. After waiting for about thirty minutes, Joe walked up to the clerk's desk and explained that he was there to get a copy of a house deed.

"What are the lot and block numbers?"

Thank goodness he could read those numbers from the deed. The clerk pulled up the information on her computer.

"Are you the owner?"

"No. My aunt is."

"Sir, where is your aunt?" asked the clerk.

Feeling badly that he had to lie to her, Joe said, "She was not able to come today due to her being hospitalized with a very bad illness."

"Sir, we are not allowed to turn over other people's personal information to their family members unless they have a power of attorney from the owner authorizing their family member to get such documents," replied the clerk.

"I'm sorry, Miss. I'm not asking for an original. I'm simply asking for a copy. I have the original here and it got messed up over the years and, as you can see, it is no longer legible to read."

"Once again, I'm sorry, sir, about your circumstances, but policy is policy."

Joe asked, "Would it be possible to speak with your supervisor?"

"Hold on. I'll see if she's available. Please excuse me. I'll be right back."

When she left, Joe did something he would never advise anyone else to do—he threw something into the trashcan and intentionally missed. While picking up the trash from the floor, he looked at the clerk's computer and retrieved the exact address of the house.

Joe noticed the clerk turning the corner with her supervisor. He pretended to be waiting patiently and he extended his hand and greeted her.

The supervisor also extended her hand and introduced herself. "Hi, my name is Ms. Black and I understand that you would like to get a copy of your ill aunt's house deed and that you came with the original?"

"That is correct, Ms. Black," replied Joe. "I would like to get all her papers in order in case something should happen to her."

"I'm sorry sir, but, as Ms. Wiggles explained, we just cannot give out that type of information to just anyone."

"It is okay," replied Joe. "I tried."

The supervisor left.

While the supervisor walked away, Joe whispered, "Miss Wiggles, can you pull up the deed and make sure the house still belongs to Aunt Lois Rose, please?"

She whispered back, "Sir, I could get into a whole lot of trouble, but I will confirm that for you. Give me a few minutes."

The clerk confirmed that the house owner was still the same.

"Thank you so much for your help. I will come back another day. Have a wonderful day."

Joe left the building with a smile on his face because his trip had not been in vain. Not only did he know that Mother Rose still owned the house, but he also found out where it was located. He headed home to try and clean up the mess that was made by the robbers. Then he remembered that his neighbor, Artie, was looking for him. He decided to go to Artie's apartment first. Perhaps he heard or saw something. Joe rang the doorbell. There was no answer, but just as he was about to walk away, Artie's door swung open.

"Hello, Joe. Good to see you!"

"Oh hi, Artie. How are you? I heard you were looking for me earlier today."

"Yes, yes. I wanted to tell you how sorry I am that your apartment got robbed and wanted to find out if you were okay."

"Yes, Artie. Thank God I was not home, but everything is fine. It just shook me up a bit."

"I'm glad because you are such a nice neighbor and I wouldn't want anything to happen to you."

"So are you, Artie. Thanks so much for being a concerned neighbor," replied Joe.

"Joe, too many strange things are happening in this neighborhood now. It used to be such a nice neighborhood, but now people are robbing, stealing and now kidnapping people in order to gain access to their money. My elder son and his wife are worried about me and want me to move to Kansas City, Missouri and so I also wanted to say good-bye. They have arranged for a moving company to help me move all of my furniture and I will be leaving in one more week."

"Ah man, Artie. Although I'm a man of few words, we always had a bond and I'm going to miss you."

"Joe, what about you? You are not getting any younger. Why don't you move in with some of your young family members?"

"I do not think so. They are all grown and have their own families now. They would not want an old man like me hanging around the house and getting in their way."

"Oh don't say that, Joe. You should try. It will not hurt to try asking," stated Artie.

Joe reached for Artie's hand, but Artie pushed his hand away and grabbed his shoulders to give him one of his bear hugs. It touched Joe so much that tears welled up in his eyes.

After straightening up his apartment, he still did not feel comfortable sleeping there. He ate something and validated how much he had in his bank account because they had some traveling to do. Joe gathered some personal items and left out the back entrance to Zach's apartment. Making sure no one saw him leave the building, Joe walked with caution, often looking over his shoulders.

After he arrived safely at Zach's apartment, Zach asked excitedly, "So what information were you able to gather today?"

"Well, the clerk refused to give me a copy, so I had to steal the rest of the information."

"What?" replied Zach.

"But, guess where the house is located?"

"Where?"

"It's located in Houston, Texas."

"What! Are you sure? How can that be? There is no way that Mother Rose would have a house located so far away. Who maintains the house? For that matter, who pays the bills? Better yet, who is occupying the house after all these years?"

"Well, Zach, there is only one way we are going to ever know the answers to all those questions and that is by getting on a flight to Houston, Texas."

"Joe, I do not know if I have enough money to book a flight out of the state right now."

"Well, Zach, it is funny that you should mentioned it because I just checked my savings account before coming over and I have enough money saved for the both of us to book a round trip, a hotel stay and rent a car as well."

Zach lowered his head. "Wow. I'm still working and do not have a savings account and here you are retired and you have one."

"No worries," replied Joe. "As I mentioned, there is enough for the both of us and you can pay me back anytime. All you have to do is let your clients know that you will be out of town for a couple of weeks."

Zach, being so appreciative, told Joe he would let his clients know that he was going on vacation. As he thought about it, he couldn't remember the last time he took a vacation. His eyes lit up with excitement. Although this was not his line of work, Zach wanted to be a part of this investigation every step of the way.

"Oh no!" said Zach, "What about Detective Kelly?"

"Well, I'm going to tell him I'm visiting my niece in Florida and I can say that I'm staying with her for a few weeks."

"What are you saying? We are going to fly to Florida first?"

"Yes, that is precisely what we are going to do and then we will travel to Houston to throw Detective Kelly off. Would that be okay with you, Zach?"

"Are you kidding me? I need a vacation in the worse way! Why in the world would I complain?" replied Zach as he danced around his living room.

"I will explain to Detective Kelly how my neighbor, Artie, is moving to Kansas City to be with his family because the area is getting so bad and that I should consider relocating as well. Then I will tell him that I'm feeling depressed about the Rose family and decided to visit my niece and her family for a while and do not know when I will return. Knowing Kelly like I do, he is going to confirm this information and use his police clearance to search the flight reservations database for my plane reservation. I think he'll believe my story. I also think that it would be best if we booked our flights to Texas after staying a couple days in Florida.

"Zach, unfortunately we will have to take separate flights. I'll book an earlier flight and you should make reservations for an evening flight. My family will pick you up at the airport."

"It is not a problem," Zach said as he walked into the kitchen. "Do you want any coffee or tea, Joe?"

"Sure, I'll have a cup of tea before I head to bed."

"Your tea is coming right up!"

"Thanks so much for taking good care of me, Zach. I really mean it. The bond we both share now is unbelievable."

Joe reached for the mug and walked into the guest bedroom.

# CHAPTER EIGHTEEN

Joe decided to go to his favorite bakery for breakfast. As he entered the bakery, he ran into one of his eating partners, named Dave. He began to share with him everything that was going on with the Rose family and how he was helping out with the case.

After Joe finished eating his breakfast, he paid for his meal and decided to go help Artie with his packing.

Joe was waving good-bye when suddenly Dave asked, "Did you run into a Detective Kelly yesterday? He was looking for you."

Joe asked, "What time was that?"

"About 7:30 or 8:00 a.m."

"Yes, I did."

Joe thanked him for letting him know that Kelly was looking for him and then left the bakery. Joe was really getting upset with Kelly because not only was he constantly calling him, but now he was also tracking his every move. How long has he been following him? It seemed like he knew all of his local spots.

Joe checked around his apartment to make sure nothing was moved, but everything seemed to be in its right place. He decided to knock on Artie's door to help him with his moving. Artie was surprised to see Joe at his apartment door. Although they had been neighbors for many years, at best, they would bump into each other and briefly talk in the hallways, but visiting each other's apartment never occurred. Joe preferred it this way. He did not want his neighbors knowing what type of work he did for a living.

"Hey Joe, I'm surprised to see you again! How are you doing?"

"I'm okay!"

"Come in and try to find a seat somewhere, and please excuse the mess. As you already know, I'm leaving this weekend."

Joe accepted the offer to sit down. "I came to assist you wherever you need me the most, if you don't mind."

"Wow! Thanks, Joe. I sure could use an extra helping hand. My son hired a moving company for me, but they called and told me that they do not box personal items or valuables and I would be responsible for packing those items myself. I have some very special items in my bedroom closet that I need help wrapping. My knees are not the same anymore. You can assist me in the bedroom area."

"Sure," replied Joe as he took two boxes and headed towards the bedroom closet which was now only full of old papers and pictures.

"Boy, does this seem like déjà vu," said Joe. Then he asked, "Artie, are you taking all of these old letters with you all the way to Kansas?"

"Yes. My son insists that I not throw anything away because they could be very important documents and frankly, I don't have the patience to read through each one of them. My son promises to go through everything when I get to Kansas and will use his shredder to destroy everything that is no longer needed."

"Oh okay. I was going to offer you my shredder."

"No need," replied Artie. "I will let my son take care of that job. Besides, we will be here all day if we had to read through about thirty years of paperwork."

Packing was very time consuming and before they knew it, it was almost 2:00 p.m. Joe decided to order some pizza and breadsticks from the local pizzeria. Artie agreed but insisted on paying the bill.

Joe declined. "Consider this a going away present—me helping you move and paying for the pizza."

They both ate until they were very full. There was still some food left over which Artie put inside the refrigerator. Joe decided to call it a night when he completed the packing in Artie's bedroom. He just could not stand to see an older man work so hard by himself. Later that evening, Joe cooked himself some dinner and decided to go to bed.

The next day seemed like it was going to be a nice day since the sun was already strong around 8:00 a.m. Joe decided that he was not going to leave the house, but just take it easy. He walked towards the window to enjoy the sunshine then he noticed a patrol car parked in front of his building. Guess who was stepping out? Detective Kelly! *Oh boy*, thought Joe, *I better prepare myself for his questioning.* He raced into the bedroom to get dressed but then thought that he should keep his pajamas on. Maybe Detective Kelly will not stay long if he thinks he had interrupted his sleep.

Sure enough Joe's doorbell rang. He decided to wait for it to ring at least two more times before answering the door. On the third ring, he opened the door and began to rub his eyes.

"Good morning, Detective Kelly. This is an early visit for you. Is everything okay? Please come in. How can I help you at this early hour of the morning?"

"Morning. Again, I'm the deliverer of bad news."

He took it upon himself to just sit down on Joe's couch without being asked. Joe fumed and thought, *something tells me he is going to be staying for a while.*

Joe sluggishly responded. "What happened now?"

"The evidence you handed over to me and I turned in a couple of days ago has gone missing."

"How?" asked Joe even though he knew that Kelly was not going to tell the truth about the DNA results to him.

"Well, it seems as if one of the examiners misplaced the cigarette butt and believes he could have possibly thrown it into the trash thinking it was garbage. The examination team searched everywhere for the butt, but they were unable to find it. Even if they do recover it, it will be badly damaged and any test results found will be compromised."

Joe, acting surprised, said, "That was our only good lead considering Fat's death. Now it will be harder finding the other suspect."

He lowered his head pretending to be disappointed.

"You are right," said Kelly. "I knew that you wouldn't take this news very well. This is why I wanted to tell you in person."

"So, what will happen now to the Rose family case?" asked Joe.

Detective Kelly, almost appearing to be delighted, said, "We will probably keep the case open for six more months and then close it. It will be placed among the other cold files that were never resolved."

By now, Joe was sick to his stomach as he watched Kelly explain the situation with no emotions whatsoever.

"I noticed there is a lot of garbage outside as if someone is moving," stated Detective Kelly.

*Wow, nice police work*, thought Joe.

"Yeah my neighbor, Artie, is moving in with his eldest son who lives in Kansas City."

"Isn't that the neighbor you said drove you around?"

Joe could not be truthful with him anymore because he could no longer be trusted.

"Yeah. His son doesn't think it is safe to live here any longer, considering what happened to the Rose family."

"I agree, Joe. If he is up in age, perhaps he is too old to be living by himself anyway. I think you should also consider moving in with your family as well."

Joe silently thanked God because Detective Kelly was making it very easy for him to share his plans without arousing his suspicions or following his every move, which Joe doubted he would do this time since he encouraged him to move. Joe knew that he had Detective Kelly down pat so he decided to share his news with him about going away.

"It's funny you should mention that because my niece has been begging me to come stay with her and her family in Florida for quite some time, just to get away from all of this drama that has been going on in my neighborhood. I just might accept her offer because first it was the Rose disappearance and now my apartment got broken into. Who knows what's next. Thank you, Kelly, I think I will take your advice and go visit my niece. I'm going to see if I can book my reservation in a couple weeks."

"Wow! That is actually great news, Mr. PI. Perhaps it will do your body some good. How long will you stay?"

"I think I'll stay for about six months."

"Mr. PI, if any evidence is found, you'll be the first to be notified or if any more leads come up, I will personally give you a call. Take care of yourself and if I do not see you before you leave, have a safe trip to Florida." Detective Kelly had the biggest grin planted on his face. "I'm glad you are looking out for yourself."

They shook hands and Kelly left Joe's apartment.

Joe lifted his eyes up towards heaven and thanked God again for making his plans run a lot smoother. Joe felt in his heart that Mother Williamson was praying for Zach and him, as well as for the police to find the family because things were just lining up in the family's favor. Joe knew that he would never receive that phone call from Kelly about finding the cigarette butt or any additional leads. It was almost as if he was glad Joe was getting out of his way. After he left, Joe wired the money to Zach and made his own reservations as well.

Three weeks passed and Joe was about to go to the airport. He gave his apartment one more walk-through to make sure everything was where it needed to be before he left. Grabbing his luggage and then locking the door, he could hear the taxi horn. He moved quickly and waved to get the driver's attention. He handed his luggage to the driver who placed it in the trunk. Then from the corner of his eyes, who did he spot parked on the other side of the street under a huge shaded tree as if he was trying to hide? Detective Kelly. But this time Joe was actually pleased Kelly was able to see that he was really leaving. It made his story so much more believable, which bought him and Zach some time to investigate the Rose case further.

Joe hoped Zach was able to get all of his reservations together for the evening's flight. When the taxi drove off, Joe covertly kept his eyes on the patrol car to see if it would move. Just as he suspected, the patrol car began to follow the taxi to the airport, but this did not surprise him one bit because that was how Detective Kelly operated. The patrol car followed the taxi all the way to the airport and left when he entered the terminal. Joe let out a deep sigh of relief as he boarded the plane.

The plane landed safely in Florida. Joe felt Florida's heat on the airplane after the pilot turned off the plane's engine. He did not take the heat too well so he turned on the fan above his head while he waited for the seat belt signal to turn off. Once the alarm alerted everyone that they could exit the plane, he took his carry-on bag from the overhead compartment and quickly departed the plane.

Heading towards the baggage claim area, Joe noticed his niece. He thought she was the prettiest girl growing up, but now she was even more beautiful as a grown woman.

"Mia!" he shouted, and waved her over to him.

Mia waved back and ushered her family to follow her. Both Joe and Mia ran into each other's arms and embraced one another for a couple of seconds until Mia's daughter, Avery, pulled on her mother's shirt, as if to say did you forget about me.

"Oh sorry, Avery. It's just that I have not seen your Uncle Joe in years. Uncle Joe, this is Avery, your great niece who is now nine years old, and this is your six-year-old great nephew, Jeffrey Jr., but everyone calls him Junior. The last time you saw the kids, Uncle Joe, they were three and eleven months old."

"Oh my goodness! You are absolutely right," replied Joe. "Where is Jeff?"

"Oh, he is in the car. We did not want to pay for parking. Let's get your luggage and meet Jeff right outside."

"Okay, these are my bags. We are all set," stated Joe.

"Let's go meet Jeff. Hopefully, he did not turn off the car because it is really hot. Uncle Joe, you told me that a friend of yours was also coming to stay with us. Did he change his mind or does he have a later flight?"

"I believe Zach's flight is scheduled to arrive around 7:00 p.m. but it could be later; I'm not sure. He will give me a call to confirm that his flight is leaving on time."

"Okay," replied Mia. "There's Jeff."

Mia pointed to the family's car.

"Hello there, Uncle Joe! How are you? You look fantastic. It seems life is treating you very well," Jeff said as he reached for Joe's luggage.

"I'm doing okay. I'm not sure if Mia told you about some PI work that I'm working on for a friend."

"In fact, she has, and that is not a problem. Hopefully you will be able to clear your head while you are with us and be able to focus better on the important things that will help you solve the case."

"Thanks!" replied Joe.

When they arrived at Mia's house, Mia gave Avery and Junior the job of showing their Uncle Joe to his room and to where his friend would be sleeping. Both children laughed as they jumped out of the car as quickly as they could and told Uncle Joe to follow them. As they ran up the stairs, Joe asked them to slow down since he could not keep up with them.

As Joe was walking up the stairs, Mia said, "Uncle Joe, I will prepare a snack for you until dinner is ready because I know they do not feed you on those flights any longer."

Sounding extremely grateful, Joe replied, "Thanks!"

Both children were now at the top of the stairs telling Joe to hurry up so that they can show him his room. He held onto his carry-on bag while Jeff carried the rest of his luggage up the stairs. As he entered the guest room, both of the kids were playing karate until their father ordered them to stop and go down stairs and help their mother in the kitchen.

Joe could smell the food. Whatever Mia was cooking downstairs, had the entire house smelling good. Joe could not wait to dig his fork into it. After putting away his clothing, his phone rang. It was Zach.

"Hey, Zach, how are you looking?"

"I'm okay. My flight is on schedule and should land at 7:00 p.m. Where should we meet up?"

"Well, it seems that Mia, my niece, does not like to pay for parking at the airport so we can meet at the baggage claim area."

"Okay, so I'll see you then," replied Zach.

Joe went downstairs and nibbled on the snack Mia prepared for him until dinner was ready. Joe felt at home around his family, as he laughed and played with the children. Time seemed to pass quickly and it was time for the last meal of the day. Mia called everyone into the kitchen and placed a dinner plate before everyone; there was much talking and laugher at the dinner table while everyone enjoyed their meals.

Joe looked at his watch and said, "Oh wow. We have to pick up my friend, Zach, in another thirty minutes; his flight comes in at seven."

"Uncle Joe, Jeff will take you to the airport because I'm going to get the kids ready for bed."

"Ah man," replied Avery, "I wanted to go see Uncle Zach too."

Both Mia and Joe smirked at each other because she referred to Zach as her uncle as well.

Mia said, "If it is not too late, we'll introduce Uncle Zach to you before you fall asleep."

She looked at her husband and knew that once the kids had a bath, it was a wrap; they would fall straight to sleep.

"Uncle Joe, let's go pick up your friend, Zach."

"I'm ready, Jeff. Thanks so much. I really appreciate you taking the time out to pick up my friend as well."

"You're welcome," replied Jeff.

Finally they arrived at the airport and Jeff stated, "I'll wait here while you get your friend."

"Thanks again. I'll only be a couple of minutes."

"No problem. Take your time!"

Zach spotted Joe as he entered the doors of the airport, but just in case, he had his cell phone in hand if he needed to call him and let him know that he had landed safely. Joe also spotted Zach afar and walked over to him. He greeted him with a handshake and hug.

"Glad to see you had a safe flight. Were you comfortable?"

Zach said, "As comfortable as one can get on those flights."

"Okay, great. If these are the only bags you have, then we can be on our way."

"Yes, this is it, Joe. I'm ready as well."

Both gentlemen approached Jeff's car.

Joe said, "Jeff, I would like you to meet a friend of mine - Zach. This is my nephew Jeff, my niece Mia's husband."

"How do you do, Zach?" Jeff grabbed Zach's hand with a firm Florida grip.

"Fine. Nice to make your acquaintance and boy, do you have a strong handshake!" replied Zach as he rubbed his hand.

"I have two kids at home who have adopted you as their uncle, so do not think it strange if they call you Uncle Zach," said Jeff.

"That's no problem at all. I love kids and most of the time they love me too."

As they drove to the house, Jeff said, "Uncle Joe, we have a bunch of family members coming over tomorrow, and they are delighted that you are in town."

"What? Are you kidding me?" Joe exclaimed.

"No, I wanted you to be prepared and they are very upset that you chose to stay at Mia's house and not theirs. So get ready because they are going to attack you the moment they see you at the cookout tomorrow. I'm just warning you so be prepared to defend yourself."

"Oh no! You shouldn't have gone through all this trouble preparing a big cookout on my behalf."

"Uncle Joe, we knew you were going to say that so we waited until you arrived in Florida to tell you. After all, no one has seen you in ages."

"So, who's coming tomorrow and why do I have to explain that I choose to visit my favorite niece?" asked Joe.

"We also felt the family was getting smaller and everyone was getting up in age, so we are taking this opportunity to have a mini-family reunion cookout for the weekend. Unfortunately, not everyone can come. Your sisters and their families will be here and your brother and his family will be here as well. In fact, your sister, Melanie, is in charge of picking up some of your elderly aunts, uncles and cousins since, as you well know, she and her husband have their own bus company so transportation was covered."

Joe was not really feeling up to a lot of company; he just wanted to come and clear his head while working on the Rose family case.

"Wow! I cannot even spend time with my favorite niece without the whole family joining in on the fun. Jeff, I do not want to sound ungrateful. I just thought my niece and I were going to play catch up, but thanks for being thoughtful."

"No problem, Uncle Joe. I guess we should have cleared it with you first."

"Nonsense," replied Joe. "This is your house and you can do whatever you want."

"Oh, Zach, before I forget, my wife saved you a dinner plate. It's on the stove, so after you get cleaned up and put away your things, Mia can heat up the plate for you."

"Oh great because I'm starving," claimed Zach while Joe looked in his direction with a no comment expression on his face.

When they arrived at the house, Zach could not believe how big the house was and said, "Jeff, you have a lovely home."

"Thanks for the compliment. Joe, can you please show Zach to his room? Zach, come down when you're ready."

"Yeah, Zach," added Joe, "I don't want my niece to feel as if she has to dedicate all her time serving us, although she probably will not have a problem doing it."

While Zach was upstairs settling down, Joe took it upon himself to go downstairs to heat up Zach's plate, but surprisingly, Mia had already beaten him to it and was setting the table for Zach.

"Hey there, Uncle Joe," she said, "I was just heating up your friend's meal in the microwave."

"Oh no, Mia, you do not have to do that. I may not know how to cook like you, but I can at least operate a microwave. Go, get the kids and yourself ready for bed. We can handle our own meals while we are here."

"No such thing! You are my guests, and I will not have it any other way. I want to make sure that you both are comfortable in my house."

Zach interrupted their conversation when he came into the kitchen rubbing both hands together saying, "Okay, what's for dinner?"

Mia graciously smiled and introduced herself as she shook his hand.

"Baked chicken served with yellow rice and black beans. Nice to make your acquaintance."

"Likewise," replied Zach, "And thanks for welcoming me into your lovely home with your family."

"It's our pleasure. Enjoy your dinner and our home."

As she got ready to leave the kitchen to attend to household tasks before going to bed, she said, "Oh, by the way, Uncle Joe, did Jeff inform you that you will have a lot of company tomorrow?"

"Yeah, I'm afraid so," he responded with a disappointed look on his face.

"Oh cheer up! It will be fun, Uncle Joe. We haven't been together since my wedding! Well, gentlemen, good night and if you should need anything, please feel free to knock on my door and let me know."

Joe got up and continued to thank his niece for allowing them to stay at her house. He kissed her good night. Zach, on the other hand, was totally oblivious to what Joe was saying as he gulped down his glass of fresh lemonade trying to rinse down a mouth full of food.

"Earth to Zach, you can come up for air," Joe teasingly laughed.

"I'm starving and I was just about to get one of those hunger headaches if I did not eat something soon."

"Okay. We'll see you gentlemen in the morning." Jeff quickly walked away.

Zach looked at Joe and said, "So you will have a house full of family members tomorrow?"

"Yeah. You'll get a chance to meet some of my dysfunctional, oops I mean, my loving family members." Joe fixed his face with a crooked smile.

"Oh come on, man. It should really be fun," replied Zach.

"Oh, you just wait and see. After meeting my family, I will be curious to see if you will still feel the same way."

Finally the late hour began to wear on them. When their eyes got heavy and they could not take it any longer, they decided to call it a night.

The next day, Zach totally regretted not lowering the shades in his room before going to bed because the brightness from Florida's sunrays felt as if they were literally lifting up his eyelids. They were so powerful. He put his head underneath the covers, but it did not help. So Zach had no other option but to get out of bed. That was when he heard a lot of noise coming from outside.

When he walked towards the same window that let in the uninvited sun's rays to his room, he saw a spectacular view of the backyard. It was beautifully decorated with tables, chairs, and different colored hanging light fixtures. Now he had a willingness to get dressed and go downstairs and help out.

"Good morning!" everyone shouted.

"How did you sleep?" asked Mia.

Zach blatantly replied, "I would have slept longer if it wasn't for the sun which interrupted my sleep."

Joe pretended to moan and groan that his eyes were hurting from the sunlight that peeked through his window also. Everyone laughed.

"Sorry that the sun interrupted your sleep this morning. Come sit down. We were about to enjoy breakfast outside," said Jeff.

"Thanks," replied Zach as he sat at the table feeling a little awkward and regretting that he appeared like a child complaining.

But then, knowing how good a cook Mia was, he quickly brushed it off. He practically devoured all the food that was on his plate as soon as she put it in front of him.

Joe, trying to distract everyone from looking at how Zach was eating, asked his niece, "So when is everyone expected to arrive?" and then shamefully lowered his head because he really did not want all of this company or attention.

"Ah come on, Uncle Joe. We are going to have a ball. It will be good to see everyone and they will especially be glad to see you too. The majority should arrive around 12:30 or 1:00. If you do not cheer up, I'm going to ask Avery and Junior to teach you how to put on a happy face."

Everyone smiled.

Mia was right. Once the whole family arrived, it was good to see everyone and they were glad to see Joe as well. They had a ball together. They laughed about the good old times. Melanie, Joe's oldest sister, told the story about Joe when he was a little boy and knew how to draw extremely well. He played an April Fool's Day joke on his parents, by drawing a picture of a television screen all cracked up.

Melanie said, "My parents were livid and the only thing that saved Joe was me running over to the television set and snatching the paper off. We started yelling, 'It was an April Fool's joke, Daddy,' as both of our parents looked dumb-founded at each other. My father went out of his way to put Joe in a gifted after-school program for talented young artists."

Everyone laughed reminiscing on the story.

To entertain the children and get them away from their cellphones, they played Twisted Me Up, a game with large colorful squares drawn on a long plastic sheet and a spinner board. The spinner had the same colorful squares drawn on it as the plastic sheet and determined where the players had to place their hands and feet after each spin. Joe figured he would show the children how to play by participating with them, but little did he know that sometimes our minds tell us one thing, while our bodies tell us something altogether different.

Melanie spun the spinner and the children placed their feet and hands on the color square she called out. Melanie spun again and she called out the color. Joe tried to move but his back locked on him.

"Help! I can't move!" he shouted.

Everybody thought that he was joking until he shouted again in a more serious tone. All of the children moved off the plastic sheet and eventually the men got him back into a comfortable position where he was able to stand. They stretched his back. Boy oh boy, all the family members with cellphones got a kick recording this event and posting it on social media.

Settling down, Joe sat still and admired how big all of his great nieces and nephews had grown over the years. He introduced Zach to his brother, John, and his wife, Monica, their son, Bruce, and, Mia who was the oldest. Then he introduced him to his sister, Melanie, the oldest, and her husband, Richard and their four children: Tia, Marshal, Richard Jr. and Russell. He introduced Zach to his younger sister, Stephanie, and her husband, James, as well. Zach fit right in as if he were a part of the family and Joe was especially proud how everyone made him feel like he was family.

# CHAPTER NINETEEN

Joe's cousin, Shirley, approached Zach. After Joe introduced them, she said, "Don't I know you from somewhere?"

Zach politely smiled and said, "I do not recall meeting you before nor does your face look familiar."

"Yes, we have met," insisted Shirley.

Zach, however, was just as adamant as she was and said, "I assure you that we have never met before. I'm good at remembering faces."

Shirley asked, "Don't you live in Florida?"

Then Joe interrupted the conversation and told his cousin that she had mistaken Zach for someone else because he lives in Atlanta, Georgia.

"Oh okay. Perhaps you are right. Maybe I'm getting you confused with someone else. Please forgive me."

"Don't worry. It happens all the time. People are constantly confusing me with someone else," replied Zach.

Joe's cousin kept staring at Zach. Then she walked up to him again and said, "I do remember you. We met downtown at a party and we dated for about two weeks and then I did not hear from you any longer."

Zach's eyes opened so wide that he thought they were going to pop out of his head and roll onto the grass.

"What! I'm sorry, Shirley, but I never dated any women in the state of Florida in my entire life. Perhaps you should join in on the fun with your family and forget you ever met me," he said as he pointed at everyone doing the electric-slide dance.

She extended her hand, but Zach refused because there was no way he was going to dance with this crazy woman who thought that they dated each other before. He shook his head no, but she stood there pleading with him hoping she could change his mind. Joe noticed that his cousin was harassing Zach again so he kindly took cousin Shirley by the hand and led her onto the grassy area where everyone was dancing.

After a few minutes, Joe left her dancing by herself since she started going off and doing her own thing. She was dancing weirdly, like she was climbing up a tree. Although Joe was up in age, he knew there was no such dance in style like the way Shirley was moving. She started bending her body forward and shaking her head back and forth as quickly as she could. She fell to the grass as she kept losing her balance. But each time, she managed to get right back up and perform the same steps over again.

Joe walked over and tilted Zach's chair. Zach had two choices: either fall to the ground or catch his balance and stand up.

Knowing that Zach would stand up, Joe said, "Everyone must join in on the family dance. Come on, join in on the fun!"

Zach tried as hard as he could to keep up with the young people, but he was lost. Seeing him struggle to keep up, Shirley tiptoed towards him. Suddenly, he felt an arm interlocking with his. He turned to see who it was and it was Shirley invading his personal space. Zach quickly pushed his arm away and found a seat in the corner in hopes that she would not find him.

But she kept her eyes on him the entire time as she laughed and shouted, "You do not want to admit it, but you know we know each other."

She let out a spooky laugh.

Joe walked over to where Zach was sitting and Zach said, "Both Mia and Jeff did an outstanding job in putting everything together. This will be a memorable moment for years to come. Just yesterday, the back yard seemed so lifeless, but not now, with all of the excitement going on. Wow, if this was just the first day, what are Mia and Jeff going to do to top this and make the second day as extravagant and elegant?"

"Only tomorrow will tell," Joe replied.

It was late and most people left. Both Zach and Joe were feeling exhausted so they made their way to their bedrooms. The women pitched in and helped Mia clean up; they put away all the food and washed the few dishes that were used.

Day two was just as delightful. "What a blast" were the only words Joe could think of to describe everything. As the sun started to set, it was obvious that everyone was anxious to return to their homes before it got too dark. Warm embraces filled the house and slowly everybody's laughter turned into grateful tears as they reminisced about the two days of marvelous family fun. As everyone said their good-byes, Joe looked around. He was happy, but he remembered why they were there in the first place. The urge of getting back to the disappearance of the Rose family laid heavily on his mind.

Jeff interrupted Joe's thoughts when he patted him on the back and said, "Now, that was not so bad, was it?"

"Not at all," replied Joe. "Actually, it was great and I'm glad I had the chance to see everyone again because my aunts, uncles and some of my cousins are really up in age now. Thank you again for all you and Mia did to make our stay here worthwhile."

Jeff said, "It was our pleasure."

He asked Joe and Zach to help him put away the large outdoor furniture.

The next morning, Zach heard loud talking coming from the kitchen area. He went downstairs to see if everyone was eating breakfast. Sure enough, everyone, including Joe, was sitting at the kitchen table eating breakfast.

"There's the sleepy head," said Joe as everyone said good morning. Mia told him to sit while she prepared him a hot cup of coffee.

"Okay thanks. I certainly can use some coffee to start the day."

Zach selected a chair next to Joe, feeling embarrassed again for being the last one to awaken.

Changing the subject, Joe asked, "Is there a public library close by?"

"Yes, there is a library just three blocks from the house," replied Jeff.

"Great," said Joe. "If you can point us in the right direction, we can take it from there."

"Actually, I can drop the both of you off if you like," replied Jeff.

"No way," Zach replied with the biggest grin on his face. "We are perfectly capable of walking three blocks on this beautiful Sunday morning. Besides, we would like to see other parts of the neighborhood."

"Okay. I get the message. You gentlemen have business to attend to and would like to be alone so I'll write down the directions. Do not hesitate to call me if you need anything."

"Thanks," replied Joe, "don't make lunch or dinner for us because we probably will not come back until after dinner time."

"Do you want me to prepare something for you to snack on?" asked Mia.

"No, that won't be necessary. Thank you, sweetie," Joe said.

Joe and Zach spent many hours going over what their next course of action would be in Houston. Each day they had a different agenda. First and foremost, they booked their flight at the most affordable price. Second, they reserved a cheap, but classy rental car. Third, they booked a hotel that was close in proximity to the Beeker Boulevard house at 175-05, the house on Mother Rose's deed. Joe was very particular about the hotel; he liked it to be very clean and upscale. Last, they spent the majority of their time researching Beeker Boulevard on the Internet and everything that was nearby. The house appeared to be on a very quiet and peaceful block that was monitored by a block association.

Before they knew it, it was time to leave. Monday finally arrived. Jeff and Mia wouldn't have it any other way, but to escort them to the airport. Knowing how stubborn his niece was, Joe did not argue. He and Zach thanked them for their hospitality. At the airport, there were good-bye hugs, kisses, some teary eyes and excitement. Joe and Zach walked through the security gate and they knew that there was no turning back. No matter what happened in Texas, they knew God was the only One who would be able to protect them.

Waking up to the sound of clicking seat buckles, Zach opened his eyes, and saw Joe removing their luggage from the overhead compartment. They had safely landed in Houston.

"It is about time you woke up, sleepyhead. I thought I would have to pour some of my bottled water on your head," Joe said jokingly. "I figured we could get the rental car first, then make our way to the hotel and grab something to eat. What do you think, Zach? Does that sound okay to you?"

Stretching Zach said, "Sure. That is perfect because I'm starving."

"Yeah, yeah. Come to think about it, you are always starving. I never met anyone who eats as much as you do."

Zach reminded Joe to call his niece once they were off the plane.

"Thanks." He pulled out his cellphone. "I better do it now before I forget or I will never hear the end of it.

Stepping off the plane and into the airport terminal, Joe and Zach noticed cowboy boots on almost everyone's feet along with cowboy hats, cowboy shirts and fancy belt buckles. Even some of the girls and women wore cowgirl dresses with cowgirl accessories. But the most noticeable was the sun's blazing heat. It covered them like a blanket in the wintertime.

*Boy it is hot!* Thought Zach.

Joe pointed to the car rental area across from the terminal and they started walking in that direction.

In Florida, they did some research and found Texas Rental Riders, which offered the best rates for a week. They reserved a black SUV. All they had to do was pick up the keys to the car. The sales representative quickly gave them the keys and thanked them for their business. They decided during their earlier conversation that it would be best to have GPS in the car to help guide them around Houston, especially to find the mysterious Beeker Boulevard house.

When they arrived at the hotel, Zach looked on with amazement to see that this retired man had booked them into a five-star, top of the line hotel. He was impressed that Joe booked them into this fabulous hotel.

Zach turned to Joe and said, "Not a bad choice at all!" He jumped out of the black SUV. "Joe, thanks for paying for everything. I just want you to know that we will settle all of the expenses when we get back to Georgia and I will pay you back every penny."

"No problem," replied Joe. "I trust you and besides, I know where you live!" He laughed.

"Isn't it strange how we both barely knew each other and have been living in the same neighborhood for years, but it was the incident with the Rose family that not only brought us together but also changed our lives forever? We've known about each other for years, but now we're traveling together as if we were traveling buddies all along."

Joe totally agreed with Zach and commented that he believed they were not meant to meet each other until this appointed time.

Joe and Zach felt at home on the 17th floor when they entered into their luxury hotel room. The living room was huge with a burgundy leather love seat and two matching chairs. The windows were extremely wide with a view overlooking a bridge and tall buildings, casting sun-setting shadows in the fading sunlight.

Zach walked into the bedroom. Joe followed. Both could not be-lieve how elegantly appointed the bedroom was. The bathroom was the largest they had ever seen. The kitchen area was a very nice size as well.

"Wow!" said Zach as he plopped his entire body onto the bed that he had chosen for himself. "This one is mine!" he shouted like a little kid as Joe smiled and headed towards the other queen bed. "The down comforters on the bed are extremely soft and I cannot wait until my body is underneath them. Joe, as beautiful as the room may be, I'm tired of looking at it, so can we go get something to eat because my stomach is crying?"

"Hey, I have an idea. Let's go to one of the restaurants in the hotel tonight. This way we will go straight to our room after we eat," suggest-ed Joe.

Zach agreed and said, "Joe, on a serious note, we need to stop and think about what our course of action will be for tomorrow."

"You're right. Maybe we should drive past the house today and see what it looks like and see if anyone is coming out of the house."

"Well, that is the smartest thing you said all day, Zach. Come on, let's take a ride and then we can get something to eat or do you think your stomach needs to eat right now?"

"I'm fine. Let's go!" replied Zach.

On Beeker Boulevard, they looked at the house with the address of 175-05. It did not look like what they had expected at all. The house was colonial and kept up very well considering Mother Rose had not lived in it for years. The house was surrounded with a beautiful gate. Surpris-ingly, there was no driveway given the size of the house. Just looking at the house, it spelled privacy and seemed lifeless and lonely. Joe and Zach watched it from the corner for almost thirty minutes. No one left or went inside; nothing was going on with this house.

Zach said, "Let's come back in the morning."

Suddenly, a black SUV pulled up in front of the house. Zach im-mediately pulled out his miniature binoculars to get a look at the person getting out, but he did not recognize the gentleman.

"Zach, do you remember the description Mother Rose's neighbor gave you of the second man?"

"Yeah. Both Deacon Brown and Mother Rose's neighbor, Mr. Harold, said all they remembered about the second man was that he wore all black."

"Well, I believe we may have found someone fitting that description." Joe took down the license plate number, and the make and model of the SUV. "This information can help identify who this individual is, or at least, who owns that car. Zach, we have enough information for the day. Let's get something to eat."

Zach couldn't agree more as his stomach kept growling quite loudly. They drove back to their hotel, and parked the car. Just looking at all the other cars, they knew they were not the only ones who felt this was a nice hotel. They entered the Steak & Grill Restaurant, which was in the center of the hotel, and soon realized that others thought the restaurant was a convenient place to eat. After being seated and ordering their food, both enjoyed eating and conversing over their meals.

"Zach, come to think about it, I have a friend who lives in Houston. Wow, I totally forgot about Oscar and you are not going to believe where he works."

"Where?" replied Zach.

"He happens to work for the Department of Motor Vehicles and I'm sure he would help me out on getting information on this guy."

"Man, I do not believe you. Tell me you are pulling my leg right now?"

"No, I'm dead serious, Zach. I will contact him in the morning and see if he will be able to dig up information on the guy or the car. This way we can place a name with a face."

"Okay, I'll believe it when you get the information. That is too much of a coincidence. I'm sorry, Joe."

Shaking his finger at Zach, he said, "You'll see." After they finished eating, Joe said, "Dinner was good and relaxing, but I think that we made pigs of ourselves."

They left the table and walked to the elevators.

Riding in the elevator, Zach said, "I cannot wait to sleep in that bed. It was calling my name earlier and has not stopped." He closed his eyes and rubbed his full belly.

Morning came. Zach slowly peeked out from under his comforter with a skeptical look on his face as he wondered if the sunlight invited itself into his hotel room like it did at Mia and Jeff's house. Confirming there was no sunlight, he mentally applauded and admired the room for its natural light and warmth. He had a hospitable night's sleep.

Joe was lying on his back in his bed thinking about the day ahead of them and wondering if this would be the day the Rose family would be found.

"Oh, you are awake," Zach said.

"Yes. I could not sleep wondering if we were, in fact, looking at one of Mother Rose's relatives last night. I also was wondering if he lives alone in the house or if there were other family members living there as well. I cannot wait to find out what his name is and how old he is."

Joe had more questions than he had answers running though his mind, but was hoping that Oscar would be able to assist.

Joe noticed, "Today seems like it will be a great day weather wise to conduct our investigation without Mother Nature interfering."

"Rain or no rain, my umbrella accompanies me wherever I go," Zach said as he walked to the bathroom to get dressed.

# CHAPTER TWENTY

Joe decided to contact his friend at the Department of Motor Vehicles.

"Hello, may I please speak to Oscar Ryan?"

"Sir, he can no longer be reached at this number. What is this call in reference to? May I help you?"

"No," replied Joe.

"What is your name before I switch you over to his new line?"

"I'm a friend and my name is Joseph Walker."

"Hold on, please." As Joe waited he tried thinking when was the last time he had spoken to Oscar. It had to be more than ten years.

Breaking his chain of thoughts, Joe refocused when he heard a male voice.

"Hello, this is Oscar Ryan."

"Hello, Oscar. This is Joe. How are you these days?"

"You mean Joe, Mr. PI Joe? Is this really you? What a surprise to hear from you. I thought you retired."

"Yes, I did retire, but now I'm helping out a close friend so you can say that I'm back in the business for a while. But I'm doing fine. How about you and the family? Is everyone okay?"

"Thanks for asking. Everyone is great. I know you want something, Mr. PI. What can I do for you?"

"Sorry, Oscar, but I really need you to run a plate for me. I believe it should be registered in Houston, Texas."

"No need to apologize. I am forever grateful to you for helping my family. Give me the numbers and I can call you back. Joe, is this your cellphone number?"

"Yes. Thanks so much, Oscar. I'll await your call." Twenty minutes later, Joe's cellphone rang and it was Oscar with information.

"Hi Joe. So here is the name of the person who the vehicle is registered to. Her name is…"

"Wait, did you say her?"

"Yes, her name is Wendy X. Harris. She lives at 175-05 Beeker

Boulevard."

"What?" replied Joe, "I saw a gentleman driving the car. What about insurance records? Can you check to see if there's an additional driver listed, Oscar?"

"I can, but as we both know, there will probably not be any additional drivers because insurance is already expensive and adding another name to your insurance policy would raise the price."

"You are right," replied Joe as he breathed with frustration. "Perhaps we will get lucky."

"Sure, give me a few more minutes and I will call you back."

Ten minutes later, Oscar called Joe.

"No other name appeared on the insurance policy; only Wendy X. Harris."

"Thanks again, Oscar. You were very helpful to me. By the way, I'm in town. Perhaps we can get together and grab some lunch before I go back."

"Yes we must. I'll keep in touch. Good hearing from you even if it was only related to business."

"Take care," replied Joe.

"You too."

Joe turned to Zach. "We still don't know who the gentleman we saw last night was, but now we have to add someone else to our list."

"Who?" asked Zach.

"The owner of the vehicle is a woman and her name is Wendy X. Harris."

Thinking aloud, Zach said, "Maybe she could be the person who kept up the house these many years."

"Yes, that is a good point. Hopefully we will see her come out of the house today. Zach, we need to watch the house for at least one full day to see if there are more than two people living there. So I suggest we go to a local grocery store and stock up on sandwiches or sandwich meat and bread. Lots of liquid to drink and plenty of snacks, but most importantly, we will need to locate some place nearby to use the restroom."

"Okay," replied Zach, "So this is what the police and private investigators call a stakeout?"

"Yes, but believe me, it is not as fun as you think because there can be no movement for five to six hours, and you must constantly watch your target or you will miss them the moment he or she decides to move."

Sounding like a rookie, Zach said, "I'm ready! Let's do this!" He slapped his hand against his chest like he was Superman or some other super hero.

Joe thought about the saying "be careful what you ask for; you just might get it." Instead he said, "Most of the morning has already gone by so the perfect stakeout day will start tomorrow at 12:00 a.m."

Zach swiftly turned his head and said, "What time?"

"Zach, we need one complete day in order to record all of the Beeker Boulevard house activities and the only way to do that is by watching the house for twenty-four hours."

"Now I see what you mean by keeping an eye on our target," replied Zach. "Boy, are we going to have a lot of fun! We better go shopping now, Joe, and pick up the things we need for tomorrow."

The alarm went off at 11:30 p.m. Both gentlemen jumped out of bed like they were being drilled in the service. Joe, moving with haste, wanted to make sure that they arrived to their destination at exactly midnight and not one minute later.

Driving ten miles per hour over the speed limit, they arrived at the house at exactly one minute prior to midnight. It seemed as if the house itself was sleeping along with its owner. In fact, all the houses on the block seemed like they were in sleep mode. Zach spotted the SUV parked in front of the house, and also noticed a white van parked next to the house as well.

Joe said, "Let me take down that information as well. Maybe this van belongs to an unknown second suspect."

Time seemed to pass slowly for Zach because he was very anxious for some action to happen. Joe, on the other hand, took this opportunity to shut his eyes for a couple of minutes. After about four hours, a light in the house came on in the basement.

Zach tapped Joe. "Oh boy! Things are finally about to happen."

They both thought that it was a very odd time of the night for someone to turn on the light in the basement. The light stayed on for at least one hour.

Two more hours went by and it was now 6:00 a.m. Almost all the lights upstairs in the house were now on, and the house seemed awake and ready to start its day. At first, there was only one shadow moving around, but suddenly another appeared and there were two people moving around in the house. One hour later, the door of the house swung open and a woman walked down the steps and slid into her black SUV and drove away.

"We should follow her, Joe. This way we will get to know more about her."

"No, Zach. I think that is a bad idea. Right now, we need to stay at this house and see all who come in and leave out! Please excuse my shouting, but I strongly believe with all my heart that many of our unanswered questions are right inside this house and will lead us to solving the case of the disappearance of the Rose family."

"No, no. You're right, Joe. I understand that we cannot be all over the place and lose our concentration. Besides, it is your professional instincts that I want to follow. After all, you are the expert here and I'm the amateur."

"Thanks for understanding. Let me give Oscar a call later and see if he can provide me with additional details concerning Wendy X. Harris." Zach nodded his head in total agreement. "So let's continue to watch the house because now we know that both a male and female are living in the house that belongs to Mother Rose."

Thirty minutes later the door of the house opened, but this time it was the young man who Zach and Joe saw yesterday. He wore only his house robe, pajamas and slippers. Zach and Joe noticed the amount of garbage he was placing in the garbage can, which seemed to be a lot for just two people. He rushed back inside the house, but suspiciously looked to his right and left before closing the door. Joe immediately picked up on how he was acting; it was almost as if he was hiding from someone.

Switching the subject and focusing on his stomach's needs again, Zach asked, "Joe, would you like a sandwich to eat and something to drink?"

"Sure. What kinds of sandwiches are left?"

Zach rummaged through the disposable cooler and said, "We have turkey and cheese, salami and cheese and roast beef sandwiches left." Apologizing, Zach admitted to Joe that he had eaten all of the tuna fish sandwiches, which really tasted great.

"That's okay, Zach. Just give me a turkey and cheese sandwich with a soda and it doesn't matter what flavor. You can just surprise me." He looked at Zach.

While eating their sandwiches, Joe saw that the young man was on the move again, but this time he was fully dressed. He opened the door to the white van that had been sitting dormant since they arrived. Zach remembered to record the license plate using some miniature binoculars that Joe brought along.

"Hopefully, we can get his name now and will be able to place a face with the license plate numbers," Zach said. As the van slowly drove away, Joe continued to eat his sandwich while still looking at the van until he could no longer see it.

"Joe, do you want me to take a look around before he comes back?"

"Absolutely not," replied Joe. "We first have to determine if there is anyone else living in the house."

"Oh okay. There I go again trying to blow our cover."

They watched the house for another two hours, but there was no movement in it at all. It was as if the house was back in sleep mode. All of a sudden, Joe spotted the white van in the review mirror.

"Duck!" he shouted. "The white van is at the light behind us Zach and it will be passing our vehicle shortly!"

As the van passed, Zach and Joe were all the way down in their seats to make sure the driver did not spot them. But the young man driving the van did not even look their way. He parked the van right back in the same spot.

Once the engine was turned off, he got out of the van, and still monitoring his surroundings, quickly walked to the back of the van, opened the doors and unloaded bags of groceries. Zach and Joe watched him unload a lot of shopping bags. They began counting the bags and there were a total of thirty grocery bags, which definitely seemed odd for just two people. Although unable to confirm their suspicion right away, they had a gut feeling that there were more than two people living in the house! They felt they were on the right path and just needed to produce the evidence.

Joe's cellphone started vibrating, and after looking at the Caller ID, Joe realized it was his friend, Oscar, with information on the white van.

"Good morning, Joe. It's Oscar. I just wanted to let you know that the van is also registered to a Wendy X. Harris under that same address."

"Wow, what a bummer. Okay Oscar, thanks again for your assistance. I thought that I would be able to answer some unanswered questions. It looks like this new job is going to be more involved and needs my undivided attention. If I do not get the chance to call you back, I will certainly give you a call when I'm in Atlanta."

"It's no problem, Joe. It was my pleasure to help a friend out. Please be careful and take care."

"Sure, I will."

"If you do not leave by Sunday, give me a call and I can arrange for you to have dinner with my wife and family. She would love to see you again!"

"Thanks for the invitation. I just might take you up on your offer. I could use a good home-cooked meal, but I will definitely call to confirm. Take care and enjoy your day."

Zach nudged Joe after he hung up the phone and told him that the basement light came on about ten minutes ago, but so far he had only seen the movement of one person.

"Perhaps he's storing food down in the basement or someone is living down there," surmised Joe. "Zach, I think it's time that we started using some of your professional skills by knocking out their electrical power, and then you can disguise yourself as an electrician so you can get into the house."

Zach rubbed his hands together and shouted, "All right! Now that sounds like a plan because I have been waiting for some major action." His eyes gleamed. "No offense, Joe, but all we have been doing is watching a house, a van and a SUV."

"Okay, calm down and listen. Here is the plan. We will still watch the house for one more complete day and make absolutely sure there is no one else living inside the house except for the young man and lady. At midnight, we will go back to the hotel and get about three hours of sleep, come back here and then confirm that their routine is the same as today. One thing we know is that there is movement in the house around 4:00 a.m. and thereafter. So, providing the young man does not leave the house anymore that day, we can probably start making plans on getting downstairs into the basement to confirm our suspicions."

As they were talking, the lights went out in the basement and there was no more activity down there until after the young lady came home around 5:30 p.m. She literally parked the black SUV in the exact spot it was in that morning.

"This block does not have much activity throughout the day. We should feel lucky because if it did, someone would have spotted us by now," said Joe.

Still watching the basement, Zach noticed that the lights came on, stayed on for two and half hours, and then they went off. Almost every light was on until about 11:00 p.m. and then the entire house was dark, except for one room that had a flickering light, which seemed to be coming from a television set. By midnight, the entire house was back into sleep mode and no one came in or out of the house while they were watching. They decided to leave and return to the hotel.

Waking up to the sound of a loud alarm clock, Zach reached for the snooze button to quickly stop the sound and then eventually shut off the alarm. He felt as if he was asleep for only thirty minutes. Although he was still tired, he was determined—his mind made up—that this work was very important. The Rose family needed him to rescue them from whomever they were with. He got out of bed and got dressed and Joe followed.

Approaching Bleeker Boulevard, all seemed to be the same as when they left hours ago. The hours passed and everything else followed like clockwork, down to the exact hour. Joe suggested they leave early and shop around for uniform stores from which to purchase an electrician uniform for Zach, walkie-talkies for both of them, and grab something to eat for breakfast. Afterwards, they agreed that they just wanted to go to the hotel and get some proper rest since they were both up in age and sitting in a car for hours at a time was starting to wear on their bodies.

Waking up to the sounds of rain beating against the windows and a strong whistling sound of the wind tossing the trees back and forth, they knew that Mother Nature was not going to be kind to them. Joe turned on the local weather channel to get the forecast for the day—rain all day until tomorrow morning.

"Oh no," moaned Joe, "this is really going to mess up our plans for today. We may have to hold off until tomorrow afternoon."

Zach said, "Maybe not, Joe. Think about it. The rain will discourage most people from looking out their windows for a long period of time; they want to see sunshine, not rain. Also, people are inclined to stay indoors, which will give us the opportunity to disrupt the house's electrical cables and blame it on the bad weather."

"Zach, you are a genius! You are absolutely right. The bad weather may really work to our advantage."

Leaving the hotel, both gentlemen got in the car, but Joe drove slower than normal. They arrived at the house a little before Wendy was supposed to leave. Joe pointed her out—she was leaving the house at the exact time she left the day before. Minutes later, the young man came out of the house, carrying folded boxes that he placed by the recycling bin, and then ran quickly back inside the house to get out of the rain.

"Okay, Zach, it is time for you to put your skills to work and play the part of a certified electrician, but please be careful."

Zach looked at Joe, as if to say, oh now you are going to tell me how to do my job, but then he said. "I will. Don't worry."

After exiting the car, he approached the gate to the house. He attempted to open the gate, but it did not open. Zach never thought that his biggest challenge would be a locked gate. Rather than draw attention to himself, he nervously ran back to the car, hoping no one noticed him.

"What happened?" asked Joe.

Out of breath, Zach said, "You'll never believe that they have a lock on the gate and you need either a code or someone has to buzz you in."

"You've got to be kidding me, Zach! Who puts a password code on an outside gate?" Joe threw his head back onto the headrest.

"Calm down, Joe. All is not lost. I will just have to cut off all the electricity in the entire house and then walk through the gate in order to continue with our plans."

Sounding miserable and very upset, Joe asked, "How are you going to get to the electrical box if it is behind the locked gate?"

Zach said, "Now watch me work my magic."

Walking back to the house, Zach climbed over the gate and walked alongside the house and found the electrical wires. Joe could not believe how fast Zach ran back to the car. It was good that Zach did run as fast as he did because Joe saw the young man peek out the window, probably wondering if he was the only one being affected by the rain or if it was some kind of blackout in the area. To the young man's surprise, all the houses had power except for his house.

Trying to get to the house before the young man called emergency services or the electric company, Zach grabbed his tool bag and was at the top of the house stairs quicker than Joe could blink his eyes. The house door was ajar with a flashlight sticking out of it. The light shone right in Zach's face. He quickly raised his arm to block the glare and shield his eyes.

"Can I help you?" the young man asked angrily.

"Yes, my name is Mr. Phillips and there is construction up the block and they hit an electrical wire, which caused some people's electricity to go out."

"Yes! It affected my home!" replied the young man.

"Okay, do you mind if I take a look at your main box down in the basement? I would like to check to see if some wires burned out or would it simply be a flip of a switch to fix?"

The young man looked suspiciously at Zach. He asked, "Exactly what are you going to do downstairs in the basement again and how long will it take?" Zach answered all of his questions sympathetically.

The young man finally gave in and said, "Okay, come inside. Wait right here until I move some things out of the way of the main box, and I will be back."

Zach thought about forcing the young man to take him down to the basement to see if there were any signs of the Rose family, but then decided to go along with Joe's plans. He was still not one hundred percent sure if he was going to stick to every step they had discussed because if he heard one of their voices crying for help, all original bets were off. So Zach tried to listen for voices coming from the basement, but all he could hear were doors slamming shut, but for a split second he could have sworn that he heard more than one person walking around downstairs.

# CHAPTER TWENTY-ONE

Suddenly, the same uninvited flashlight was shining in his face again.

"Do you have ID on you?"

Zach was hoping he was not familiar with the Atlanta's badges as he said, "Sure. Here it is."

The young man barely read the badge because the bottom line was he wanted his power back on.

"Please follow me, sir," he said as he watched every movement Zach made and lead him to the basement. Zach had not prayed since he was a little boy, but fear gripped him and he felt a need to reach out for God's help now. Zach asked God that if this was where the Rose family was being held to please show him a sign. If they were, he asked God to make the young man leave his sight, which would give him time to check things out in the basement.

While leading Zach to the main fuse box, loud thumping sounds began coming from upstairs; they eventually intensified. The young man now had a worried look on his face.

"Sir, can you please excuse me? My dog must have locked himself inside one of the bedrooms upstairs and is trying to get out."

"Sure," replied Zach as he looked up and thanked God and let out a sigh of relief. Then he remembered that most dogs bark when a stranger enters their home so Zach knew that the young man was lying and he had to move fast.

He whispered into the walkie-talkie. "Joe, can you hear me?"

"Yes, I'm here, I did not want to say anything earlier and risk blowing your cover."

"Yeah, thanks for that. There is something happening in this house, but I'm not sure what! I'm alone in the basement for a couple of minutes. The young man fabricated some story that his dog locked himself in one of the bedrooms upstairs. But what if that is where Mother Rose and the girls are locked up? Should I take on the young man and confirm my suspicions?"

"No Zach! In order to fully investigate someone, you must gain his or her trust. What if the young man overtakes you? Then everything will be jeopardized. Just take this time to learn about the setup of the basement. Tell me what you see in the basement."

"It is very dark down here and I have a little flashlight and I cannot see very much," replied Zach.

"Are there any signs of someone living down there?"

"Well, I do not see any furniture if that is what you are referring too."

"Look for doors and check inside to see if there are any indications that someone is living in the basement."

"No, it just looks like wooden panels across all the walls. I do not even see any open water bottles, paper plates, leftover food or blankets and pillows. Joe, there is no real evidence that someone is living down here. Maybe it could just be that when we see the light down here, the couple is enjoying their basement."

"Zach, you mentioned that all the walls have panels on them."

"That is correct."

"Okay. Try knocking on each wall softly so that the young man does not hear you, but hard enough to distinguish between a solid and a hollow wall."

"Sure, that is a great suggestion, Joe!"

"Because all the walls should sound the same, and let me know if you hear a spot that sounds different, but hurry because you're running out of time."

Moving as fast as he could, Zach went around the entire basement and when he knocked on the last wall, it slightly shifted.

"Joe, I think I found a wall that sounds different because it shook when I knocked on it."

"Good, Zach. What do you hear upstairs or better yet, do you hear him coming back down the stairs?"

"No, he is still upstairs because I can hear him walking around."

Just as Zach told Joe the young man was still upstairs, almost immediately, he heard a loud voice shout, "Sir, are you okay?"

Zach quickly replied, "Yes, I'm fine. Thank you. I just need a few more minutes."

"Okay," said the young man. "Please hurry. I'm really getting tired of bumping into things!"

Zach flashed the light onto the area where the wall shifted and sure enough, it appeared to be a doorway. Quietly, he tried to open the door, but it made a loud squeaky sound. He, however, managed to peek inside and it confirmed his worst thoughts—there was definitely someone living down there. Then he noticed there was a padlock hanging from the door that he did not see before due to the darkness in the basement. A television and three cots were inside the room. Strangely, an apple that was bitten into was lying on top of a box that looked like a makeshift nightstand between the cots. Zach heard footsteps walking down the stairs and quickly closed the door as quickly and quietly as possible.

Once again, the young man shined his flashlight directly into Zach's face. "Have you figured out the problem yet?"

Panicking, Zach replied, "Yes! The emergency switch automatically shut off because it sensed danger, but it should be working now. Let me go outside to check if the main junction box has been restored."

"Great! Now that is the best news I received all day long!" replied the young man.

When they reached the front door, the young man said, "So when you get down the steps, turn right just before leaving the gate and the box will be up against the lower part of the house wall." He extended his hand and said, "Thank you, sir, for your help." They shook hands.

"My pleasure!" While walking away, Zach was smiling inside because he already knew where the box was located. "Oh by the way, I probably will not come back inside the house once you give me the thumbs up that you have lights."

"That's fine," replied the young man. Then unexpectedly, he asked, "Do I need to sign any paperwork?"

Zach had not thought to bring paperwork with him. "No, you will receive an official letter from the electric company in a few days. On behalf of the company, we would like to extend our apologies and sorry for any damage that may have occurred during the power outage."

Zach turned on all the switches he previously turned off and walked back to the front of the house. There was the young man standing in the doorway with a huge grin on his face and his thumb up in the air. Zach went out the gate only this time, he simply strolled out. He did not know if the young man was still watching him, so he started walking in the direction of where he told him the construction was taking place.

Minutes later, Joe pulled off slowly and turned down the next block and met up with Zach. Very eager to speak with Joe, Zach started speaking into the walkie-talkie while he was walking.

"Joe, I know that the Rose family is there and I know that they are being held against their will in that basement room. I can just feel that they are all alive and we have to do something before it is too late! I must go back inside that house again and rescue them! I know that he moved them all to another location before he let me down into the basement which explains the several footsteps I heard coming from upstairs."

"Okay, Zach. Please calm down. We need to be positively sure because the police can only get a warrant if there is probable cause that someone is being held in the house. Let's go back to the hotel and discuss our next steps with a clear head. We would not want to come this far and blow everything because of assumptions, unverifiable evidence and mistakes."

"Thanks for bringing me back to reality, Joe. Let's lay all our cards on the table and discuss this further."

While driving back, Joe decided to follow-up with a few more questions from Zach. "Are you certain that you heard several footsteps while you were waiting?"

"Yes!" replied Zach.

"You are also certain that someone occupied that room?"

"Yes!" replied Zach. "I'm absolutely sure of everything I saw!"

"Okay," replied Joe. "Now, was there food of any kind inside that room?"

"Yes! Oh, but I did forget to tell you there was also a bowl that had fresh fruit like apples, bananas, grapes, and plums on the makeshift nightstand. One of the apples was bitten into and I know it was a fresh bite because the fruit had not begun to oxidize!"

Joe was finally convinced that there was definite activity of life occupying that room downstairs in the basement.

"Come to think about it," Zach continued, "I also remember seeing a pitcher of orange juice and a cup and saucer with a tea bag hanging from it."

"Could you see if the tea had steam rising from the cup?"

"No, it was dark."

"It's okay, Zach. You did a really great job today on your own and I'm very proud to be working with you and sorry that I keep questioning you. It's just that we need to make certain and not accuse innocent people."

Zach lowered his head as he received accolades from Joe and thanked him.

"So, we now are both confident that someone is living in the basement," Joe said. "We just need to be positive that it is the Rose family. We know that every morning around four, Wendy or the guy goes down into the basement, perhaps to feed them. If we could just find out the young man's identity, perhaps it will link him to Mother Rose."

"What do you suggest, Joe?"

"I'm thinking we go back to the house and see if we can get him to sign a document of some sort. Do you feel up to this again, Zach? If not, I will totally understand because he may get suspicious and get on the defensive side."

"What are you kidding me? I'm perfectly fine with going back inside the house especially if it will help us find out if the Rose family is there. I'm all for it!"

"Okay here are my plans. Hotels today have business centers with a computer and printer where their guests can print out boarding passes. Let's draft up a letter in the room and go downstairs and print it. We need to create some type of official letterhead from the electric company. In the letter, I think that we should indicate that the electric company is sorry for any inconvenience that the loss of electricity may have caused everyone and would like to compensate them for any losses. It needs to have a place for him to sign. This is just to throw him off and get his signature. What do you think?"

"That's a fantastic idea," replied Zach. "What kind of compensation do you have in mind?"

"I'm not sure, Zach. Maybe we can purchase a gift certificate of some sort. We can offer him a gift card to compensate for any food that may have gone bad during the outage. I'm sure he would accept the gift card even if he has to sign for it."

"Okay, I think the hotel receptionist mentioned that there is a super warehouse called Bulk-By-Bulk nearby. Maybe we can get a gift card from there."

After creating an official document, they looked up the exact location of Bulk-By-Bulk.

"Okay, Joe. Talking about food made me hungry. Do you think that we can get something to eat?"

Zach noticed that Joe's facial expression changed and Zach already knew what he was thinking.

Then Joe got serious. "I think we will stand watch one final night and then we will make our move to try and confirm our worst nightmare."

"Okay, you are calling the shots. Everything has worked out so far and I do not want to change things now."

It was midnight and Zach and Joe found themselves right back in familiar territory—staking the house they had now become familiar with. Suddenly, the front door opened and an older man stepped out of the house. It was hard to make out what he looked like because his hat was pulled down on his head and the collar of his trench coat covered most of his face.

"Look, Zach!" Joe said as he pointed towards the house. "I see we have another person in the mix. I wonder who he could be?" Joe watched his every move. " There's something familiar about his walk."

"Do you want to follow him once he gets into his car?"

"No," replied Joe. "I think we should stay focused on the house because he could just be a neighbor or even a relative stopping by who is innocent. We should focus on trying to free the Rose family if they are the ones who are occupying the room downstairs in the basement."

The older man approached his car, which was parked a block away. This seemed very odd to Joe since there were so many empty parking spots closer to the house. He quickly dismissed this thought, considering the man could have parked earlier when the spots were all filled. He noticed the lights in the entire house were now turned off.

Once again, the house and all the other houses were in sleep mode. Considering nothing changed, except for an unexpected visitor, Joe decided to leave.

"Let's get a good night's rest and pray that God will be with us tomorrow as we try to regain entry into the house."

As they drove away, Joe could not help but think about that figure of the man leaving the house and how his body build and walk reminded him of someone he knew, but who? Tiredness got the best of him and he just brushed the idea from his thoughts.

Zach felt ambitious and powered up in the morning. He was ready to take on the world. He knew that if they did not get answers soon, he would burst. Wanting to confirm if the Rose family was in the basement, he could not wait to go to the house again. They drove to the house rehearsing what to say to the young man and what not to do so he would not get suspicious. Zach felt this would be his chance to fully observe the inside of the house and notice everything since the lights would be on. When they arrived, Joe, once again, asked Zach to be careful. He parked the car in a different location across the street from the house this time.

Zach, with his work gear on and a writing tablet stocked with a pile of papers, headed for the house. When he got to the house, he remembered that the gate was locked and he couldn't just go through and knock on the door. He pressed the intercom button.

A male voice asked, "Who is there?"

"Sir, this is Mr. Phillips. I was here a couple of days ago and fixed your electricity in your home."

"Yes, I remember. How can I help you?"

"Well, the electric company would like to provide all of the residents in this neighborhood with a complimentary gift card to Bulk-By-Bulk Super Warehouse."

"Oh really? And how much is the gift card worth? I would like to know if it is worth me getting out of my warm bed."

"Well, if your lights were off for thirty minutes, you are entitled to a two hundred fifty dollar card."

"Wow! Do you have a record of how long my lights were off?" asked the young man.

"Sir, the electric company will give a five hundred dollar card to anyone whose electricity was off over thirty minutes. You are entitled to a five hundred dollar card because your lights were out for almost fifty minutes. So if you will sign for your gift card to Bulk-By-Bulk Super Warehouse, I will be on my way."

"What?" shouted the young man, "I will be right down!"

He buzzed the gate open. No sooner than Zack walked up the stairs, the house door flew open. When he stepped into the house, he realized the young man was speaking very softly as if he was preventing someone from hearing him talk. Joe slid all the way down in his car seat as he looked from a distance. As the door closed, he knew that the first part of the plan worked.

While the young man looked over the paper work, Zach took the opportunity to quickly look around the house for pictures, but there were none to be found. The young man asked Zach if he had a pen. Zach began patting himself pretending to search for a pen.

"Nope. Must've left it in my car," said Zach although he had a pen in his jacket pocket.

He hoped the young man would go find one so he could have time to look around.

"Okay," replied the young man. "I have to run upstairs to get one. I'll be right back."

Zach nodded his head. As soon as he heard the young man's feet hitting the first step, he jumped up and started looking around for any clues that would tie him to Mother Rose or the girls. There was nothing in plain sight.

Joe sat frantically in the rented car not knowing what was going on and wished that Zach would have taken the walkie-talkie just in case he got into trouble. Then from the corner of his eyes, he saw a male figure approaching the gate. It was the same man he saw yesterday. The man slowly turned his head and pressed the intercom button to the gate. Joe's heart nearly jumped out of his chest. Now he knew why the man's gait was so familiar. The man was his longtime friend, Detective Kelly!

Joe's mind raced one hundred miles a minute with all kinds of questions. Now he was very concerned about Zach's safety even more. Had Kelly ever seen Zach up close? Did he know that they had been watching the house for days? Could it be that he is on to them? Should he call the police now and blow Zach's cover? Trying to use some of his professional skills to calm his nerves, Joe decided to wait it out as someone opened the front door to the house and Detective Kelly went inside.

Zach was about to stand up not knowing who the individual was entering the house, but changed his mind even though he was nervous because he wasn't sure if anyone discovered that he was an imposter.

"Hey Kelly, surprised to see you!" said the young man. "I did not know you were stopping by this morning. I thought you planned to stop by later tonight."

"Well after shopping, I decided to stop by considering I was already near your house."

Zach heard the name Kelly in various conversations with Joe. *Wouldn't this be something if this Kelly were Joe's Detective Kelly?* Zach thought. His hands began to sweat with the thought that it could be possible so he tried to leave.

Zach said, "I see that you have company so I'll just come back some other time."

Kelly immediately noticed him sitting there. "Who is this gentleman sitting in the living room?"

"Oh," the young man explained, "I just received a gift certificate for $500 because my power went out for almost one hour the other day and the local electric company wanted to reimburse me for any damages it may have caused. This is Mr. Phillips who works for the electric company."

Kelly looked Zach squarely in the eyes. "Hello, Mr. Phillips. Nice to meet you," he said as he extended his right hand, but with a concerned look on his face. "Wow, that is sure generous of the electric company to give everyone such a nice reimbursement. So, what electric company is this?"

Thinking, Zach remembered the name of one of the local electric companies he and Joe had looked up and quickly said, "We Got The Power Electrical Company located in the downtown area."

"Please excuse us for a moment."

Kelly walked away grabbing the young man angrily by the upper arm and pulling him to the side. Being brave, Zach extended his head to hear what they were talking about.

Kelly hissed, "I thought we made an agreement not to allow anyone inside the house for any reasons whatsoever."

The young man angrily shot back, "Get your hands off me!"

Zach heard a thump and guessed that Kelly pushed the young man's back up against the wall.

"Do you have any idea what is at stake here?" Raising his voice louder, he said, "For one thing, my career is on the line and secondly, we both can wind up in jail for a very long time. What were you thinking, or were you thinking at all?"

The young man explained in a fearful tone, "I know, but we had no lights the other night and when he offered a gift certificate for $500 to the local super warehouse, I thought we could use the extra money for food. Kelly, I was just going to sign this document and in return, he was going to give me my gift card and leave."

Zach heard Kelly snatch the document from the young man's hands.

"Let's look at what you were about to sign." Then he said in a low stern voice, "This document is a fake!" Having many years in the police department, this was his expertise—spotting false documentation. " I went to special training for two years to learn to detect these types of phony documents and I'm telling you that this document is a fake!"

Zach overheard that this Kelly person worked for the police department and wondered again if this could be the same Detective Kelly who knows Joe. If so, what was he doing here in Houston at the exact time that they were in this state? This Kelly had figured out that the letter was a fake. Zach knew that they were on to him. Once again his hands began to sweat. He decided to excuse himself again.

"You seem preoccupied. I can come back another time."

Reaching inside his pocket and flashing his badge, Kelly introduced himself. "I'm Detective Kelly," he said while looking Zach squarely in the face without blinking an eye. "May we see your identification, Mr. Phillips?"

Oh no! Surely, this was the Detective Kelly who knew Joe. Now, it all made sense—why he was following and questioning Joe. He was in on the kidnapping! This is the Kelly who Joe suspected of hiding evidence and potentially providing information to the kidnappers. Now wishing that he was wearing the walkie-talkie, Zach reached into his pockets acting as if he had lost his ID card.

"Oh no. I left my ID in the car parked out front."

Zach thought that if he was going to get out of this house alive, he had to tell them something believable. Sweat began to drip down Zach's face. Almost immediately, Detective Kelly picked up his body language and looked squarely at Zach.

"Do you know how much time you can get for impersonating a city worker or, for that matter, anyone?" threatened Detective Kelly. "Let's stop playing games. I know that your document is not real and I know that you do not work for We Got The Power Electrical Company, so who are you really? Let's start by getting your real name because I know that it is not Mr. Phillips. It would be in your best interest if you started telling the truth now. It will make everyone's life easier. Are you working alone?"

Zach knew that he had been caught, but he refused to sell anyone out. He lied, "I do not work for anyone. I heard that the people living in this house were rich and I was trying to see if that was true by gaining access to their house. My name is really Phillips. If you would just let me get my wallet from my car parked out front, I can prove it to you." He stood up.

"No. Sit down." Detective Kelly shoved him into the chair. "You are not going anywhere!"

Zach remembered what Joe said about Detective Kelly—how he was capable of anything, especially when someone got in his way. The young man was standing by and observing everything. He was just as nervous as Zach.

He nervously said to Kelly, "I think you are getting way out of hand here. I think that we should stop and think about what we are going to do here. I do not think this man knows anything and we need to let him go before things spiral out of control."

"Shut up!" screamed Detective Kelly. "You are the one who messed up everything in the first place. I told you and you agreed that we would not let anyone in the house under any circumstances, but no. You got tricked by the lure of a $500 gift card!"

# CHAPTER TWENTY-TWO

"I'll prove to you that I'm not getting way out of hand," barked Detective Kelly. He pulled Zach out of the chair and pushed him to the back of the house. "Walk toward the basement door on my right," he ordered while pointing in that direction.

The young man grabbed his head with both hands. "What are you doing Kelly? I need you to stop right now or the whole deal is off!"

Kelly reached for the young man's throat and started choking him. "Don't ever threaten me again! Get out of my way!"

He pushed the young man to the side and proceeded to pull Zach down the basement stairs.

The young man was tired of Kelly calling all of the shots. He had just as much say as Detective Kelly. He brushed past Zach and began pushing him back up the stairs.

"Kelly, I'm not going to let you do this without a fight. Now think about what you are doing before you regret it!"

"I'm not the one who is going to regret anything! I understand your frustration and concerns, but if you just let me prove that this guy knows more than what he is telling us, you will see for yourself!"

Zach knew what Detective Kelly was trying to do, but the young man could not see it yet. Kelly started apologizing for choking him and pleaded with the young man to allow him to pass so he could prove that he was right all along about this Mr. Phillips character. Pausing for a moment, the young man finally agreed and allowed them to pass.

He said to Kelly, "Some things cannot be reversed!"

Detective Kelly pushed Zach towards the same doorway he discovered before in the basement then ordered him to stand there while he unlocked the door. The door swung open. There was Mother Rose, who seemed to have aged at least ten years, placing her arms around both girls who looked distressed. Then Mother Rose grabbed her mouth in complete shock. Could this be Zach, her handyman from Atlanta, or was she seeing things after being lockup in such a small place for so long?

As Detective Kelly pushed him inside the room, Zach tried to pretend like he did not know the Rose family, but his body language gave him away. He, nevertheless, tried to prevent Mother Rose from admitting that she knew him or saying his name. Unfortunately, Mother Rose was so shocked to see her neighbor and there was very little light in the room that she did not pick up on what Zach was trying to do.

"What in the world, Zachariah? What are you doing here? Are you okay? Did they capture you too and bring you here to Houston against your will?"

"See, I told you!" shouted Detective Kelly as he turned to the young man.

"Yeah, you are right Kelly. How did he track them to this house? Who are you and what are you doing here in Houston, Mr. Phillips, or should I say Mr. Zachariah?" grilled the young man. He was upset that he had been bamboozled into Zach's scam. "You better start talking Mr. Phillips, or whatever your name is, or someone is going to pay the consequences!"

Mother Rose jumped up to shield the girls with her body. "No one is going to touch my baby girls because you will have to go through me first!"

Laughing out loud, the young man angrily said, "Remember, Mother, these are my babies, not yours! You stole them from me and my wife, Wendy. She is their real mother. Do not forget that!"

Zach could not believe what he was hearing. All this time, he thought that those girls were Mother Rose's daughters. Now he was starting to fit all the pieces of the puzzle together. This young man was Mother Rose's son. The picture he and Joe saw was her in her younger days holding him when he was a baby. But he was still unclear as to how Kelly and this young man knew each other, how they met and how they planned the kidnapping of the Rose family.

Almost reading Zach's mind, the young man started blabbing, "I have searched for months trying to find my precious little twin girls who I lost fifteen years ago." Upset, he continued, "I was your son. Why did you do this to me? Why would you steal our babies? Mother, you have never been a good parent to me. I could feel how you hated me. Do you know what it feels like when a child knows that his own mother does not really want to be bothered with him?"

"Rick, Jr.," Mother Rose innocently replied, "where is all of this coming from? You tried to suffocate one of your daughters when she was just an infant. I did nothing but give you the best in life and love you until there was no end, but all you ever gave me was trouble."

"I knew you would deny it! Well, at least I was able to lean on Uncle Brad. He not only came to see me more times than I can count, but he also drove to North Carolina to pick me up after I was released from prison, and drove me back to Houston. You knew while I was locked up, Uncle Brad was there for me. He would come and see me all the time. You only showed up one time!"

"Junior, you would not take my visits. What was I supposed to do? Keep wasting my time coming to see you when you would just reject me?" shouted Mother Rose. "Son, I'm glad that you were able to get out of that horrible place, but as I always said, Junior, you are sick and need help. Unless you turn your life over to God, nothing you do will ever work out for you." She turned her head away from him as if to say I'm done talking to you.

"Okay, okay enough about who hurt who or whose kids are whose!" shouted Kelly. "I want that money and the only way we are all going to get the reward money, is if we keep a cool head and not get caught up in this baby mama drama because we haven't finalized our plans in collecting the reward money yet!"

Detective Kelly rubbed his face to maintain his temper.

"But Kelly, she knows that I'm telling the truth!" shouted Rick.

Mother Rose said, "Now, Rick you know that's not true. Rick baby, you crossed the line when I saw you almost suffocate one of the twins because she would not stop crying on your command. We had to get away from your violent and abusive behavior, to someplace that was safe for all of us."

"No! Mother, you made the whole ordeal out to be more than it was so that you could steal my children and raise them as your own! But thanks to the Internet, anyone can be found, Mother. All I had to do was post an ad online about a young man who lost his birth mother years ago and was desperately seeking to reunite with her. Also, when you are willing to pay the piper, all the little mice are ready to dance to your music. Right, Kelly?"

Suddenly Rick released this crazy loud laughter. "Now you will pay for all of the pain and misery you caused me and my wife to suffer for fifteen long years! If you thought I treated you badly when I was young, you have not seen anything yet!"

Mother Rose began to pray silently and asked God to help them get out of this nightmare. Then she asked Rick, "What are you going to do with your own daughters? Rick, tell me. Please do not harm them. They did not have anything to do with our dysfunctional family issues. It's just between you and me!"

"Mother, don't you worry your ugly little head off," sneered Rick. "I have big plans for bringing my family back together again and they do not include you! My wife and I will become the perfect parents and raise our daughters the way we had intended in the first place!"

Now Zach was able to complete the puzzle. Detective Kelly must have tried to make some extra money on the side so he answered Rick's ad. Suddenly, they heard another set of footsteps coming down the stairs to the basement. It was a woman because Zach heard the sound of high heels.

Rick grabbed her by the hand and kissed her on the lips. "This is my wife, Wendy. Honey, can you prepare a meal for everyone?"

Wendy looked in Zach's direction. "Wait a minute. Who is this man?"

Rick explained, "Wendy, he tried to rescue Mother Rose, but Kelly spotted him a mile away. Now we have another mouth to feed since we can't let him go."

"Oh, you are asking me to cook for another person? What is this? No!" shouted Wendy. "Honestly, I'm tired of cooking for this woman who stole our daughters from us and now you want me to cook for some-one who was going to help her? What am I? Your maid or your wife? In case you are having a memory loss—I'm your wife! Remember me?"

"Honey, come on. I do not need this type of aggravation now. We need to feed everyone until Kelly and I decide how we are going to finalize retrieving the reward money."

Detective Kelly ordered, "Get back upstairs and do as you were told and prepare a meal for everyone."

Feeling frustrated, Wendy decided not to look in Mother Rose's direction anymore and stomped her way back up the stairs.

As Rick locked his mother and his daughters inside the room, he thought it would be best if he separated his mother and her friend because he did not want them talking to each other. He taped Zach's hands behind his back connecting the tape to the basement poles. He also taped his feet.

He was about to put a piece of tape on his mouth when Zach said, "My friends and family members are going to get worried about me and eventually come looking for me."

Rick snarled, "Be quiet! If anyone comes looking for you at this house, they will find themselves sitting right beside you taped up on the basement floor."

# CHAPTER TWENTY-THREE

Detective Kelly was getting very irritable because nothing was working out as they had planned; everything was taking its own course.

He asked Rick, "What are we going to do about your mother and this guy because I did not sign up for hurting anyone?"

"I have been working with this doctor who told me for the right amount of money, he plans to place my mother in a mental institution for the rest of her life. I will take ownership of everything that she owns and, with the money I receive from my uncle's property, money will not be a problem when we leave the country."

"Okay, what about this guy?" asked Kelly.

Rick started scratching his head. "Is there any way you can arrest him on a bogus charge back in Atlanta? A charge that will get him locked up for a long time?"

"Wow, that really is not a bad idea. To really make it stick, I just need to make sure no one believes his story."

"Okay, what about the girls? They are of age. How would you prevent them from talking to anyone about what really happened?" asked Kelly.

"Well, that same doctor is also going to prescribe some kind of pills to cause the girls to lose their memory. During that time, we will have to try and win them over and gain back their trust as their parents."

Mother Rose had her ear pinned to the door and was listening to every word they were saying. She told the girls that they must continue to pray that God would abort the plans of the enemy. Meanwhile, Zach was sitting on the basement floor and also listening to the dialogue. Fear overtook him and he hoped that, by now, Joe realized he was in trouble and had called the police.

Rick excused himself and told Kelly to stand watch as he went upstairs to make some phone calls and also to see if Wendy needed any help bringing the food to the basement. But as soon as Rick stepped his foot on the bottom step, the basement door suddenly swung open. Wendy came running down the stairs.

"We are busted!" she screamed at the top of her lungs. "The house is surrounded with the police! Someone called the police!"

"Who?" replied Rick. "Maybe this guy is not working alone. Who is this guy in our house anyway? Something tells me he works for the police!"

Kelly flew past both Rick and Wendy while they were talking. He ran out of the house with his hands up flashing his badge to convince the police that he was one of them and not one of the criminals.

A detective shouted, "Hold your fire! He's one of us!"

Joe got the attention of a detective near him. "He's working with the criminals. Don't let him fool you! He is not a good cop! His name is Detective Kelly and he works for the Atlanta, Georgia police department. He withheld information that could have led to the arrest of these kidnappers!"

The detective directed Joe to stand back and out of the way of danger. He ordered Detective Kelly to keep his hands in the air and slowly approached him.

"Sir, I am going to take you into custody," he said as he read Detective Kelly his Miranda rights.

Kelly could not believe his eyes when he saw Joe standing in the crowd because Joe was the last person on this earth that he expected to see in Houston. With his hands still in the air, he knew only Joe could make the police believe that he was in on the kidnapping. He started looking for a way of escape. He spotted a vacant alleyway nearby and ran. He ran as fast as he could.

A detective shouted, "Stop or we will fire!"

Detective Kelly quickly turned the corner into the alleyway. Suddenly, someone grabbed him by the neck, flipped him onto his stomach and handcuffed him. He did not know that a police officer was hiding in the alleyway. He did not want to surrender and wrestled with the police officer, but other officers came to assist.

At this point, Kelly shouted, "I'm innocent!"

A detective escorted him to a nearby police car and placed him inside as he read him his Miranda rights again.

Joe approached the police captain nearby. "May I talk with Detective Kelly? I'm a PI working on this case."

Hesitantly she said, "Yes, but I must accompany you."

Kelly looked at Joe. "I thought you told me that you were going to Florida to visit your family. You really tricked me this time."

Joe said, "Yeah, it's a skill set that I acquired over the years, but you should be the last person talking about someone tricking you."

"Joe, please, if our friendship means anything to you, I beg you not to say anything to the police against me. Please think about my family."

"What?" cried Joe. "You should have thought enough of your family not to have participated in all of this foolishness. Even if I wanted to help you, my other friend would not agree to it. Was it really worth it to lose everything, including your family? You only had two years left on the force. You blew your entire career, pension and freedom. And for what?"

"Joe, please don't turn your back on me now," he sobbed like a little boy about to be punished.

Joe shook his head and walked away with tears in his eyes because he was hurting for Detective Kelly's family.

Kelly, still not willing to accept what he had done, kept saying over and over again, "This is all a misunderstanding. I demand that these handcuffs be removed! This is ridiculous! I am an officer of the law! I'll have your badges for this!"

Back inside the house, Wendy began pulling her hair. "I cannot and will not ever go back to prison!" She looked at her husband, Rick, who was clearly in no better shape than she. "What are we going to do? Obviously, Kelly is only thinking about himself and has abandoned us. He is sitting in the back seat of the police car handcuffed."

Wendy ran back into the kitchen to get any kind of sharp object or weapon. She reached for the sharpest kitchen knife she could quickly get her hands on and ran down to the basement.

She ordered her husband, "Unlock the door to where the girls are. My only way out now is by taking a hostage with me. Come on, Honey, hurry up before the police force their way into the house. I'm taking Eva hostage and I'm getting into my car and driving out of the country. How much money do we have?"

Rick, still in a daze, said, "I'm not sure. Just take everything and get as far as you can because I do not have it in me to run anymore."

Eva touched Mother Rose's back and said, "Let me go, Mommy. God will take care of me. I'm no longer afraid."

Wendy said, "Yeah, listen to your granddaughter, old lady, because I'm running out of time!"

Mother Rose kissed Eva on the cheek and told her that she loved her and to continue to trust God.

Wendy roughly grabbed Eva from Mother Rose's arms and placed the knife near her neck. "If you try anything, I will hurt you."

Rick retrieved all the money he had in the house and handed it over to Wendy. She told him to place it inside her pocketbook. He kissed her for the last time and placed the car keys in her hand.

"I love you, Wendy. You have always been the love of my life and perhaps we will see each other again someday. I hope you make it safely wherever you go with our daughter."

Rick ran his hand down Eva's face. "I'm sorry that things never worked out for us."

Wendy grabbed his hands. "I love you too. I will never forget those days when we first came home from prison. I wish we would have left things the way they were and met our daughters when they got older."

Wendy told Eva to start walking up the stairs slowly and to open the front door. The police were focused on the open door and had their weapons drawn. Wendy and Eva's bodies were close together like those of Siamese twins.

Wendy shouted, "I'm not going back to prison. If you want Eva to remain alive, then back away from the black SUV parked right outside."

After walking down the stairs, Wendy told Eva to slowly open the car door and slide over to the passenger side of the vehicle. The police captain realized that this was a residential neighborhood and decided to let Wendy leave in the car. She ordered the police to immediately move out of the way and Wendy was able to slowly drive away from her house and out of the crime scene area.

Then Wendy suddenly pressed down on the gas and off she went speeding down the street, hoping that there was no traffic in her way.

Eva began crying and prayed that God would prevent accidents and allow them to reach their final destination safely, wherever that may be.

Eva pleaded with Wendy, "Slow down before you kill us both!"

She prayed that the police would apprehend Wendy soon. Wendy was really scared now. Sweat dripped down the sides of her forehead. She could see about five police cars in her rear view mirror. Eva also noticed them from the passenger side mirror. Wendy did not have a chance of getting away. At any moment she was going to get blocked in.

Eva gently said, "Mother, I love you and I do not fault you for not being in my life. If you stop the car and surrender, I will continue to love you."

Wendy began to slow down. Finally the car jolted to a complete stop. Eva silently thanked God for getting her mother to listen to her, but she soon realized that it was not her encouraging words that made Wendy slow down as she watched her start to pound on the steering wheel—the car ran out of gas!

"Why didn't I fill up the gas tank before I came home? Why?" she screamed. She scooted over to the passenger's side behind Eva. "Open the door slowly and get out of the car," she ordered.

As they were getting out, Eva in the front and Wendy behind her holding her arm, Eva took her elbow and jabbed Wendy in the side of her stomach. Eva broke free from Wendy's grip and ran towards the police car. Wendy lost her balance and fell to the ground. Several officers with guns drawn ran towards her while she was on the ground, still holding the knife in her hand.

"Put down your weapon and slowly stand up with your hands in the air!" ordered the police captain.

Wendy knew at this point that she was caught and that she did not have it in her to try to run on foot. She dropped the knife and slowly got off the ground with her hands in the air. An officer kicked the knife away and another cautiously stepped behind her, handcuffed her and read her Miranda rights.

A female officer took Eva to her patrol car. "Are you all right?"

Eva said, "Yes, I'm fine and ready to go see about my mother and sister back at the house."

As they drove off, Eva looked sorrowfully at her birth mother. She was in handcuffs seated in the back of the patrol car with her head down. Eva thought to herself that her mom was going back to the only home she ever knew her entire adult life—prison.

From the basement window, Rick noticed that his baby girl was now in police custody. He knew he only had two choices, either give up or try to fight for his freedom. He realized that, in the basement, it was three against one so he started tying his mother against a pole like he did her friend, Zachariah. While he was tying her up, Ava secretly freed Zach's hands and when she tried to remove the tape from his feet, Rick caught her in the act. He pushed Ava to the basement floor. Zach managed to finish removing the tape from his feet and wrestled Rick to the floor. Ava raced for the tape that Rick put on the nearby table and began helping Zach bind both of his hands and feet. Then she untied her mother's hands. When her hands were loose, Mother Rose ran over to assist in binding up her son. Both Mother Rose and Ava sat on his back while Zach called for the police. Rick, Jr. did not have a chance nor did he have enough strength to free himself, so he stopped struggling and laid on the floor.

He began sobbing. "Okay, I give up."

Tears fell from his eyes. Mother Rose knew that no matter how bad or disturbed a child was, most mothers just do not stop loving their own.

"You need help and, unfortunately, I will not be able to help you. Only God can," she said soothingly as she stroked his head. "I love you, my long lost son."

Zach flew up the stairs and slowly opened the front door with his hands in the air. He told the police that the last perpetrator was tied up inside the house. Joe stood by and confirmed that Zach was a friend of his and that he was being held captive along with the Rose family.

An army of police came running into the house. They arrested Rick, Jr. and put him in the police car.

Rick, Jr. yelled out the car window, "If anyone needs to be arrested, it should be my mother. She stole my daughters fifteen years ago and my wife and I were just trying to get them back! She is the guilty one!"

Zach stood at the top of the house stairs with a little smirk on his face because he helped apprehend the perpetrators. From a distance, Joe put his thumb up as if to say we did it. They walked towards each other and embraced. They were glad that after all they had gone through, everyone was still alive and unharmed.

"Joe, how did you know I was in trouble? I know it was you who called the police, right?"

"Yes, Zach. I knew the moment I recognized Detective Kelly. That's when I knew you were in great danger. So I decided to wait a while to see if you would come out of the house and when you didn't, I called the local police. I told them that an entire family had gone missing in Atlanta and they possibly were being held against their will in this house. I also left messages on both Detective Thomas' and Detective Lee's phones telling them that you and I were in Houston and had tracked down the people involved in the kidnapping of the Rose family. I asked them to call me back as soon as they could.

"Detective Thomas finally returned my call while I was outside waiting for everyone to come out of the house and that is when I told him that everyone in the Rose family was alive and well. I told him that I had one of the twins, Eva, right by my side."

Zach said, "It turns out that the young man the cops arrested was Mother Rose's son and his name is Rick. Apparently, years ago he had a melt down and tried to kill one of the twins as their real mother encouraged him. Thankfully, Mother Rose was able to intervene and had both of them arrested for attempted murder. That is the reason why Mother Rose went into hiding with the girls and moved to Atlanta. She had stopped him from suffocating his own daughter, Ava."

"Wow!" replied Joe.

"I do not have to tell you who agreed to help for a price," said Zach.

"Yeah, I know—my friend, Kelly," stated Joe with sadness.

Finally it was all over. The people who kidnapped the Rose family were in custody to be arraigned and charged with kidnapping. Mother Rose was pretty shaken up, but glad everyone was alive. Her daughters cried as they clung to her sweaty body but they were glad this horrible event had come to an end!

Joe went over to Mother Rose and the girls and gave them a big hug.

"The worst is already over," he said, "and soon you will be back home enjoying the comfort of your home."

Joe walked over to Zach and patted him on the back. They both had big grins on their faces.

He said, "We really did it!"

At the station, Mother Rose and the girls could not wait until the questioning was over because all they could concentrate on was going back home. They were in the interrogation room for what felt like hours because the police had to confirm and record everyone's statements. The police confirmed that Mother Rose did in fact have legal custody of the girls and that Joe and Zach were who they said they were.

An officer said loudly, "You are all free to go!"

Walking towards the exit, one of the detectives said to Mother Rose, "Unfortunately, you will have to come back to Texas and testify against your son and the others."

Mother Rose cleared her throat and asked in a sad tone, "Will he ever be released from prison?"

The detective replied, "Miss, I do not have the answer to that question. The courts will have to decide whether or not your son will be eligible for parole again. But I will say this, kidnapping is a very serious crime and I would not count on him being released anytime soon."

Mother Rose lowered her head in sorrow and Joe placed his arm around her shoulders and said, "Although he has given up on himself, God has not given up on Rick so be encouraged!"

It had been a little over three months and there still was no news of the Rose family. During each church service, Pastor Paul encouraged the congregation to keep the faith because God may not come when you want Him, but He is always right on time! He told them to continue to pray and fast believing that a breakthrough was on the way.

Before he started to pray, Pastor Paul heard his phone ring. He answered it.

"Hello, Pastor Paul. It's Zach, Mother Rose's neighbor."

"God bless you, my son. How are you doing?"

"I'm fine. I just wanted to give you an update on the disappearance of the Rose family."

"Zach, I pray it's good news."

"Yes, Pastor Paul, it is. Joe and I decided to take matters into our own hands from day one and we followed evidence that led us to Houston, Texas."

"Texas! You mean the state of Texas?"

"Yes, the state of Texas and guess who we found there?"

"No! You could not have possibly found the Rose family in Texas, right?"

Excitement was in his voice. Zach said, "Yes we did! You are absolutely correct and they are all alive and well!"

Pastor Paul dropped the phone to the floor and began to give God praise for protecting and keeping them safe. Then Zach could hear his footsteps as he ran to tell the other members of the church how God had answered their prayers! Zach knew that this was an exciting moment for everyone so he decided to give Pastor Paul all the time he needed in thanking God and telling the congregation.

Eventually, Pastor Paul came back to the phone and made no apologies. "Thank you, Zach, for your heroic act and for allowing God to use you in finding the whereabouts of Mother Rose and the girls. Oh, I forgot to ask you, are both you and your neighbor, Joe, okay?"

"Yes, we are all fine as well. Nobody got injured during the whole ordeal."

"Are they back home in Atlanta yet?"

"No, not yet but Pastor Paul, there is more to this story than anyone would ever believe."

"Oh no! Do you have time to talk now? Are you at liberty to discuss it with me?"

"Yes, everything is on the news here in Texas. I'm surprised you haven't seen any breaking news reports in Atlanta," stated Zach excitedly.

"It probably is on television, but everyone that would have informed me is here at the church praying," replied Pastor Paul.

Zach began telling Pastor Paul all the details that transpired in Houston.

"Once the police straighten out all the details, Joe and I will personally escort them back home."

"Young man, you must come to our church. The whole time you were telling the story I sensed God's calling on your life and we both know that He has His hands on your lives. Would you accept a special invitation to come to my church and let me pray a blessing on your life? Although you helped in saving the Rose family, God wants to use you in His kingdom to also save lost souls."

"Yes, I accept the offer and I know Joe would be delighted to accept it as well. Now that you mentioned it, we felt a peace with us and knew the church was praying for us."

"That's great news! I must let my congregation know all the details on how God answered our prayers. God bless you. Oh, by the way, I will have a special event welcoming the Rose family home and it will be held at the church so expect a phone call from me inviting both you and Joe to come."

"Thanks, Pastor Paul. We will be delighted to attend."

Pastor Paul knew that Joe and Zach sincerely loved Mother Rose and the girls because not once did Zach even mention anything about how much was collected for the reward money nor did he ask for it. For them, it wasn't about the money at all, but about finding a neighbor they both had grown to love over many years.

Pastor Paul thought, *this is true friendship and I would love to have them under my leadership. It's hard trying to find people who dedicate their lives to helping others the way those two gentlemen did.*

At the church service, Pastor Paul was excited as he began telling the congregation about Mother Rose's and her daughters' rescue in Houston and how they were all safe and would be home very soon. The entire congregation began to praise God for His faithfulness towards them. When he got the congregation to settle down, he made another announcement that the celebration committee should start preparing for a welcome home party in honor of the Rose family.

The pastor stated, "This time Mother Rose will not be spearheading anything. This celebration will be in her honor and I'm going to put everything into the capable hands of Mother Williamson."

Unfortunately, he had no way of telling Mother Williamson the good news because she was being held in some undisclosed location under strict protection. Pastor Paul could not keep the congregation quiet for too long. They listened to what he had to say and then once again began to give God praise as everyone sang spiritual hymns with joy in their hearts.

# CHAPTER TWENTY-FOUR

Detective Thomas called Mother Williamson but she could barely hear what he was saying. She thought she heard that they found her, that she's safe. She asked him to repeat what he said and he repeated it again.

"She is safe! The whole family is alive and well!"

Mother Williamson began to praise God with all that was in her. The joy she felt inside was unexplainable. Now she knew how David must have felt when he danced out of his clothes. She shared the good news with Detectives Jackson and O'Brien. They too began to praise God right along with her.

Mother Williamson ran back to the phone. "Does that mean I can go home now? I want to see my friend!"

"Yes, you can head home today, but you will have to wait awhile before seeing Miss Rose and the girls. They are being detained by the Texas police for routine questioning."

"Texas?" Mother Williamson repeated. "What were they doing in Texas?"

"It's a long story, Miss Williamson. I have to explain it some other time. But for now, let's concentrate on getting you back to your apartment."

Ending the conversation, Mother Williamson could not move fast enough. All she wanted to do was take a hot bath and relax in the comfort of her own home. *Alone*, she thought as she looked at both detectives. Jackson was moving as fast as Mother Williamson. She missed her husband and son so much, especially her son because she had not seen him since the doctors diagnosed him cancer-free.

When Mother Williamson arrived home, her apartment had a smell of absence; there was no life in the apartment. She gave God praise as she walked around the apartment, making sure everything was as she left it. Detectives Jackson and O'Brien each gave Mother Williamson a hug and told her they needed to check with the precinct before going home to their families.

She asked them if they would come to her church because she was sure that Pastor Paul would be planning something special for the family and it would be an honor if they would come and join in the welcoming home celebration. They both agreed to come and to pass the information on to Detective Smith.

Mother Williamson immediately called Pastor Paul. "I'm home safely and am glad to know that Mother Rose and the girls are safe as well."

"Yes, Mother Williamson, I'm glad to hear that you are okay and back into your home. I would like you and a team to get together to arrange a homecoming celebration in honor of the Rose family. But if you do not feel up to it, then I can assign one of the other Mothers from the cooking committee to spearhead the event."

"Nonsense, Pastor. I felt in my spirit that you were going to have something in their honor. It would be my privilege to coordinate that event."

"Okay, great! I would like it to be this Sunday."

"Okay, I will call the committee and we will show the Rose family how much we really missed and love them."

Mother Rose reminisced about life with Rick, Sr. She just could not believe how wonderful of a husband and father he was to her and their son, Rick Jr. She always tried to live by the Bible all her life. Although she did not consider herself a perfect person because she made many mistakes along the way, she could not figure out where she and her husband went wrong with Rick, Jr. It was as if he was someone else's baby. Like he was switched at birth. She and her husband had not given their parents any trouble while growing up, and most parents would have wished for children like them. Mother Rose remembered Rick, Jr. as a little boy:

*When he was around seven years old, he wanted his father to buy him the latest bicycle for Christmas, which we could not afford that year.*

After staying up all night to wrap his presents and celebrate Christ's birth with praise and worship music, we went to bed. No sooner than we shut our eyes we were awakened by Junior crying outside our bedroom doorway. He walked into our room and stood beside our bed with an angry look on his face.

"Where is my bicycle?" he asked angrily. "I do not see it under the Christmas tree."

Confused, I got out of bed and said, "Junior, watch your tone and apologize to me and your father for acting like a selfish spoiled brat."

"Sorry," Junior replied. "I'm serious! Where is my new bicycle?"

My husband could not believe that our son was acting this way over a bicycle when he had so many other gifts downstairs.

"Well, Junior, I could not afford to buy you a new bicycle this year. Besides, the one you have still works fine."

"No, no! I do not want that piece of junk! I want a new bicycle!" Junior screamed at the top of his lungs.

"Okay, just for that outburst, young man, you will not be getting any gifts," responded my husband. "Your mother and I will be taking those gifts back to the store and you will not be getting anything at all for Christmas this year. Plus, you will be grounded for one month!"

"I don't care," cried Junior. "I broke them all up anyway."

I held my hands to my mouth in shock that he would do such a thing. We went downstairs to witness everything.

Then we heard Rick, Jr. scream, "I hate the both of you!" as he ran into his bedroom and slammed the door.

As time passed, we realized we had not heard a peep from our son so my husband checked in on him and he was sound asleep.

My husband called down to me and said, "Our son is upstairs sleeping like a little angel."

After taking in everything that transpired, my husband and I decided to treat Junior with the same disrespect as he had shown us. So while he was sleeping, we rudely woke him up and my husband took one of Junior's belts and began to spank him while I held him so he would not run away.

We were confident that when God got a hold of him, Junior would be what God had created him to be. But as the years grew, so did Junior's temper. He became meaner than when he was young. As my husband was getting older, Junior grew stronger so punishing him became a difficult task for us. Rick, Sr. was diagnosed with liver cancer and eventually died at the tender age of forty. One of the things my husband told Junior before he died was that he was the man of the house now and should take care of me. I think that really went to Junior's head.

If only I was a little more cautious when I answered the apartment door on the night of the church's fiftieth celebration, the girls and I would not have been abducted. I thought that Deacon Brown circled back around to return something the girls or I left in his car. Suddenly there was a light tap on the apartment door.

Cautiously, I asked who was at the door and the voice said, "It's me. Open up the door. You dropped something."

I tried looking through the peephole but all I could see was the top of someone's head. Given Deacon Brown's height, the person could've been him.

I opened the door to whom I thought was Deacon Brown, but the voice belonged to a person I really did not ever expect to hear for the rest of my life. It turned out to be my one and only son Rick, Jr. My heart sank to my feet. There he was standing right before my very eyes. I could not believe what my eyes were seeing—my son, Rick, Jr. was finally released from prison.

Frantically, I tried closing the door and called out to the girls to lock themselves in their bedroom. Then I noticed there was another gentleman walking in the hallway.

My son's familiar voice said, "Hello, Mother. Are you surprised to see me? I bet you thought that you would never lay eyes on me in this lifetime."

He blocked the door with his foot.

I did not know that the gentleman walking in the hallway was with my son so I called out to him. "Call the police! My family is in danger!"

He immediately replied, "Sorry, I do not have a cell phone."

I asked, "Can you at least protect us from this gentleman who is trying to force his way into my apartment?"

"Sure," he replied, "I'll protect you and your family."

My gut feeling started telling me that this guy was helping my son. I tried closing the door but their strength was much too strong for little old me. The girls were so concerned. They did not hide in their room. They tried to help me close the door, but we were no match against two strong men.

"What now?" asked the gentleman. "We cannot take them down stairs to the van because someone will see us."

"Calm down," replied Rick. "We will wait until the wee hours in the morning about 3:00 a.m. and then we can leave the building and not be seen. Okay? So let's all try to get some rest because we have a long drive ahead of us."

"What do you mean a long drive ahead of us?" I asked. "Where are we going?"

"Mother, did you forget that fast? We are from Houston, Texas!"

As the time passed, I noticed that Junior and the gentleman were fast asleep. I whispered in both of the girls' ears that I was going to get help. They grabbed both of my arms begging me not to leave them with the strangers. I explained to the girls that Junior would never hurt them, but if he had the chance, he would definitely harm me.

I quietly got up from my chair to go to the bathroom and managed to unlock the apartment door along the way. Both gentlemen were out cold when I returned from the bathroom. I started quietly wheeling my bicycle out of the apartment. I knew that God was on my side because I did not make one sound as both men snored. I carefully closed the apartment door as both girls looked on with fear in their eyes and clung to one another.

I realized it was raining heavily, but I did not care! I rode my bicycle down the disabled ramp. I headed for the local police precinct, which was only three blocks away. I saw lights from a car behind me. I prayed that it was a police car passing by. Suddenly, I heard the loud squealing sound of brakes as a white van splashed water all over me. It pulled up beside me.

Junior was screaming at the top of his lungs. "Pull over! If you do not pull over, I will be forced to run you off the road with this van and I doubt very strongly you will survive!"

I had two choices: obey Junior or keep peddling as fast as I could for one more block. Thinking about Junior and what he would do to me, I decided to trust God and kept peddling and hoped someone, even the police, would pass by.

# CHAPTER TWENTY-FIVE

Mother Rose remembered that the white van sped up and got in front of her and abruptly stopped, which caused her to slide and press down on her brakes so that she would not crash into the back of the van. Rick jumped out and grabbed her upper right arm and threw her in the back of the van. Now looking from the back window, Mother Rose just watched her bicycle lay on the ground blocks from her apartment building. Thank you God, she thought, someone will definitely notice my bicycle. She looked at both girls' frightened crying faces.

Rick knew that his mother would be well-known in whatever church she worshiped and people eventually would worry about her when she did not show up to church on Sunday morning, but he did not care. He asked the other gentleman to stop and get a bucket since they could not take any chances being seen in the public restrooms. The other gentleman suggested that they should not feed or give Mother Rose and the girls too much to drink until they arrived in Texas.

Hours later, the van arrived in Houston and everyone was certainly glad that the long journey had finally ended. It was an extremely long trip to Texas in a van with few stops and everyone was completely exhausted. They parked in front of a house.

Rick had really thought this process through because the van was equipped with a mattress and some blankets and pillows along with handcuffs and chains. Now parked, he did not feel comfortable taking his family inside the house right away and decided to wait another hour.

Unlocking the handcuffs from their hands and feet, Rick helped them out of the van and warned them, "If anyone tries to scream for help, I will hurt you."

The other gentleman stood outside the van when the back doors opened and he immediately threw a sheet over Mother Rose and the girls. Wendy opened the front door and watched to make sure no one saw them.

While guiding Mother Rose and the girls toward the basement stairs, the other gentleman advised Rick not to feed them too much for about two weeks.

"This way, they will become weak and they will be easier to handle," he said.

*Little did Rick and the other gentleman know that they were accustomed to not eating because their church fasted on a regular basis! By now, Mother Rose was feeling extremely tired and felt like she was going to collapse while walking down the basement stairs. But one thing that Mother Rose did best was trusting God during wilderness experiences. He had never failed her yet. Mother Rose had no doubt that her prayer partner, Mother Williamson, and The Love Church of God Assembly would be praying for her and her precious girls.*

*Sitting in the dark for hours, Mother Rose was surprised to learn that when you do not utilize your sight, your other senses get stronger, especially hearing. She was able to hear a full conversation among the three individuals about how they plan to split the reward money. Rick and Wendy also mentioned that they would all have to leave the country at the same time with the girls because if the police caught one of them, everyone would be at risk of getting caught.*

⚬≈≈⚬

Snapping out of her daydreaming and coming back to reality, Mother Rose wanted answers. Why would her own flesh and blood treat her this way? She prayed, "Lord, please give me the courage to go see my son, Rick, in prison after this kidnapping so that I can tell him that I forgive him. Also give him a receptive heart to hear the words that You, oh God, will speak to his inner man. Thank you, Lord for going before me and setting the atmosphere and I thank you in advance for melting Rick's stony heart."

Suddenly, Mother Rose felt a spirit of boldness rise up within her. She was determined now, more than ever, to witness to her son. "God, please help him understand and see that he is missing out on the greatest gift ever given to mankind—salvation! God, how can I be so bold in approaching strangers in the street, but now that I have to minister to my own son, I'm getting cold feet?"

After the news of their kidnapping and rescue hit the local news stations, Mother Rose and the girls were offered rooms free of charge in a five-star hotel with 24 hour room service and all kinds of perks. They were also given free airline tickets to travel back home. Almost everyone on the plane recognized them. The people were kind to them. They had first class seats and were served large, healthy meals. They also received free movies and phone service to take advantage of while in the air.

Settling down in her seat, all Mother Rose could think about was how their journey to Texas was so degrading, regrettable and embarrassing, whereas their journey traveling back home to Atlanta was uplifting, memorable and appreciating. Not only had the hotel offered transportation to the airport in Texas, but there was also a car waiting at Atlanta's airport to take them home.

Before they knew it, the plane landed and the family didn't know what to expect once they exited the aircraft. They felt *really* good being back on Atlanta soil. Mother Rose thought there was a lot of attention surrounding them at the airport in Texas, but what was waiting for them in Atlanta won hands down! There were cameras, reporters and photographers from almost every news channel, trying to get first dibs on their story. The girls looked around with excitement and noticed a huge "Welcome Home Rose Family" sign and a lot of strange faces. Instantly, Ava spotted Pastor Paul and other church members among the crowds of people. She tried to inform her sister, Eva, and her mother by pointing in Pastor Paul's direction, but she could not get their attention. There were all kinds of flashing lights shining in their faces along with all shapes and sizes of microphones aimed at their mouths.

Joe and Zach pushed through the crowd and tried to shield Mother Rose and the girls from the paparazzi and press by waving them away. Detectives Thomas and Lee appeared and helped with shielding the family from the mobs of people. Quickly escorting them to the limo, Joe and Zach could hear people say as they walked past that they were glad they found the family alive, and that the son should be placed underneath the prison. People were saying that he was crazy to treat his own mother and daughters so cruelly.

Joe happened to look Mother Rose's way, and he saw tears streaming down her face while she covered the girls' ears as much as she could to prevent them from hearing cruel statements about their parents.

Mother Rose shouted to the girls, "Do not listen to any of this negative talking because God's Word teaches us to forgive others and not hold bitterness in our hearts."

Eva said, "We know, Mommy. We still love our parents. We will pray for all these people who are saying bad stuff about our parents and pray that they stop judging them and let God be the judge."

Finally the limo arrived at Mother Rose's apartment building. There was another huge welcome sign posted across the rooftop of their building.

As they got out of the limo, the crowd began to clap their hands and some made whistling sounds. Others were hanging out their windows, standing on the benches in front of the building, and unbelievably, sitting in the trees! It seemed everyone wanted just to catch a glimpse of the Rose family coming home for the first time after their horrible experience in Texas. Reporters and photographers from numerous television and radio channels were outside the building trying to capture their arrival. There were several police cars surrounding the area to make sure the crowd did not get out of control. They were doing everything they could to keep the people from approaching the family.

All waved to the crowd and thanked them for being so supportive. A shrine was built in front of the building! Floral arrangements, stuffed animals, and lit candles built a memorial to the whole family. Detectives Thomas and Lee made sure that the paparazzi did not get inside the lobby or try to sneak up to their apartment using the elevators or staircases.

Finally, Mother Rose and the girls were home, a place that brought them peace and serenity. They did not have to deal with the crowds of people. Everyone meant well, but it was overwhelming for them especially after what they had gone through. As they looked around the apartment that they missed so much and adored, all kinds of emotions went through their minds considering that it all started here. It would be an emotional roller coaster ride for months to come until things died down.

Unfortunately, the building security was not allowing anyone who did not live in the building to gain access so Pastor Paul and the other church members were unable to visit Mother Rose and the girls. Joe asked them if they would like to stay at his place for a while until they felt comfortable staying by themselves.

Mother Rose declined. "No thanks, Joe. You all have been so very kind to me and my family and I will never, ever forget your selflessness."

Joe, pointing to the constant ringing of the phone, said, "You will have to deal with this every day. Is that what you want?"

Mother Rose briefly reconsidered his offer, but the girls persuaded her to stay in their own home because they missed sleeping in their own beds.

Mother Rose said, "Thank you for the sweet offer, Joe, but we will pass and try to regain our lives."

Detective Thomas said, "Okay, Miss Rose, we will have a patrol car in front of the building for about a couple of weeks just to make sure no reporters attempt to do anything crazy or illegal just to get an exclusive snapshot or story. Also, we were told that building security would be standing outside your apartment door making sure no unwanted visitors try to ring your doorbell or enter your apartment. I'll be going now. Please just let the phone ring or you can unplug it. At least eighty percent of the calls will be reporters. Miss Rose, these reporters love to marry scandal to the media and will stop at nothing to get an exclusive story from you."

"Oh do not worry, Detective Thomas. I will not open the door. We are going to get ourselves settled down for bed now, and I will let the good Lord watch over us for the rest of the night."

Zach asked, "Mother Rose, would you like to hold onto my cellphone for the night so that you can call some of your loved ones?"

"Oh how sweet! You know, I think I will take you up on that offer," replied Mother Rose. "Considering my house phone will not stop ringing, I will have to unplug it. Just show me how to operate this type of cell phone, and if you do not mind, I will make my personal phone calls on it. Thanks so much, Zach. You all have truly been a blessing sent from heaven. Gentlemen, you may go. Don't worry. I will be fine."

The men nodded their heads in agreement.

"Call me whenever you want to go anywhere and I will drive you," offered Zach as everyone exchanged hugs.

"Okay, I will definitely take you up on that offer because the crowd is just too much for the twins. They are not used to living like this."

"You know, I'm right in the same building so you can call me anytime of the day," replied Joe.

"Yes," said Mother Rose. "You know, I would like to see you and Zach tomorrow so please stop by. I'm telling you in advance, so I will not have to call you."

Detective Thomas looked at Joe and Zach. "What you did was dangerous, but very heroic. I'm honored to have met you. All of the reward money belongs to you and once everyone has been convicted and sentenced, you come down to the station and claim the reward you rightfully deserve. The total amount collected from the precinct and from Miss Rose's church is five hundred thousand dollars."

Both gentlemen's eyes almost popped out of their heads when they heard how much the reward money totaled.

"How could that be?" asked Zach.

Detective Lee said, "It is unbelievable, but this story really hit the hearts of many people."

Detective Thomas added, "Several people gave thousands of dollars in one shot. Once the story of the Rose family's disappearance was aired on the news, it seems as if the precinct was getting all kind of donations. A lot of wealthy people were really touched by this whole ordeal and wanted the suspects caught as soon as possible! One individual, who would rather remain anonymous, gave one hundred thousand dollars with no strings attached. This case received so must website attention. All it took was some more wealthy people with love in their hearts and that is how we wound up with a half of a million dollars.

"Detective Kelly was fully aware of how much was pouring into the Rose family reward account because he monitored it on a daily basis to make sure no one was tampering with the funds. I believe that he would have hurt anyone who tried to get in the way of him getting the reward."

Gratefulness was written all over the two detectives' faces as Detective Lee said, "Yes, it's a lot but no one else deserves that money more than you two gentlemen. If anyone deserves all the accolades and if there were medals to be handed out, it would certainly go to you two without thinking twice."

As everyone was leaving and going their several ways, Detective Thomas offered Zach a ride home since the reporters saw him come out of the car with the Rose family and they would follow him home just for a story. He accepted Detective Thomas' offer. He also knew that Joe's and his life would be different as long as this was the top story in the headlines.

Mother Rose decided to make all her phone calls while the girls were preparing for bed. Their beds would take them to another level of peace. In comparison to the hard cot they were made to sleep on, their beds felt like sleeping on a cloud. The first person Mother Rose called was her pastor and filled him in with all the details of their kidnapping and rescue.

Realizing they had been on the phone for more than an hour, he asked, "Can we pray together?"

"Sure," replied Mother Rose.

After praying for the family, Pastor Paul did not want to prolong the conversation any longer and told Mother Rose to get some rest since she sounded very exhausted. Then she called Mother Williamson, but there was no answer. Although she wondered where she could be at that hour, deep down inside Mother Rose felt a little relieved because she did not know how much longer she would be able to keep her eyes open. Just being home, she was feeling a lot better inside and a peace that surpasses all understanding rested upon her; she no longer felt afraid. Although her apartment had been violated by uninvited guests, nothing could take this moment from her. She was caught up in the heavenly realms!

Mother Rose peeked in on the girls. They were peacefully sound asleep in their own beds, and at that moment, she could not stop giving God all the praise. After praying, Mother Rose thought it was now time she gave her body some rest as well. She ran a hot bubble bath, turned off all the lights in the apartment and lit a scented candle. The bath was so relaxing. She closed her eyes and felt the same peacefulness the girls felt sleeping in their beds.

Then she heard a voice. "Hello, Mother. Are you surprised to see me again? Did you think that I could not break out of jail and find you again?"

Mother Rose could not believe her eyes. She called on the name of Jesus. "Lord, please help me! My son is trying to kill me and kidnap my granddaughters again!"

Rick Jr. said, "No need to call Him either because He definitely will not be able to help anymore."

She tried to get out of the bathtub, but she was unable to move any part of her body—he had poured quick-setting cement inside the bath water.

He sneered. "Don't try to fight it because it works just like quicksand - the more you move, the quicker you'll sink and the quicker the cement will expand and set. Then you will no longer be able to breath. So relax. You will soon be with your Maker, the God you worshiped all your life. He can't save you now."

Using her last breath, Mother Rose began calling on Jesus to save her. The water around her throat was turning solid and squeezing out every ounce of air left in her body. While she was grasping for air, Rick, Jr. walked away laughing. He headed towards the girls' room. He waved good-bye to his mother whom he hated and told her that he was glad that he would never ever see her face again.

Suddenly, the bathroom was filled with mist and Mother Rose could no longer see her son. Then she saw a nailed-scarred hand reach out to her.

She heard a voice say, "Grab my hand!"

Mother Rose now was able to move her arm and she grabbed the nailed-scared hand. The hand pulled her all the way out of the bathtub. As she grabbed a towel, she was able to see a bodily figure wearing a long white robe walking away; the figure disappeared in the mist.

Immediately, she realized that her son was heading towards the twins' bedroom. She raced past the fading figure and ran straight into their bedroom. It was empty. Then she noticed the apartment door was wide open and the security guard was lying face down on the hallway floor.

Mother Rose began screaming at the top of her lungs that her son had kidnapped her girls and she did not know where he had taken them!

Running back into the apartment and getting rid of the towel that she held so tightly against her body, she dressed as fast as she could. Remembering that a patrol car was downstairs in front of the building, she ran down the hallway to the elevator. On her way, she banged on her neighbors' doors screaming for help.

All of a sudden, she felt a hand shaking her. "Mommy! Mommy! Mommy, wake up!" Are you okay?"

Mother Rose opened her eyes and regained consciousness as she lifted her body up from the bathtub and quickly grabbed a towel. Both girls were standing near her with tears in their eyes. They knew that she had a bad dream about her son - their father. As they hugged each other, Mother Rose apologized to the girls for waking them from their peaceful sleep and frightening them.

"I'm sorry, girls. I dozed off and had a nightmare. Go back to bed. I'm going to do the same. The hour is really late."

She kissed both girls and told them she loved them. Before getting into bed, Mother Rose asked God to send His angels to watch over them throughout the night because that dream seemed so real. She turned off the light in her bedroom. As she drifted off to sleep, she was almost positive that she saw a huge shadow with wings holding a sword in his hands standing at the foot of her bed. She managed to say thank you God before she fell asleep.

Morning always made Mother Rose feel happy so she decided to turn on the television. All she could see was the news about her and the girls on every news channel.

"Hello my name is Monica Boxer," a news reporter declared, "and this morning we have breaking news! The Rose family is finally home after their disappearance and the controversy surrounding it. One would never have guessed in a million years that they were found in Houston. Yes, Houston, Texas! In turns out that Miss Rose was originally from Houston and had tried to raise a son on her own after her husband passed away. Miss Rose's and her son's relationship spiraled out of control and, years later, she had her son and his girlfriend arrested for trying to kill one of their twin daughters.

"The state awarded Miss Rose custody of the twins and fearing for her life, she fled to Atlanta where she has been raising the girls. Here are some of the clips of the family leaving the house where they were held captive in Houston. There are claims that the house is still owned by Miss Rose. Here you see the family safely exiting the plane and arriving home in Atlanta along with their brave neighbors, Joseph Walker and Zachariah Cooke. These neighbors risked their lives to find the Rose family. Boy, do they have a hefty reward waiting them. Miss Rose's community and church collected five hundred thousand dollars. Yes, a half million dollars. Once again, I'm Monica Boxer. Back to you Jim!"

Mother Rose could not believe what she was hearing. Did she just say the reward money was five hundred thousand dollars that the church and the local community collected for her family? Crying was a norm for Mother Rose but now she could not help it because she was so over-whelmed that the people cared so much for her and the girls. It seemed as if she had shown this community nothing but love and now they were turning the tables and showing her the same generosity. She thought, *may the hand of God pour out a blessing that they will not have room enough to receive.*

Noticing her two daughters getting up, she reached for the remote to turn off the television to try to protect them from all of the cruel publicity about their parents. Then she decided to no longer hide any-thing from them going forward. The maturity they displayed during this whole ordeal was evidence that they were no longer little girls, but mature fifteen-year-old young ladies.

After Eva watched the news, she asked, "Mommy, who is going to get all of the reward money?"

"Well, baby, it looks like both Mr. Joe and Mr. Zach who saved our lives will receive that reward money. Correction, the men God used to save our lives."

"Mommy, what are we going to do with the house in Houston? There is no one to care for it now, nor live in it either," said Ava.

As she drew both girls closer to her on the couch, she said, "That will now be a decision we will all have to make as a grandmother and granddaughters. So, girls, what do you think? What should we do with the property in Texas? Should we keep it or should we sell it? I never sold it because your Great Uncle Brad was maintaining it for me and I was willing to let Junior keep the house when he was released from prison. Girls, we have the option to rent the property out as well."

Both girls giggled at the adult decision that they were faced with. "We don't know."

"Okay," replied Mother Rose, "you do not have to answer right away. Just pray about it and we can all discuss it at another time."

"Mommy, I just want you to know that I understand why you didn't expose us to the truth. It had to be a hard decision to keep us away from our real mother and father," replied Ava. "But Eva and I were talking and we would like to get to know them as our parents. Do you think we can go to the prison and minister to them?"

"Oh, babies! I was hoping you would say that. God is so awesome! He can use you two girls to reach a son that his parents could never reach. Praise God!"

"Not trying to change the subject, but I just realized," Eva exclaimed, "the phone stopped ringing!"

"No, baby. I unplugged it last night or we wouldn't have gotten any sleep. I also do not want you to go anywhere near the windows. I've pulled down the blinds on all the windows. So, ladies, what do you say if we order in for breakfast?"

Almost immediately there was a knock at the door. Mother Rose slowly looked through the peephole expecting to see both Joseph and Zachariah. But all she could see was Detective Thomas' face.

*Wow, he is early,* she thought.

Cautiously, she opened the door and saw a bunch of people from the church, including Pastor Paul, Mother Williamson, Deacon Brown, Zach and Joe, standing outside her apartment with bags and bags of groceries. They decided to go food shopping for Mother Rose and the girls, knowing whatever food was in the house was definitely spoiled by now.

Everyone shouted in a loud voice, "Welcome home Rose family! We are glad you are home safe and sound!"

Mother Rose started to cry again. "That is why I did not get any answer this morning when I called you for prayer, Mother Williamson!"

Pastor Paul laughed and said, "Yes, we went shopping last night, cooked up some meals for the family, and decided to shut-in at the church last night."

Everyone took turns greeting each family member by hugging and kissing them. It seemed like it would never end. Mother Rose's two-bedroom apartment was a little crowded when there were just three people in it, but now it was holding at least forty people. People were in every nook and cranny. They were just glad to be in her presence because they all loved and missed her so very much. They could not wait until Sunday to see her worshiping with them.

They prayed, ate breakfast and laughed together, just like in the good old days. Mother Rose and the girls felt surrounded with love; they thanked the Lord for His many blessings. Pastor took the time to witness to Zach and Joe, as well as Detectives Thomas and Lee. After that happened, they were ready to receive the Lord as their personal Savior. Then the saints welcomed them into God's family. Since they just made the best decision of their entire lives, there was even more rejoicing in the apartment.

# CHAPTER TWENTY-SIX

Joe stood up and asked if he could say something and everybody gave him their full and undivided attention.

"I know that many of you are aware that both Zach and I are eligible for the reward money." Joe looked at Zach who was nodding his head in agreement. "However, we both would like to split the money with Mother Rose and we want to purchase a van for the church so that all the senior members can be driven home safely on late night events."

Deacon Brown began to play as if he was doing a spiritual dance across the floor. Everyone burst into laughter and held their stomachs. It wasn't what he was doing, but how he was moving as if he was some performer on a stage.

Pastor Paul said, "Joe and Zach, not only are you heroic individuals, who gave of yourselves to save others, but you are also generous in your giving. God will bless the both of you for even thinking of Mother Rose and the church."

"Well, that is not all," Joe replied. "We also would like to open an account to take care of the van's insurance for the next five years and gas for one year."

Pastor Paul could no longer contain himself and he began his spiritual dance unto the Lord, but his dance was serious because he was also praising God for the many blessings He had provided. Mother Williamson was crying uncontrollably. She just could not believe how someone could love the Lord so much that they gave abundantly and unselfishly. Praise was in the air as everyone gave thanks unto the Lord for the many blessings He had given them.

Afterward, while everyone was getting ready to go home, Deacon Brown, still being comical, said, "I wish we had that van now. I would drive everybody home!"

Everyone laughed. They began hugging and kissing the girls and Mother Rose again, and told them that they would see them in church on Sunday, God willing.

Pastor Paul turned to Joe and Zach. "It is a great privilege and honor that you are now a part of God's family. Trust us when we tell you, you will never regret this decision. I also want to tell you that we are having a welcome home celebration at the church this Sunday and are expecting you both to attend."

They nodded in agreement.

Joe said, "Absolutely. We wouldn't miss this for the world."

Now that everyone had cleared her apartment, Mother Rose sat and thought how the devil meant evil, but God turned it around for everyone's good. The names of four new souls were written in the Lamb's Book of Life this wonderful day all because of what her family had to go through. She mumbled a quick prayer under her breath to God, "Lord, please do not forget my son, Rick and his wife, Wendy. They need you like never before. God, I thought that some things I have gone through in life were hard. But God, testifying against my only son and daughter-in-law will be the hardest thing that both my granddaughters will ever have to do. Please give us strength. Amen!"

⚯

It was a beautiful sunny Sunday morning in Atlanta. Mother Williamson and her team could not ask for a better day. Pastor Paul had informed all his members that service would start two hours earlier than usual so they could get a seat. He was expecting a lot of spectators, as well as reporters and camera crews wanting to question the Rose family and he definitely did not want his own church members to be turned away for a lack of space. Pretty much every member was inside the church before the crowd outside grew. The crowd only wanted to lay eyes on Mother Rose and the girls and waited with anticipation. In fact, it grew so large that the ushers and deacons started turning people away. The church was packed and the street was overcrowded.

Due to all the publicity and the crowd, the Rose family was brought into the church hours before the service started. Thanks to Detectives Thomas and Lee, a diversion was created as they were led into the church through the back. They were allowed to rest in Pastor Paul's sleeping quarters. Once again, Mother Rose and her granddaughters felt like this shifting around would never come to an end. They really wanted it to be all over.

Downstairs, Mother Williamson and the team decorated the basement with all kinds of welcome home/welcome back signs with matching decor. Upstairs Pastor Paul asked the people to be seated and to clear the aisles. Respectfully, everyone made their way to their seats and there was silence throughout the church. They sat in anticipation as they were eager to hear the Rose family's testimonies.

Pastor Paul began, "Now we all know that God has safety brought back our beloved Rose family." They all stood and waved their hands as a sign of thanksgiving. Once again, Pastor Paul had to wait until the crowd grew quiet. "Now I wanted to start this service early because I would like to give certain people a chance to acknowledge the Rose family. Unfortunately, everyone will not have a chance to speak, so for starters, I would like to call Deacon Brown, who played a key role in providing critical information in helping to solve this case."

Deacon Brown made his way to the front of the church wearing a shiny gray and black pinstriped suit. While holding his Bible, he reached for the microphone but before completely handing it over, Pastor Paul reminded him that he had only ten minutes to share his thoughts.

Deacon Brown positioned the microphone and boastfully shouted, "Praise the Lord everybody! Praise the Lord! I would like to take this time to give God all the praise once again for bringing my best friend and her family back home safely!"

As the Rose family was seated in the front row of the church, Deacon Brown softly whispered that he loved them, and they whispered back that they loved him too. "I prayed day and night for their safe return, and today I'm rejoicing with the saints and friendly community because they once were lost, but now they are found."

Deacon Brown dedicated the song, *Keeper of My Soul*, to them. He eloquently sang the words: "God is the keeper of my soul, He watches over me every day and night, God is the keeper of my soul!"

When he finished, everyone stood up, applauded and rejoiced with Deacon Brown as he did a little dance back to his seat. Pastor Paul called Detective O'Brien to speak.

Detective O'Brien moved nervously and quickly to the front of the church. He, too, gave God praises and told the Rose family it was an honor to finally meet them.

"Because of them, my life has changed forever. I had the wonderful privilege of meeting Mother Williamson and many others. God decided that, through your wilderness experience, many would form friendships. I pray that God continues to watch over you and keep your minds in perfect peace as you continue to walk with the Lord. God Bless you!"

He then hugged each family member and gave each a welcome home kiss. Pastor called Detective Jackson and her family to say a few words.

"Praise the Lord everyone!" Detective Jackson greeted, "I'm glad to stand before you today."

Everyone replied with a loud, "Praise the Lord!"

"Mother Rose, you do not know me, but I was assigned to guard Mother Williamson during your kidnapping and she talked so much about you and the girls that I feel as if I know you already."

While talking, Detective Jackson was extending a handshake to the girls, but when it came time for her to shake Mother Rose's hand, Mother Rose stood up and embraced her instead. Officer Jackson began to talk with tears in her eyes.

"This is the first time I have ever given a testimony. Pray for me. As I mentioned, I was one of the detectives assigned to guard Mother Williamson after the threatening phone calls and scary visits. But I thank God - because of Mother Williamson, I can stand here and say, I'm saved and have accepted the Lord Jesus Christ as my personal Savior."

The church members jumped up and began to praise God as the musicians encouraged them with dancing and shouting music. Pastor Paul calmed down the congregation and told Detective Jackson to continue.

"During our times together," Detective Jackson continued, "Mother Williamson began to teach me how to study the Bible, pray and even to turn down my plate, which I now know is called fasting. Each day I began to grow spiritually and to increase in faith, all in a short period of time."

To Mother Williamson, she said, "I will never ever forget you; you will always be my spiritual mother in the Lord."

Then she walked over to her and gave her a kiss and the biggest hug. More clapping and praising God continued for a moment with the saints.

"Because Mother Williamson shared Jesus Christ with me, I began to witness to my husband, Marcus, and shared with him how Jesus saved me. I also began teaching him about Jesus. Every night, we would read the Bible together and then one day he told me, 'I want to know this Jesus too.' I walked him through the steps of salvation and I can say on his behalf that he is saved today!"

Not wanting to speak, he just stood next to his wife and raised both hands, giving God all the praise.

"So far, I testified how God saved both me and my husband, but now I would like to share with the church how I began to know God as a healer. I also shared with Mother Williamson that my son, Marcus Jr., was suffering because he had brain cancer. Being new in the Lord, I just did not know if God could solve a cancer problem, but Mother Williamson started praying with me and told me to start speaking life over Marcus' body. She explained to me that there is nothing too hard for God and that with God, all things are possible if you only have faith to believe!"

Now, the church was so in-tune with Detective Jackson's testimony, you could hear a pin drop on the carpet. Even Pastor Paul knew that she had gone over her time but he just could not interrupt her captivating testimony.

"Saints, God has completely healed Marcus Jr. from cancer, saved both me and my husband, so no one can tell me that I do not serve a powerful God!

"Later, I witnessed to my son, Marcus Jr. and he also accepted Jesus Christ as his Lord and personal Savior!"

Marcus, Jr. stepped forward and waved at the congregation with tears in his little, precious eyes.

The church stood again with praising and dancing before the Lord.

Pastor Paul joined the worship as well. At this time, Detective Jackson, her husband, and their son were all hugging the Rose family and thanking them for allowing God to use their bad situation to bring about salvation and healing into their home.

Detective Jackson looked at Mother Rose with tears in her eyes. "I know that you must have gone through a lot, but I want you to know if it had not been for your disappearance, I would never have met Mother Williamson and my family probably would never have gotten saved and healed. Thank you for being the person you are because God knew that he could trust you with this wilderness experience and now look at the end results. God bless you! Pastor Paul, I know that I have taken a lot of time, but thank you for teaching your church members to spread the Word of God. It is so important that we all try to reach the dying world. God bless everyone!"

They walked back to their seats. The church gave the Jackson family a standing ovation and almost every member had tears in their eyes while looking at Marcus Jr., a walking miracle. Pastor Paul tried speaking, but he could only beckon for Detective Thomas and his family to come and share.

They made their way to the front of the church with their heads lowered and when he began to speak, it was in a shy, low tone.

"Hello everyone. I'm Detective Thomas and this is my wife, Emma. When I was first called on duty to assist with this case, I never expected it to turn out like it did. I'm a cop, living in the real world. Most kidnapping cases are hardly ever solved or they end up badly. So to stand before the Rose family today is a blessing and that they have suffered no physical harm is a double blessing. I, too, would like to thank someone and that person is Pastor Paul for leading me through the steps of salvation. Today, I can truly say, I'm saved and my wife has come here today because she would like to receive Jesus Christ as her personal Savior as well. I shared with my wife how God's hand was all in this case and that I have never seen anything like it before. I told her it was as if God staged a play and He was using us as actors and actresses and when the play was over, we were all blessed in some way."

Again, the congregation could no longer contain themselves. Some ran around the sanctuary in excitement while others "fell out" under the anointing. Some ushers made their way to the front of the church and escorted Emma into another room to walk her through the steps of salvation. Everyone clapped as she walked away.

Detective Thomas walked towards the Rose family and said, "God has turned your tragedy into triumph."

He hugged them and walked back to his seat. By now, Mother Rose had to be given a bottle of cold water and a fan because she could not stop crying and blessing the Lord. Pastor commented on some of the testimonies.

"We don't always know why God allows some things to happen in our lives, but what the enemy tears down, God can build up again—and build even better. It is all about timing."

The Rose family was now crying tears of joy. Next, Pastor Paul called Detective Lee and his wife to speak.

Also nervous, Detective Lee spoke in such a low tone that some of the members shouted they could not hear him and asked him to put the microphone closer to his mouth.

"I want to thank God for saving me through Pastor Paul and my wife would now like to receive salvation."

They embraced each other. Ushers took Mrs. Lee into the same room as Emma Thomas. The church members clapped their hands because another soul was won for the kingdom.

Detective Lee agreed with his partner that it was a miracle. "God's hand of protection was around the Rose family and for that, now I know what an awesome God my wife and I will be serving." He hugged the Rose family with tears in his eyes. "You are miracles from God and however you bless God today, He will be pleased because Mother Rose your family's experience has changed many lives today. God bless you all!"

Mother Williamson noticed Detective Smith with his wife, Sarita, in a wheelchair in the back of the church. She asked Pastor Paul to call them to share their testimony.

Pastor Paul agreed. "Detective Smith and Sarita, please come to the front of the church and give a testimony about what God has done in your life."

Detective Smith slowly pushed his wife's wheelchair through the crowded aisle. Everyone began applauding to encourage them as they made their way to the front of the church.

Ava turned to her mother and said, "Mommy, none of these people go to our church. What church do they attend?"

Mother Rose said, "You are right, but because God decided to use us, they all will probably be attending our church now."

Detective Smith cleared his throat. "God is so good."

The congregation responded, "All the time!"

He said, "All the time!"

The congregation finished. "God is good!"

"I want to thank God for never giving up on me even when I gave up on Him. I grew up in the church, but I found excuses to turn my back on God. But, thank God for His mercy. I could have died in my sins, but God said not so! I thank God for Mother Williamson. This little giant of a woman seized the moment to grieve for her best friend and family, but also saw an opportunity to win souls for the Lord and that she did!"

Detective Smith's voice got stronger as he spoke. "We serve a mighty God, people! Saints, my testimony is not just about God saving a backslider like me, but my wife has a testimony as well."

He handed the microphone to his wife, Sarita. "Praise the Lord everybody." She had a strong Spanish accent. "I would like to give my testimony. My husband found out a couple of months ago, prior to meeting Mother Williamson, that I had given my heart to the Lord. He did not like it 'cause he said that I should have told him first before making a decision that would affect our lives. But how many of you who are married know that we have to have a personal relationship with God for ourselves?"

The church said, "Amen!"

"So when I told this to him, he became very angry with me and began to stay out very late every night. But I know it was the devil trying to make me leave Jesus. No, no, no, I would not and I kept praying that God would save my husband again. Saints, sometimes you have to be careful what you ask for 'cause you never know what you will have to go through to get your prayers answered. Are you willing to suffer? Are you willing to trust God until your change comes? The devil knew I was determined so he tried to kill me by running me over with a truck."

Shouts of "Jesus!", "Oh, my Lord!", and "Father, keep me near the cross!" came from the congregation.

Sarita stood up, with her husband's assistance, and began to walk around the front of the church without holding on to anything. The congregation was astonished and the people stood to their feet and praised God.

Sarita stopped and threw up her hands. "The doctors said I would never walk again and they also told me that I would never have use of my left arm." She waved her left hand in the air. "Whose report will you believe?" She shouted at the top of her lungs.

The congregation shouted in reply, "WE SHALL BELIEVE THE REPORT OF THE LORD!"

Sarita made her way back to the wheelchair. She personally thanked Mother Williamson for fasting and praying for her while she was on her sick bed. She also thanked her for taking the time to witness to her husband. God heard her prayers and now she and her husband are saved and living for the Lord.

Lastly, she looked at the Rose family and said, "We suffered together during this time, but we made it by God's grace!"

The music started again and it seemed like the whole church was praising and worshiping God, including Mother Rose, Ava and Eva. Once the church saw that the Rose family was up on their feet giving God praise, all who were not standing rose to their feet as well.

The pastor once again tried to hold back his emotions as he called Joe and Zach to the front. Joe decided to let Zach go first. As he introduced himself, Mother Rose and the girls were smiling because they knew them. God had truly used these gentlemen to help rescue them!

Zach began, "I've known Mother Rose for many years; I cannot even begin to tell you how many. I have known the girls mostly all of their lives. We have been neighbors who always took time to communicate with one another and make sure everything was okay with each other. Mother Rose was always feeding the birds in the morning and witnessing to as many people as she could. One of the things I like best about her is that she would never try to cram the Lord Jesus down anyone's throat, but gently ask if you did not know the Lord, and would you be willing to accept Him as your personal Savior? Mother Rose, I want you to know that after all those years of witnessing to me, I finally accepted Jesus Christ into my life."

Tears rolled down Mother Rose's face and she thanked God for finally saving her neighbor and friend.

Zach said, "Mother Rose, it took a bad situation to make me see how real God really is, and for that, I will always be grateful to you. God bless you!"

He went over and gave them the biggest hugs and kisses and told them that he truly loved them as they said the same to him.

Joe took the microphone. "I would like to piggy back off what my friend, Zach said. Mother Rose would choose the right words to say to you, words that made you really think about what she was saying concerning the Lord. Unfortunately, it had to take this circumstance to let me really understand what she was telling me about Jesus Christ all those years. I, too, have accepted the Lord Jesus."

The congregation shouted, "Praise the Lord!"

"There was never a time during the kidnapping that I thought of the kind of harm I was putting myself or Zach into. I was very determined to find my friendly neighbor who would give you the shirt off her back; a neighbor who took the time to befriend me when others would pass me by. A neighbor who did not care if you called her crazy, but was only concerned about winning souls for the Lord. Everyone, I really want you to know that Mother Rose is a special neighbor and dear friend to me."

Then someone shouted from the back of the church. "Did you do it for the reward money?"

A bright flash of light temporarily blinded Joe. Pastor Paul immediately stood up and asked that one of the male ushers kindly escort the reporter out of the sanctuary. He kept yelling, "Did you do it for the reward?" until his voice trailed off in the distance.

Joe continued to speak, "Mother Rose, both Zach and I already told you that we were sharing the reward money with you since the subject came up."

Everyone who did not know already was shocked. Joe and Zach looked to Pastor Paul.

"Zach and I already told you that we would also like to purchase a church van and open an account that includes five years of car insurance and gas expenses for a year."

The congregation was back on its feet thanking God for such a generous gift. Joe and Zach had a group hug with the Rose family and went back to their seats.

The pastor stood. "It would be robbery if we did not allow Mother Rose's best friend to come and share a few words."

As Mother Williamson was already sitting at the front of the church near her friend, she stood up and said, "God bless you, Mother Rose. No one can relate to what you and your precious daughters endured. Even I endured a great ordeal myself, but it was not in vain."

Her feet were hurting after preparing for this celebration almost all night long, but she remained standing and looked the Rose family in the face. She missed seeing their pretty smiling faces.

"My God, my God, how great and excellent are Your ways. Who in all of the earth can compete against You? You are so wide, no one can go around You. You are so high, no one can go over you. Church, we serve a mighty God who cannot fail. When I think how He kept Mother Rose and the girls, it makes me wonder, who are You God that everything and everyone obey you? Mother Rose, I just cannot stop praising God. Every time I think about what could have happened, I just go into praising God all over again."

Suddenly, two more flashes came from the back of the church where more reporters snuck in to get pictures of Mother Rose and her family. As with the previous reporter, they were escorted out of the sanctuary.

"I love you and I'm glad my buddy, my best friend, my prayer partner is back," continued Mother Williamson. "Right now I'm just short on words and full of emotions, but I hope you and the girls really appreciate how much everyone took the time to come together in your honor.

God bless you! Oh, before I forget, some of the Mothers prepared a little food downstairs in your honor, so once Pastor gives the green light for us to eat, please everyone come downstairs and enjoy."

Mother Williamson hugged and kissed the Rose family and excused herself while several other members left the sanctuary with her to check on the food.

Pastor Paul asked, "Choir, please give us two beautiful song selections."

The choir was dressed in their powder blue choir robes with navy blue trim. Hearing the songs "God Has Got Your Back" and "God Has Carried You All The Way" made one feel as if one were already in heaven. The entire congregation was on its feet singing along with the choir because, after hearing those testimonies, who could remain seated?

When the choir finished, Pastor Paul announced, "Thank you for coming to celebrate this very touching and special occasion. It's now time to go downstairs and celebrate!"

Ushers quickly escorted the Rose family downstairs so they could be settled and in place to greet the people. After everyone was seated, Pastor Paul took the opportunity to share his testimony.

"The Rose family has been with this church for many years and it took so much out of me when I heard that they were missing. So all I could do was depend on God's promises, and I knew that He would never leave them nor forsake them. I just waited until God said it was time and suddenly it was all over. Now we are here to tell the Rose family how much we really love them."

Everyone lifted their glasses of sparkling cider, toasted and welcomed the Rose family. The sound of clinking glasses filled the air. Pastor Paul wanted to give Mother Rose a chance to share her testimony so he called her to the microphone before the food was served.

Mother Rose stood as she shouted, "Hallelujah! Praise God for all of the many blessings He has bestowed upon me and my granddaughters!"

Everyone was on their feet joining in on the praise because not only was the Rose family a walking miracle, but they also had become a living testimony to anyone who ever doubted the power of prayer and the assurance of trusting God.

Tears began to soak Mother Rose's face. Ava and Eva clung on to each arm to assist her in walking. She reached for the microphone but she was still full of praise. Eva took the microphone and testified instead about the goodness of God.

"I would like to give God all the glory that is due to His matchless name. Not only have I had a true, miraculous experience of our great God, but I also now know how the Israelites felt when they were chased to no end and God came through for them in the nick of time. I know that I am still young and have many more years to see the awesome power of God, but I stand amazed how God can lead someone from Atlanta, Georgia to Houston, Texas and have that person wind up solving a kidnapping case. God is a good, good God!"

The church was in total praise. Eva gave her sister a chance to say a few words.

"Praise the Lord, everybody."

Everyone replied, "Praise the Lord!"

"I completely agree with my younger sister, Eva," Ava said as she looked her way with a mischievous smile. The congregation laughed.

"I repeatedly heard my mom say while I was growing up that God is so high, you can't go over Him; He is so low, you can't go beneath Him; He is so wide, you can't go around Him. So I always knew that God was with us, and would dispatch His angels to watch over us. During the kidnapping, I remembered when my father would come downstairs in the basement where we were being held captive and he would try to pick fights with my mother about their past. I was just sitting there listening to the conversations take place. I could see, no matter how many times he tried to stir up trouble, God would block it! So, devil, where is your victory?"

Everyone clapped in response to what Ava said.

Finally, Mother Rose was ready to give her testimony. She started singing and concluded with more praises to the Lord for His goodness in and through her life!

"What an experience my daughters and I had. We were subjected to a makeshift bedroom in a basement where we were made to sleep on cots. I do not have to explain to you how uncomfortable it was sleeping this way. Saints, how would we really know God as a protector if He has never protected us from harm and danger? How would we really know God as a healer if He never healed us when we were sick and the doctors could not explain it? How would we really know God as a provider if He never came through for us when we did not have any money to buy food or pay bills? Some may say, just take God at His Word because He is not a man that He should lie! Meanwhile, others may say when you have truly been healed, provided for and/or protected by God, you will know God on another spiritual level!

"Saints of God, after going through my wilderness experience, I can truly say that I know God on another spiritual level. He is my rock of salvation! He is my shield and buckler! He is the lifter of my head! I'm so glad that I know Him for myself and not by what others testify about Him. Today, I can boldly stand before each and every one of you and declare: He is my bridge over troubled waters; He is my ever-present help in the time of storms!

"Young people, you should learn from now how to walk with Jesus while you are still in your youth because the tests will only get bigger as you grow in God. The devil is like a roaring lion seeking whom he may devour. He does not care about your spiritual gifts. He is not impressed by the great relationship you currently have with the Lord. His tactics have been proven over time and so he is patient; patient as he waits for the best time to attack! He will wait for any signs of weakness and if you are not careful and prayed up, he will try to destroy you. That is why the Bible tells us not to be ignorant of his devices.

"Adults, you should know that the devil is definitely playing for keeps. He comes to kill, steal and destroy! He does not care what title you may have and he will use any member in your household—whomever is the closest to you— or whatever you cherish the most to bring you down.

"Saints, you never know when your wilderness experience is coming. Be encouraged my brothers and sisters because greater is He who is in you than he who is in the world. So be blessed and look to God and He will never ever fail you!"

As Mother Rose and the girls walked back to their seats, the people began to shout out, "We love you! We love you!".

The food was served banquet style. Everyone ate, laughed and enjoyed each other's company. After they had their fill of the delicious food, it was time to go home. Pastor Paul made sure that all the seniors had a ride home and were safely escorted to their doorways.

# CHAPTER TWENTY-SEVEN

Mother Rose, the twins, Joe and Zach were all summoned to Texas to testify against Rick, Wendy and Kelly. It was a hard thing for them to do. Day by day as they went to the court to testify, their hearts broke to see their family this way. Rick, Wendy and Kelly were eventually charged with kidnapping and attempted murder. Rick and Wendy were sentenced to twenty years with the possibility of parole. Kelly, however, got slapped with the most time because he was supposed to be upholding the law and not breaking it. He faced thirty years without the possibility of parole.

Months went by. Joe and Zach were still on fire for the Lord. They joined The Love Church of God Assembly and helped wherever their hands were needed. One day, Joe felt the Lord was leading him to go visit Kelly in prison, but was afraid that he would reject his visit. Nevertheless, being obedient, he made arrangements to fly to Texas and asked Zach to go with him. Both men went to Texas to witness to Kelly to see if he would be open to salvation.

When the guards told Kelly he had visitors, he wondered who would come to see him. Most of his family and friends were in Georgia and had turned their backs on him. Even his wife and children did not have anything to do with him. When he reached the visiting area, Kelly looked into the very men's faces who were responsible for placing him in prison.

Kelly shouted to the guards, "I do not wish to see these visitors!"

But Joe returned the shout. "Wait! Please, give me a moment to just share some good news with you!"

Kelly paused and thought to himself, *"Good news about what? I haven't heard from a single family member since I've been in here. No one's come to visit me - and now THESE guys? What could they possibly have to say?"* He slowly turned and waved to the guard that he had changed his mind. He sat down on his side of the plexiglass wall.

Speaking into the phone, Joe said, "Kelly I know that I am the last person you would ever want to see again, but I came to share some good news with you and this news will change your life forever."

Kelly responded, "Good news? What is this about? The only good news you could bring me is to tell me I'm getting out of here."

Zack replied, "No. Something happened to us that we need to share with you. During this ordeal with Mother Rose and her family, we had a spiritual awakening that has changed our lives forever."

Kelly was furious. He jumped up with force, pushing back his chair. He leaned into the plexiglass and said in a low, stern voice, "You mean to tell me you came here to preach to me? You guys are something else. First you get me locked up, then you come all the way to Texas just to tell me what random preachers come into prison to shove down our throats? I don't need this!"

Joe quickly snapped back, "Listen, you wanted to retire, but you were disgraced. You wanted the reward money, but you didn't get it. This is different; this is huge. This makes up for ALL of that. You have nothing left to lose!"

Kelly slowly sat back down in his chair. His breathing slowed and he was shaking. He was angry but he was also ready to listen. Stone-faced, he asked, "What?"

After ministering to Kelly for a straight twenty minutes, he began to cry. "Why, why did I do something so stupid and dumb?"

Joe assured Kelly that everyone has, at least one time or another in their life, done something regrettable and wished that they could undo it. "Here is where you can make all of your wrongs, right with God and your family."

Kelly whimpered, "Joe, my family won't take any of my phone calls. I wrote them a bunch of letters, but they have not responded. Joe, please tell me how I can make things right again with God and my family. I'm so lonely, lost and confused."

"Kelly, my friend, I'm glad that you asked that question because we had to surrender our lives to the Lord Jesus Christ. He is God's Son who died for mankind's sins and we can lead you to Him if you are tired of living in sin."

"Yes!" Kelly began to shed tears. "Joe, please forgive me for all of the dishonorable things I have done to you. I knew that you were on to me so the only way I could try to throw you off track and not harm you was to know your every move."

"I do not understand what you are trying to tell me, Kelly. What are you saying—that you intentionally tried to stop me?" asked Joe.

"Yes, that is actually what I'm trying to tell you. That I was responsible for several different things like paying someone to make all those phone calls to Miss Williamson's home."

"But why, Kelly? Why? Mother Williamson didn't have anything to do with this case at all."

"I know, but I thought that if I could convince her that someone really kidnapped the Rose family, then she would convince Detectives Thomas and Lee as well. It worked. I needed someone to believe that a real kidnapping had taken place."

"Kelly didn't you think that you were going to get caught once you picked up the reward money?"

"Joe, like we always talked about, there really is no perfect crime, but you do not think about that at the time you are plotting one."

"Okay, what about the cigarette butt—did the DNA evidence really get lost or did you destroy it?"

Holding his head down, Kelly felt like he was being arrested all over again. He managed to lift his head up and said, "I'm afraid I'm guilty of tampering with evidence as well. I'm sorry, gentlemen. You have no idea how regretful I am each day."

Zach saw how sorry Kelly really was. It was not a sorry that he got caught, but a real genuine sorry for hurting so many people he cared about.

"Kelly, were you also the one who broke into my apartment and took everything including all of the evidence I found?"

Bending his head down in shame again, he began to nod, "Shamefully, I paid-off two young people to break into your apartment and once they were inside, I asked them to call me. Joe, I was not really after the other clues that you found, but Rick and I needed the deed to the house in order to sell Miss Rose's house. God, I am truly sorry for all that I have done. Please forgive me, please. I hope that you and Zach can forgive me."

Those words made Joe and Zach feel glad inside as they put their hands against the glass window.

Joe said, "Kelly, my friend, please place your hand on the glass also."

Kelly looked at Joe and said, "After all that I have done to you and your friends, you would still consider me a friend?"

Joe looked Kelly squarely in the face without batting an eye. "That is correct, and soon you will become my brother in the Lord when you surrender your life to Christ."

They walked Kelly through the steps of salvation. Tears began to flow from his eyes as he realized that he had not been forgotten by God. God sent his old friend from another state to walk him though the steps of salvation; no—he wouldn't rot or be forgotten! He could feel the heaviness being lifted off his shoulders and for the first time since he had been locked up, he felt free inside. Joe looked at Kelly, this once strong, respected man he used to know, and now he saw a humbled and weak man with whom God could work.

"Kelly, I love you and I'm going to reach out to your family. I cannot promise you anything, but I'll try to make them see that you need them now more than ever."

"Time's up!" shouted the prison guard. "Visiting hours are over!"

Joe waved the guard over and asked if they could give a Bible to Kelly. The guard took the Bible from Joe's hand and said that they would have to examine it first and then give it to the inmate. Joe thanked the guard and told Kelly that they were not sure when they could return, but they would write as often as they could to encourage him in his new walk with God.

Arriving in Atlanta, Joe and Zach had one thing on their mind and that was to contact Mrs. Kelly. Searching his address book, Joe finally found Kelly's contact information, which included both his home phone and his address. Joe and Zach decided that it would be a good idea to visit his wife and not call ahead. She would probably hang up or just not answer. Moreover, Joe felt it would be better if a woman like Mother Rose or Mother Williamson, came along to share the blessing of salvation to Mrs. Kelly.

Joe gave Mother Rose a call and asked if she would be willing to take on this task. She agreed delightfully as she would try to save the whole world if she could. She told Joe that she would give Mother Williamson a call to see if she wanted to help and would wait for him to contact her about the date and time. Joe knew that they had a challenge on their hands because they were dealing with someone who was broken and did not have anything else to loose.

Weeks passed and both gentlemen felt that they were familiar with Mrs. Kelly's schedule and decided to call Mother Rose to give her a date and time to visit the home. Getting acquainted with her schedule was not difficult because she tried very hard to avoid her neighbors since she was still embarrassed by her husband's actions.

The day to visit Mrs. Kelly finally arrived. Both Mother Rose and Mother Williamson had been praying for weeks that God would intercede on their behalf and melt Mrs. Kelly's stony heart and give her a heart of flesh so that she could receive Jesus as her Lord and Savior.

Mother Rose knocked on the front door as Mother Williamson stood beside her. When the door opened, they introduced themselves. When Mother Rose stated they were friends of her husband, Mrs. Kelly tried closing the door.

Mother Williamson said, as she gently held the door open, "Please, please, Mrs. Kelly, may we have just one moment of your time?"

"No, I do not want to hear anything about that man! He has messed up my families' entire life. Please let me close the door." Sobbing now, and weak, she blurted out in anger, "We do not have food and we are going to lose our house. I cannot afford to pay the mortgage and all our bills are past due. To add salt to my wounds," she sniffed, "I have no one in my family to turn to because my husband has disgraced the family name. His income was much larger than mine and he paid for everything. My income alone is not enough to support the household." By now, they could see that Mrs. Kelly was distraught.

"We know how you feel," Mother Williamson said, looking at Mother Rose, "We've felt loss in our lives, but we know who you can turn to for help and He will supply all your needs."

That got her attention and she slowly opened the door and asked that they come in. She began thinking that they could provide resources to assist her with her financial needs.

Mrs. Kelly led them into her kitchen, which was a complete mess. It was the only place in the entire house that had space to sit. It looked like no one had cleaned up since Mr. Kelly's arrest and trial months ago. Mother Rose and Mother Williamson made room wherever they could and sat down. Mother Williamson started off by letting Mrs. Kelly know that she was not always financially stable, that there were times she did not know where her next meal would come from, but because she trusted in God, she never lacked for anything.

"When I needed food on my table, God provided. When I needed my bills to be paid, God provided," she testified.

Then Mother Rose shared with Mrs. Kelly that she was raising two beautiful girls on the single income she received every month. "There are times when I have extra and there are times we just make it. But God always provides because He promised us in His word that He would supply all of our need according to His riches in glory. Do you know Jesus as your Lord and personal Savior?"

Mrs. Kelly shook her head and said, "I would like to know Him."

In their witnessing to her, they did not have to convince her any further because she felt she had nowhere to turn.

Mother Rose said, "Why not let Jesus be the Lord in your life? Mrs. Kelly, repeat after me, 'Lord Jesus forgive me of my sins, and I believe that you died for my sins. Please come into my life and I accept you as my Lord and personal Savior. Amen!' Do you believe that you are born again Mrs. Kelly?"

"Yes I do!" she replied.

After they hugged and welcomed Mrs. Kelly into God's kingdom, they pitched in and started straightening up the house as much as their older bodies would allow them.

Being led by God, Mother Rose did not share what she was about to do with Mother Williamson. She felt God was leading her to be a blessing to Mrs. Kelly by using some of the reward money Joe and Zach gave to her.

She asked, "Mrs. Kelly, which bills need to be paid immediately?"

Mrs. Kelly was so shocked. "You would do this for me, a complete stranger?"

Mother Rose grabbed her hands and said, "No, you are not a stranger to us anymore. You are now our sister in Christ and we always help one another."

"God is so awesome!" said Mother Williamson because she knew that only God could have led Mother Rose to perform such acts of kindness towards someone she hardly knew. Mrs. Kelly started pulling out all her bills. The ones that needed addressing first were her mortgage, light and gas bills. Mother Rose took them from her hands and began to pray that all her debt be erased and gave her the money to pay them in full.

Later, Joe and Zach stopped by Mrs. Kelly's house and introduced themselves as well while Mother Rose and Mother Williamson were still there. Then Joe asked if there was any place that she needed to go and that they would take her.

"Well," replied Mrs. Kelly, "my bank is open now and I would really like to get the mortgage paid right away. It's six months past due and the house will be going into foreclosure in a few days."

Then Mrs. Kelly gave Joe and Zach a big hug.

"Give me a few minutes while I get myself together."

She thanked God while she ran upstairs to change. Within what seemed like seconds, Mrs. Kelly was back downstairs and ready to go. Mother Rose decided to accompany her for spiritual and friendly support. They took the ride to her bank. Mother Williamson, however, decided to go back home and took the bus.

Because her mortgage was so far behind and the house was about to go into foreclosure, Mrs. Kelly had to wait to be seen by a loan officer. When the loan officer came out to greet Mrs. Kelly he asked that she and Mother Rose accompany him into his office. His demeanor was unpleasant.

"Hello, Mrs. Kelly. I know that you are here for more time, but unfortunately, I'm going to have to start foreclosure proceedings this week."

"Mr. Cummings, I'm not coming here to get another extension. I would like to know my overdue total in order to bring it up-to-date."

Mother Rose knew that he was treating Mrs. Kelly unprofessionally because of her husband's criminal behavior and wanted her to know that he did not respect him as a person anymore.

"Yes," added Mother Rose, "can you please just tell us the total amount past due? Thank you so much!"

Mr. Cummings looked at both of them as if they had three heads on their shoulders. He could not believe that he was not going to get the chance to throw Detective Kelly's family out onto the streets.

Mother Rose asked, "May we speak with your supervisor?"

Mr. Cummings said, "Excuse me, but who are you and why are you in my office with Mrs. Kelly? This is a personal matter that does not concern you."

Mother Rose got up and walked out of his office and began asking the tellers who was in charge over Mr. Cummings.

"Hello, Miss, you seem to be very upset. I'm Mr. Steins and I'm the branch manager. How can I help you?"

"Yes, I'm trying to help out a friend of mine get past a very difficult situation, but we are being disrespected by one of your loan officers named Cummings!"

"What? Let's go into Mr. Cummings' office and get to the bottom of this. Our bank has zero tolerance for that kind of behavior!"

Mr. Cummings, seeing Mr. Steins coming towards him from afar, began speaking to Mrs. Kelly in a more polite tone.

"Mrs. Kelly, is there a problem with Mr. Cummings?" asked Mr. Steins. "Are all of your matters being addressed in a professional manner?"

Mrs. Kelly had gone through enough and did not want to bring any more attention to her situation so she said softly, "Everything is fine now."

But based on her comment and knowing who she was, Mr. Steins decided to handle her financial transaction, so he asked that they follow him to his office.

Mr. Steins profusely apologized again for how Mr. Cummings made Mrs. Kelly and Mother Rose feel and wanted to help them in any way he could.

"Mrs. Kelly, our records indicate that you are really behind in your mortgage payments. How can we help you today? Would you like to bring your mortgage current today?"

Mrs. Kelly looked at Mother Rose to make sure that it was okay. She said, "Mr. Steins, I will pay the entire past-due amount today in cash."

"Yes, we would like to know how much is currently owed so that we can pay it in full," added Mother Rose.

Mr. Steins started smiling. "Well, Mrs. Kelly, if you are going to pay in cash, I might be able to save you some money. I'll be back. Give me a moment to work out some numbers for you that will make your mortgage payments more affordable for you and your family's budget."

Mother Rose grabbed her hand. "See, God is already working on your behalf! He is deeply concerned about everything that goes on in your life."

Mrs. Kelly agreed.

Minutes later, Mr. Steins came back with the biggest grin on his face and slid a piece of paper across his desk. "Here is what you owe the bank. We dismissed all late fees and interest charges, but it will have to be paid in full today. I also took the liberty of taking advantage of our forgiveness program and removed one month's payment. We also did a calculation based on your salary and have reduced your monthly payment to fit your budget until you are able to increase your income."

Mother Rose and Mrs. Kelly could not believe their eyes. God had given Mrs. Kelly favor by reducing the amount she owed to the bank.

The mortgage paperwork was updated. Mother Rose paid the bank for the past due mortgage. She was also able to pay off all three past due utility bills with less than half the amount of money originally owed! They both walked out of the utility company thanking God for all He had done.

The next day, Mother Rose came back with some younger women from the church and they cleaned Mrs. Kelly's entire house, not missing a corner. They also received financial donation from the church so they went grocery shopping for the family. They would have something to eat for at least a month. The sisters made lunch and they had a good old time fellowshipping with Mrs. Kelly and her family.

Mother Rose told Mrs. Kelly, "Now that all your bills are up-to-date, the church's lawyer is working on getting Mr. Kelly's pension signed over into your name. He is still entitled to his pension that he worked for all those years."

Mrs. Kelly could not believe that a God who cared so much for her had not been in her life sooner. She was grateful that she accepted Christ into her life and had a church family who cared and prayed for her family as well.

Mrs. Kelly said to Mother Rose, "If there is anything I can do for you, please let me know and I will not hesitate. I will do it in a heart-beat!"

Mother Rose simply smiled. "If I had to ask you to do anything for me, it would be to forgive your husband, even as Jesus has forgiven you of your sins. You must forgive others who have done you wrong. I will even pay for you and the children to go see Mr. Kelly. Maybe our lawyer can also petition to have him transferred to a closer prison location, but that would take some time."

Mrs. Kelly mumbled with embarrassment. "You are right. It is time for me to forgive him. I must also tell him about all of the wonderful things God has done for our family."

With excitement written all across her face, she grabbed Mother Rose and kissed her on the cheek.

"Yes, I have to forgive my husband. No one has ever done anything like this for me before. The world is so cold and people always seem to be angry."

Mother Rose said, "You are saved. You must show the world that there are people who care and that there is a God who is deeply concerned about His creations, but just hates their sin."

"Yes, Mother Rose. I want to be like you while I'm still alive—caring for the dying and hurting people in the world by making a difference."

Mrs. Kelly looked at how neat the house looked.

"Thanks to all of you who volunteered to clean our house, buy our groceries, make our lunch and just be with us. Thank you because I can't remember the last time I had company over and enjoyed myself like this! Thank you all for being a blessing to me and my family!"

After coming to the church for several Sundays, Mrs. Kelly and her family felt at home and decided to join The Love Church of God Assembly. After she finished the beginner's class, she joined two ministry groups in the church. Pastor Paul did not believe in the saints of God joining more than two groups because they would become overwhelmed and eventually burn out.

# CHAPTER TWENTY-EIGHT

Finally, it was time for Mrs. Kelly and her children to visit Kelly in the Texas Correctional Prison. She remembered how her husband would always talk about how bad prison was and would tell their children to never go to such a bad place. She began to cry, feeling her husband's pain. She just could not imagine seeing him inside a facility like the one he had sent criminals to.

When they arrived, the guard called Mr. Kelly who was in his cell through the PA system and told him he had visitors. He had grown spiritually over the months, reading his Bible every day and praying that God would forgive him of his sins. Most importantly, he had prayed that God would save his family and allow them to forgive him for hurting them.

Kelly was expecting to see his friends, Joe and Zach. He could not believe his eyes when he saw his wife and kids sitting behind the plexiglass window. Pausing for a while to make sure he was not dreaming, his eyes filled with tears. The guard asked if he wanted to decline the visit because of his hesitation.

Kelly immediately said, "No!" He wiped his eyes and pulled himself together. "Sir, please this is my family whom I love and have not seen in months. I'm okay. Please let me see them. I'm sorry for any confusion I may have led you to believe."

As the door to the prisoners' side of the visiting area swung open, his wife and kids all stood up and sadly watched the man who had provided and loved them for years now walking in a bright orange jumper with cheap looking sneakers on his feet.

"Daddy! Daddy!"

His children placed their hands on the glass with tears in their eyes and his wife held her hands to her mouth with tears of unbelief streaming down her face.

Kelly walked up to the glass window and began to cry and to say that he was so sorry for what he did to them and hoped they would find it in their hearts to forgive him. Directing them to be seated in the chairs in front of them, he picked up the phone so that he could hear what they were saying; his wife followed.

"Hello baby, I'm so glad you came to see me and brought the kids too," Kelly said. "I prayed every day to God that you would forgive me and come see me."

"Honey," replied Mrs. Kelly, "did you say prayed?"

"Yes, baby. I gave my heart to God and I know that you may see me locked up behind bars, but I'm free in my spirit because God has shown me a better way. God has been keeping me, baby. He has introduced me to others in prison who also made some mistakes in life, but have now accepted God as their Savior and are free in their hearts and minds. We pray and read the Bible together when we can, which is a huge encouragement to us."

Surprised, Mrs. Kelly could not believe how her husband was talking because he never believed in God before. He always felt that he could handle anything that came up in his life and did not need God's help.

"Yeah, baby. Do you remember Joe, Mr. PI, who I invited to the house for dinner a couple of times with his wife years back?"

"Yes, he was one of the two men who were responsible for your capture. Okay, that Joe," replied Mrs. Kelly.

"Well, he and his friend, Zach, received God into their lives and came back to Texas to minister to me."

Mrs. Kelly said, "Look at God! Honey, did you know they came to see me at my lowest state and prayed with me as well? Mother Rose and Mother Williamson also prayed with me and led me to the Lord."

"What?" replied Mr. Kelly. "You mean...?"

Mrs. Kelly nodded her head yes. "I'm saved as well, honey, and the kids are too. We all have been going to church for a couple of months since we gave our lives to Christ. We came to tell you that we forgive you and that we still love you."

As he placed his hand on the glass and began thanking God, his family did the same. The Kelly family was praising God for what He did for them as other visitors just looked.

"Honey, Mother Rose is the one who paid for our trip with the reward money."

Then Mr. Kelly lowered his head in shame because the main reason he was sitting in prison was because he was trying to get that money so he could retire earlier and take care of his family's obligations.

Mrs. Kelly said, "Hold your head up again because God has forgiven you and so have we. We want to move forward and forget about the past."

He was so grateful to hear his wife speak with such boldness and authority. It made him believe that if she could still love him after all he had done to hurt this family, then he had to forgive himself.

Both his children desperately wanted to speak with their father as well, but they also knew their mother needed to clear some things with him first. They decided to be patient and wait for their chance. They wanted more than anything in the world for their parents to reconcile with each other so they could feel like a family again.

"Honey, guess what else they did with the reward money?"

"What, baby, what?"

"Mother Rose paid off all our past due debts!"

Mr. Kelly rolled the chair back that he was sitting in and buried his head in his lap and began to cry like a little baby.

The guard came over. "Is there a problem?"

Kelly regained control immediately and saw the look on his children's faces. They had never seen their father break down like that before.

He looked at them and said, "This is what God will do for you—break down your stony heart and then give you a heart of flesh." He told the guard, "Everything is okay. I just received some good news."

"Baby," Kelly asked his wife, "what bills did she pay? I was so worried we were going to lose the house."

"Well, we were on the verge of losing the house. All of our bank accounts are still frozen because the police needed to make sure that the money in the accounts came from us and that you were not involved in any other illegal activities."

"I assure you that I was not and that is all honest savings."

"I know, honey, but we have to wait it out. Mother Rose paid off the past due mortgage and all of the other outstanding bills. Then some Mothers and Sisters from the church stopped by and helped clean up the house from top to bottom. For days, I had no reason to get out of bed, never mind clean up the house."

"Baby, you know it had to be God who led her to perform these acts of kindness towards the family of the very man who held her captive for months. God is the best example of forgiveness and teaches us how to behave the same way. God is real whether others want to acknowledge him or not! He is a great God!"

"Honey, I thought I was losing my mind, but God stepped in! If it had not been for the Lord on my side, where would I be?"

"Our side," corrected Kelly. "Our side now that I have you back in my life. God has taken care of the both of us and every day I would sit in my cell and ask what did I do to deserve His love. I did not want anything to do with God and He still loved me anyway."

"Honey, we are serving a loving and forgiving God! One who loves us unconditionally in spite of how messed up we are as individuals."

"Yes, baby, I know and I'm so glad He saved all of us and brought us back together as a family."

"I know it's not going to be easy for you and the kids, but if we continue to trust God, even on our worst days, He promises to see us though all of our trials and tribulations."

"Yes, dear, we all must trust God going forward."

"Honey," Mrs. Kelly said, "God has allowed us to obtain a lawyer free of charge from the church to help get your pension funds straightened out and unfreeze our savings accounts. The best news of all, this lawyer from the church is going to see if you can be moved to a closer location, hopefully to one of the Atlanta prisons, so we would not have to take a plane to see you which will become costly over the years."

"Wow, God is so amazing!"

"Yes, so let's pray about these changes for our lives and believe that God will come through for us."

"Yes, baby, I will and I love you, but before my time is up, let me speak to my kids!"

"I love you too and will let you know the next time we can visit.

Maybe we can also spend time together as husband and wife for the weekend."

Mrs. Kelly's eyes lit up just imagining that she would be able to hold her husband in her arms again.

"By the way, honey, can you please send me some personal items and if permitted some of my favorite snacks as well?" asked Kelly.

"Sure I will do that, baby," replied Mrs. Kelly.

After Kelly had spoken to his entire family, the prison guard shouted that their time was up. But he did not care because he felt like a new man all over again. God had saved and restored his whole family, people who he would die for. They watched him until they could not see him anymore then they exited the building and headed back to their hotel. Unlike other prisoners, Kelly had a stricter punishment. Based upon his crime, he was only allowed a visitor once a month. Kelly was expected to be a good example when he was on the police force, but now he was looked upon as an embarrassment to law enforcement.

As she wondered how everything went with Mrs. Kelly and her family, Mother Rose and the girls started packing for their trip to Texas. Hopefully, Mr. Kelly was still saved and walking with the Lord. Unfortunately, Mother Rose would not be able to find out the answers to her questions until she got back home from seeing her son, Rick. She knew that God was in the midst of everything, but for the first time she was nervous about witnessing. She had been doing this for so many years and it became second nature to her, but this time it would be different. She now had to minister to him once again, but inside the prison. This time, she was bringing teenagers to him, in hopes that he would accept them back into his life and, more importantly, accept God back into his life.

The girls seemed to be as nervous as Mother Rose because they wanted to get to know their parents and wanted their parents to want to get to know them as well. As Mother Rose and the girls exited the plane, they all felt like they were reliving a nightmare, but knowing God as they did, they began to flush out doubt and fear from their minds and trust in Him.

After settling down in their hotel room, Mother Rose suggested to the girls, that once they hailed a cab to go to the prison, they should pray. Ava was able to flag down a cab and Mother Rose gave directions to the cab driver.

They all held hands in the back seat of the cab and Mother Rose began to pray.

"Jesus, we know that it is not your will that anyone should perish, but only to have eternal life. So, Jesus, we need You to be in the midst of this visit. We need Your presence to go before us, even right now. Jesus, You already know what we are up against, but we take authority over every disobedient spirit. We abort any plans that the enemy may try to use against us. Jesus, we thank you right now for the peace that surpasses all understanding and we thank you in advance for salvation. We call those things that are not, as though they already are. In Jesus' precious name we pray, Amen!"

As Mother Rose opened her eyes, she could not help but notice that the cab driver was looking at them through the rear-view mirror.

Mother Rose introduced herself to the cab driver and asked, "What is your name?"

"Oh, my name is Khurrah. It is a pleasure to meet you."

"Likewise," replied Mother Rose. "Do you know the Lord Jesus Christ as your personal Savior?"

Khurrah said, "No, I do not know Jesus Christ."

Mother Rose smiled at him and said, "Let me share with you, the life of the Son of the living God."

Immediately, Khurrah paid attention as she began to share how God sent His only Son, Jesus Christ, into the world to die for mankind's sins.

"Over 2,000 years ago, God chose a virgin named Mary to be impregnated and gave birth to His Son named Jesus. Although Mary was engaged to be married to Joseph at the time, they had not known each other yet. Because she was not married and was pregnant, this caused conflict between Mary and Joseph who both loved God. So God sent an angel to tell Joseph that Mary had not been unfaithful to him, but God had chosen Mary to miraculously carry His only Son.

"Jesus grew up and loved everyone and enjoyed helping those in need. He performed many miracles such as giving sight to the blind, making the deaf hear, the dumb speak and the lame walk. There were so many more miracles that Jesus performed while here on earth that showed He really cared for mankind. Jesus always taught mankind about His Father and how man must be born again to become a child of God. Jesus explained to the people that although you were birthed by earthly parents, in order to be accepted into God's Kingdom, they had to be spiritually born.

"Jesus chose twelve ordinary men to become His disciples and as they followed Him, they witnessed Him healing the sick, walking on water and raising the dead. So many people began to believe in the Kingdom of God that it eventually caused uproars among the religious leaders. Jesus, knowing that He was sent into the world to die for all mankind's sins, warned His disciples that He would be taken away by evil soldiers. Although God had given Jesus all power in His hands, He was sentenced to death. He humbly carried the very cross on which He was nailed. Some people believed that they forcefully took His life, but He kindly and willingly laid it down for all mankind's sins and died.

"Jesus promised His disciples that after His death, on the third day, God would raise Him from the dead. As promised, on the third day the tomb Jesus was buried in was in fact empty and there was no sign of His body. Jesus was alive. Jesus was raised from the dead!"

"Oh come on, lady!" shouted Khurrah. "First of all, how can God, who is a spirit, impregnate a human being?"

His response did not come as a shock to Mother Rose. She knew that he would question that.

She just gently smiled. "Do you believe in God?"

"Well," replied Khurrah, "I was born and raised in India and I have been in this country for seven years. I was taught from a little boy the ways of Hinduism. Most people in my country believe there are many gods. Let me now explain my religious beliefs to you."

Mother Rose listened patiently.

"We believe that each living being is a unique manifestation of god. We believed in ancient times and still believe that there are 330 million deities or gods of Hinduism. But out of the 330 million gods, there are only two gods who claim to be superior over all of the other gods. They are called Krishna and Durga.

"So, I do not understand how you claim there is this one true God over all mankind. But how can that be? Does this one God have eyes everywhere? Does this one God know who is sick or who needs money to pay their bills? He would have to be everywhere, at all times."

Mother Rose smiled again. "Well, as a matter of fact, God is omnipresent, which means that He is everywhere at the same time. There is one God we serve, a Triune God—the Godhead consisting of God the Father, God the Son - Jesus Christ - and God the Holy Spirit and they all have their special functions in the Godhead."

Mother Rose then began to explain to Khurrah what each represents. "First, God the Father reigned during the Old Testament times and still does. Second, God the Son, Jesus Christ, became known during the New Testament times, is the Savior of the world and died for the sins of the world. Jesus is alive and is coming back again one day for His people, a prepared people. Third, the Holy Spirit is our mediator who controls today's times."

Khurrah replied, "So you believe in many gods like we do. Since I have been in this country, many people have tried to persuade me to believe that there is only one God who has complete control over the entire universe. But I never gave them a chance to discuss the matter any further and I would just wave my hand at them and keep walking. That is why I have never heard of this Jesus Christ you were referring to earlier."

Mother Rose asked him, "How could you believe in so many gods that do not offer any guarantees? Can all of these gods show that they care for you personally? Do all these gods care if you live a righteous life or care how you live? God forbid, He sent His only begotten Son into the world to die for your sins and mine, which shows that He is very much concerned about our lives. My Bible tells me that after death God is going to judge your life. We do not believe in reincarnation or purgatory; its either heaven or hell period!"

Khurrah pulled the cab to a stop. "We are at your destination."

Mother Rose wanted so desperately to finish her conversation with him, but she was totally committed to reaching her lost son. She reached into her pocketbook to retrieve a tract about a story line where someone was witnessing to a person of Hindu beliefs. It explained about God, His Son Jesus Christ, and the Holy Spirit.

She asked, "Khurrah, could I pray with you before I leave the cab?"

"Of course you can. I never turn down prayer!"

Mother Rose reached for his hand through a small opening in the makeshift glass window and reached for her daughters' hands as well.

She began to pray. "Jesus, if it is possible, please allow us to meet again. God, You said in Your Word that he that wins a soul is wise, so Jesus I pray that You open the eyes of Khurrah as he takes the time to read this tract I gave him. Give him clarity of thought and remove the scales from his eyes and ears so that he may comprehend everything that he needs to know concerning You and Your kingdom. Father, we thank You for seeing it through. Thank you in advance for his salvation and determination in wanting to learn more about You. In Jesus' name, Amen!"

Khurrah nodded his head. "Thank you for those kind words. The total will be $54.80."

Mother Rose gave him sixty-five dollars and told him to keep the change and that she hoped they would cross paths again someday.

"Thank you, Miss. Thank you for praying for me!"

After entering the main building, Mother Rose and the girls had to sign in, remove everything from their pockets and were patted down before going into the visitation area where her son was waiting. Rick was sitting in a chair thinking that his lawyer was coming to see him because he needed to finalize his paper work with him. But when he looked up, he saw his two daughters coming through the door. Mother Rose and the girls planned that the girls would be the first ones to have their moment with their father and then she would come in after about thirty minutes. Inmates only had one hour of visitation time.

Rick could not believe what his eyes were seeing. Guilt began to swell up inside him as he lowered his head. He thought to himself that if they were here to tell him off, he deserved it and would just take it like a man. Both girls sat down.

Ava, being the bolder of the two, grabbed the phone and pointed for Rick to do the same.

Rick nearly dropped the phone when he heard his daughter say, "Hello, Daddy!"

He totally did not expect that from her so, at first, he was speechless.

Then he said, "Hello, my daughter. Then embarrassingly, he asked, "Who are you?"

"I'm Ava, Daddy, and I know you are wondering why we came to see you, right?"

"Well yes. I'm very surprised and even more surprised that you address me as your daddy," replied Rick. He was not expecting her next statement.

Ava said, "Friends you can change, but family is forever."

His eyes began to swell up with tears, but no tears fell yet.

He said, "My, how grown up you are."

"Daddy, I came today to tell you that I forgive you for what you have done and that I still love you even though I really do not know much about you."

Rick was so relieved in his heart that his daughter could still love him after all he put them through. He decided to let her vent.

"Daddy, I want to get to know you and Mommy. That is why I came and I want to know if you feel the same way."

"Yes, oh yes, I feel the same way. I wanted this so much, but I went about it the wrong way. I should have tried to reconnect with my mother, your grandmother, first and then get to know you girls instead of doing what I did."

Mother Rose was in hearing distance. If Rick had not accepted them, then she would have told the girls they were leaving because she refused to put the girls through this whole ordeal with their father trying to harm them again. But God was answering her prayers. She began to get emotional.

Rick looked at his daughter. "Will you forgive me for all the wrongs and for being an absent father to you?"

Ava quickly said, "Yes, I forgive you, Daddy. Would it be okay if I wrote to you from time to time so that we can get to know each other better?"

"You did not even have to ask that question," replied Rick. "I'm so lonely and to have my family back into my life again means the world to me. Does your sister, Eva, feel the same way?"

"Yes, Daddy, she does. I love you and I'll let you talk to her now."

He quickly said, "I love you as well."

Ava passed the phone to Eva who had the biggest grin on her face as she took the phone.

Sounding a little younger than Ava, Eva said, "Hi, Daddy. I'm so glad that you still love us after we testified against you during your trial."

"Oh no! I'm glad that you are not still mad at me for what I did to you girls."

"Daddy, I do not want to revisit the past. I just want to move forward and establish a relationship with you. I've always wondered about you, Daddy. We were always under the impression that our grandmother was our real mother, but we always wondered what happen to our real father. But we do not have to wonder any longer."

"No, you do not, my baby. I want to always be in your lives from now on." His time was almost over so he decided to blow a kiss to both girls.

"Did my mother come along as well?"

No sooner than he completed his sentence, Mother Rose came towards him with tears in her eyes. She could not remember the last time her son was willing to speak with her, let alone the girls. The last words Rick had spoken to her were in court when he said that she was dead to him and that he no longer had a mother. Rick was still upset with his mother. He looked at her and then lowered his head. He noticed, however, how both girls stood up to greet her as she walked through the doorway. He began to show signs of relief since he now knew his mother was no longer angry with him. He wanted desperately to make-up with his entire family. Mother Rose went for the phone.

"Hello, Junior. I know you are very surprised I would ever show my face in this place. I know you are surprised that I would come now and not before when the girls were younger."

Rick was crying now because he knew that his mother was the only one who could read him so well.

"Son, I always thought about bringing the girls to see you, but they were so young and I didn't want them to have it on their minds that both their parents were locked up and did not want to have anything to do with them."

Rick lifted his head and surprisingly mumbled, "I know you were protecting the girls."

Mother Rose, with gladness in her heart, said, "Yes, baby. That was all I was trying to do—protect the children."

Another unexpected statement came from Rick's mouth. "Mom, can you ever forgive me for treating both you and Dad the way I did?"

Mother Rose's heart was now smiling because she knew at that moment her son was ready for salvation.

She replied, "I already forgave you years ago through God's grace."

"Mom?"

"Yes, my son?"

"Can you please also forgive me for kidnapping you and the girls?"

"Son, that too is a thing of the past. I love you, Junior, and you will always be my son."

# CHAPTER TWENTY-NINE

Mother Rose said, "Son, I wanted so much for us to get along and have a good mother and son relationship. It broke my heart every day until God showed me how to let go and trust Him."

"Mom, if it's any consolation, my heart was also broken. Every time I would see a mother and son visitation in prison when meeting with my lawyer, I thought of you. I'm taking counseling sessions now and they have taught me to forgive and not hold bitterness in my heart."

"Good, Junior. I'm also so proud of you for coming out to speak with your daughters and I also would like...what I mean is that the girls and I would like for you to get reacquainted with God and His Son Jesus."

"Mommy, I know this is what you were always trying to get me to do, but I just wanted to do my own thing."

"Yes dear. This is what your father and I wanted. I also wanted you to hear what the preacher would preach every Sunday—having a personal relationship with God."

"Mommy, the enemy had my mind all messed up and all I could think about was hurting you and if the girls did not want to have anything to do with me, I would hurt them as well." He looked in their direction. "Mommy, I'm tired of living this way. I know I put Daddy in an early grave. I don't want to do the same to you. Please forgive me. I'm ready to turn my life around for God so He can change me from my sinful ways. I do not want to hurt the people I love anymore. I want to love them. Please help me, Mommy, please!"

"Son, I cannot help you, but let me reintroduce you to God's Son, Jesus, who died for our sins! The Bible declares in John 14:6, 'Jesus saith unto him, I am the way, the truth, and the life; no man cometh unto the Father, but by me.'"

Mother Rose walked Rick through the steps of salvation and prayed with him.

Rick said, "I feel lighter, like my problems are now all gone. I cannot explain it, but it feels like a weight has been lifted off me."

"Praise God!" shouted Mother Rose.

The guard looked directly at her with an expression of disbelief on his face, indicating that Rick was probably just pretending.

Mother Rose looked Rick, squarely in the face. "There will be many doubters around you but, Junior, I do not want you to look at the faces of the people, nor do I want you to try and convince people that you have changed. Just keep living for the Lord and your life will be a witness to many. Walk by faith in God and not by sight." She and the girls were also concerned about his personal cares. "Do you need anything?"

Anxiously, he asked, "Can you go visit Wendy, and save her too?"

Once again Mother Rose corrected Rick, "Son, I do not have the power to save anyone, but I do know who has all power in His hands and His name is Jesus! Only He can save Wendy if she is willing to accept Him as her Lord and personal Savior."

"Thank you so much, Mom. Thank you!"

He looked relieved. Mother Rose and the girls asked him again if he needed any personal items or desired a taste for anything while they were in Texas.

"Actually, I do have a couple of requests. Can I get your home number so that I can call and speak with everybody more often? Also, would it be too much to ask if you can come see me at least once a year? You might be able to see me two or three times during that one trip. Lastly, I would love to write a list of all the personal items I need before you go back home. Most are already listed in the documentation the guards will hand out before you leave."

"Sure," said Mother Rose. "Here is our number. Remember it." She said each number slowly and then repeated it several times. "I'll write it down too and ask the guard to give it to you. We would also love to come and see you once a year. That will give me time to save up for the trip. I will also speak with the guard and ask him for the document so we will comply with the prison rules."

"Great," replied Rick, "but I forgot one request. Can you also send me some pictures of you and daddy - and some baby pictures of Ava and Eva? I would like to hang them on my wall to remind myself how precious my family members are to me."

Mother Rose began grinning from ear to ear and said, "Junior, the girls beat you to it. They thought of that already so before we leave, we will hand them over to the inspection department for you."

"Mommy, have you ever noticed that when someone says 'this is the last request', that they usually have another one?"

Mother Rose nodded her head. "What is it, baby?"

"Well, I would love for you and the girls to have something that may help out with the cost of living and perhaps the girls' college education. I'm going to speak with my lawyer and ask him to give you access to my savings account and the money from Uncle Brad's home once it is sold."

Mother Rose said, "Son, I'm so proud of you to suggest that. God bless you!"

Rick realized that his time was over when he noticed other inmates getting up to leave. He quickly placed his left hand on the plexiglass window while holding the phone with his right hand. He told them that he was so grateful they came and that he loved them. He blew a kiss to them and they touched the plexiglass window where his hand was. They blew kisses back to him.

The guard shouted, "Visiting hour is over! Come on, start moving in line with the other inmates, even you, Rose."

Rick left the visiting room. As he walked down the corridor towards the inmates' cells, he held his head down in shame because he realized that God had given him all the opportunities to change but he didn't. He remembered the numerous times his mother tried to lead him in the right path when he was younger, but he did not want to listen. And then there was his father whom he thought was just trying to spoil all his fun and make him live a boring life. Why didn't he just listen to someone? He now knew that his mother and father had his best interest at heart.

Oh, how could he forget Uncle Brad, especially after their last conversation while traveling back home after being released from prison? Uncle Brad told him that when there's a calling on your life, no devil in Hell could stop God from getting a hold of you and using you for what He has created you to be! Rick thought that, once again, he was in this familiar setting, a correctional facility, where his life did not matter to anyone; they just saw him as a number. But God saw something in him worth saving. He didn't give up on him or allow him to give up on himself. He thought, *God I'm now ready to totally surrender my life to you. Here I am God. Use me for your glory!*

The girls held on to each other with tears in their eyes as they watched this fatherly figure, who did not exist to them most of their lives, disappear again, as he walked through the doorway. But Mother Rose could not cry anymore. She was just so overwhelmed by an awesome God answering prayers. It was amazing when you trust God for so many years and see the manifestation of His work through time. As she paced back and forth with praise in her heart, she thought, *God, You are marvelous and magnificent is Your name!*

On exiting, Mother Rose and the girls spoke with the guards at the General Information Booth about the pictures they wanted to leave with Rick and about other personal items the inmates could have in their possession. Mother Rose also asked the guard if they could make arrangements for a car service to take them home.

"No!" replied the guard angrily. "We're not in the business of catering to visitors nor do we allow commercial traffic to come onto prison premises. You will have to call information and get your own car service. Meet them at the approved designated pick-up and drop-off area about a mile away."

Profusely apologizing, Mother Rose said, "This is all new to me and my daughters. Please forgive us and thanks for your assistance anyway. God bless you!"

"Yeah, yeah whatever!" replied the guard. "Everyone says God this and God that, but live like the devil all day long." He handed them the documentation they requested. "Keep moving along!"

"Mommy, he seems very upset. Why is he so angry?" asked Eva.

"Baby, not everyone is able to cope with life's disappointments, but the difference between the saved and the unsaved, is that we have God's peace upon our lives which surpasses all understanding."

"But, Mommy, we have disappointments in our lives too," replied Ava, "and we're not going around trying to bite everyone's head off."

"I know, babies, but when you have God in your life it makes a huge difference. We can cast all of our cares upon Him because He cares and when you do not have God in your life, you are trying to solve life's problems all by yourself which can become very burdensome. God never intended for us to take on the cares of the world ourselves. That's why He told us in His Word to cast all our cares upon Him; because He cares for us. All God wants from us is to acknowledge Him as the Creator and acknowledge His Son, Jesus, as the Savior of the world. Sadly, the world does not have a problem with God. It is Jesus, His Son, they have a problem with and do not want to accept."

While walking to the designated pick-up area, the girls took delight in making a mental note of all the items from the list the prison guard handed to them that they wanted to purchase for their father. "Can we stop at the local discount store in our neighborhood to make the purchases?" they asked.

"It would be cheaper if we purchased the items here in Texas. This way, we can save on shipping and handling and Junior will receive the package much quicker."

"You are right, Mommy," replied Eva. "I do not know what I was thinking."

"It is okay. You are excited."

Still reminiscing, Mother Rose thought about how good God was and wanted to give Him all of the praise, glory and honor for all His wonderful works He did today. So while sitting at the local pick-up area waiting for the cab, Mother Rose and the girls began to give God praise for saving Rick's soul. Mother Rose was also hoping that they would get the same cab company, and Khurrah would be their driver again.

The sound of a loud horn drowned out their voices of praises. They stood up from the bench and started walking towards the cab. To Mother Rose's disappointment, they had a different driver. As they rode back to their hotel, the girls could not stop talking about what they were going to purchase for their father whom they had come to love.

It was a tiresome day for everyone, so after shopping and dropping the package off at the post office with almost every item on the list and extras, it was now time for them to visit their biological mother, Wendy.

Eva, bouncing around on all of the beds like a little five-year-old, said, "I can't wait until our mother accepts Christ as her Savior too."

"Yeah," replied Ava, "We will be one big family again, I cannot wait."

Mother Rose knew in her heart that one of the main reasons Junior had stopped going to church was because Wendy did not want to go any longer. She looked at both girls and was so happy because now everyone would be taking their rightful place in the girls' lives. She wanted what was best for her granddaughters and was not afraid that they might no longer love her. Preparing for bed, Mother Rose asked the girls to shower and she would take hers shortly after.

"Girls, we need to believe God for Wendy's salvation so we will get up and pray at five in the morning until seven. Are you up for that, my little prayer warriors, because we know that prayer changes things?"

Eva gently wrapped her arms around Mother Rose and said, "Mommy, this is also what we want. There is no way the enemy is going to win this war. The devil had control over their minds long enough and now we're taking our family back in Jesus' name!"

Ava agreed. "When we stand on God's Word and trust Him, He said that He would save our whole household and that is what we'll believe."

Morning arrived and the alarm clock went off at five, waking everyone up, except for Eva. Mother Rose was the first to get out of bed and Ava followed. Finally, Eva slowly made her way out of the bed. Although she was sleepy, she was still determined to pray for her mother's salvation.

Mother Rose began to praise God and the girls followed. Then each one prayed for Wendy separately—that God would save her. This went on for two straight hours. They, however, recognized that they were in a hotel praying early hours in the morning and were very sensitive to their surroundings. They kept the tone of their voices very low. They knew that God was able to hear any type of sincere prayers.

After prayer, Mother Rose recommended that they go back to bed for another hour. She suggested that they fast until after their visit with Wendy at the Texas Women's Correctional Prison. Besides, visitation did not start until two in the afternoon, so they had plenty of time to get extra rest.

Waking up in a cold sweat, Mother Rose began to rebuke the dream she just had. She struggled to remember each detail of it since she felt God was trying to tell her something or warn her about something. Grabbing some paper and pen from the hotel desk, she began writing about the dream:

*It seemed that I was shopping in a grocery store and a teenage girl was standing outside with this sad look on her face just watching everyone in the store. Almost everyone had compassion for her and invited her inside to buy her something to eat but she refused. It seemed like she became very upset when men would offer to buy her something to eat by angrily shouting "No!" But each time a woman would offer her something to eat she would kindly say, "No, thank you."*

The dream puzzled Mother Rose and she wondered what it meant. She got out of bed to read her Word and decided to keep the dream to herself because she did not want to confuse the girls.

Ava and Eva were so excited about seeing their biological mother again. They could hardly wait for the cab. It seemed to be taking a lifetime, but it finally arrived. Still concerned about last night's dream, Mother Rose prayed that God would keep His hands of protection over the girls. She felt in her spirit that something was not right so she found herself rebuking every unrighteous thought that tried to overtake her thoughts with fear and doubt. She began to hum a hymn.

The cab driver interrupted her praise. "You sound very lovely. We have reached your destination."

"Thank you, Sir," Mother Rose put the fare inside a Bible tract. As she gave it to him, she said, "Keep the change. Have a blessed day."

After getting checked into the prison, the guard asked that they be seated in a waiting room. This prison did not have a glass wall separating the prisoners and the guests, just table and chairs. After waiting for about twenty minutes, they heard the sound of a gate opening and releasing dozens of inmates. Wendy was among them. As she turned the corner to the waiting room, to her astonishment, she saw her two daughters and mother-in-law. They looked excited as they were anticipating God to work through them for Wendy like He did with Rick. Wendy, however, turned around and told the guard that she did not want to see her visitors.

Mother Rose, having compassion for the girls, quickly shouted, "Your daughters want desperately to see their birth mother and they will only be here until the end of this week. Please, Wendy, please! If not for me, at least do it for your daughters!"

Wendy kept walking as if she did not hear Mother Rose. The girls held each other as they were led out of the waiting room crying. All of the other inmates and guests looked on in sympathy.

Mother Rose's heart felt like it was being torn in pieces as she watched both girls get rejected again by their natural mother. She placed her arms around them and they left the building.

"It's okay girls. I tried to hide this from you for such a long time. Now that you have decided to still meet with your mother, I will not blame you, if you never want to see her again."

"No, Mommy, no! I will not give up on her. Jesus did not give up on us and He would not want us to give up on Wendy. This was our prayer this morning—that we would continue to reach her because God said He would save our whole household," replied Ava.

"So what do you both want to do?" asked Mother Rose.

Eva replied adamantly but respectfully, "We want to fight for what belongs to us and show Wendy what true family love is all about—never giving up on each other. God told us to plant the seed and He would do the increase. I want to go back again. Visiting days are Sunday and Wednesday, and I want to go back on Wednesday."

Mother Rose looked at Ava. "Do you feel the same way as your sister?"

She said, "I don't want to give up on Wendy either because it would be like we are giving up on each other. Mommy, you always told us we are supposed to make the difference in the world. Just because *she* gave up on herself doesn't mean *we* should give up on her."

If there was ever a time Mother Rose was proud of the two girls she raised, that time would be right now. Mother Rose opened her arms.

"This calls for a group hug! Come here, my babies. I have an idea.

Let's find out what things we can buy for your mother and put a picture of the family inside the gift box."

Ava smiled. "Oh boy, that sounds like a great idea, Mommy. Let's do some shopping today. Do you remember some of the things she liked when she was living with you?"

"Ava baby, that was so long ago. I cannot begin to remember what she liked."

"Okay," said Eva, "we will just ask God to bring it back to your remembrance."

Mother Rose giggled and walked towards the visitation booth to inquire about what products would be acceptable to purchase.

.

# CHAPTER THIRTY

It was Wednesday morning and everyone was looking forward to seeing Wendy's reaction when they visited. The Bible says some things only come by fasting and praying, which was what Mother Rose suggested to the girls. They fasted and prayed for three days believing God that not only would their mother speak with them, but that they would be able to usher her into the heavenly family.

They checked in. Not knowing what to expect, they were nervous, but were still trusting God because He had everything under control. Once again, the guard brought them into the waiting room and asked that they wait until the inmates were brought in. They patiently waited for about fifteen minutes before the inmates were led into the room. When Wendy laid eyes on them again, she turned to leave the room.

Mother Rose shouted, "We left a gift bag with personal items including family pictures with the guards!"

Then both Ava and Eva shouted, "We love you, Mom! Please do not leave!"

Wendy stopped and slowly turned around. She looked at the girls with surprise in her eyes. "But you don't even know me! How can you love someone you don't even know?" she asked with skepticism.

Ava decided to address Wendy's question first. "No, we do not know you, but the God we serve knows and loves you. God instructed us to love and not hate, so it is our duty to love you whether we know you or not. I choose to love you, not because God told me to, but because you are my flesh and blood."

Mother Rose dared not interrupt the girls and wanted God to use them to win their mother to the Lord.

"Mommy, you are the one who carried us for nine months and brought us into this world. That's another reason why we love you! Besides, you are family and family sticks together and always look out for one another." Ava did not know what else to say.

Wendy just stood there after hearing those words coming from her own daughter's mouth and began to show a breaking. Tears welled up in her eyes but she fought them back. Mother Rose and the girls were not permitted to touch the prisoners. They had to wait out her emotional moment and hope she would join them at their assigned table.

Then the guard yelled at Wendy, "What are you going to do? You need to make up your mind!"

Cautiously, Wendy headed towards their table, sat down and slowly in a soft, barely audible voice, began apologizing for all the things she had done to the family.

"Why would you want to come back and see me, especially in a place like this? Why?" she cried.

They strained to hear what she was saying. Mother Rose felt the girls needed to address their issues with her first, and then she would clear the air between Wendy and herself.

"Mommy, I'm Eva and I do not like the idea of you being in this place any more than I like coming here. But, at the present time, we have no other choice. I've chosen to make the best of it and spend time with you."

Wendy was choked for words. What words could she say to her teenage daughter who appeared to have more sense than she had as an adult?

Eva continued, "Mommy, look at us. We want you to forgive yourself. The only one who is still upset is you. Let it all go."

"Well, what about her?" asked Wendy referring to Mother Rose.

"Who me?" replied Mother Rose. "I'm not angry anymore. Wendy, God removed hatred from me years ago and He can do the same thing for you too."

Wendy looked at Mother Rose and solemnly said, "I believe you will forgive me, but why would you want to have anything to do with me? Look at what I have done with my life and to you and the girls."

"Wendy, I'm not here to judge you or condemn you for what you have done in the past. I'm here because I love you and desperately want you to get to know your beautiful daughters."

"Miss Rose, I do not trust people who talk about God except you. People make you believe that they have your best interest at heart, but then they take advantage of you. I don't trust church people."

"No, my daughter. That's not always true," replied Mother Rose. "We do care about you and what happens to your soul."

"Maybe you're of the few who do care, but the rest are not living a godly life. They just take advantage of others," as she visibly began to get angry.

"Wendy, I do not know where all of this is coming from. What about others who are not living a godly life? I do not understand," replied Mother Rose.

"Let me share with you why I stopped going to church and listening to people who talk about God. It is a bit disturbing. Do you want the girls to hear?"

"Yes. They're growing up now and need to know that this is a cruel world out there and they need God's protection at all times. Please, go on."

"This minister approached me at my old church and told me there was bible study on Tuesday nights at his house for the young adults. I decided to try it. This was before I met Rick. When I got there, the minister was standing at the door with candy in his hand and welcomed me. I accepted the candy and went inside, but immediately noticed that there was no one else there besides me at this so-called 'bible study.' The minister pretended as if he was waiting for more people to join us, but he knew darn well that he planned for it to just be us!

"I started getting nervous when I heard him lock the door. I tried to leave the house by saying that I needed to make an important phone call outside, but he blocked my path and said that I could make the call in the house. He started making inappropriate moves towards me, and I realized that this minister was not right. I began screaming and fighting my way out the door and never went back to that church!"

As tears streamed down her face, Mother Rose wanted to hug Wendy.

"I am so sorry for what happened to you. Wendy, I just want you to know that all Christians are not like that. I will go as far and say that man was not a true man of God at all, let alone a minister of God! Let God into your life and He will show you that He has forgiven you as well. As the saying goes, every saint has a past but every sinner has a future! God does not care about the sins you committed as long as you are asking Him for His forgiveness, and have a sincere and a repentant heart. God will hear your prayer and wash away your sins forever and throw them in the sea of forgetfulness."

"I do want to repent because I'm truly sorry for all of the bad things I have done to you and the girls! Do you all forgive me?"

Mother Rose and the girls nodded.

"Yes, we all do. We have already forgotten them, but now we would like to make amends." Mother Rose asked, "Do you want to accept Jesus as your Lord and personal Savior?"

Wendy said, "I would love to accept Jesus but I need a moment to think."

They silently prayed as Wendy sat and pondered the question. She lifted her head and said, "Okay, go ahead. I'm listening."

Mother Rose walked her through the steps of salvation like she did with her beloved son. She told Wendy that Rick had accepted Jesus Christ as well and wanted them to visit her and display the same kindness of God's love they showed him.

Wendy began to cry so loud that everyone in the room was staring at her to make sure she was okay. If she was making a disturbance then she would not only be spoiling visiting hours for everybody, but she would need to be immediately removed and returned to her cell.

Wendy, trying to control herself, said, "My husband is now saved? I love my girls so much and really want to get to know them and I would like your help Miss Rose in getting to know them better. I was a terrible mother! I don't even know what mothering looks like. Miss Rose, I'm going to need your help, please."

"I would be delighted to assist!" replied Mother Rose.

Ava said, "Mommy, we all will take it one day at a time."

Wendy let out a big laugh. "Look how grown up you both are which is not surprising to me. Look who raised you! When are you leaving?"

Eva said, "We were leaving at the end of this week, but decided to stay one additional week. Do not worry. We will be back to see you one more time before we head home. Besides, Mommy said that we can come back to see both you and Daddy at least once a year."

Wendy hearing for the first time, that her daughters were calling their grandmother Mommy, replied, "That is terrific news!"

She smiled because it made sense for them to call Miss Rose 'mommy' because she really had been a mother to them.

Mother Rose told Wendy that they also included Rick's address in the package with the guards so that they could write and encourage each other during their imprisonment.

Wendy now felt comfortable calling her 'Mother Rose'. "Oh thank you, Mother Rose. I miss him so much!"

Visiting hours ended. Everyone said their good-byes and told Wendy that they would be praying for her and to keep her faith in God. Mother Rose and the girls kept their promises to Rick and Wendy by visiting them again and bringing them approved gift baskets full of all their favorite goodies.

On the plane heading back home, Mother Rose suddenly thought about the dream she had. It was God's way of warning her of Wendy's past experiences with the church.

Back home in Atlanta, Pastor Paul felt in his spirit to allow Mother Rose to share the word at the next Friday night service. Also knowing that she had just come back from visiting her son and daughter-in-law in the Texas prisons, he felt God would use her past experiences to encourage everyone if they too were having a wilderness experience. He called to see if she would accept his offer. She was honored and humbly accepted his invitation.

Friday was quickly approaching. Although Mother Rose was fasting, praying and trusting God to use her to share a word to encourage His people, she still felt butterflies were using her stomach as a playground. She knew it was her nerves trying to get the best of her because she had been laying before the Lord since Pastor Paul asked her to share. She became her own worst enemy. Each time she envisioned herself standing before the whole congregation, the sight would essentially wipe away all boldness she had been praying for. But then she thought,

*Now that is not such a bad thing because if I shared God's Word and am too confident, it means that I am more than likely operating in my own strength and not relying on God's strength.*

On Friday night, Pastor Paul wanted nothing more than to move out of the way so that God could have His way. He gracefully introduced Mother Rose as the speaker and asked everyone to stand.

"Welcome this great woman of God to the podium. Without further ado, please put your hands together for Mother Rose!"

Everyone began clapping and praising God for allowing Mother Rose the opportunity to once again preach the unadulterated Word of God!

Mother Rose nervously took the microphone from Pastor Paul's hands. He noticed that she was shaking, so he whispered into her ear words of encouragement telling her to take her time and allow God to use her. Mother Rose thanked him for trusting her enough to stand before God's people again.

She started. "Praise the Lord, saints! Praise the Lord! Saints, thank you all for your showers of love that you have continually poured upon me and my family since our return. It is one thing for someone to tell you that they love you and it is a totally separate thing when someone shows you how much they love you. All of the blessings have just melted my heart. May God bless you!

"If everyone can remain standing for the reading of God's Word, and if you have your Bibles, please turn with me to the book of Numbers and we will begin reading chapter 26 verses 52 through 55 and also chapter 27 verses 1 through 11. When you have found them, please indicate by saying Amen!"

A small group of people said, "Amen" while others were still turning the pages of their Bible. Mother Rose told the congregation that she would give them some more time. After the reading of God's Word, Mother Rose asked the congregation to remain standing as she prayed.

"Father, it is in You that I live, move and have my being. Father, I ask You to hide me behind the cross that only You may be seen. God, please allow this Word to encourage Your people. In Jesus' name Amen!"

"Saints, if permitted," she began, "I would like to use for a subject today 'Desperate Times Require Desperate Actions'. Saints of God, I have great news. My son, Rick, and my daughter-in-law, Wendy, have accepted the Lord Jesus Christ into their lives. Hallelujah!"

Everyone stood again giving God all of the Glory! Mother Rose waved at them to sit while she continued.

"Before this bad ordeal took place not only was I living from paycheck to paycheck, but I literally did not have enough money to keep a savings account open. Now I know most of you are thinking that anyone could at least put a dollar or two aside in case of a rainy day. But I'm here to tell you that I was not able to save that. I was really struggling to survive from month to month. But God not only saw fit to save so many souls during my bad ordeal, but He also managed to bless me financially and I'm so thankful for all that He has done!

"My first financial blessing came my way when my neighbors, Joe and Zach, were kind enough to split the reward money and give me two hundred and fifty thousand dollars. I will forever be thankful to them for blessing me financially, and also for risking their lives.

"My second financial blessing came my way when I was offered five hundred thousand dollars to do an exclusive interview about my kidnapping experience. I prayed about it and humbly accepted and I'm sure that most, if not all of you, have seen it aired on television.

"My third financial blessing came my way when the girls and I decided to sell my property in Houston. My brother-in-law took care of it all these years and we were able to sell the house for seven hundred thousand dollars. We have made a family decision to save this money for both Ava and Eva's college education. Saints, God is good, good, good!"

Everyone, in thanksgiving, gave God praise and glory!

"My fourth financial blessing came my way after Rick and I mended our relationship by God's grace! Rick told me that his Uncle Brad, my husband's younger brother, willed his house to him and he wanted to give me everything that his late uncle saved for him, which is in his savings account. Both the girls and I have been meeting with my son's lawyer and we managed to sell his uncle's house for seven hundred and fifty thousand dollars. Praise God!

"Saints, I stand here today to tell you that I no longer have to rely on elevators to get into my home, but I can boldly say that I can drive my brand new car into my brand new house garage! I do not have to worry about paying a mortgage because it is paid-in-full! God has taken my poverty situation and turned it into a prosperous one. He is so good! I stand before you all as someone who lived from paycheck to paycheck, but now I'm a millionaire. Thank you Jesus!

"When God allows trials and tribulations to come your way, saints, He is setting you up also for a blessing and that is what God was doing for me. He took a bad situation with my son and saved a whole lot of people along the way.

"Moving on, I kept asking God to give me a Word for His people and I just happen to be reading at that time about Moses and the children of God in the wilderness and I stumbled on this story in the Bible. By the raising of your hands, how many of you know that I did not just happen to be reading the Book of Numbers, nor did I stumble upon this story? It was God sent!"

As Mother Rose raised her hand in the air, she asked this question, "How many people believe that you can change the heart of God Almighty?"

Everyone raised their hands and shouted, "Amen!"

"How many of you also know that when you have not received your answered prayer from God, that it does not mean 'no'?"

Some from the congregation stood to their feet in agreement as testimony that they are still waiting on God to answer their prayers.

"But saints of God, there are moments when desperate times require desperate actions and this time was one of them! Here in the book of Numbers chapters 26 and 27, it speaks about an inheritance about to be passed over a whole generation. God spoke to Moses in chapter 26 saying, 'And the Lord spake unto Moses saying, unto these the land shall be divided for an inheritance according to the number of names.' So Moses shared with the people what God spoke about dividing the land by lots according to the tribes of their fathers' inheritance because the population of the people in the wilderness was growing.

"Saints, we all know that laws are set in place so that they can be followed. Although we may not agree with all of the laws being put in place, everyone must obey the laws of the land or you will be considered disobedient to your leadership and breaking the law. During the Old Testament days, God got sick and tired of the children of Israel murmuring and complaining about every little, single thing. God could no longer deal with the sinful ways of their disobedience. God destroyed the older generation so that they would not see the promise land.

"But here is the key part—God spoke to Moses and told him this was how He wanted him to proceed with the dividing of the land with the children of Israel. Another interesting part is that back in the Old Testament times the Israelites did not have the privilege that we have today of coming boldly before the throne of God. They had to go through their appointed leadership whether it was the priests or Moses and this was the only way they could speak with God concerning their prayer requests.

"Now, as Moses shared with the people what God spoke about concerning dividing the land by lots according to the tribes of their fathers' inheritance, it caused a big problem for the five daughters of Zelophehad. Their father Zelophehad died in the wilderness because of his sins and he did not have any biological sons, only five daughters whose names were Mahlah, Noah, Hoglah, Milcah and Tirzah.

"Just think about it. You hear that all of the other families will receive lots based on their father's inheritance and your father had ceased to exist! Now their whole generation was about to be passed over because a law God put in place, not Moses.

"During my ordeal, there were times when I was not always in a praying mood and I could not understand why God was allowing all of this to happen to me. But God is a God who knows all things and nothing happens that He is not aware of. When I went through my wilderness experience, I did not know at the time that so many people would turn their lives over to God, but God knew the bigger picture and He also knew that He could trust me to hold on until He told the devil to back off!

"The five daughters were desperate and could not sit back any longer and watch their father's inheritance be passed to another family, so they decided to approach the whole congregation, including the priests and

Moses, about their father's inheritance. They asked that their father's portion be given to them.

"These five sisters did not just go before the whole congregation to complain. They went there with a purpose in mind and that was to change the mind of God! What could these daughters possibly be thinking about changing the mind of God Almighty? They were fully aware that Moses was God's mouthpiece. They also knew that whatever laws God set for His people, He expected everyone to follow. But these sisters did not feel God's law was fair and was hoping that by going to Moses, he would be persuasive enough when presenting their cause before God. Now keep in mind the order in which everything took place. God approached Moses to divide the land because it was getting crowded. God gave him strict instructions to distribute by the tribes of the fathers' names. The five daughters heard and brought their situation before Moses. He must've agreed and decided to take their request before God. God agreed with the five daughters and changed the law to recognize both genders.

"God's ways are past finding out. I do not know why God went this route with Moses. He knew perfectly well that there was a family within the congregation that no longer had males in it. God knows all things and there is nothing that happens He does not know about! He is our Creator and knows us better than we know ourselves. Why would He tell Moses to divide the land based on the fathers' inheritance knowing that there was a family that only consisted of women? Many thoughts come to mind. Women did not have a lot of say back then. They were only to be submissive to male authority. Maybe God wanted to show the women that they mattered to Him as well. Also, this could have been a test for Moses to see if he thought the five women were worthy enough to even bring their cause before God. Whatever the reason, God decided to create the law in the first place and then change it, only He knows.

"So you see saints, we serve a God who not only loves us, but He cares about how we are being impacted in life. Now I'm not saying that God will change every law to fit your circumstances, but the fact that God cared enough to consider their request and agreed to change the law says a lot about the God we serve. Here is a God who is above all creation, a God who took the time to create man with His own hands, and is also willing to sit down and talk with His creation. As He politely stated at Isaiah 1:18, 'Come now, and let us reason together, saith the Lord.' That says a lot about our God!

"Now these five daughters were not concerned how they looked, or what people would think about them not having any males in their family, but they knew that if they could not change the mind of God during these desperate times, their father's inheritance would be lost forever.

"Saints, my son did not allow me and my granddaughters to do anything while we were being held captive, but I still knew how to pray and bring my request before God. I was desperate and it required desperate actions. The girls and I bombarded heaven with cries of help every chance we could! Ladies and gentlemen, who knows when your day of desperation will come? Just remember to make your requests known to God and He will hear your cry and answer your prayers!

"Desperate times require desperate action and these five daughters took action before they lost their father's inheritance. Will you trust God through your desperate times? When you pass the test and come out of your desperate times, God will elevate you and take you to another level in Him. We must also remember when we are going through, God is essentially telling the devil that He can trust us until the end, just like He so boldly told the devil about His servant, Job! We did not know when God was going to deliver us from the hand of the enemy, but timing is everything. Had these daughters just waited until someone else took their inheritance, they would have lost it all. Timing and waiting on God is very important, the Bible clearly states in Ecclesiastes that there is a season for everything.

"God, the Father of time, who exists outside of time, still controls the universe as the Creator. God is not a part of earth's time zone, so patiently waiting is something we *must* learn as we walk and develop into mature Christians. The Bible states in 2 Peter 3:8, 'But beloved, be not ignorant of this one thing, that one day is with the Lord as a thousand years, and a thousand years as one day.'

"Even when we pray and ask God for something, we must see things from God's perspective. If we see with our natural eyes, we cannot see

God's will for our lives clearly. When we see with our spiritual eyes, we are more in tune with God's will and can see much clearer. Also, most people know that God has the ability to answer their prayers, but God, being an all-knowing God, sees the bigger picture. So ask yourself this question: does answering your prayer involve answering someone else's prayer first? Although desperate times require desperate actions, wait I say on the Lord!

"God bless you for listening to me tonight and I hope that this message made a difference in your hearts! Remember saints, God may not come when you want Him, but He is always on time!"

As Mother Rose took her seat, she felt tremendous pride as she pondered all that had taken place over the course of several months. God took a bad situation, which the devil thought he had under control, and turned it around for everyone's good! Thank God that He saw the desperate times and decided to send His Son, Jesus, to redeem mankind from their sinful ways. Desperate times required desperate actions!

After everything settled down and Mother Rose's story became old news, Pastor Paul saw how God was really using all of the new, as well as the long-time, members in his church. Mother Rose, Mother Williamson and Deacon Brown were filled with zeal and had committed to visiting as many nursing homes, hospitals and handing out bags of food to the homeless as they could.

Brother Joe and Brother Zach were totally sold out to prison ministry, determined to reach many souls for Christ. They dedicated themselves to helping inmates understand the Word of God. They worked with the prisons in and out of the state to show inmates how to have a better life for themselves outside of prison. They were involved in building housing for some of the inmates who did not have any place to go when released from prison. Sister and Brother Jackson, and Sister and Brother Smith got permission to start an outreach program in the police department to mentor troubled youth, giving them a second chance to turn their lives around. The program was very successful.

While Ava and Eva had been totally involved in the church in the past, Pastor Paul saw a change in Ava's behavior. Mother Rose also saw a change in her demeanor around the house; she was becoming distant from her and Eva. Mother Rose decided to speak with Pastor Paul about her concerns, and he told her that he saw the same thing in her and was also becoming very concerned. Both Pastor Paul and Mother Rose could not figure out what was exactly happening to Ava or who was causing her spiritual and social life to change. It seemed as if after writing to both her parents, her behavior started changing for the worse. Or maybe she was just being a teenager. Teenagers act moody sometimes, right? Could it be because some of the boys in church were starting to pay more attention to Eva than to her? Or was she starting to blame Mother Rose for taking her away from her parents? What was in those letters? Time would eventually tell.

## THE END

# REFERENCES/BIBLIOGRAPHY

Scripture quotations were taken from *The New Scofield Study Bible, Authorized King James Version*. Copyright © 1967 By Oxford University Press, Inc., *The Scofield ® Reference Bible*, Copyright 1909, 1917; copyright renewed, 1937, 1945, By Oxford University Press, Inc.

Scripture quotations were taken from the *New International Version/ Amplified Version/King James Version/Updated New American Standard Bible Comparative Study Bible, Corporative Study Bible, Revised Edition;* Copyright © 1999 by the Zondervan Corporation, All rights reserved.

Definitions were taken from *The Three-In-One Bible Reference Companion, Concordance, Topical Index, Dictionary;* Copyright © 1982 by Thomas Nelson Publishers.

Definitions were taken from *Webster's Universal College Dictionary,* Gramercy Books New York; Copyright © 2001, 1997 by Random House, Inc.

Definitions were taken from the internet encyclopedia website *"WIKIPEDIA", The Free Encyclopedia;* Copyright © 2001, by Jimmy Wales and Larry Sanger.

# TIME

*God the Father, knowing that the world He created was full of sin and needed a Savior, sent His only begotten Son Jesus to become a part of time. Clothing Himself in the flesh, He came to dwell among us.*

*Although time has many different meanings, and can take on many different forms to each of us, how would you personalize your own bullet below?*

- To an Achiever, time can mean – waiting, during uncertainty;
- To a Bishop, time can mean – praying, salvation for people;
- To a Christian, time can mean – eternity, with the Father;
- To a Doctor, time can mean – medicine, healing to the body;
- To an Examiner, time can mean – reflection, of past & present;
- To a Farmer, time can mean – harvest, or growth;
- To a Gardner, time can mean – planting, for flowers to blossom;
- To a Heavyweight, time can mean – rounds, winning the fight;
- To an Inquirer, time can mean – answers, waiting on results;
- To a Judge, time can mean – ruling, for sentencing;
- To a King, time can mean – royalty, provider for the people;
- To a Leader, time can mean – direction, for guidance;
- To a Militant, time can mean – duty, years of service;
- To a New-Believer, time can mean – cleansed, renewed mind;
- To an Opportunist, time can mean – exploring, new adventures;
- To a Pilot, time can mean – duration, for arrivals or departures;
- To a Quitter, time can mean – giving up, too long of a wait;
- To a Racer, time can mean – practice, for starts and finishes;
- To a Swimmer, time can mean – exercise, short or long lapses;
- To a Trainer, time can mean – elevation, for growth;
- To an Unbeliever, time can mean – damnation, eternity in Hell;
- To a Victim, time can mean – healing, restoration of mind;
- To a Worshiper, time can mean – praise, glorifying God;
- To a Xenophile, time can mean – learn, more about foreign cultures;
- To a Youth, time can mean – maturity, years to adulthood;
- To a Zealous-Person, time can mean – excitement, about the future.

# ACKNOWLEDGMENTS

To God be the Glory! God, because of Your encouragement and guidance, "I'm In Time" was birthed. Thank you so much for trusting me with this project even when I doubted myself so many times. You knew I could do it. God, I think we, as Christians, forget that when You call us to do something, You already know that we have what it takes to complete the task. The hard part was just convincing myself that I could do all things through Christ who strengthens me. As I began to trust You more each day and believe that You would not tell me to take on such a big challenge, and then leave me, this is when my confidence began to build up. You are everything to me God. Just to think, that one day I will behold the beauty of Your face; what a day that will be!

I thank my mother, who trusted God, instead of lecturing me every single day about surrendering my life to the Lord. Mommy, I knew it could not have been easy for you when I rebelled and wanted to go a different direction, but thank God you were obedient and waited. Because of that, you were able to see the manifestation of your prayers, and God is not through with me yet! The half has not been told in my life, all of what God wants to do in and through me, all because you trusted and waited on God. After all, God is my Creator and He knows me best. I miss you Mommy and love you and I cannot wait until I see you again!

I thank my father, who always talked to me and tried to instill good values into my life. Many times I did not fully understand everything he was trying to say to me at a particular moment. But as I grew into adulthood, those sayings began to come alive. After he had given me a couple of dollars, he used to always say things like not to spend everything all at once, but hold on to some of it for a rainy day. Of course, later on in life I found out about those rainy days. Now I know he was teaching me to save my money and not consume it all at once.

I also remember when he lectured me about how I should get good grades in school and make something of myself. Strangely, I distinctly recall him telling me that I should always work hard for the things I wanted in life because if not, I would do *anything* to obtain those things I desire. I used to get so upset because to me it always seemed like he was reprimanding me about something, but he was just looking out for my best interest.

Also, I especially recall him taking me out on my first date, and teaching me how a man is supposed to treat a woman. I remember him opening the door for me as I walked into the restaurant. I also remember him helping me take off my coat and pulling the chair out for me to sit. I thank you, Daddy, for those short, but memorable and beautiful times we shared together.

These descriptions may not really mean anything to a lot of people reading this book but losing a father at such a young age, and not having many memories of him, is very dear and precious to me. So rest in peace, Daddy, and one day I will see you again, but until then, I will continue to carry you in my heart and mind each and every day. Love always, your baby girl.

I thank God for the prayers for the salvation of my older sisters, Cheryl and Anita, who have been walking with the Lord much longer than I have. They are my spiritual pillows. Whenever I need a supporting word, a hug or a kiss from them, they are right there to extend their love. It's truly a blessing to have other saved members in your immediate family because they are the ones who will intercede and stand in the gap on your behalf when life tries to get the best of you. Thank you for lifting my head when I get depressed or when I need correction. You are amazing sisters. I deeply love and appreciate the both of you!

Lord, I also know that You have heard my mother's prayers for the salvation of my older brothers, Darrell and Rodney. I know that You would leave ninety-eight sheep to look for two lost ones, so God I thank You in advance for allowing their limits to become Your opportunity to turn their lives around. Even as my mother trusted You for my salvation, I too will wait and trust You for my brothers' change as well. Darrell and Rodney, I love you dearly and I cannot wait for the both of you to really experience God's love for you!

To all my loving nieces and nephews, I love you just the same. My prayers for all of you are that you will experience God's true love in your lives and that you will one day say that you have accepted Jesus as your Lord and Personal Savior before you leave this earth. The end is near and who knows, I may not be around to see all of you living for the Lord, but just know that I have great confidence in God that He will hear our prayers for you.

I dare not begin to call out all of my other family members for the fear that I will leave out someone's name. So I thank God for all of my aunts, uncles, cousins, in-laws, and extended family members too! As we are all getting up in age and becoming a smaller family circle, let's continue to stick close together. There is nothing like family, but it is even more important to be a part of God's family. My prayer is that God will save those who have not accepted Him into their lives. I also pray that God will keep those who know Him, knowing that one day we will all be a part of God's kingdom.

To all my saved friends who bring joy into my life as we journey along this Christian walk—what an inspiration you all have been to me in some way or another, knowing I do not have to call you when I'm going through something but, because you are sensitive to the Spirit, you are already there for me. You intercede on my behalf. What a blessing to have spiritual friends in my life to get a prayer answered. I love you all. I also do not want to forget my unsaved friends either, those who have not yet surrendered their lives to God. My prayer is that God will grab a hold of you and never let you go, literally! I pray that you will begin to experience how much God truly cares for you. He is concerned where you will spend eternity. I love you, but God loves you more.

I thank God for all of the pastors I have encountered over the course of my salvation. I remember Pastor C.R. Johnson when I first stepped into Brooklyn Tabernacle Deliverance Center over thirty years ago. What a change took place in my life! That beautiful feeling that I felt each time made me want to come back more and more. I remember you preaching the Word in such a way that a babe like me could understand the Bible. I thank God for using you during my times of growing spiritually. Although I grew up in a Baptist church, it was this Pentecostal church that gave me my spiritual foundation and taught me so many things about walking with the Lord. The 50-Days Consecrations, the washing of the feet during Communion, bible school, ministering in song with the choir, ministering in the hospitals and witnessing to lost souls on the street gave me my foundation. Rest in Peace!

I also remember Pastor James Copeland, whom God chose to be the next man of God in charge, one who walked strictly by faith. I clearly remember attending one of his faith classes and, boy, did my life change forever. You not only taught the class how to walk in faith, but you also walked the walk as well, which was very important because so many people say one thing and live a totally different life. Because of your teachings, I've learned to develop such great faith in God, to lean on Him and not to depend on what my eyes may see. I've learned how to take God at His Word, and never ever settle for what the enemy says! Your preaching and teaching faith had such an impact on my life that it will always be memorable as long as I live. My faith in God has been strengthened because of you. Rest in Peace!

Last but certainly not least, I thank God for the pastors of the Caesar generation. When I first came to Bethel Gospel Tabernacle, I came into the church and would hear this great man of God who had this distinct voice when preaching the Word of God. He had such a way of teaching the Word that you were immediately mesmerized and locked into his messages, just like a sponge soaking up everything! Although I did not sit under his leadership for long, just the short times that I did before his illness took over his body, had a huge impact upon my life. There were times he would be sitting on the podium without using a Bible, wearing dark sunglasses (because his vision was fading) and preaching the Word of God from memory. My God what a blessing! Then there were times he was unable to make it to church and would deliver a message to the congregation over an audio system, which was even more of a blessing because you could hear the anointing in all his messages! Rest in Peace!

Passing the baton to his son, Dr. Roderick R. Caesar Jr., has impacted my life also and he too has a way of drawing you into his messages by eloquently delivering God's Word. Pastor uses words that you need a dictionary to define, but once his message is over, you are inspired, empowered and encouraged to hold on until your change comes! Pastor I love you and all that you do to encourage the congregation. Both you and Pastor Beverly are a blessing to so many people—blessings you may never know about! God equipped the both of you to teach the congregation to stand our battles and not to waver or compromise. Because of your leaderships, I can boldly say today I am more than a conqueror! God has appointments and opportunities waiting for the both of you.

Bishop Caesar is still around, and has groomed his son, Pastor Roderick R. Caesar, III to receive the baton; and as the saying goes, the apple does not fall far from the tree. In other words, this young man of God is already a powerhouse like the generations before him. He is definitely born for this time and season! So Father, allow him to be fearless in battle, and to never forget that You have got his back all the way —just as with the generations before him! Even as his father's sister, Pastor Beverly Caesar Sherrod, whom I admire so much, took a warrior's stand by her brother's side all of these years, let it be so with the sisters of Pastor Roderick R. Caesar, III as well. Roderick, God bless you on your pastoral journey!

# ABOUT THE AUTHOR

Lisa Walden was born and raised in Brooklyn, New York. Most of her life she was raised by her single mother. Losing her father at the tender age of thirteen was difficult, but she still had her mother and other siblings to lean on whenever she needed their support or guidance in life. She now knows God had His Hand upon her life as well and had His angels watching.

Lisa, the youngest of the girls, grew up in a large household that consisted of her mother, five brothers and two sisters. Sadly, three brothers have gone on to be with the Lord and only two brothers and two sisters are in the land of the living.

Her mother tried to instill in all her children godly values while they were young and as they grew into adulthood. Her mother made sure that they attended church on Sundays from a young age, even though she was not really sure if her children understood why they were going to church.

Although Lisa decided to walk away from the godly values she was taught when she was sixteen, it did not stop her mother from praying and bombarding heaven on her behalf. During 1986, her mother was finally able to see the manifestation of her prayers when Lisa developed a real spiritual relationship with God.

God began to use her in the church where she sang in the choir for many years. Then she joined the Tract Team—going out into the streets ministering to the unsaved and dying world—the Hospital Ministry, and the Prison Ministry. She also attended bible schools where she received an Associate Degree in Theology from Bethel Bible Institute (BBI). Lisa loves reading Christian novels, and is now being led by God to join in with other Christian novelists to entertain God's people through her writing.

Since 1986, there have been many hills to climb and lonely roads to walk, but God has kept His hands upon her life and she is now confident more than ever that no devil in Hell will be able to pluck her out of God's Hands.

Lisa will be the first to state that she has not always done things right and has also made a lot of mistakes along her Christian journey. But every day she is still fighting battles and running for her life to stay in this Christian race!

Lisa says, "One day when I have given up this earthly body—what a day that shall be to behold the beauty of God's face and ever reign with the Lord!"

***To God Be the Glory!***